SIMON'S WIFE

L. M. AFFROSSMAN

SPARSILE BOOKS LTD

Acknowledgments

My thanks to Jennifer Muller, previously of the DHH Literary Agencyfor her untiring help.

Also, my thanks to Mitchell Waters of Curtis Brown Ltd, New York for his extraordinary insight and encouragement.

And, finally, my deepest gratitude to Professor G. Fuks of the University of Haifa, Department of Jewish History, whose generous help allowed this story to be grounded in fact.

Contents

Historicus Personae 7

Prologue 9

Chapter I 11

Chapter II 19

Chapter III 27

Chapter IV 34

Chapter V 44

Chapter VI 51

Chapter VII 59

Chapter VIII 67

Chapter IX 82

Chapter X 92

Chapter XI 102

Chapter XII 114

Chapter XIII 122

Chapter XIV 133

Chapter XV 140

Chapter XVI 149

Chapter XVII 159

Chapter XVIII 165

Chapter XIX 176

Chapter XX 189

Chapter XXI 205

Chapter XXII 215

Chapter XXIII 222

Chapter XXIV 231

Chapter XXV 240

Chapter XXVI 249

Chapter XXVII 260

Chapter XXVIII 269

Chapter XXIX 276

Chapter XXX 290

Chapter XXXI 300

Historical Note 317

Glossary 318

Tables 320

Further reading 321

For a love that once lighted the way

Historicus Personae

Simon bar Giora
(Also known as Simon ben Gioras). Leader of revolutionary forces during the Jewish-Roman War in the 1st century Judea.

Shelamzion
The unnamed wife of Simon referred to in Josephus' Bellum Judaicum.

John of Gischala
Leader of Galilean forces.

Eleazar ben Yair
Leader of the Sicarii. He held out the longest against the Romans.

Titus Flavius Sabinus Vespasianus (Vespasian)
The most noteable of Roman Emperor Nero's generals, Vespasian was sent to put down the Jewish Revolt.

Titus Flavius Vespasianus
Elder son of the General/Emperor Vespasian.

Cestius Gallus
Governor of the Roman province of Syria and Florus' superior.

Gessius Florus
Roman procurator.

Flavius Josephus
The author of The Jewish War, the only eyewitness account of the war that survives

Prologue

You! Yes, you. I am talking to you with the tongue of a dead man. Sit up; look around. What do you see? The dawn of a new millennium. The inevitable march of power and progress. But look further. Don't you smell it? A faint stench. A stink of rotting below the fabric of the world. The lies are seeping through.

Now turn eastwards. Yes. See how it teeters on the verge of destruction. Fanatics everywhere claiming God as their own. We've been here before. Two thousand years ago, more or less. What's that? You're growing bored. You've heard this story a thousand times before, and never liked its moralising tone. But you're mistaken. This is not the story of Yeshua, the carpenter's son. He has been born and has died his horrible death by the beginning of this tale. But he is not yet famous. His story has still to be mixed up in the mythology of other men, and no emperor of Rome has yet chosen him as a vehicle of power.

The men and women of this story are barely known to you. Yet they shaped your world. This seething mass of humanity of which you are a part. A helpless part, watching the gathering storm approaching from the east. You are dismayed. How can things have gone so wrong? You don't understand. Well, the answer is in your hands. Simply turn the page

Chapter I

At certain fated times the entire world is subject to conflagration, and then is reconstituted afresh.
Plutarch, De Stoicorum Repugnantiis

Jerusalem, September, 70 CE

The sun, a blinding orb, threw flames across the sky above the ancient city. But its scorching light revealed an uncertain landscape. Seared stone walls, fallen archways, colonnades with their roofs smashed, their shattered pillars littering the cracked and dislodged paving stones that had once lined the streets. And in between the pyramids of rubble and the charred, broken beams the city was peopled by figures stranger than the landscape itself. Mostly they lay on the ground, their twig-like limbs held stiffly, their heads rolling back, as though Death had come amongst them and persuaded them to dance a macabre jig. Those whose bodies had not been torn apart by starving dogs, that is.

Not all Jerusalem's inhabitants were inanimate. Here and there the sunlight caught the crown of a dented helmet or the surface of a cuirass turned rust-coloured with blood. The men who wore these were dressed in tunics the colour of mercuric sulphide. They had sallow, vicious faces, and the hard, well-fed figures of soldiers. In their hands, they wielded the deadly *gladius* of Rome, and they marched steadily through Jerusalem, tearing her apart.

Sometimes screams pierced the air or a building crashed to the ground with a rolling sound, like a tremor in the earth. Rarely, other inhabitants of the city were exposed. Bands of stringy Jerusalemites, moving quickly past, glancing everywhere with the haunted faces of wolves. And shortly afterwards the screaming would begin again.

In the midst of this chaos a woman and a small boy, barely out of babyhood, were running for their lives. They were not running to safety. There was no safety to be had. Torn from where they had been hiding in the tunnels and sewers under the city, they were as helpless in the sudden light as the first creatures of creation struggling out of the earth. Nor were they running in the hope of evading their captors, because they were already captured, and making them run was simply the way the legionaries had of making sport.

The woman's name was Shelamzion bat Judah. She was nineteen years old. And until a few days ago she had been the most important woman in the whole of Jerusalem. Now she was nothing. A faceless captive in a defeated city. Holding on to her child, dragging him behind her. A gash on her inner thigh oozing blood down her leg. Daggers of breath tearing at her breast. Hopeless. Nowhere to go. Everything gone. Jerusalem in flaming ruins about her. The mighty temple destroyed.

'Simon!'

She called out his name, knowing it was useless, knowing that the End of Days was upon them. Still clinging to that last vision of him being dragged away on the orders of the Roman commander. Pleading with God, who must surely come now, to spare him.

Her shins collided with hard stone—the ruins of a pillar—and she stumbled, almost letting go the precious fingers that clung to hers.

'*Imma!*' Mother.

She did not answer. Her eyes had found the smoking remnants of the Sanctuary. And she looked up towards that place, where millions had come to pray. To be near the inner sanctum, that holy of holies where the spirit of the deity dwelt, seeing only crumbling stone and charred rafters, and a huge, blank emptiness, a colossus of nothing that went on and on, reaching all the way to the sky and beyond. And she understood then, more than any of them, that the dream was over. The Jews were no more. God had abandoned them …

Two Months Later
Rome, November, 70 CE

Abandoned, yes. The flaring image of the Temple wavered then collapsed behind Shelamzion's fluttering eyelids, and was replaced by a yawning maw of blackness, so thick it seemed to press against her eyes. The stench of it crawled over her skin, confusing her senses for a moment, so that time wound backwards and she thought herself still in the ruins of the Temple Mount. At once she reached out for her son. But the chain around her wrist cut the movement short, drawing her widening eyes towards what she could not see. Then instantly all the horror welled up again. Rome. They had brought her here in the last days of the war. When everything was lost. Half mad with grief and terror they had brought her. Because she was Simon's wife, and her death was a morsel to be savoured.

Later, her jailor, who was known as the *custos*, fastened the chains about her wrists. Ghastly as a grinning skull in the torchlight, his was the last face she saw. Then it was the spiralling darkness for company, except for those rare, unguessable moments when her water bowl was refilled or a morsel of food was pushed alongside it.

Gradually, as the days passed and horror grew over her, like a numbing scab, she began to wonder what had happened to the other prisoners. Those with luck on their side had probably been sold as slaves. The unlucky ones would already have met their deaths in the arenas and theatres. Or was it the other way around? She shuddered and drew her knees close in to her chest. What a world to live in, where the dead were more fortunate than the living.

The mist rolling up from the Tiber had an evil smell about it. Along the walls of the basilica ragged beggars huddled against the dank archways, while sooth-sayers and penniless prophets hissed out words of doom into the yellow air. Late in the morning a hired litter passed them by, moving laboriously along the *Clivus Capitolinus*, before finally setting down in front of a low, uninspiring building, known to the citizenry of Rome as the Carcer; the state prison. After a few moments, the elderly occupant of the litter made his exit with more than the usual degree of stiffness, and stood self-consciously in the middle of the road, his head turning slowly to look back the way he had come. He seemed undecided.

Above him the sun appeared briefly, imprisoned behind the curtain of dense vapours and blank-faced as an uninscribed coin. The same sun that had beaten down, like a relentless harpy, on the legionaries' heads all through the long war in Judea. Hard to believe it of this pallid disk. And, for a brief moment, he wondered if the prisoner might not be thinking the same thoughts. Then he smiled at his foolishness. Given where they were holding her, there wasn't much chance that Shelamzion bat Judah was looking at the sun.

The fog was lifting his skin in a patina of tiny bumps. It made his bones ache. He had slept poorly, as old men do, kept awake by pains in his legs and thoughts of the prisoner. She would surely be in chains; the mighty bandit queen brought low. And he found the thought did not displease him. He took a step towards the Carcer. As her interrogator, it was fitting that she should be humbled before him. But he had not come here, as if on Nike's wings, for vengeance. It was a story that had drawn him. If he was right, she held within her a tale, like a searing flame, Homeric in breadth, alive with battle and bloodshed, the cries of soldiers over sun-blackened landscapes, hubris, lust, and the dreadful, harrowing echo of a toppled god. *Anthropos versus Theos.* The clash of the mortal with the divine.

He drew a deep, shuddering breath. To hear such a tale would be to remember it forever. And for weeks now it had existed right under the long noses of the literati, there for the taking, yet he alone, Fabius Cornelius Grammaticus, a humble schoolmaster, had been graced with the wit to see it.

At once a great contentment washed over him, and he forgot the evil in the air. Indeed, so certain was he of the gods' favour that he could almost feel it, like a warm breath upon the back of his neck. Boldly he mounted the steps and beat out a commanding tattoo on the Carcer's door, all the while thinking, Only let the muse of Hellas linger on my tongue. And they will hear me sing more sweetly than Theocritus. The door opened and he stepped inside.

The *custos*, a small, wizened individual, with an incongruous pot belly, was waiting for Cornelius. They stared at each other for a moment and Cornelius was forced to ask, 'Do you know who I am?'

'Fabius Cornelius Grammaticus, your honour. Our new assistant governor,' the *custos* answered. He gave a bow, which was obsequious enough, though Cornelius noticed that it was somewhat shorter than decorum demanded.

'You may have heard of me,' he suggested.

'Indeed, sir.'

Cornelius bestowed upon him a small smile. And, encouraged, the man continued, 'You are the cousin of our esteemed governor, Fabius Quintus.'

Cornelius' smile vanished and his voice became icy. 'It is my humble opinion that I am an *historicus*.' And when the *custos* stared up at him with filmy, uncomprehending eyes, he added wearily, 'I am a writer of histories, a scholar of … some reputation.' He heard the self-doubt in his voice and wondered if the *custos* had heard it too. But the man only shuffled from foot to foot, then scratched his arse. Cornelius sighed. 'You understand your orders?'

'Yes, sir.'

Nonetheless he repeated them. 'As Fabius Quintus' assistant, I will be taking his place on the weekly visitations. Understand, it is not my intention to make these visits on a regular day or time, or to provide you with warning of my arrival.' He paused, raising an eyebrow to see if the *custos* took his meaning, and the man nodded and bowed again. Cornelius continued. 'I may also decide to inspect a particular prisoner from time to time, or even to conduct interviews with them. If this is the case, I am not to be disturbed except on matters of the utmost importance.' Again, he paused and the *custos* twisted his hands into an ingratiating knot.

'Yes, sir.' He ran his tongue over rotten teeth. 'Fabius Quintus gave me to understand that you would be speaking with the prisoners. And that you had a most particular interest in our new arrival.' Cornelius stiffened, but the *custos* did not seem to notice. He cocked his head over his shoulder towards the dark passage behind him. 'Been keeping her nice for you. Though I'm afraid, sir, she's been got at. Legionaries most likely. They're good lads, but rough.' He glanced up unexpectedly and something in his leering expression made the colour in Cornelius' face drain away then rush back in, like an angry tide.

'I will see her now,' he said sharply.

The *custos* seemed on the point of saying more then changed his mind. He gave a soft chuckle, and took a limping step into the passage.

'This way, sir. This way.' With the aid of a smoking lamp, he led Cornelius to the end of the corridor, and then down a flight of filthy steps. 'Mind where you step, sir. Prisoners aren't too mindful of what they leave behind.'

Cornelius followed silently, appalled as any spirit entering the underworld.

Only let her be beautiful, he thought. It was said that Bouddica had been beautiful. But then they'd said the same thing about Cleopatra, quite in contradiction with those who had known her. Perhaps it didn't matter. The nobility of her spirit would transcend any earthly shortcomings. As he followed the *custos* down the narrowing passageway it occurred to him that he had, in fact, made that very point to his cousin Quintus when he had agreed to take on the role of assistant governor. Naturally Quintus had laughed, pointing out in his usual languid manner that an enemy is never more virtuous than when he lies dead at one's feet. Did not Scipio weep for Carthage just after he'd sown its ruins with salt?

The *custos* had stopped before a low door and was beckoning to him. He flinched and did not move. The *custos* nodded, as though he sympathized. 'Only I need you to hold the light, sir. Easier to pull the bolt back with two hands.' Understanding, Cornelius jerked to life, and took the lamp. The *custos* released the bolt, and with the moan of ages, the door began to swing open slowly under its own weight. Cornelius looked to the *custos* for instruction, but already the man was gazing back the way they had come. 'I'll leave you the lamp, sir. Know this place like the back of my hand, I do.' And when Cornelius still hesitated, he added, 'She's chained, sir. Can't cause you no mischief.' Then looking for all the world like old Charon returning to the gates of hell, he limped past the new assistant governor of the Carcer and was lost in the thickening darkness.

Cornelius felt a number of emotions looking at the bandit queen, the primary one being disappointment. He had hoped for beauty, been prepared for ugliness, but somehow, he had not considered how very, very ordinary a legend would appear in the flesh. He stared wonderingly at this wild-haired woman, amazed that no touch of the divine tinged her drabness. And while there was pity in his thoughts, there was also distaste, and a powerful feeling of justice well done at the sight of her degradation. She might have been part of a tableau by Skopa or Veio depicting Psyche's humiliation in the wilderness, entitled 'Defiance Conquered'.

'Stand up.' He spoke to her in the clipped Latin of his class, which, at first, she did not seem to understand. Then, with difficulty, she got to her feet and stood before him, hands clasped, eyes downcast. He moved closer, covering his nose and mouth to protect them from the stench. After careful deliberation, he chose not to speak, partly to demonstrate his power over her, partly because all the grand speeches and clever epigrams he had composed in Greek did not seem fitting in this place of filth. Not what I expected, he thought. No, not at all. Yet what did I expect? The flame-haired queen of the Iceni, bare-breasted, her loins girded in the skulls of men, or the venomous sensuality of a Cleopatra? She was none of these. Young, yes. But well past the first, coltish bloom of youth. Her features were too strong for any classical dimensions of beauty. She seemed to be all dark-ness and tension, poised like a young hind, nostrils quivering, ready for flight. But there was something broken there too. There were marks of suffering upon her, a few silver threads of hair woven through the black, and a livid scar below her temple, which wound its way towards her ear. Without thinking, Cornelius reached out to touch it. She held very still, but her mouth opened in a gasp, and he saw the ragged edge of a broken tooth towards the back.

Her gasp broke the spell and he let his hand fall. At once he saw his mistake in coming here. This was no Arsinoë to be paraded through Rome in chains, beautiful and sad. He had been promised a queen, the remnant of a long and noble line, around whom he would weave his story. *Bellum Romanae*. His mag-nificent history of the Roman war in Judea. After all, had he not said to Quintus that too many accounts of great individuals were written after their death, pieced together by self-seekers and enemies alike? This was an opportunity to reach out and touch the living flesh of history. And make his name too, though he hadn't said that. And Quintus had agreed, even flattered him on his insight. How typical. He would have said anything to get out of his duties as governor. The man had no scruples.

Well, he had gone too far this time. This ragged, dirty little Jewess was more urchin than queen. So he would tell Quintus when he resigned first thing tomor-row. For the moment, there was nothing to be done but to complete the duties of the day as quickly as possible. Coldly, he asked, 'Do you know why you are here?'

She answered without looking up. 'To die.'

He made an irritated sound at the back of his throat. 'Of course.' Only a fool would think otherwise. He closed his eyes for a moment then continued in the weary, deliberate tones he reserved for the slow-witted. 'To be made an example of. You should now consider your life a warning to those who harbour revolt in their hearts. And, you may be assured, your death will merely strengthen the glories of this empire yet further.'

He paused, hoping for a reaction in that narrow, downcast face, but it was immobile. And, knowing of great men who balked at the first mention of their mortality, he softened his tone somewhat as he continued. 'When your husband returns in Titus' entourage, you will be witness to—'

'Simon! Then ... he lives?'

Cornelius dropped the hand he had been discretely raising to his nose. He was taken aback. Had she not known? Yet it was possible. She had been shipped back to Rome while Titus set off on his victorious tour of the East. So in keeping with the man's character not to miss a chance to rub his enemies' noses in it. Not much of the poet in that one, it was clear. Cornelius avoided her eyes, which were now turned upwards, beseeching him to answer.

'You ... will be witness to the justice Rome bestows on traitors and rene-gades.' He was faltering despite himself, and he grasped at cruelty. 'Judgement has already been passed. Simon bar Gioras will be thrown from the Tarpeian Rock at the end of the Triumph to mark the return of the Emperor's son.'

He expected her to flinch then, to scream, to fall to her knees. She did none of these things. But two tears, plump as pomegranates, budded at the corners of her eyes and rolled down her cheeks. And Cornelius stood rigid before her, surprised by the vividness of his captive's pain. Quite at odds with the dogged inflexibility of his classical upbringing. True, there had been pity when his wife died. Had she not combined the best virtues of her class, modesty and austerity? And he missed her presence in much the same way he missed a beautiful Corinthian vase he had once owned. But this woman seemed to draw her pain from a deeper, more tragic source, then form it into an arrow, which she aimed straight at his breast. He did not know yet that this was her gift, the ability to pierce men's souls. And he felt only the sudden violation of her intrusion. He took a step back, more to emphasise her humiliation than to distance himself, asking, 'Do you know who I am?'

She looked steadily into his eyes and he looked back, oddly experiencing none of that mixture of pity and loathing the freeborn feel instinctively for the captive, but rather one of those strange moments of perfect communication, which he had read of in Plato's *Respublica*, but had always assumed only existed between men. For an instant he felt perfectly understood, and he whispered again, 'You know who I am?'

She cocked her head to one side, studying him, then nodded, and whispered back, 'A very lonely man.'

Her comment struck him like a slap —what had she seen?— and his jaw fell open under its impact. A huge anger seized him and it was only his need to demonstrate the uniquely civilized cast of his nature that made him rain down words instead of blows. 'You will know me,' he spat over numbed lips. 'I am your gaoler. Every crumb of bread, every drop of water you receive in these last days of your life is dependent upon me. If you do not wish your husband's last view of you to be a crawling skeleton, remember that.' He drew breath and had the satisfaction of spying a slight quivering of her chin. What had disturbed her when the thought of death left her unmoved? The husband? Yes. There was the Achilles' heel. He drove the point home. 'Perhaps you regret the day you allied yourself with a bandit, whose sole intention was the destruction of the finest civilization on earth.'

She had lowered her lids at his first assault. Now she looked up, eyes flashing with unearthly lights. 'What do you see, Roman? A blind woman? A heap of ashes?' She took a step towards him and her chains groaned to restrain her. 'Look again.'

Cornelius blinked. Perhaps it was the guttering light that made the shadows shiver back, like the raising of a curtain. Or perhaps it was the lowering of that soft voice almost to a growl that suddenly made Shelamzion bat Judah something more than a piteous heap of rags crushed into submission in the stinking bowels of Rome. She was tall and gaunt in the half-light, the stamp of her nobility unmistakable. Here was the queen he had come looking for. And how she despised him.

Her lips curled back. 'Look again, Roman. Did you think me a child, following my husband in deed and thought without question? How little you understand. Aye, my husband was the enemy of Rome. Would that you had seen how the legions trembled before him. Their name for him was *Excisio*. Destruction. And I was his bride.'

Cornelius stood transfixed. Did those who sought the cavernous secrets of the Sybil feel this strange loss of power? He gaped at the bandit queen. And suddenly all the pride went out of her and her head slumped forwards. 'Have you got what you came for, Roman?' Her voice was quite different now, small and empty, like a child who has known nothing but pain. Cornelius shook his head.

'This is not why I came.'

She barely lifted her eyes.

'Then … why? Has all Rome not done goading me?'

'That is not why I am here.'

She turned away as far as the chains would allow, and hunched her shoulders against all the weight of her sorrows. He thought she would not speak again. Her eyes were closed. But she shivered suddenly, as though the ghost of her thoughts walked through her, and asked, 'What do you want of me?'

'I want—' He paused, not knowing how to go on. Some instinct warned him to go no further. In a breath of clarity, he had seen her as she was, touched by a source magnificent and terrible. And to get too close would be to burn. *Cave quem di diligent*. Beware whom the gods love.

'I—' he started again, reaching out to her even as he made the sign against evil. She opened her eyes and his hand fell.

'I want you to live forever.'

Chapter II

I will shew unto thee the judgement of the great whore that sitteth upon many waters.
Revelation 17:1

Sores had formed round Shelamzion's ankles, where the metal chafed, and she welcomed the small diversion of pain. Better to feel pain than to go on torturing herself with thoughts of the Roman and his impossible promises. That way lay misery or madness, or—she dragged her hands down the sides of her face—worst of all tortures … hope. Although he was gone, the Roman had invaded her thoughts. Simon! Alive! She had been so certain when they led him away that it was to his death that the words of the Roman seemed miraculous. Unthinkable. Deceitful? She stopped in her tracks and her soul failed a little. A trick. Why not? Were the Romans not filled with treachery? Why should this one be any different? She thought of the moment when he had looked into her eyes, asking, *Do you know who I am?* She had said the first thing that came into her head. Yet hadn't she sensed something? Or was that a trick too? Had she simply wanted to see some hint of his loneliness in the midst of all her own?

But what if he spoke the truth?— Of course she had refused him, dismissed him with her silence. But … if Simon was alive. Then there was still hope, wasn't there? Her heart fluttered within her chest. She had seen him cheat death so many times. For a moment, she was entranced by a vision of him as he had once been. A man amongst men, addressing the thousands, ready to shake the foundations of the world. Her breast swelled. Surely not even the chains of Titus' army were enough to hold him. He will be free, she told herself fiercely. And not daring to think of rescue. He will be free for both of us. But then her heart darkened. Where would he go? Where could a man go, who had defied the limitless power of the Empire? Nowhere that Rome touched would he be safe. And the whole world was Rome.

Furious with his bandit queen's refusal and a thousand times more furious with himself, Cornelius crawled into his litter and ordered the slaves home at double time. The *custos* came running after him, enquiring whether he should punish the prisoner, but Cornelius ignored him, wanting only to get away from the stench and the filth. The humiliation of failure.

Now back in his home, a view of the villas on the Palatine visible from the front windows, Cornelius felt restless. It had been an ugly trick, he realized. To offer her immortality when it was more truly his own that he sought. Yet wasn't that the storyteller's artifice? To hold a soul captive behind bars of ink. How else might it be prevented from slipping forgotten into the next world? Even so, it had pained him to see the look in her eyes when he had explained the true meaning of his words. What had she hoped for? For a moment, he had sensed that there was something …

He sank heavily into a chair and sent for Atticus, ordering wine—plenty of it. Yet when it came, he found he had no thirst. With grim determination, he forced down a cup. But though it was an excellent vintage—the herbs fresh and newly mixed—it was powerless to sweeten the sour humors rising from his spleen. Nor had it the power to prevent his gaze from creeping forlornly towards his desk.

On top was laid a fresh roll of papyrus. Knowing it for weakness, but unable to resist, he went over to it and stared down at the unspoilt fibres. The first page, waiting in readiness to record the beginnings of his history. Only now there would be no history. No mention of him in the Senate. The dinner invitations would not come. He would be left to obscurity.

In despair, his hands reached out across the pristine sheet. Old hands they were. He seemed to be seeing them for the first time. The liver spots sprouting, like edible fungi, between the knuckles, the fingers clawed and crabbed. How right the Greeks were when they said old age was a wound that could not be healed. What spiteful trick of the gods had led him to believe that there was still time to grasp at glory? Mediocrity, that was to be his fate. Shelamzion bat Judah had seen to that. He watched his hands, as though they were not his, suddenly spasm into fists, crushing the papyrus into a yellow pulp. Then he straightened, and calling Atticus back, calmly told him to hire a litter. He would visit the baths. Yes indeed, the baths. Where else do old men go to while away the hours?

Her hands trembling, Shelamzion lifted her water bowl and tried to lick the bottom. Impossible. Her tongue had swollen. And besides, the bottom of the bowl was cracked and dusty. As well try to lick up the desert. She let it drop, and crouched against the wall, wrapping her arms around herself. Let her mind find something else to think on besides her thirst.

The Roman had said that Titus was bringing Simon to the city for the Triumph. Would they first bring him here? Might she see him again? The thought made her blood run hot then cold. What would he think of her? To see her in this place, dirty and defiled. Had he not honoured her and raised her up? Made her his queen. She could not bear the thought of him seeing her brought low, held in the darkness with the maggots and the worms and all the crawling things of the earth. She had wanted to give him, as every young girl dreams of, the gift of her beauty, and without thinking she started to draw a hand through the tangle of her hair. But it was filthy and alive. Revolted, she stopped.

What would be worse? Never to see him again? Or to see him look at her then turn away? And yet he would not turn away because she was filthy and degraded. That much she knew of him, and she did him insult to think otherwise. Surely there was but one reason he would turn from her. She had failed him. The precious gift he had entrusted to her care was gone, and with it all their hopes. She closed her eyes, wanting to flee into the barren desert of sleep. But her mind's eye, subversive to will, opened wide on blinding white light, on the soaring columns of Jerusalem's breath-taking Temple, soot-blackened now, their broken capitals, like daggers, piercing the sky …

'*Imma!*' Mother.

No time to answer. Keep running, Jathniel. Hold mama's hand tight.

She blundered forward. Beads of sweat obscuring her vision, the sun glaring through the smoky air, turning everything to sparks of white fire. Where am I? The laughter of the legionaries was behind her now. Or was it? Perhaps she was running towards them? Everywhere, bitter smells, charred wood, dust. Corpses littering the ground. Corpses where moments ago there had been living men and women. People who had struggled as she had struggled, who had wept and raged and laughed and prayed alongside her. Dead now. Making it hard for her to keep her feet.

She was lost. Dragged from her hiding place. Pushed and jostled and turned about until she might have been a hundred miles from where she began or back where she started. She put out a hand, feeling her way, like the blind beggars pleading for alms round the Nicanor Gate. What is this place? The Royal Portico? Or further in. The Court of the Women? Why didn't she know? She who had lived all her life in the shadow of this temple, who was as much a part of it as though her bones were the great supporting stones and her blood the sacrificial blood that flowed from its altars. But panic had transformed the place into a Roman hell, filling it with choking shadow and crackling flame.

She slowed her pace, aware that the world was beginning to grow solid. Details emerging from the glare. A smouldering staircase. A broken arch. And there was a strange smell in the air. Different from the hot, metallic smell of new blood and sizzling flesh.

'Imma!'

'Shh … not now. Not now.'

The little fingers were growing slick in her hand, and she struggled to hold on to them, even as she hesitated in an agony of indecision, her head turning this way then that. Where am I? What is this place? But she knew. In her heart, she knew. The Court of the Priests. Magnificent. Forbidding. The vast courtyard, surrounded by great halls and chambers, facing the holiest building of all, the Sanctuary of the One True God. That smell, the blood of numberless sacrifices permeating the stone. Animal blood spilled before a jealous deity so that He might not spill the blood of men. But she should not be here. Not *here*. In this place of immaculacy. This place of men. Even now her presence must be a violation.

A sharp, unexpected jab in her back. The butt of a legionary's *pilum* pushing against her spine. She gasped and stumbled forward, her breath coming out in dry little sobs. There was a broken, hiccoughing noise from behind, and she glanced back to see the man's distorted face. Was he laughing at her? They were all over the place like this now, Roman soldiers, drunk on victory and the spoils they had looted from caravans trying to supply the city. Now that Jerusalem's head was severed, they were swarming over her corpse, intoxicated by the smell of blood and booty.

Shelamzion turned southwards and began to run towards the Chamber of Hewn Stone. What ill fate had driven her to take this path? But her heart rang out with the certain knowledge of why she had come. She had needed to see for herself. Needed to know if Simon was wrong. Surely this couldn't be the end. Mightn't it yet all be part of the Lord's great plan? But her answer stood before her. Gone. The Sanctuary, that last haven where she might have pushed her son to safety. In its place, a charred ruin, black and smoking, gaping like the mouth of Sheol. And the One True God—Nowhere to be seen.

Im—possible. She staggered, feeling her knees go weak. She'd thought if she might only reach here that everything would be resolved. She would know what to do. But Simon had been right. God was not with them. And now all that was left to her was to save her child.

Gathering up her skirts, Shelamzion started to run again. There was a way. A way out if she could but reach it. Swiftly, she threw a glance over her shoulder, trying to count the number of legionaries behind them. *Kkhad. Treyn. Tlotho. Arv'o.* The Aramaic tongue burned against the parched roof of her mouth. Only four. And their attention had been drawn by a group of snarling, desperate men who had emerged from the Court of the Women and thrown themselves upon the Romans. Good. There was a chance.

'Come!' She tightened her grip around Jathniel's wrist, making him cry out.

'No, Imma. No!'

She ignored him, keeping her watering eyes on the altar up ahead. The great altar where the High Priest laid burnt offerings before the House of God. Well, the Romans had offered up the whole Temple as a sacrifice. Perhaps that was the reason God let them rule the world. She forced the bitter, blasphemous thoughts from her head and began to work her way along the side of the altar, keeping Jathniel tucked behind her, past where the huge, bronze *laver* stood waiting to be filled with clean water. Strange to be so near what she had only glimpsed from afar. But she did not look at it. Her eyes were trained to the ground, following the drains that led from the altar, past the place of slaughter then into the Parwah Chamber.

'Beneath the Parwah Chamber,' Simon had said, 'Down in the Chamber of Salt, you will find a sewer that will lead you below the Temple and out into the Kidron Valley.' It was the Parwah Chamber, wasn't it? Why hadn't she listened better? She risked another glance backwards. The legionaries were already dispatching the Jewish fighters. So little time. She ran harder, the soles of her sandals slapping against the hard stone. Jathniel was failing, his breaths coming in little whimpers. It tore at her to be unable to comfort him. But she had no breath left for words. Time enough for that when they were safe.

The Parwah Chamber was within sight. Its door torn off. If she could only make it inside. A shout from behind. The legionaries had spotted them. Don't stop! Don't look back! Keep running! Tears of exhaustion pouring down her face. Jathniel losing his footing. Dragging him behind her. Eyes burning. Lungs bursting. A rush of air past her ear and a *pilum* burying its deadly force in the side of a fallen timber. She swerved round it, sobbing, like a child. Blinded by tears. Stumbling and crying out her terror. The last few steps … And she was over the threshold.

For a single, luminous instant she believed they were safe. As the cool dimness closed around them she knew they had only to slip down the steps into the Chamber of Salt and they would disappear into the blackness of the sewers, never to be found. Free, if only with the freedom of a rat. But she would have taken it willingly. Eagerly she started towards the staircase. And it was then he appeared. A legionary climbing up from the Chamber of Salt. A huge man with a stupid, brutal face, which cracked apart in a gap-toothed grin when he caught sight of them. The smile confused her. Will he let us pass? She looked pleadingly into his face, whispering in Greek, 'Please …'

The grin did not waver, but his hand came down and unsheathed the *gladius* at his side. He advanced towards them, blade first, part of the Roman killing machine. The blood in her veins turned to ice, but she pushed Jathniel behind her and began to back away from him, still pleading softly in Greek. 'Please … You need not … No one will know.'

He didn't understand. Was still coming towards them with his *gladius* at point, and she did not have enough of the legionary's gutter Latin to reason with him. But there must be something. Some way to distract him. A bribe she could offer. Already they were back at the threshold, exposed. Something—

Cold metal touched the back of her neck. And she froze, knowing it was over.

The legionaries out in the courtyard had caught up with them.

For a moment, nothing happened. She felt the hot rays of the sun on the back of her head. The slow descent then rise of her eyelids as she blinked. A pulse of blood beating against her forehead, and the heat of the little fingers cocooned, like nesting dormice, in the safety of her hand. Then there was a guttural bark of Latin over her head and the world changed forever.

A tug. A wrench. More painful than any pang of childbirth and her son was gone. She was screaming, but the rush of blood in her ears deafened the sound. They were dragging her out across the courtyard. And words, meaningless to these ignorant Roman street boys, spilled over her lips as she pleaded and bargained with them, desperate to find some spark of human feeling in their empty, greedy faces.

'Not my son, my baby … Take me … Take me.'

They paused. One of them, a sharp-faced lad with large ears, like an intelligent mongrel, seemed to follow some of what she was saying. He said something to the others and their cracked, stubble-fringed lips broke into smiles. The sharp-faced one spoke to Shelamzion in a slurring, wine-soaked Latin she could not understand, but he was nodding and smiling so she nodded and forced herself to smile back, trying to show she was willing.

'Yes … yes. Take me.'

She let her glance go from face to face, fighting revulsion, unable to meet their eyes, wondering when it would start. Yet they did not move, waiting to see what she would do. So slowly, her hands trembling, her breath coming in ragged, convulsive moans, she lifted her skirts, like any street whore. Like an unveiled woman. A *tim'ay*. Filth. A ripple of something too strained and ugly to be called laughter went through the men.

'Hold!'

Whirling round she saw a weary-looking centurion coming towards them. His face was grey with ash, his armour dulled with dust and streaks of rust-coloured blood. Not until he was close did she see that he was young.

'What's going on here?'

The intelligent mongrel jerked his head uneasily towards Shelamzion.

'Dealing with prisoners, sir.'

The centurion drew a blackened wrist across his forehead. 'Then dispatch them and move on.'

'Sir!'

Shelamzion saw a blade raised towards her at a killing angle.

'No. Please.' She was on the ground, pleading at the centurion's feet. She did not know how she had got there or what she was saying. Overhead the sun had grown sulphurous, its poisonous illumination lighting her way to ruin. But she was possessed by demons that would not allow her to accept the dusty road down to death. Where was Jathniel? She heard him cry out to her. But saw only the hard flesh of the centurion's ankles. She gripped them as she might a graven image, face to the ground, pouring out her soul before this temple of blood and bone. 'Please … anything … anything—'

'Don't touch her. Leave her be!'

Turning her head, she saw one of the Jerusalemite fighters—wounded, but not yet dead—dragging himself towards them. Through her tears she recognized him. Ephraim was his name. A cheesemaker until he took up soldiering late in life. One of her husband's generals; she had thought never to see him again. But there he was, battered and nearing death, yet still crawling towards them, shouting out, 'Are you all fools and blind men? Can you not see? That is Simon's wife.'

One of the legionaries took a step towards him, but the centurion shook his head. 'No, this bears investigation.'

Hands found Shelamzion's shoulders, pulled her to her feet. She stood in their grip, mute now. The centurion regarded her doubtfully. 'You heard what that man said. Is it true? You are bar Gioras' wife?'

She dared to shake her head.

'Simon's wife might live …'

It was a trap. She knew it, but her eyes betrayed her in a pleading upwards glance. Too late she lowered her head. Then came the words she was in dread of.

'Where is the boy?'

'No. … No, not that … Jathniel—' She struggled in the iron grip of the legionaries, eyes searching wildly.

Ephraim lay still now, his arms outstretched as though reaching towards a little bundle of rags. The *pilum* that had grazed her ear was still sticking out of the fallen timber a little beyond them. She looked again. Men. Rags. *Pilum*. Was he hiding? Men … Rags—Her eyes stopped, as did her heart. She tried to take herself back. To see nothing but a pathetic little heap of tattered cloth. Too late. Her mind had caught the fragments and leapt forwards to form the whole, the small, dirty foot sticking out of the bottom, the dark puddle spreading red across the stone slabs …

'Jathniel!'

The word tore from her throat with a wild, inhuman pain, and she wrenched herself free, staggering forwards, calling his name again. He was lying on his back, head turned towards the Sanctuary, so that all she saw was the silky fleece of his hair and the delicate curve of an ear.

'Jathniel?'

Her legs were lead. She threw herself down beside him and gently lifted his head. It lolled helplessly in her hands and she nursed it to her breast, certain he was safe now. Would he not open his eyes? For his *imma*. She began murmuring soothing, childish nonsense, taking him back to the beginning so that she might give him life again. Yet for all her boundless love he lay still.

'Jathniel.'

A whisper this time, a sound so soft it did not carry, and falling from her lips was instantly extinguished.

'Jathniel.'

Cruel hands clamped around her arms and started dragging her away. She did not resist. Her head fell back, the sky darkened and the sun filled with blood.

Chapter III

History is philosophy from examples.
Dionysus of Halicarnassus,
Ars Rhetorica, Ch. 11, Sect. 2

Cornelius entered the fuggy, scented atmosphere of the bathhouse in a mood of depression. And it did little to improve his temper when he spied Quintus already relaxing on the water's edge. He would have preferred to delay a reunion with his cousin until he could rely upon himself to speak calmly. But he could hardly afford to ignore his benefactor. So, with ill grace he undressed, leaving his effects with his body slave, and waded over to greet his cousin.

It pleased him still less to discover Quintus engaged in conversation with the fleshy —yet unmistakable— figure of Aulus Gratidius Festus, a man of no consequence, and certainly no family, who was beginning to make a name for himself as an importer of human cargo. They glanced up as he approached, and he greeted them politely, trying to hide his annoyance at the careless way they received him.

'Ho, Cornelius, how goes it?' Quintus asked, then without waiting for a reply he turned to Festus. 'My cousin, Fabius Cornelius Grammaticus.'

'The *historicus*, eh.' Festus gave a disinterested shrug. 'Don't have many dealings with historians in my line of work. Not much use for them.'

'Nor would I presume to suggest otherwise,' Cornelius said coldly. 'Equally, I must confess that the intimacies of the flesh markets prove quite impenetrable to my untutored sensibilities.'

There was a brief, hostile silence. Quintus stretched languidly in the water. Cornelius moved his gaze to the entrance of the *caldarium*. Two slaves appeared. Both young, scarcely more than boys. They had sad, doe eyes and woolly heads. And while it was hardly remarkable to observe sadness in the eyes of a slave, something in their stiff, averted heads attracted Cornelius' attention. Something more than the familiar stance of deference before their masters. Some look of disbelief in amongst the horror, as though they were genuinely shocked. But of what—in this place, with its clean, smooth tiles and the sleek, hard bodies of young men bathing—Cornelius couldn't begin to imagine.

'Jews,' said Festus.

'I beg your—'

Festus gave a baleful nod in the direction of the two slaves. 'Everywhere now. There's the real tragedy of the war if you ask me.'

Cornelius turned to Festus with new eyes. 'You believe our victory over Judea came at a price.'

'Be a fool not to see it. Markets flooded. Between the *kalends* of one month and the *ides* of the next, price of a slave's more than halved. And, mark my words, we haven't seen the half of it. They say the emperor came back with a hundred thousand Hebrew slaves in tow. And his son is coming back from Judea with twice that number.' He rubbed thoughtfully at the hairy dome of his belly then spoke in lowered tones. 'Wouldn't surprise me if he's out before the *Veneralia*.'

Cornelius gasped. 'Vespasian overthrown by— '

'Hush. Not so loud.' Festus threw a glance at Quintus as if to ask whether *historicus* was a synonym for feeble-minded. 'All I'm saying is, we've seen three emperors come and go in a year. And people don't forget what Vespasian's men did here while they were chucking out old Vitellius. Made himself a lot of ene-mies when the temple of Jupiter burnt down.'

'But he was quick to order its rebuilding. And, besides, wasn't it his brother, Sabinus, who caused all the uproar trying to take it. Vespasian was still fighting the war in Judea.'

'Cornelius is writing a history of the war,' Quintus said.

'I—' Cornelius started to correct him, then realizing this was not the time broke off. 'I have not yet begun.'

'It's a marvellous undertaking, the writing of a history,' Quintus continued, then spoiled the compliment with a yawn. 'Yet I always find myself wondering, how do you decide exactly what was said at the height of a battle?'

Cornelius smiled. 'Naturally I choose to follow the advice of Thucydides and to compose speeches appropriate to those who made them and to the occasion. For example, when the rebel leader, Simon bar Gioras, turns the heads of his people against Rome, I intend to borrow from—' He had meant to go on, but Quintus had stopped listening. Festus began a lurid description of a new mural he was commissioning.

'An entire wall, facing the bed,' he was saying. 'Rape of the Sabines. Twenty female figures in all. And all of them very—' He cupped the air with his hands as words failed him. 'Couple of satyrs too.'

'Satyrs?' Cornelius asked.

Festus gave the mischievous grin of a schoolboy, which sat uneasily on his corpulent face. 'Just to spice things up. Artist didn't want to do it. You know how these creative types can be. Bleating on about balance and harmony. But I told him, "While the gold's still in my purse, to hang with harmony. I know what I like, and satyrs it is." ' He leaned forwards confidentially towards Cornelius. 'I mean, if a man pays for that much tit and ass on his wall it isn't harmony he's after, is it? He wants to see more—'

'You know, I can never remember,' Quintus interrupted, his sleepy eyes on Cornelius' scandalized face. 'Who was the woman who opened the city gates and betrayed Rome to the Sabines? Talaitha, wasn't it?'

'Tarpeia?' Cornelius corrected, still looking at Festus. 'She was crushed to death by the shields of the Roman soldiers. You surely know that the Tarpeian Rock was named after her.'

'Don't they intend to cast your rebel leader from it when Titus returns?' Quintus observed. 'To mark the end of the Triumph.'

Cornelius did not answer. The chilling echo of his words to the bandit queen suddenly hammered in his ears.

Judgement has been passed. Simon bar Gioras will be thrown from the Tarpeian Rock at the end of the Triumph …

It was Festus who spoke next. 'If I'd had my way, every whore's son of them would have been pushed off it last time they tried something.'

'Tried something?'

'Arsonists and bandits,' Festus said vehemently. 'Every last one of them. Not enough for them to burn down Rome. Now they want to set the whole world alight.'

'Wasn't that those new Jews?' Quintus stretched and blinked sleepily. 'The followers of Chrestus.'

'Christus,' Cornelius corrected automatically. 'My knowledge of them is scant. Though I seem to recall they have a particular affinity for fish. Their leader was a poor man … a fisherman, perhaps.'

Quintus laughed. 'Once a schoolteacher, always a schoolteacher.'

'Old Jews, new Jews, scratch the surface and they're all the same,' Festus said moodily. He made a snapping motion with his fingers and one of the woolly-headed slaves hurried forwards carrying a jug. He poured a golden stream of liquid directly into Festus' cup, keeping his eyes averted all the time. And watching, Cornelius felt an old fact shake itself loose from the dusty shelves of his brain. The Jews' distaste for nudity, even the perfectly acceptable kind between men. Such superstitious nonsense. But there was no denying that they were a peculiar race. And suddenly he wanted nothing more than to be at home. Away from these strange, black-eyed slaves, who looked towards him with sorrowing eyes, as though it was he who was somehow responsible for their fate.

He made as if to get to his feet. 'I must take my leave.'

'Wait a while.' Quintus' arm restrained him. 'You've yet to tell me how the new assistant governor of the Carcer fares.'

Reluctantly, Cornelius sat back down. He shot a sideways glance at Festus, who by some surprising quirk seemed to understand what was wanted and, downing the contents of his cup in one slobbering draught, lurched to his feet with many compliments aimed at Quintus. But his final words he reserved for the ears of the *historicus*. Bending low he murmured, 'This history of yours. Whose side do you come down on?

Cornelius stared. 'The side of truth.'

'Ah.' Festus straightened up and stretched the overlapping folds of his flesh. 'Best choose your audience carefully.'

After Festus had left they sat in silence, Cornelius filled with a desire to express his outrage in defence of his history only to recall that there would be no history. A thought, which made him morose and uncommunicative until Quintus remarked casually, 'Was the place as dreadful as I suggested?'

He had intimated no such thing, but Cornelius gave a grim nod.

'And your little Jewess, has she furnished you with all the lurid details you need to write your history?' Quintus eyed Cornelius through sleepy lashes. Embarrassed, Cornelius dropped his chin on to his chest and started to mumble something about the responsibility being more than perhaps a man of his limited experience was justified—

Quintus cut him off. 'My dear Cornelius, you're not suggesting our little Jewess sent you packing with your tail between your legs?'

Cornelius began to grow flustered. 'Not in so many words—' He wished his cousin wouldn't speak so loudly, but Quintus was propped up on his elbows now, the sleepiness of his face quite banished. This was not a good sign. Cornelius strove to make amends. 'You misunderstand me. She did not reject *me*. I simply found her less suited to my task than … I might otherwise have been led to believe.' He meant this last barb for Quintus, who appeared not in the least affected by it.

'I'd have thought letting her dance on the end of a *flagrum* for a bit would help loosen her tongue.'

Cornelius stiffened at the rebuke. 'Must you speak so coarsely? I think you're spending too much time in Festus' company these days.'

Quintus laughed. 'So you don't want her whipped. Really, Cornelius, you're far too tender-hearted. But you're wrong about Festus. He wouldn't recommend the whip.'

'Indeed?' Cornelius turned to Quintus in surprise.

'No. He favours the use of nettles.'

'Nettles?'

'Yes. Apparently he got the idea from an Eastern trader. The one he buys all the Nubians from.'

'But … but what does he do with nettles?'

Quintus raised an eyebrow. 'For a man who hopes to make his name through words you are singularly lacking in imagination. Think on it. There are only so many cavities through which to enter the human body without making a wound.'

He paused to laugh at Cornelius' affronted expression. 'Allow me to lighten the burden for you, cousin. He does not have them eat them.'

Cornelius opened his mouth, but nothing escaped, except a faint gasping sound, like an infant struggling to catch its first breath. Quintus was relentless.

'Come now, Festus would tell you to look on the bright side. After all, your Jewess affords you twice the opportunity of any of his Nubian males. And she didn't cost you a penny.'

'Really, Quintus! That is enough.' Cornelius could not contain himself any longer. 'I will not allow you to continue in this indecent manner. Your father may be a wealthy man and astute in matters of business, but he was sorely swindled when he paid for your education in morals.'

Quintus looked at him sadly. 'I fear, Cornelius, you lack cruelty. It is hardly surprising, therefore, that you are always disappointed in your ambitions.'

'If you are suggesting that all ambitious men are cruel,' Cornelius replied in a voice that shook, 'I could not help but agree. But if you are suggesting that there exists some universal law justifying such moral dereliction—that, in some way, it is the natural order of things for baseness to be found amongst the highest as well as the lowest—you are not only mistaken in your logic, but mistaken also in the belief that you and I share anything beyond the coincidence of our family name.' He got to his feet. But once again Quintus' arm restrained him.

'Cornelius. Dear cousin. I have offended you.'

Cornelius sniffed, but he did not remove Quintus' arm. Quintus spoke to him gently, his contrition almost comical in its exaggeration. 'Sit with me again, Cousin, please. I will make amends.'

With a show of reluctance, Cornelius resumed his seat. He expected Quintus to offer some formal words of apology, but instead he sat looking at him, lost in thought. After a while he said, more to himself than Cornelius, 'So she won't talk.' He fell into silence, drumming his fingers against the tiled steps. Then a light broke across his face. Cornelius looked at him questioningly. 'Well?'

'Well,' answered Quintus. 'Everyone has his price.' He held up a hand to stave off the inevitable eruption from his cousin. 'No. I do not mean to bribe her. If torture won't move the bandit queen, I doubt gold would tempt her.'

Cornelius moved closer. 'What do you mean?'

Quintus met his eyes. 'Well, they say where there's life, there's desire. Even a man nailed to a cross has wants.'

'And you think there may be something she wants … something she would bargain for?'

Quintus nodded. And Cornelius grew thoughtful. 'There was something. Just for a moment. I thought she wanted to ask me—' He shook his head. 'But nothing came of it. And she would deny it if I asked.'

Quintus smiled. 'Then don't.' He leaned forward, close as a lover, his breath hot in Cornelius' ear. 'A little bird has it that someone will be arriving shortly who knows all there is to know about her.'

Sh'ma Israel, Adonai Elohainu, Adonai Ahad. Hear O Israel, the Lord our God, the Lord is One.

Words. Familiar as the smells of childhood. Trying to form in the dry cavern of her throat. Instead, they wedged there, like blown sand. Choking her. She woke, gasping from her dream of evil only to find that it had followed her out into the waking world. She was incarcerated in stinking darkness, a faceless prisoner still, swallowed up in the belly of Rome. How much longer would they keep her here, now that her body was skeletal, her mouth a desert of ashes ready to cover her bones? I am dying, she thought, and took comfort in the knowledge. Slowly her eyes closed.

Light—

Shining in her face. And someone saying her name over and over again. Blinking weakly, she tried to sit up, but the effort was too much and she slumped back. Beyond the light the cell was in darkness. Day or night? There was no way of telling.

'Shelamzion!'

Who was calling her? She struggled for conscious thought and Cornelius' face swam into focus inches from her own. Roman. She made a weak, flailing motion with her hands, trying to push herself against the wall, ready to tear out the stones with her nails rather than let another Roman misuse her.

But he made no motion towards her. Instead he turned his head and spoke to someone out of sight. 'When was the last time this woman was fed?'

She heard the voice of the *custos* reply.

'Won't eat, sir. Give it to her regular. But she don't touch it.'

There was a clink of something at her foot and the Roman spoke again. 'This food bowl is dry as dust. There hasn't been a crust in it for days. Bring me a rag soaked in wine, then get some hot soup down here.' His voice hardened. 'And not that execrable slop you normally dish out.'

Shelamzion closed her eyes. Almost instantly something pressed against her lips, and a warm sensation dribbled down her throat, which immediately made her choke and push it away. It was brought back, more gently this time, and held there until she had managed to moisten her lips and swallow enough to feel a warm sensation spreading through her belly. All at once the world to which she had been growing less and less attached solidified around her. The Roman's arm was around her shoulders and she struggled to be free of it. She felt no sense of gratitude. She had been revived before, and there was always a price.

Cornelius waited until she was able to sit up independently before removing his arm. He crouched at her side, looking into the gaunt, filthy face.

'Shelamzion,' he whispered. Then louder. 'Shelamzion?'

Her eyes opened and rolled towards him. 'No.'

'Don't speak yet.' His voice was soft, but she bared her teeth. 'I'll tell you nothing, Roman.'

'Won't you?' He smiled at her sadly, like a wise teacher disappointed in a favourite student. 'Not even if I could bring you word of your child?'

Chapter IV

Simon, son of Gioras, a Gerasene by birth ... superior in physique and daring—the quality which caused Ananus the high priest to turn him out of his toparchy of Acrabata ...
The War of the Jews, Book IV

Three days had passed since Cornelius had given the order to revive Shelamzion bat Judah, and now she stood before him, cleansed of her prison stink, her hair washed and combed, hanging loosely down her back, like a dark mantle, a fresh robe covering her body. She was no longer shackled. But her face was still pale and there were deep lines of suffering etched upon her brow and in the corners of her mouth.

The *custos* had brought her here to this bare, unadorned room. It was almost as small and dark as her cell, but it was clean and dry, and there was light from a grating high in the wall, and a small fire crackling in the hearth. A stool was set in the centre of the room, opposite a rough wooden table, behind which sat the assistant governor. He was watching her, his shrewd face thoughtful, yet betraying nothing of what he was thinking. His gaze filled her with a sinking unease; other men had looked at her that way, trying to get the measure of her thoughts and it had never led to kindliness. She stood very still, holding herself erect. Let him see that she was no slave to stand with head bowed.

After a moment something flickered behind his eyes and he smiled faintly. 'Have you been well treated?'

She let her gaze travel down to the barely-healing sores that ringed her wrists, and knew that he was watching. She heard him cough. 'But you have been given food ... water?'

She nodded.

'And your cell? I gave orders that you be moved.'

She looked him squarely in the face and answered in unaccented Greek. 'I have been granted more hospitality than I first received.'

Cornelius lifted an eyebrow, and would have said more, but he noticed the bandit queen had begun to sway slightly and the colour had drained away from her face. He inclined his head towards the stool.

'Please, sit.'

Shelamzion obeyed, still watching him warily. This sudden concern for her well-being was more frightening than the threat of punishment. And to hide her confusion she turned her head and gazed into the fire. Little demon-tongues of flame crackled and spat at each other, like the hissing mouths of pagan gods. Yet it was good to be here, to be warm again. Then, in a rush, words Simon had spoken came back to her: *Fear Romans most when they would bestow favours upon you.* In panic her hand gripped the rough fabric of her tunic. She must take care. But when she turned back the assistant governor was smiling.

'Perhaps,' he began amiably, 'you have had time to reconsider.'

She stiffened, but did not answer. The assistant governor nodded, then continued.

'You recall my request for your help in composing a history of the war?'

Shelamzion kept her face immobile. 'Why come to me? It is my husband you want.'

'Titus intends to display his star captives on a grand tour of the east. Naturally he wishes to relish his victory, (He kept to himself the opinion that Vespasian wanted his son— a man who knew more about soldiering than politics— at a distance, while Rome adjusted to its fourth emperor,') Many months may pass until they reach our shores.' Cornelius leaned across the desk. 'No. It is your help I need.'

'I will not help you, Roman.'

His jaw tightened and he drummed his fingers on the desk.

'Not even to save your son?'

She closed her eyes against his words, then took a deep breath. 'My son is dead. I saw him murdered with my own eyes.'

Cornelius glanced down at the papers on the desk before him then back up again. 'Yet it was not so.'

Her eyes flew open and for a fleeting moment there was a look of intense yearning on her face. Then her expression hardened. 'You think to trick me.'

'No indeed.' Cornelius tapped the papers before him. 'I have the accounts of two legionaries of the V Macedonica. Good and reliable men according to their commander. They had heard that in the last days of the siege a centurion came across a small boy near the place you call the Sanctuary. He was wounded and near death, but the centurion took pity on him and brought him to one of the camp's physicians—'

Shelamzion interrupted him, her hand outstretched. 'I would see for myself.'

In surprise, he handed her the documents and watched as she read the reports. It was bemusing to find that the bandit queen was educated, and it secretly pleased him to have made this discovery. He watched as she read the documents through twice, then laid them back on the desk.

'This could be any boy,' she said. But her voice trembled as she said it.

Cornelius gave a small shrug. 'That is true.' He made a show of gathering up his papers. 'There must have been many small boys lost to their mothers in those terrible times.'

She was silent, then she said quietly, 'Not so many.'

'Yet it may mean nothing.'

She did not answer him, and Cornelius nodded. 'But, doubtless, you are correct. The documents could have been referring to any boy.' He glanced at the door. 'Guard!'

The door opened and a burly man, Cilician by the look of him, entered. He looked at Shelamzion then turned to the assistant governor. Cornelius gave a slight nod, and the guard took a menacing step forward.

'No … Wait.' She wasn't ready to go back. She jumped to her feet, knocking the stool over, and it fell with a crash against the flagstones. But it did not halt the Cilician, who marched towards her, his face set in a dull repose of malice. She backed away, the heat scorching her back, and her eyes sought the assistant governor's face.

'Please—'

He frowned, adopting an air of puzzlement, and she said quickly, 'I would hear more.'

For several heart-stopping seconds he did not answer. Then he glanced at the Cilician and shook his head. The guard made a small salute and took his leave of the room without a second glance at the prisoner. After the door banged shut, Cornelius and Shelamzion were left in silence, each watching the other, like two lions circling, until Shelamzion ventured, 'Is there not … more?'

A bright, naked hope was burning in her eyes, but it seemed to disturb the assistant governor. He shuffled his papers and cleared his throat several times. 'There are some additional facts my sources have provided.'

'Tell me … I beg you.' Her body was tilted towards him, poised, as though suspended by a single, fragile thread, and her eyes were two bright spots in the otherwise dead pallor of her face. Cornelius blinked, and for a single ghastly moment felt unable to draw his plan to its conclusion. Only the thought of admitting to Quintus how he had got his fish to take the bait but failed to land her gave him the strength to continue. He coughed, then pretended to study the topmost scroll before saying, 'It would appear that the child was between one and two years of age.' He heard her sharp intake of breath and plunged on. 'He was too young to provide information concerning his parentage. But he answered to the name of Jared or possibly Javan.'

'Jathniel,' she said softly. 'His name is Jathniel, *the gift of God.*'

'Then the news is good.' Cornelius leaned back in his chair and rubbed the back of his neck. 'You have found your son.'

For a moment, her face lit up with an almost celestial light and she took a half-step forward, arms outstretched, as though to embrace him. Then understanding clouded her features and she froze, as though the dark horror underlying his words could not be made real if she did not speak it. Cornelius watched her carefully then said blandly, 'A joyous occasion is it not, when a mother discovers that her child is alive?'

He expected his words to provoke a frenzy. Instead she stood very still, her face immobile. Only her eyes moved rapidly from side to side, as though she was trying to decipher a difficult passage in a book. When finally she spoke, her words fell dull and hard, like little drops of lead. 'Have you found him?'

Ah, so that was it. She was cleverer than he had supposed. He would have to tread carefully on the narrow path between half-truth and deceit.

'As yet we do not know his whereabouts,' he admitted. 'But I am assured that it is only a matter of time.'

She said nothing, and now her calmness began to grate on him. He got to his feet and came round the desk to face her. There was not much difference in their heights, but he made a show of bending down and speaking close to her ear. 'What is wrong? Are you a mother to stand silent as the grave when you receive news of your child?'

She did not look at him, but stared straight ahead, as though talking to someone he could not see. 'You will kill him.'

He closed his eyes briefly then opened them again. If he wanted her co-operation he must not waver.

'Can you be so certain?'

'He is Simon's son,' she replied dully. 'How can you let him live?'

He did not answer at first, but stepped back so that there was distance between them once more. 'Perhaps there is a way.'

She did not seem to hear him—stood shaking her head, her eyes lowered—and he was forced to say again, 'There is a way … to save him.'

She looked up, eyes black with loathing. 'You lie!'

Cornelius reddened. Should he stand here, a citizen of Rome, allowing himself to be subject to such insolence? A prickle of perspiration broke out on his forehead, and he dabbed at it. A curse on Quintus and his stupid schemes. The bandit queen was to have been on her knees by now sobbing in gratitude, not standing before him like a vengeful fury, accusing him of deceit. He tugged at an earlobe. Little wonder that the Jews were a nation bent on self-destruction if this was what their women were like.

Her eyes had not left his face, and he saw now that he had been wrong to approach her as an eager supplicant to his goodwill. He must use more cunning. Dropping his gaze to the floor, he allowed himself a moment to regain his composure, and when he looked up again he was smiling, and his voice was quite steady as he asked, 'You Jews enjoy a bargain, do you not?'

It was a clumsy opening, but it would have to do. He watched the iciness of Shelamzion's expression crack and uncertainty show through. She was frowning, and, taking this as a good sign, he continued, 'As an historian … of some repute,

I deem it my duty to chronicle the events that led to the unhappy demise of your nation with the utmost clarity and detail. Too many baseless and inconsistent stories abound. And even the most astute writer may struggle to differentiate truth from fabrication.'

He paused. Words which had resounded with a certain grandeur when he spoke them to the admiring ears of dinner-party guests sounded hollow and faintly ridiculous now that he was faced with the one person who could truly appreciate his meaning. He coughed and massaged the base of his throat. 'I mean to write a history … ' he began again more slowly. 'Not in the manner that has become so fashionable of late, where every fault of the victor is overlooked in order to praise his achievements without hint of offence. Rather, it is my intention to write a history that does not idly flatter the conquerors while at the same time finding nothing but fault with those they have conquered.'

She was staring at him intently, but he could not tell what she was thinking, and he went on hurriedly, 'It is my ambition to produce a work never before accomplished, though it be compared with any of the great minds: Hieronymus, Plutarch, Pliny—A work that reveals the world to itself in all its ugliness and beauty.' He had forgotten his fear of ridicule, and let his hand fondly caress the sheets of papyrus on the desk. 'This will be my masterpiece, a melting pot of base motives and noble sensibilities, of matchless jealousies and exalted acts of courage. I shall bring them together in a single sublime and eloquent undertaking that will lift the veil from men's eyes and draw them ever closer to that one marvel of flawless purity they are forever seeking—' He broke off, then spoke the last word almost in a whisper. 'Truth.'

As the sound died on his lips, Cornelius found that he was almost panting. Shelamzion had drawn back a little, and though her face was immobile, something flickered behind her eyes, and he found himself thinking, *If she dares to laugh, by the gods, I swear I will wring the life out of her with my bare hands.* But she did not laugh. She furrowed her brow and asked, 'But what has this to do with me?'

She had taken the bait. His relief was so great that he had an absurd notion to go to her and take her hands in his. Instead, he walked round the desk and sat down heavily, nodding sombrely to underlie the gravity of his words. 'The proposition is simple. You have something I want. I have something to offer.' There was a Euclidian elegance to the pact that pleased him immensely, and he looked at her expectantly. He was met with blankness.

'I have nothing to offer.'

'Not so!' Cornelius cried, almost tripping over his words with excitement. 'It is true that your sex makes you ill designed for the nature of the task I wish you to undertake. But, as the wife of Rome's foremost enemy, you are in a unique position to provide me with eyewitness accounts and insights into the mechanisms that led your nation to insurrection.' He did not add that his previous interrogations of Jewish slaves had met with sullen evasion or helpless inability to communicate in a foreign tongue.

She was watching him closely. 'And in return?'

Cornelius blinked, having almost forgotten his role in the bargain. 'In return?' He did not quite meet her eye. 'I will find your son and guarantee his protection.'

To his surprise, she laughed, albeit a thin, echoing laugh that did not reach her eyes. 'And who are you to stand against the might of your emperor's wishes?'

He flushed. 'I am a respected citizen,' he said stiffly. 'And I have many powerful … connections in Rome, people who understand that necessity must sometimes be sacrificed to expediency, and who will appreciate the wisdom of my decisions—' Hearing the almost treasonable tone that had crept into his words, he broke off and could not help glancing towards the door. It remained firmly shut, and no guard burst through, shouting *Treachery!* But when his eyes returned to Shelamzion bat Judah he found she was considering him with a narrow, cynical expression, which suggested that she had not believed a word he had uttered. Indignation made him brutal. 'The question is not whether you can trust me,' he said, laying cold emphasis on each word. 'But, given that your son's life hangs in the balance, whether you can afford not to.'

She flinched, and he watched her glance from side to side, as though desperate to escape the trap he had set for her. Then she sighed and her whole body relaxed. She turned to him, half smiling. 'You have brought my husband back to life. Now you offer me my son?'

Cornelius nodded. He was leaning forward across the desk, holding his breath, and she looked down at him, shaking her head slightly. His heart skipped a beat.

'And the only thing you ask in exchange is the only thing that has not been taken from me … my history.'

He was afraid to look at her, afraid she might look into his soul and see that it was riddled with deceit. But she closed her eyes and her lips moved. And he was not sure if she argued with herself or prayed.

'Will you do it?' he asked, hoarsely.

Her eyes opened. 'I do not know if I can trust you.'

'Have you heard nothing—' Cornelius blustered, but she ignored him, and went on speaking softly, almost to herself. 'I do not know if I can trust you. But I will do what you ask. For the sake of my son, and because, when you talked of your love of truth and beauty you made me remember that once, long ago, I loved those things too.'

'Tell me about your husband.'

Two weeks had passed since Shelamzion had agreed to divulge the secrets of her past, and Cornelius had visited every morning, installing himself behind the *custos*' chair, papyrus spread out, reed pen poised and ready in his hand. She was surprised that he did not employ a scribe. After all, labour was cheap to the Romans. What citizen of Rome would wipe the food from his mouth if there were a slave nearby to do it for him? Yet she did not dare to ask him. He was still the enemy. It was his key that locked her into darkness each night.

Cornelius tapped the side of his nose with his pen and repeated his request. 'Your husband, tell me what you remember.'

She put her hands to her temples and sighed. Two weeks and always the same: Tell me about your husband. What was he like? Did men love him? Were they willing to die for him? She lowered her hands and, standing straight, tried to uphold her side of the bargain. 'My husband was a great man. He led his men with both honour and courage—'

'No. No. No,' Cornelius broke in, rapping his pen against the desk. 'We have been through this. Anyone of note might be described as honourable and coura- geous by his own kind. It tells me nothing of the man or his motives. You say he was a great man. Yet is it not true that he slew his own countrymen without pity, that he destroyed food stores, that he executed men without benefit of trial?'

'No!'

'No?' Cornelius raised his eyebrows. 'These things did not happen?'

Shelamzion began to pace up and down, twisting a fold of her tunic between her hands. 'I did not say that.'

'Then explain.'

'How can I? War is not what you think, some noble game to swell the hearts of poets. War is like a demon that takes over the souls of men. Even the most high-minded may find themselves forced to commit acts of a loathsome nature—'

'And this is how you justify your husband's tyrannical actions?'

'Yes … No. You twist my words.'

Cornelius put down his pen and pinched the bridge of his nose. Two weeks. Two fruitless weeks. He had taken in every word the bandit queen had to say for herself, filled countless papyri with studious note-taking … yet something was still missing. He stared sourly up at Shelamzion, saw her lick her lips. Was she holding something back from him? If he found she was, then by the gods he'd— No. No, he must stay calm. She had spoken freely enough. It wasn't that.

But his instincts as an historian warned him that the growing mountain of facts and platitudes he had collected so far amounted to nothing more than a sorry jumble of tiresome detail and bland anecdote. The dullest imagination might write of war, quoting exact figures about anything and everything, from which legions lined the battlefield to the quality of bread the *praefectus castrorum* provided for the troops' dinner on a particular day. But such histories were as colourless as clods of earth. The heavens knew he had heard enough of them read out by dull-witted boys during his days in the schoolroom. What of passion? Of hubris or heroism? Quintus would call him an old fool for these thoughts.

His eyes travelled over Shelamzion bat Judah. She had fallen silent and was staring at the floor. Would she too think him a fool, this humbled, captive queen? Suddenly Cornelius felt loneliness weigh heavily on his heart. He thought of returning home, of giving the whole project up as foolishness. But what was there for him at home? Empty rooms. The dead eyes of his slaves. Reluctantly he picked up his pen.

'You have not explained to me how a man of such intelligence and moral character chose to ally himself with those of a rebellious nature against the ruling elite who had shown him nothing but kindness.'

She began plucking at her tunic again. 'I cannot.'

Cornelius felt himself seized with a wild fury. 'You cannot or you choose not to?'

'I cannot!' She surprised him by showing a wildness of her own. In two steps she was at the desk, grasping its edge, as though she intended to hurl it and its contents across the room. Cornelius stared, dumbfounded, but after a moment she breathed more easily and her hands slipped to her sides. 'I cannot explain,' she said quietly. 'You do not understand. You know nothing of our lives.'

Cornelius leaned forward, suddenly excited. 'Then teach me.'

She shook her head. 'Can you think it so easy?'

They stared at each other, both sensing that a point of no return had been reached. Then Cornelius' face broke into a slow, contemplative smile and he leaned forward on to his elbows. 'I think I have been wrong. You cannot tell your husband's story.'

Fear flashed across her eyes.

'I can tell it. You have only to give me the chance—'

Cornelius shook his head. 'I have asked you to tell me the story of your husband. But you do not know it.'

She was trembling now, seeing her child slipping beyond her grasp. Her eyes pleaded with him. 'I will try harder, *archon*. Please, it is the only story I have to tell.'

His eyes narrowed; she had called him 'lord'. But he began rolling up his papyrus. 'No. You cannot. And I was wrong to ask it of you.'

She started to speak then stopped. She dropped her gaze to the floor, then looked back up at him, eyes glistening with a measureless pain.

Cornelius' expression grew kindly. 'Do not distress yourself. Now I think on it, the fault is surely mine. I have been asking you to tell the wrong story.'

She took a step backwards, shaking her head. 'What else can I tell?'

Cornelius sat back in his seat and let his eyes travel slowly across her frightened face. 'Tell me about yourself. Of your childhood in Judea. How you met Simon and came to be his wife.'

She stared at him blankly. 'But what use is that? It is not his story.'

'No indeed.' Cornelius agreed, half smiling. 'It is yours. And in the end, what other story do we have the right to tell?'

The next day she was given a mean breakfast of grey, gritty bread, then taken straight to the assistant governor's room. It was still cold. The heat from the fire seemed puny, failing to warm anything but a narrow pie-slice of room directly in front of it. The assistant governor had pulled his table up close to the hearth, though he was dressed in a thick, woollen mantle. Every so often he put down his pen and frowned at the fire, as if to chastise it for poor performance. Shelamzion kept to the far end of the room, despite the chill on her back. She did not like to get too close to the flames. She saw faces there.

The assistant governor frowned again, then lifted his pen and licked the end of it. 'We will begin at the beginning. Where were you born?'

She bit her lip and glanced one last time towards the door, before answering, 'I was born in Jerusalem. My father's house was in the new city, in the district of Bezetha. And I was born there in the ninth year of the reign of Tiberius Claudius.'

Cornelius nodded and his pen began to scratch along the surface of a fresh tablet. 'And your family? Do you claim a distinguished lineage?'

She seemed surprised by the question. 'I claim no privilege by birth.' Then seeing his frown she added quickly, 'But my family was not without wealth. My father was a doctor of the Law—'

'I see.' Cornelius nodded without looking up. 'And that is how he made his living?'

She gave a short laugh. 'Indeed not. Some of the poorest men in Israel are doctors of the Law. It is said of my grandmother, that when she heard my father wished to be a Pharisee, she blessed the Lord for showing him the way to piety and cursed my grandfather for not teaching him a better way to earn his bread.'

'Then your father did not have the means to provide for his family.'

She looked at Cornelius sharply. 'I did not say that. My father was a gentle, moderate man, greatly respected in our community. Perhaps because of this, he married well, and the dowry my mother brought was wisely invested. My brothers were much taken up in overseeing the family's interests in our date-palm orchards, and then there was the harvesting of balm from the plantations in Jericho and the deals to be struck with merchants from Peraea. My brothers, Menachem and Judas, ran everything. And this left my father to his greatest pleasure … that of teaching.'

Cornelius glanced up without raising his head. 'Then he must have been a most remarkable man. I, myself, spent many years in the classroom teaching the merits of Homer and Theocritus to small boys. And never once would I have described it as an act of joy.' He had not intended the sentence seriously. But she stood, biting her lower lip, considering the matter for some time.

'Perhaps,' she said at last, 'that was because you were compelled to take your pupils regardless of talent or commitment. The young men who came to my father fought for the privilege of becoming his disciples, and he always exercised the utmost caution in making his selection.'

'Perhaps,' Cornelius agreed in a hollow voice. 'Then, doubtless, between the good fortune of your mother's dowry and the satisfaction your father's employment brought him, yours was a happy childhood.'

A shadow passed over Shelamzion's face. 'It was happy ... at least I remember it being so ... until the riots began in Caesarea.'

Chapter V

… in the toparchy of Acrabata Simon, son of Gioras, collected a large band of revolutionaries and gave himself up to pillage. He not only looted the houses of the rich, but ill-used them personally and it was evident from the start that his aim was despotism.
The War of the Jews, Book II

Ah, Jerusalem. Jerusalem on high. Exalted beyond all delights. The thrones of justice are there. May those who love you prosper! Your golden age is yet to begin. As time went by, and this enduring message drew the thousands and the hundreds of thousands into Jerusalem's eternal embrace, how could the growing population of priests and scribes, bakers and cheesemakers, pedlars, silk merchants, artisans, pilgrims, prophets, lepers, thieves and beggars be sustained? And so a new city was created on the north side of the ancient walls, almost doubling its size to more than four hundred and fifty acres, and this was known as the Bezetha suburb.

On the roof of one of the better houses in this suburb stood the tall, straight-backed figure of Shelamzion bat Judah. She had come up here to be alone with her thoughts, and also because she hated the women's work of spinning. Here she could catch any chancing breeze that might fleetingly stir the air, and though it was almost always her choice of refuge the roof seemed to be the last place any-one ever thought to look for her.

There was no breeze today. The air had a heavy, aromatic quality and it was impossible to take a breath without the ticklish sensation of inhaling fibrous layers of thick, unwashed wool. Shelamzion did not mind. She was sixteen years old and filled with the unshakable confidence that life was merely a fragrant dish waiting to be sampled. In this she was no different from any other child of sixteen summers. Her destiny was as certain as her soul, and lacking either form or shape, it was limitless, soaring. It made her restless, and more and more frequent-ly chased her up on to that roof, to the only place she could be alone.

'Shel—amzion. Daughter of the house, where are you?'

The voice, thin and appealing, was coming from the courtyard. Stupid old Sarai. A slave all her life, half bent over with age. Why did she never look up? Shelamzion stole a last look over the rooftops of Jerusalem. But the scene was so familiar, the landmarks so much the background to the canvas of her life, that she accepted it all without emotion. Not even the alabaster blaze of Herod's great temple atop Mount Moriah or the grey Antonia Fortress, its slabbed sides failing to change even in the golden sunlight, made the slightest impression. Jerusalem was her home, her bedrock, her birthright. And she took it utterly for granted.

On the stairs that led down from the roof she was careful not to be seen by the ancient Sarai. Instead she chose to slip indoors and make her way through a series of rooms to her father's study. The latticed windows let light into the room in long, slanting pillars, illuminating certain objects—the fine old writing desk, the wax tablets lined up on chests filled with papyrus scrolls—and leaving others in shadow, and thus when she entered the room the sitting figure of her father was not immediately visible. Instead she went over to the desk and examined an opened scroll, held in place with four smooth, round stones. It was written in Greek and she read with ease,

> *In the tenth year of Emperor Nero Claudius Caesar Augustus, in the procuratorship of Gessius Florus before the nones of Artemisios, hereby called Sivan in accordance with the custom and practices of the people of Jerusalem…*

But she got no further, because a powerful sense of being observed made her lift her head sharply, to find the watchful eyes of Rabbi Judah ben Eliad fixed upon her.

'Father.' She felt pleasure at seeing him, but also a little guilty at having been caught prying. She rubbed the polished wood of the floor with the sole of her foot, waiting for him to speak.

'I'm glad you came. Did Sarai tell you I was looking for you?'

Her mouth took on a slightly petulant look, an air adolescence had recently added to the library of her expressions. 'I didn't hear. I was on the roof.'

Rabbi Judah's eyebrow rose a fraction, and she went on quickly, 'You wanted me, father?'

He shrugged a thin shoulder and shifted uncomfortably in his chair. Anxiously watching him, Shelamzion felt a pang. He seemed so very old. Not a young man when he had married, children had been a late blessing to the union. And now as Shelamzion, the youngest, took her first long-limbed steps into womanhood, his flesh seemed to shrink and the shadow of eternity could sometimes be detected in the far-off focus of his eyes. He was stroking his beard, a prelude to serious pronouncement, but all he said was, 'We will wait till your mother gets here.'

Not old enough to have learned to keep her own counsel, she babbled, 'Is it about the spinning? The fault was not mine. The spindle broke.' She looked at him appealingly. 'I know I often drop it, but—'

'A spindle must fall many times before it breaks,' he remarked shrewdly.

She dropped her gaze to the floor and did not answer.

'Yet in the story of Moses, do we not learn that, All the women who were wise-hearted did spin with their hands … '

She looked up then, all the childish petulance gone from her expression, to be replaced with the firm mouth and steady eyes of a young woman ready to speak her mind. 'You taught me to read and to write, father. To understand the Law and interpret the commentaries. Have you not often said that I am more accomplished than Menachem and Judas?' She studied his face earnestly. 'You will not deny it?'

Rabbi ben Eliad stroked his beard. 'I will not deny that you have shown more dedication to your studies than your brothers.'

'Then why must I spend my time rubbing my fingers raw to make cloth that looks as though it was made with hooves rather than hands?'

Her father evinced surprise. 'Will your husband then go naked beneath the sun?'

'Husband?' The thought made her burst with laughter. And in a rush of affection she ran forward, crouching down at her father's feet and hugging his knees. 'I will never—' A sound from behind made her break off and turn her head towards the door. Into the room had come her mother.

The rabbi's wife was a tall, bony woman, with her daughter's wide, dark eyes. But where the daughter's eyes were filled with a clear, uncompromising intelligence, the mother's were clouded by the constant shadow of a deep-seated bitterness—too many babies lost in the early years of the marriage. Hopes dashed. Joy buried over and over in the cold ground. And now the wife of Rabbi ben Eliad was always looking over her shoulder, waiting for disaster.

And though she would have admitted it to no one, least of all herself, when her fears proved founded it gave her a strange sense of fulfilment, in truth a kind of sexual release. Her three surviving offspring had not brought her the joy she had expected. When they had not died she found herself comparing them unfavourably with the saintly characters of their dead siblings, almost as though they had cheated her of her pain. And she was often remote with them, secretly blaming them for escaping their fate.

With Shelamzion this resentment manifested itself in harsh criticism. Had Shelamzion been a biddable child, eager to please, pity might have eventually tempered resentment and mellowed their relationship. But Shelamzion, so it seemed, cared only to thwart her mother in all matters of advice and instruction. She dressed carelessly, often forgot to comb her hair, could not be persuaded to control her spindle or to grind corn to the desired texture. And if left to her own desires would fritter the day away in reading or conversing with her father in Greek.

In vain her mother had tried to put an end to these unfeminine devotions, but Rabbi Judah was an indulgent father, who, recognizing the more plodding nature of his sons' souls, found a mirror of his own quick mind in the shining eyes of his daughter. To his wife's objections he often waved a dismissive hand. 'Peace. Are we not commanded to turn our ear to wisdom and our hearts to knowledge?'

And, with neither learning nor natural humour to counter these arguments, she was forced to submit to the indignities of defeat. It did not make for an easy relationship between mother and daughter. And as Shelamzion's learning increased, so did the doubt in her mother's heart that a learned daughter could feel anything but contempt for an illiterate mother. Standing in the doorway, hearing them chattering easily in a language she could not begin to understand, she thought, *No more. I shall put an end to this.*

To her husband she asked, 'Well, does she know?'

Rabbi Judah had been smiling at his daughter. Now the smile left his face. He loosened Shelamzion's grasp on his knees and motioned for her to get up. A little hurt to be so abruptly cut loose, Shelamzion scrambled to her feet. Already she sensed that there was more to this summons than the usual admonishments for domestic ineptitude. She avoided the stony face of her mother, focusing her gaze, as always, on her father.

'What should I know?'

Rabbi Judah looked at his daughter with guilt in his heart. He had lived something of a double life with her, allowing her mind to range wild and free in the confines of their conversations. It had given such pleasure to his old age. When it came to learning, his sons, Menachem and Judas, were like sand, absorbing everything, yet remaining essentially unaltered. Shelamzion was like the earth, lapping up learning like water and sprouting back beauty and splendour wherever words touched her.

But this splendid flower, this rose of Sharon he had so carefully cultivated within the walls of his home suddenly seemed too exotic a bloom to survive in the rigid matrix of society outside. A woman was legally and morally a minor in the eyes of the law, and while it had been his secret joy to coax a female mind to independence he now saw, with an old man's hopelessness, where his selfishness had led. To his daughter he said, 'We are pleased to tell you that we have found you a husband.'

She blinked at him stupidly. As though, for all her knowledge of Aramaic, Hebrew, Greek, even a little Latin, she could not find the intelligence to translate his words. Rabbi Judah coughed, then forced out a smile. 'Do not look so thunderstruck. You—we both knew this day must come.'

Shelamzion's eyes had filled with tears. 'Who?' she managed to stutter out at last.

Rabbi Judah glanced at his wife, not trusting himself to speak. And feeling the power of being deferred to, for once, she became business-like. 'Don't think it was an easy choice. Men do not flock to find a wife with talents such as yours.

Did you think we could announce to the world that our daughter, Shelamzion bat Judah, wife to words and mother of fine letters wishes a husband who can cook and spin and keep house for her—'

Balling her hands into fists in an effort to control the frightening disorder of her thoughts, Shelamzion interrupted her mother, asking again through gritted teeth, 'Who is he?'

Her parents exchanged glances, both acknowledging that this was no maidenly response, though in her father acknowledgement was tinged more with sadness than condemnation. Avoiding his daughter's eye, Rabbi Judah said, 'He is a fine young man of faultless virtue and good character. Your mother has done well to find him.'

Shelamzion stayed silent and her silence spoke more eloquently than her interruption. Rabbi Judah heaved a sigh and went on. 'His name is Saul bar Akiba, the eldest son of a family whose fortune is in silk and cotton … ' He continued to speak, aware that he was selling this young man, like a street hawker eager to impress a cynical customer. But for all his efforts, Shelamzion, who was listening with a face set like stone, heard the details only in part.

There was a noise, like a howling gale, inside her head. It was the sound of her voice screaming, *No, no, no!* And her father's words were scattered upon it. She gathered that Saul's father had been dead many years. That his mother had remarried, and that he had a younger brother, Simon … Business was profitable. And Saul … No, Simon was making a career for himself in politics. Already governor of Acrabetene—

'Acrabetene?' she whispered. 'So far.' To any Jerusalemite Acrabetene was little more than a wild province in the north, hardly civilized since the days of the wandering tribes. The blow of Exile more crippling than the revelation of marriage.

'No, no. You misunderstand.' Rabbi Judah got shakily to his feet, gesturing to his wife to hand him his stick. 'Saul has no desire to stay in his mother's house. He hopes to expand the business here in Jerusalem. He has plans for Judas to join him when he finishes his studies. After all, Menachem has long complained that there was not enough work for two at the plantation.' He smiled at her, and she felt the first stirrings of hope.

'And, if I marry him, where will we live?'

'Here. Under this roof.'

'Of course,' interjected her mother, 'You will be expected to behave like a wife. Saul will not want you spending your days with your fingers dipped in ink and your head in the clouds.'

Rabbi Judah pushed out his bottom lip. 'Yet I must say that he struck me as a very genial young man, open to new ideas perhaps.'

Shelamzion's mother folded her arms across her breast to show how little she thought of this. 'A man wants a woman who bakes him bread and bears his children—'

The thought of children made Shelamzion, barely out of childhood herself, rear up like a frightened mare. 'But what if I don't like him?'

Like him?' Her mother exploded with the rage of those who have made a virtue out of accepting their own fate unquestioningly. 'Foolish girl. We did not choose him for you to like. We chose him to provide for you and protect you.'

'Peace.' Rabbi Judah felt the need to quench the flames that were igniting around him. 'It is as well that she knows the truth.'

Shelamzion glanced at her mother then quickly back to her father.

'The truth?'

The truth was this. Rabbi Judah's disciple, Yohanan, had disappeared. Of the five boys who came to study at the household of Judah, Yohanan, at fourteen, was the youngest and most studious. Several weeks ago he had stopped coming to his lessons, nor had he sent word. Thus far the story was familiar; much was made of the disappearance at the time. But now it appeared that, after repeated enquiries, the whereabouts of Yohanan had been discovered. Or at least, if not exactly the *where* then the *who* of his new location was understood. 'You see,' Rabbi Judah said softly, 'Yohanan was from Caesarea.'

There had been riots in Caesarea; this much Shelamzion knew. She waited for her father to go on, but he swayed a little and leaned heavily on his stick. 'For this I will sit, I think,' he said, and eased himself back into his chair. He moved so stiffly; it tore at her heart. 'On the eighth day of Sivan, Yohanan's family home was overrun by Greek pagans. Not a single soul survived, may they find eternal rest.'

'And Gessius Florus does nothing,' his wife interrupted angrily. Shelamzion said nothing. It was not news that Florus had not lifted a finger. Pagan procurators rarely took the job for the love they held of their Jewish charges. A thought struck her. 'But if Yohanan's family has gone, why does he not return here? Surely he could not think you would be angry with him?'

The innocence of the question made Rabbi Judah's eyes wash over with sadness. 'He could not return. He has gone to join the Zealots.'

Shelamzion's mouth fell open. Zealots were criminals and madmen known for raiding the properties of the rich and killing the owners. Fanatics who turned their religion into a holy war and then made war on anything they pronounced unholy. Would Yohanan really become one of the dagger-wielding Sicarii, who had the temerity to abduct the Captain of the Temple's own scribe? It seemed impossibly far-fetched. Like the tales Menachem brought back from Greek traders, of pagan gods who put on the corruption of mortal garb to chase after beautiful youths. She half expected her father to burst out laughing and claim it all for a joke. But he did not, and when he spoke again, it was with a quaver in his voice.

'I am an old man—'

'No.'

He held up his hand. 'Peace. It is no more than the truth. Why should I be afraid of the truth?' His eyes held hers, and she saw in them the extraordinary intelligence that made him one of the great sages of his day. He went on gently, 'You are so young. You do not remember a time when there was an emperor other than Nero on the throne. You think it is the way of Rome to squeeze out the life blood of a country in taxes. And to ignore the scales of justice while they stuff their hands full of gold.'

At this his wife glanced anxiously towards the door, but Rabbi Judah's voice was soft. 'When your brother travels on business he sees the way the peasants are being thrown from their land. How they flock to the towns and cities, and not a person lifts a finger to help them, because who has a coin to spare when Rome has taken everything? I have lived long enough to know that when men are unhappy they forget everything they have in common, and remember only the differences. I fear the riots in Caesarea may only be a beginning. The pagans are testing the waters, and they have seen that there are no consequences for killing a Jew.'

He paused to draw breath and Shelamzion became aware of a pain at the base of her belly, like a tightening knot. She wanted to scream out, *But what has this to do with me?* The answer came soon enough.

'Your mother and I have talked,' Rabbi Judah said, glancing at his wife. She responded with a prim nod. 'There may come a time when the unrest reaches Jerusalem.' Ignoring his daughter's round-eyed disbelief, he pressed on. 'It would be a good thing to have a son-in-law who is well connected outside the area. He might be our salvation.' And seeing the flash of protest in the girl, who stood before him so pale and stony-faced, he moved to reach her another way.

'It would ease the conscience of an old man to know that his only daughter would be cherished even when he, himself, is beyond helping her.' He did not add that he could see no life for her outside marriage. In these last days he had started to question the roles open to women, the dry spinster, the pleading widow, even—may the Lord forgive him—the painted whore. And nowhere could he find a place for his daughter. His clever daughter, with a mind like a man, trapped in the fragile vessel of her womanhood.

He reached out and took her hand. 'All we ask is that you meet with him. If he is not pleasing to you, we will find another. I promise.'

She nodded, curling her fingers a little tighter around his. But all the time thinking, None of this matters, for whoever he is, I won't like him. And that will be an end to the matter.

Chapter VI

Now is the time. The mountains shall be thrown down, and the steep places shall fall, and every wall shall fall to the ground. ... every man's sword shall be against his brother ... And the land will run with pestilence and blood—

Ezekiel 38

Cornelius put down his wine cup so abruptly that the surface of the liquid shook and heaved, and little droplets of amber fluid flecked the back of his hand. Struggling to control his voice, he said, 'Quintus, the question was very simple, and I cannot understand the difficulty you seem to encounter in answering it. Were the depositions given by the legionaries of the V Macedonica concerning Shelamzion bat Judah's son true?'

Quintus gazed at Cornelius sadly. 'That depends.'

Cornelius glanced down briefly, and a little enviously, at the gorgeous mosaic of Faunus in pursuit of Sirynx across an Arcadian landscape that stretched the full expanse of the room. The similarity between the goatish god and his cousin's satyric looks was not entirely lost on him. 'Depends on what?'

'It depends, I suppose, on what you consider the truth to be.' Quintus ran his finger lazily around the rim of his cup and seemed disinclined to continue.

'My dear Quintus,' Cornelius said acidly. 'I never took you to be a Sophist. Either the depositions were true or they were false.'

Quintus looked at him sharply. 'And I am equally surprised to find you, cousin, such an advocate of Heraclitus. Truth is not an absolute. You know that. Even Socrates admitted it.'

'I have read the *Apologia*. But you are missing the point. The truth behind any proposition can only be discovered through logical enquiry, *elenchus*. So I ask again, were those depositions faked?'

Quintus looked his cousin squarely in the face. 'No.'

Cornelius' eyes narrowed. 'No?'

'They swore honestly to what they had heard.'

'But had not seen with their own eyes?'

Quintus held up his cup, and his body slave hurried to fill it. 'What can I tell you, dear cousin?' He took a sip of wine and pulled a face. He held the cup towards Cornelius. 'A gift from Festus. Sadly the man cannot tell the difference between cost and quality. Still he's generous enough. It may be worth cultivating his taste in the hope of better things to come.'

Cornelius swirled the pale liquid round in his cup. When he looked up his face had a hard, determined look. 'The reports suggested—'

'The reports!' Quintus groaned and rolled his eyes. 'Must you be so persistent? You're like Jove on the tail of a comely nymph. I have a headache, you know. Another debt I owe to Festus' generosity.'

Cornelius ignored him. 'The reports suggested that a physician may have looked after the boy.'

'What of it?'

'Well, have we no further information concerning this physician? Did he cure his patient? What happened to the boy when he left his care?'

'Questions, questions.' Quintus snapped his fingers and another slave appeared with a basin and towels. *Really*, thought Cornelius. The number of slaves he employed was pure ostentation. Quintus stayed silent while the slave rolled the towels into sausages then dipped them in the water before applying them to his master's head. Then he lay back on his couch, eyes closed, groaning. 'Leave me alone, cousin. Can you not see I am dying?'

Cornelius, who could see no such thing, went on. 'It has been five weeks since my discourse with Shelamzion bat Judah began—'

'Who?'

Cornelius sighed. 'The bandit queen. You may recall, she is the wife of one of our chief adversaries, Simon bar Gioras.'

'I know, I know.' Quintus opened his eyes a sliver. 'What of it?'

'I made a bargain with her. News of her son in return for her co-operation.'

'And?'

'And she has been co-operating. Admirably so.'

'Then what, if I might be so bold as to ask,' Quintus replied, half sitting up and brushing off the eager slave who rushed to adjust his towel, 'is the problem?'

Cornelius breathed in deeply, lifting his shoulders then letting them fall sharply with his exhalation. 'The problem is simple. I cannot keep my part of the bargain.'

'So that's it.' Quintus slumped back on an elbow. 'Really, cousin, I can scarcely believe men as innocent as you exist outside legend. There is no problem. Tell her what she wants to hear. Tell her you've found the physician. But be vague. Not too much detail. Leave her begging for more.' Here he smirked, and Cornelius understood that it was to more than captive queens that Quintus applied this rule.

He took a sip of the disagreeable wine to stay his temper before saying firmly, 'I will not lie.'

Quintus looked at him more in sorrow than in anger. 'Really, Cornelius, you are too fastidious. I am not asking you to lie. Simply use the truth at your disposal more intelligently. Be a little more imaginative in the way you deploy it. Come now, you are the one who wants the whole civilized world to sit up and pay heed to this marvellous history of yours. Is it not time you learned to use words a little more to your own advantage?'

Cornelius closed his eyes and counted up to ten in Phoenician before replying. 'Even,' he began slowly, noticing with a sinking feeling that compromise was beginning to creep into his voice. 'Even if I was willing to enter into this subterfuge by extending the truth a certain degree, I would still require some grains of fact on which to base my extension. As yet, you offer me nothing substantial.'

Quintus surprised him by raising a finger, as a gladiator might in defeat. 'You have me down. Your persistence has beaten me. I concede.'

Cornelius shifted uncomfortably in his seat. 'I wish you would take this matter seriously. I need to speak with your sources.'

Quintus smiled. 'And so you shall.'

Cornelius opened his mouth to argue then shut it again, not sure he had heard correctly. Quintus gave a little, gratified nod. 'It was always my intention to introduce you to him.'

Cornelius leaned forward. 'Him?'

'Yes.' Quintus' sleepy, clever eyes were wide open now. 'He should be very useful to you. He fought during the war.'

'Indeed?' Cornelius' interest was growing. 'With which legion? Is he of distinguished rank?'

'He is a Jew.'

Cornelius blinked, and his next question faltered on his lips. 'I don't quite—'

'Of course you don't,' Quintus agreed kindly. 'Why should you? In answer to your question, he is of distinguished rank. He fought in Galilee … Unsuccessfully.'

'Then where is he being held?'

Quintus stretched and the towel fell from his forehead. 'He is not being held anywhere. He is a guest of his patron, our esteemed emperor, Titus Flavius Vespasianus.'

Cornelius stopped with his wine cup half way to his lips. 'Do you—Can you possibly intend to suggest—'

Quintus nodded. 'Joseph ben Mattathias, or as he currently prefers to be known these days, Flavius Josephus. Are you not pleased?'

Cornelius did not answer. He sat, staring down at the oily surface of the wine in his cup, the forefinger of his free hand circling against the pad of the thumb. At last Quintus grew impatient.

'Cornelius, did you hear me?'

Cornelius raised his eyes.

'I heard you.'

'Then you understand … what this means. What I am offering you.'

'I understand.' Cornelius said slowly. 'You are offering me the chance to meet with a traitor.'

Shelamzion watched, arms stiff at her sides, as the assistant governor entered the room and removed his cloak. He was carrying a small bundle in his arms, which he placed carefully on the table, before taking his seat and checking the sharpness of his pen. All this he did without acknowledging the bandit queen in any way, and only when he had straightened the wax tablet before him and smoothed the folds of his tunic did he raise his head and offer her his usual, formal greeting.

'You are well, lady?'

'I am well.'

He nodded, satisfied. Then enquired, 'And your food, it is still sufficient?'

'It is.'

'And they allow you to bathe regularly?'

'Yes.'

'Good.' He turned to his scrolls and she waited with growing impatience until she could wait no longer and blurted out, 'What news of my son?'

She saw him stiffen, and he did not look her in the eye as he replied. 'Be patient. These things cannot be rushed. I have told you this before.'

He was right, of course. She knew that. But he did not understand. How could he? Was he there to watch as she paced her cell every waking hour, her lips aching with the fervour of her prayers? Did he watch as she wept because she was starting to forget the details of her child's face? How could she tell this Roman that she had begun to love and fear and hate him all at the same time? Her life was running out. And this remote, arrogant citizen of the Empire was her only conduit to those few things that still truly mattered. She tried to rein in her disappointment, and forced herself to say, 'Very well. Let us begin the day's business.'

He reached out to lift one of his scrolls, then seemed to remember the bundle he had placed on top of them.

'Here.' He held it out to her. 'I thought you might use this.'

She stared at him quizzically then came forward with a slow, hesitant step. He half rose, pushing the bundle into her arms, then resumed his seat. Without looking up, he began to thumb through the scrolls, looking for a particular reference. The abruptness of the transfer left her gaze fixed on the strands of thinning silver on the crown of his head, and it was some moments until she looked down and saw that she was holding a fine woollen shawl.

It was such a long time since her hands had held anything of beauty that the tips of her fingers actually tingled at its touch. She glanced back at Cornelius, but he was still busy with the scrolls, so carefully, almost guiltily, she unfolded it, and found a lady's shawl of thick, creamy lamb's wool. It spilled across her arms, like a foamy stream of fresh milk. Slowly she tore her eyes from it, and this time found Cornelius watching her. She gestured with the shawl.

'I—I do not understand.'

Cornelius gave a small shrug. 'It is cold in here, and I have noticed you shivering. I thought the shawl would offer some protection against the damp.'

Shelamzion did not answer. Her thoughts were filled with the knowledge that she should return this extraordinary gift, that it did not belong on a creature grown dry and dusty all alone in the darkness. Then a fierce instinct took over, and she drew it tightly about herself. She would keep it. Her body remembered a time when beauty did not feel strange to the touch, even if her mind was forgetting. When she looked again on Cornelius there was no gratitude in her expression, simply a cool acceptance, and the smallest hint in the shifting of her eyes that the gift troubled as much as it pleased her.

Cornelius, seeing only that she had accepted his offering, was eager to begin the day. He tapped his pen on the table.

'Now we have established much about your early years in Jerusalem.' He consulted his notes. 'You have described many of the rituals associated with the Temple in, I may say, exemplary detail. And yet … ' He paused. 'It is in my mind to move on from here. I wish to know—' He paused again, looking full into her face. The pale aura of the shawl softened her, and it was almost like seeing a different woman, or at least a different side to the same woman. For the first time, he saw her as the bandit king had seen her, and began to understand a little of the seductive nature of those clear, intelligent eyes looking back at him. 'I wish to know—' He coughed. It had been in his mind to ask her about Flavius Josephus. What did she think of the general of the Galilean campaign turned sympathizer to the Eagle's cause? Yet looking at her, he found himself saying, 'Tell me how it was when you first met Simon.'

In the tenth year of Nero's reign, Rome was devastated by fire. Later, looking out over the ruins—aware that there were those who suspected he had started it himself—Nero vowed that the city would rise again from the ashes. But not as it had been before: dark streets, rickety tenements frantically hugging each other for support. A grander, more visionary plan was needed. While the mob's attention was diverted with the hunt for those deemed guilty—aliens, foreigners, those strange Jews who followed Yeshua the carpenter's son—the most magnificent changes began to occur. Architects began to dream of vast, elegant palaces, connected by parklands and wide, tree-lined boulevards, and the gold from Nero's coffers breathed life into these dreams and clothed them with flesh.

By contrast, Jerusalem had never been planned. As the centuries turned, like pages, houses were built on the ruins of previous dwellings. And it wasn't uncommon for a traveller, pressing his way through the narrow confines of a street, to find it meandering as randomly as any stream, only to end suddenly in an arbitrary building or blocked-off archway. Even the richest homes had a certain practicality about them. And Rabbi Judah's house was no exception, with its flat, tiled roof, its limed walls and central courtyard, which was home to a single jasmine tree emerging from the hard, trodden earth.

Earlier, Rabbi Judah had sat beneath the tree, teaching the day's lesson to his disciples. Now he was gone, and Shelamzion had come to sit alone beneath the contortion of its branches, hugging her knees to her chest, and letting the lacy shadows filigree her bare arms and feet. Her face was troubled, and from time to time she closed her eyes in silent prayer. What to do? Her situation was impossible. So easy to consider rejecting this first impudent attempt to gain her hand. But then what? Would they stop? Or, more likely, her parents would bring another suitor, then another, until she was worn down into accepting. And wasn't it rumoured that the first bite of the cake was always the sweetest? At least this Saul was from a respectable family, willing to live in her father's house.

She shifted position a little, letting her head flop against the tree's rough bark. And what of other considerations? Did she want to give up all thought of marriage? To live the life of a stale maiden aunt in the home of one of her brothers. After all, she was not completely without sexual awareness. True, she was innocent in an age of innocence. But she was three years into her womanhood, and there were the dreams. A pale, young man with flowing hair. A prophet. He came to her in the restless hours of Jerusalem's suffocating nights.

She had seen him once in the grounds of the Temple, preaching to an enthusiastic crowd. Using dangerous phrases that stirred the eager gathering: 'I say, who amongst you does not know that this is a time when the Temple must be cleansed … Only lift up your eyes for the Kingdom of Heaven is upon us.' The air thrilled with nervous excitement. And even Shelamzion, who had an innate, unconscious dislike of following the herd, was drawn into the electric atmosphere. For days she dreamed of pale skin and flowing hair. Of words that were as powerful as deeds. And often she awoke, mouth dry, thighs pressed together, feeling that she was on the brink of something wonderful and strange.

Then, one day, the prophet disappeared. Judas, flush-faced and panting, came running back from the Temple with the news that a squadron of hard-faced legionaries had dragged him unceremoniously into the Antonia Fortress. The orders had come from the commander of the garrison who, understanding the phrase the Kingdom of Heaven to represent an end to Roman rule, had taken it to be a synonym for rebellion.

Brother and sister had looked at each other. 'No one helped him,' Judas went on. 'The crowd, who hung on his every word yesterday, melted away at the first glint of a burnished shield.'

Shelamzion looked down at her feet, shaking her head. 'But what if—if he should be—' She did not dare put the thought into words.

Judas looked troubled. 'The messiah? Is that what you think? I thought it too. As soon as it happened I went to father—'

'What did he say?'

'He looked at me. You know how he does, with a twinkle in his eyes, and said, Another one? And mother was there. She said, Who was it this time? James, the son of Salome the Galilean, no doubt. Always talking, like a madman, and she can do nothing to stop him.'

Shelamzion lifted her eyes to meet her brother's gaze. 'This one was different,' she said defiantly.

Judas nodded sadly. 'I felt that way about the last one.'

That night Shelamzion went to bed, her thoughts filled with Saul, but it was the prophet who came to her in her dreams. His words were honeyed, leaving a trail of raised flesh along her body, vivid as fingerprints. Yet she was still ignorant of fulfilment, gasping in the darkness after a release that did not come. But this time it was the sound of strangeness that roused her. Voices, not altogether familiar, raised in the darkness.

She sat up, with a lustre of sweat coating her limbs and the bedclothes tangled around her bare legs. Again it came. The low rumble that was her father's voice followed by others. Menachem? Judas? Or was it one of the disciples? Her mind worked rapidly. She reached out for her shift and pulled it over her head. Who was down there? There seemed only one likely explanation. Yohanan, returned from Caesarea. The prodigal home once more. Lured by the lateness of the hour and premonitions of strangeness, she threw a blanket over her shoulders and padded out of the room towards her father's study.

Even as she neared, the voices were low and urgent. Where were the exclamations of joy? She hesitated outside, too much a maiden of her time to enter a room possibly occupied by strangers. Glancing back the way she had come, she thought how easy it would be to slip back to bed, unheard. But curiosity had been allowed to thrive in the fertile soil of her maturing mind, and she had never learned the woman's trick of suppressing her needs.

With a hand trembling, more with excitement than fear, she reached for the door. But it was all for naught. The door was suddenly flung wide and her father stood illumined in a narrow rectangle of light. He seemed unsurprised by her presence, but Shelamzion's jaw dropped and her eyes grew round. She had never before seen her father openly weeping.

'I—heard voices,' she said in confusion. 'I thought Yohanan had returned.' Suddenly the notion seemed absurdly childish, and she looked away, shamefaced. But her father reached down and patted her shoulder. 'Poor child,' he murmured. 'Poor child.' He stepped aside to let her enter, and, in a daze she followed him over the threshold.

She had been right. Menachem and Judas were waiting inside. They did not smile as she entered, and as one, their eyes turned towards the room's fourth oc-cupant. A man. Dark where the speaker in the Temple had been pale, and without his beauty. Yet something in his face, the very stillness of his eyes, like the calm surfaces of deep, dangerous pools. Looking at him, Shelamzion felt a quick, sharp stab of fear that made her blurt out, 'Are you Saul, my betrothed?'

She felt her father's hand on her shoulder, the thin fingers digging into her flesh. The stranger had not answered. He looked towards her father, as though she had not spoken, and it was Rabbi Judah who murmured, 'Daughter, this is Simon bar Gioras, Saul's brother. He has come all the way from Acrabetene to bring us the most terrible news. Saul, your betrothed, is dead.'

Chapter VII

Josephus' description of [Simon] as a bandit in Acrabatene in north-east Judea, and later at Masada, is usually taken at face value.
Martin Goodman, The Ruling Class of Judea

The day that followed the news of Saul's death was fierce with smouldering light. Above Jerusalem's limed houses the air rippled like smoke, and shadows shrank to pinpoints or clung tenaciously to the heels of those who had business abroad. From the roof of her father's house, Shelamzion watched the white-faced sun appearing behind the cool walls of Herod's Temple and felt a kind of shapeless disbelief for what had happened during the night.

Saul was dead. Should she weep? Should she sing? She had awoken the next day to discover how death changes everything. Her parents, her brothers, even the family slaves, treated her with a kind of grave, sympathetic expectancy, as though she might suddenly tear at her clothes and pour ashes on her head in grief.

But Shelamzion felt nothing. Saul had merely been a word, not yet made flesh. And now he never would be. Stolen away by a fever and the mysterious will of the Almighty. When condolences were proffered she lowered her head in sombre response, but only because she was beginning to sense how little effect men's wants and desires had on the frightening chaos of the world. To make sense of it all she had climbed up on to the roof to watch the sun make its westwards journey across the city, which it was doing unimpeded by the death of an unknown man in Acrabetene.

A soft footfall from behind made her whirl round.

Simon was standing at the head of the staircase. Simon bar Gioras. Simon the convert's son. She had not known that the second marriage of Saul's mother had been to a proselyte, and she felt the natural superiority of those who are born with a birthright over those who are forced to earn it. But that was not the matter at hand. It was hardly seemly for them to be alone together, and she assumed he had come, as she had, for the solitude of the rooftop, not knowing she was there.

Avoiding his eye, which was no difficulty given that he stood half a head taller than Menachem, the giant of the ben Judah family, she cast herself in tragic lines and awaited his condolences. When it became obvious that no such consolation would be offered she said awkwardly, 'I grieve for your brother.' There was a silence in which she glanced up, and found Simon looking at her, brow arched. 'Why? You did not know him.'

Such candour struck her like a blow. And, not knowing how to respond, she dropped her gaze and hurried past him down the steps.

It was several hours before Shelamzion dared to climb the staircase again. Simon had not come down. But some time ago Menachem and Judas had taken refreshments up to their guest, and they had been joined by several of the disciples. There was no reason why she should not go up. The roof was a place of work as much as leisure, and there was a string of laundry hanging out to dry that had not yet been taken in. At the top of the stairs she hesitated, but the men were lounging over on the eastern edge, and paid no attention as she made her way to the washing line.

'Seventeen or seven hundred. It makes no difference,' Micah, one of the youngest disciples was saying. 'That a Roman procurator can demand those talents from the Temple is the issue.'

There were thick striped blankets of wool hanging from the line. A hot, lanolin smell rose from their fibres, and Shelamzion began to run her hands over them, checking for dampness.

'He claimed there was a shortfall in the year's tribute,' Judas put in mildly.

'An even worse excuse. If he is going to be a thief, let him at least be an honest thief.' Micah looked round his companions with an intense, angry expression. 'Something should be done.'

'And what would you have us do?' asked Menachem. He was filling his cup, and did not look up. Micah's brow darkened. 'We cannot allow Gessius Florus to plunder our holiest site and do nothing.'

Judas and Menachem exchanged looks. 'Nothing can be done,' Judas said with a shrug.

'But it can.' The voice was Simon's.

Shelamzion felt her fingers tighten around the woollen fibres. She peeped round the edge of one of the hanging blankets and watched as Simon lifted a bowl from the table and held it out toward Micah. 'Are there no alms you can spare for the pride of Rome?' As he said it he smiled, a thin thread of a smile that showed no teeth and raised only one corner of his mouth.

He said no more, but left the image of the fat, buttery procurator, a begging bowl clutched in his greedy, bloated paws, to float in the imagination of his audience. It was enough. A few titters of laughter fell, like the pattering of rain, then a cloudburst of bellows as the tension tore in the air like a thunderclap. Yeshua, a strong lad from Emmaus, clapped Simon on the shoulder so heartily Simon winced. Then Menachem reached for the bowl, pretending to be the impoverished procurator, and it was passed from hand to hand with gleeful exaggerations and embellishments.

The laughter irritated Shelamzion, as laughter that cannot be shared often will. Giving up her pretence at domestic duty, she began heading back down the stairs, when Yeshua suddenly said, 'It is a pity Yohanan is not with us.' At once the laughter died and the atmosphere grew charged.

'Yohanan?' Simon asked.

Shelamzion willed herself still. She was in plain sight, but the men did not seem to notice.

'Yohanan was my father's disciple,' Menachem explained. 'The pagans murdered his family in Caesarea.'

'Now he is a Zealot,' added Judas. 'And who knows what he may be doing?'

Menachem gave an angry jerk of his shoulders. 'Storming rich men's houses with the rest of his zealous band? Or perhaps he has plans to throw the uncircumcised out of Jerusalem?'

'And who is to say he is not right?' It was Micah who had spoken.

Holding her head stiff and unmoving, Shelamzion longed to turn to get a better view, but dared not move an inch.

'What do you mean?' Menachem asked, and there was a warning in his voice, which Micah chose to ignore.

'Only this. You know as well as I do that I have great respect for your father's teachings. But we are young men, and—' He hesitated a moment, gathering his courage. 'And your father is a … a man of his generation, and does not see the signs.'

'What signs are these?'

'That innocent men die, while wicked ones go free. That poverty chases the honest man from his land—'

Watching from the corner of her eye, Shelamzion could not make out Menachem's expression, but she saw his dismissive shrug. 'When has that not been the case in Israel?'

'But this is the fourth oppression!' Micah's voice was rising, and Shelamzion wondered how much wine he had drunk. 'It is all there in the book of Daniel. First Babylon, the lion, then the Persian bear. Third was the Seleucid leopard, and now—' He paused to draw breath. 'Rome the monster. My brothers, do you not see; the beast is tearing at us with its teeth of iron? Yohanan is right. Now is the time to act.'

There was a shocked silence, then Yeshua whispered in an awed tone, 'You believe this is the End of Days?'

Micah's chin was tilted in defiance. 'It is written that the messiah of Aaron will come among us and there shall be a time of peace and blessing, glory and joy, and long life for men of righteousness.'

It was all Shelamzion could do to stay silent. Images of apocalypse filled her mind, an endless darkness lit up by gorging rivers of fire and the bright, despairing screams of men. Faintly she heard Judas asking, 'But who is a man of righteousness, the one who wields a sword or the one who prays for him to put it down?' It was obvious he was comparing Yohanan with the gentle Rabbi Judah, and, at once, a heated argument broke out. Shelamzion listened, biting her lips, longing to join the debate and knowing she could not. Then someone asked, 'But what does Simon think?'

There was a surprised silence, and several people broke off mid-sentence. Simon put down his wine cup. 'I think our brother, Micah, is right.'

A babble of excitement rose up then quickly died away when it became apparent that Simon was still speaking. 'I think he is right when he talks of peace and glory, and the messiah of Aaron. But let us not forget that the passage also talks of the messiah of David, a king who will come amongst us to lead us into battle.' His voice hardened. 'We should not forget that it is written that on the day when the Sons of Darkness fall there shall be a battle and horrible carnage before the God of Israel. Those who pray ardently for the coming of the Kingdom of Heaven must bear in mind that it will be forged in fire and blood.'

' … in fire and blood—' Shelamzion broke off and frowned. 'Why are you smiling?'

Cornelius, suddenly aware of his upturned lips, answered a little self-consciously, 'The hubris of the Jewish mind never ceases to astonish. You see yourself as a jewel in the desert, the pivot upon which the rest of the world rotates, while our generals see you as nothing more than sand-covered rabble-rousers. And emperors and greedy procurators think of you as a treasure chest to empty as the desire takes them.'

Shelamzion's pale cheeks grew hot. 'Such men know nothing of God's will.'

'Such men consider themselves above the will of the gods.' Cornelius' smile faded. 'Even yours.'

'And you? Are you such a man?'

He had anticipated the question, but still he pondered it, rolling his pen between his fingers to give himself time to think. 'No,' he said at last. 'I am not. There are things I have done, certain mysteries I have participated in that have allowed me … ' His eyes narrowed, and he paused, wondering whether to trust her. He gave himself a little shake. Why not? She would be beyond this life soon enough and able to judge for herself. Why did he keep forgetting that? He cleared his throat. 'Mysteries,' he continued, 'that have allowed me to catch a glimpse of the existence of the godhead.'

Her lips parted, but she did not speak, and encouraged, he went on. 'With the help of the priests of Mithras I have been privileged to experience a state of *ekstasis.* Pure being. No knowledge of self. Everything given up.' His grip tightened on the pen and his voice lowered. 'I did not know what would happen. Yet I am certain, as certain as I am speaking to you in this room, that I felt the god draw near.' He shook his head. 'Can you imagine what it is like to give yourself up utterly? To be absorbed by something magnificent … something quite beyond reason … the Eternal.'

He paused, a little breathless, and waited for her reaction. Her eyes were kind, but she could not keep the hint of scorn from her voice as she answered, 'That is the difference between us. You Romans, with your bacchanalias and your Greek philosophies, are always trying to lose your selves. Whereas, when we Jews turn to God, it is to find who we are.'

'And it has served you well, has it not?' he replied a little crossly. 'In following your god, you find yourself under sentence of death. Your country reduced to a cinder. And your people enslaved.'

She flinched from his words. 'That was not God's will.'

'Indeed. Then who do you blame for the conflagration of an entire country?'

He waited for her to lay the blame at his feet, to name collaborators or traitors. She did neither. Smiling a little sadly she said, 'I blame my brothers.'

As the bright white days of the month known as Sivan settled seamlessly into each other like the great stones of Herod's Temple, Simon continued to stay on in the ben Judah household. And though it was noted that he seemed in no hurry to return to his sorrowing mother, it was put down to a young man's enthusiasm for the metropolitan lifestyle of the capital. That he was grieving for his brother was in no doubt. Several times he began saying, 'When Saul hears—' then broke off, leaving the phantom outline of his words to fade into the appalled silence.

To Shelamzion's growing frustration he spent much time on the roof, gazing up at the pristine walls of the Temple, or sitting there, with her brothers and the disciples, discussing points of theology or politics. When drawn into conversation he was a capable, erudite speaker. But, she noted, while he was often the voice of arbitration in a dispute, he was rarely the instigator of debate.

And the longer he stayed, the more contrasting and unreadable the elements of his personality became. Several times she had caught him in strange acts of humility, carrying logs for old Sarai, listening to stories of her childhood near Nain before she was sold in lieu of a tax debt at the age of twelve. The poignancy of this behaviour, coupled with an intuitive grasp of the barren emptiness that follows loss, led Shelamzion in an attempt to convey her sympathy with warm looks and understanding smiles. But her efforts were met with such blank, flat indifference that she soon retreated into an offended silence.

As daughter of the house he treated her with civility, but for the most part he did not acknowledge her at all, often looking through her, as though she were no more than the motes of dust twinkling in the air. It was therefore a shock to eventually discover that she had been the focus of his thoughts all along.

On the twenty-first day of the month, Shelamzion rose from her bed and went down to breakfast. She took the stairs leisurely, having as yet no premonition that the familiar mosaic of her life would shortly shatter into a million pieces. The first thing she noticed was the absence of any smell of cooking. And, now she thought of it, wasn't the house unusually still? No shrill orders from her mother or good-natured cries from Menachem and Judas. Where were the slaves? She hesitated, one foot dangling in suspense over the next step, head tilted to one side in an attitude of listening. There were footsteps coming towards her.

A moment later her father appeared. She saw at once that his normally genial face was strangely grave.

'Father, what is it?'

Rabbi Judah noted the challenging tone in his daughter's voice, how she did not wait to be addressed, and inwardly the burden of his guilt grew heavier. Aloud, he said, 'Come with me.'

They went into the large, airy room that was used for family gatherings. Menachem and Judas were there already. As she entered, they looked up, then quickly averted their eyes. In her surprise, Shelamzion took a moment to see that her mother was also in the room. She was dabbing at her eyes with the sleeve of her shift, and had not noticed her daughter come in.

'Sit down.' Rabbi Judah nodded at the cushion-strewn floor, and set the example by stiffly lowering himself into a seated position. Shelamzion sat next to him, facing her brothers. A heavy silence then followed, in which flickering glances were exchanged, but nothing decipherable passed. She fidgeted with the hem of her robe, unable to escape the vague sense of guilt that always assailed her in her mother's presence. At her side, Rabbi Judah tapped the tips of his fingers together, and instantly all eyes were upon him.

'Daughter,' he began with an air of weary finality, 'I have come to a decision … You will be wed tomorrow.'

In dreams, words have no meaning. Understanding can be grasped at, but never attained. So it was now as Shelamzion looked into her father's face. Her lips moved, but no sound came out. Rabbi Judah was watching her closely. 'Have you nothing to say?' The blankness of her reaction was more terrible than the outbursts he had imagined. At last she gave him a quick, fever-bright smile, and muttered, 'Impossible … Saul is dead.'

Rabbi Judah shook his head. 'You do not understand. Several days ago your brothers committed an act of great foolishness—'

'It was but a prank,' Judas interrupted.

'Silence!'

Shelamzion jumped. She had never heard her father speak so harshly. The old rabbi closed his eyes and pinched the bridge of his nose for a moment, before taking up the story's thread. 'Some nights ago, your brothers took it upon themselves to partake in a celebration with friends. Simon did not go with them. But amongst their number was Eleazar ben Ananias.'

The Captain of the Temple. Shelamzion knew him well, a hawk-faced youth who strode about the Temple as though he was the High Priest himself.

'It seems,' Rabbi Judah went on coldly, 'that your brothers remember little of what went on that night. But the next morning they were found at the Gate of the Pure and Just passing round a bowl and asking for alms on behalf of our impoverished procurator.'

'People laughed,' Menachem muttered. 'They cheered us because we spoke righteously.'

'*The lips of the righteous feed many: but fools die for want of wisdom,*' Rabbi Judah snapped. Judas and Menachem hung their heads and Rabbi Judah went on sadly, 'It might have been well. It might have passed as nothing more than the folly of young men. But Simon has been abroad and listened to the prevailing rumours, and thinks not.'

Shelamzion frowned. Simon. Was he not the first to have likened the procurator to a beggar? *Are there no alms you can spare for the pride of Rome?* Menachem had taken the bowl and pretended to collect alms. But the words came from Simon … She looked into her father's face, wanting to tell him, but he ignored her pleading gaze and continued. 'Florus has arrived in the city.'

Shelamzion's eyes grew round. The procurator. Here in Jerusalem? 'But what has that to do with me?'

Rabbi Judah looked at his daughter with the anger that is born of too much love. 'You are young, but you have studied our history, and cannot claim ignorance now. Is peace in Jerusalem anything but a glimmer of light in the darkness? Florus has taken up residence in Herod's palace, and he has surrounded the place with his own troops. Simon has discovered that Florus intends to set up a tribunal tomorrow. He has given orders that our most eminent men, priests and nobles alike, be brought to attend.'

Out of the corner of her eye Shelamzion saw the hand resting in Menachem's lap clench into a fist, but she did not dare to let her attention stray long from her father's face. Rabbi Judah continued in a flat, grey monotone. 'Florus will demand the names of those who dared insult him by portraying him as no better than a beggar.'

'But they will not give them!' Shelamzion cried out despite herself.

'No,' Menachem answered quickly. 'They dare not. Too many sons of noble blood were amongst the jesters.' But he did not sound sure.

'They dare not,' Rabbi Judah repeated grimly. 'Yet a man may say many things when put to torture.'

Menachem gasped and Judas seemed to shrink in on himself. Shelamzion turned to her father. 'But these are eminent men. Surely not even the procurator—'

'Florus is a Roman. His only god is greed. While his predecessor understood restraint, Florus has plundered whole cities. Now that his pride is hurt, he will stop at nothing until the perpetrators are hanging from crosses.'

Shelamzion's mother, who had remained silent until this moment, let out a moan of despair and began to weep loudly, rocking back and forward into the cup of her hands. And, watching her, Shelamzion understood that her mother's reddened eyes were not for the thought of a daughter torn away by unwanted marriage, but of sons given up to a gory death. Judas had begun to weep too, and suddenly the air seemed to stifle. Shelamzion bit her lips and drew in a long breath. 'What is to be done?'

Rabbi Judah's eyes narrowed very slightly at this unexpected poise. He was beginning to realise that, for all his teachings, he had only scratched the surface of a deep and complex mind, and he grew more afraid for her. Tugging at his beard, he announced in a dry, choking tone, 'You will be wed to Simon bar Gioras tomorrow.'

That it was Simon who was to step into the dead groom's shoes should not have surprised her—*Yibbum*, the duty of the living brother to marry his widowed sister-in-law. And she, Shelamzion bat Judah, who was knowledgeable in the Law, could not deny it—Yet somehow hearing the words on her father's lips made her insides turn to stone.

Even as she accepted that she must be sacrificed to save her brothers she could not face the thought of being bound to that strange, cold youth, who looked through her with dark, impenetrable eyes. The very idea added a layer of horror to her grief. Pathetically, she leaned forward and took hold of her father's robe. 'There was no union with Saul—' She was struggling, grasping at words to save herself. 'Simon has therefore no obligation—'

'He thinks otherwise. You were betrothed to his brother. In the circumstances it is enough.' Rabbi Judah cleared his throat. 'Once the ceremony is over, you will leave with your brothers as escort for Acrabetene. Simon will make them welcome guests until it is judged fit for them to return.'

For them to return, Shelamzion thought with bitterness. But not me. I am the sacrifice for their folly. She lifted her eyes to meet her father's. Let him see the magnitude of his betrayal reflected on her face. She was rewarded with the anguish that inscribed itself, like the flowing lines of a confession, across his old forehead. But before he could move to offer reassurance or solace, she dropped her head in a dramatic parody of submission. 'Your will be done, father.'

Chapter VIII

You were united to your wife by the Lord. In God's wise plan, when you married, the two of you became one person in his sight.
Malachi 2:15

It was the custom of the day that a bride should ride to her wedding in a litter. The experience was new to Shelamzion, and in other circumstances one she might have enjoyed. But it was one thing to submit with words to the unthinkable, and quite another to carry the action through to its conclusion. She had enough honesty to know that she had intended to shame her father with the melodrama of her agreement, never truly believing that he would allow her to go through with it. And that in itself lent the day a dangerous kind of make-believe. It had been possible, she discovered, to act in a manner not at all like herself, with no qualm of conscience, because essentially nothing was real.

Before the litter arrived she had waited in her room, swathed in the embroidered folds of the floor-length veil known as the *tsa'iph*. It was not an obligation to wear it before the ceremony. But already she was acting, playing a role in defiance of herself. As the door to her room opened she looked round in surprise. Her father entered. To do what? Offer his advice? Wish her well? She could only see him dimly, and nothing of his expression. Already the *tsa'iph* was doing its work, separating her physically from the world of childhood until she was ready to emerge from its embroidered cocoon, a butterfly bride fluttering at her husband's side.

Deliberately she turned her back on her father, excluding him from the world she now found herself in. Sensing his helplessness provided perverse satisfaction. She was new to cruelty, but she was learning fast. Not until she heard his hesitant footsteps leaving the room did she pause to doubt herself. Then she rallied. She still loved her father, deeply, passionately. He was the man who had guided her faltering footsteps towards what she had been certain was a constant, ever-growing light. Her anger at him could not last. But he had hurt her, and she was not ready to show forgiveness. Time enough to thaw once the nuptials were over and done with, she decided.

As Simon had no residence in Jerusalem, the wedding was to be held at the home of his uncle. The house was not far from the marketplace. Yet they might have been walking all the way back to Acrabatene as far as Shelamzion was concerned. In the swaying litter, the journey seemed endless. She clung to the sides, feeling sick with the strangeness of it all. Outside, family and friends were singing the marriage hymns, while drums were beaten, and every so often the air parted to the haunting note of a *shofar*, emerging from its twisting ram's horn shell like a musical curl of smoke. To be the focus of such attention should, Shelamzion understood, have been glorious. After all, for many women marriage was the pinnacle of their life's achievement. Yet she felt nothing. Only a flat resignation that masked the deeply buried spark of her rebelling soul.

The litter suddenly jolted to a stop. Shelamzion sat bolt upright. Have we arrived? No, it was too soon. Her heart began to throb painfully in her chest, hoping desperately for fate to take her in another direction. The next moment the curtains of the litter were tweaked aside. But the dimness cast by her veil made it hard to see who it was. 'Who's there?'

Her mother's voice replied, 'Peace. Someone has spotted the king's litter.'— The king. Agrippa II, in whom it was said the inheritance of Herodian blood ran thin. No longer king of a reunited Israel. Rome had snatched the kingdom from his limp fingers almost before Agrippa I exhaled his last breath. The son now found himself king of a tiny principality, more insult than acknowledgement of his royal blood, his father's dream of a Jewish empire in ruins about his feet. But still he was a king, and a Jewish one at that. The people loved him, even as they despised the true power of Rome's procurator, Gessius Florus—Shelamzion felt her mother's hand grip her through her veil. 'The king wishes to come this way. We will need to go back … No … Wait—'

'What is it?'

There was a gasp. 'The king has halted. We are to pass.' The grip tightened on Shelamzion's arm. 'To think, Agrippa of Tiberius has halted *his* retinue to let us continue.'

Shelamzion had never heard her mother so excited. 'That was kind.'

'It's an omen. A good one. I can tell.'

'How can you tell?' But already her mother's hand had slipped away and the procession was underway again.

The atmosphere of excitement was growing. Well-wishers swelled the ranks of the wedding party, and the hymns, so demure and reverent to begin with, were becoming discordant with merriment. Inside the litter, Shelamzion saw nothing but the play of shadow and light against the curtains, and her gaze followed this display with a kind of entranced desperation, as though it might suddenly become readable, like the fading pages of a forbidden manuscript.

The heat was something she could not ignore. In the enclosed atmosphere it was difficult to breathe, and rivers of perspiration began to run down her neck and gather between her breasts. The silken dress—her mother's pride—wrinkled against the dampness of her legs. Thoughts roaming wildly, she was beginning to think that it would be worth the pain of marriage just to be allowed to remove her veil, when the litter stopped and she came down to earth with a thud.

There was a silence. The singing had stopped. Holding her breath, Shelamzion waited for the curtains to be drawn aside. And when this did not happen, she took matters into her own hands and pulled them open herself. Piercingly strong sunlight assailed her eyes, but she was protected by the veil, and able to sum up the situation in a single glance. An unfamiliar courtyard, bedecked with flowers and ribbons—the house of Simon's uncle. The well-wishers had melted away and only the wedding party remained. Strangely, they were gathered in knots and clumps, gaiety drained from them, the bolder ones casting furtive, sidelong glances towards a small knot of roman legionaries, who—she now saw—stood blocking the entrance to the house.

Shelamzion slipped from the litter unnoticed. The pupils of her eyes were round and full of fear, but the rest of her face was impassive. Up ahead, Simon and her father were speaking with the legionaries. Their conversation could not be heard, but Rabbi Judah's shoulders were slumped and he was leaning heavily on his cane. And something in the very stiffness of Simon's back, the bridal crown on his head flaring in the golden light, served as a warning against those who might have drawn near. A warning to Menachem and Judas to come no closer, thought Shelamzion. Suddenly the veil was suffocating, and she tore it from her head. Her mother, standing defensively between her sons, caught the motion and glanced towards her daughter in surprise, as though she had forgotten Shelamzion's presence and now was startled to see her there.

They stared at each other helplessly across a skewed plane of time, the few seconds since their arrival already seeming like hours. Then a guttural Latin bark rose over the soft words of her father. Simon shook his head violently. But Rabbi Judah put out a hand and laid it gently on Simon's arm. Making a gesture of acquiescence, he turned, allowing two of the legionaries to escort him from the courtyard. The remaining legionaries followed. The paralysis of shock held Shelamzion and the other guests rooted to the spot, as the old man made his way past, his face held in a deliberate mask, looking neither left nor right, acknowledging no one.

There was a scramble of movement as soon as the door to the courtyard shut behind the last legionary. Everyone crowding round Simon, demanding to know what was going on, while leaving him no space in which to answer. Somewhere in the confusion it emerged that Florus had set up a tribunal, ordering priests, scholars and eminent men alike attend. Simon's uncle was already there, and Rabbi Judah's presence was also required.

'Then he is not arrested,' Judas said with evident relief.

'No,' Simon agreed. 'But it would be wise for you to go home and gather every ounce of gold you can find. Florus has ever reckoned that justice belongs to the highest bidder, and I doubt diplomacy will be enough to satisfy him now that his ego is bruised. Here—' He took the wedding crown from his head and tossed it to Menachem. 'You have more need of this than I.'

His gesture was light, indifferent, and through her shock Shelamzion experienced a slight stab of pique that the marriage should mean so little to him. Then again, she reminded herself, what was this affair but a sop to Simon's conscience? He was the one who had begun the whole monstrous joke. Now that her father had gone to deal with Florus face to face, he had doubtless gotten cold feet. She looked towards him with narrowed eyes, watching as he sent away the guests. At his bidding, her mother made ready to leave, hurrying towards the door, and calling to her sons to go with her. Shelamzion took a step after them, but Menachem blocked her way.

'No.'

She could scarcely believe her ears. 'No?'

'Simon orders that someone must stay. There was no time to make arrangements. If the Almighty is with us, father may return before the bribe is gathered, and it is meet that he will come here.'

She shook her head, trying to clear it. 'Simon orders? You are head of the family when our father is not present.'

He pursed his lips in exasperation. 'Please don't be difficult. You will be safe here. Simon assures us that his uncle's slaves are loyal. They will not abandon you.'

Safe? She looked at him despairingly. Did he think she was worried about her own safety? Protests rose in her throat, but Simon, who was almost at the door, threw a scowling glance over his shoulder. 'Come,' he called sharply, and Menachem turned, meek as a dog, to follow.

Shelamzion's lips were still parted as the courtyard door slammed shut. It was suddenly very quiet in the garden. A capricious little breeze ruffled her hair and the fine silk dress she was wearing. A growing sense of numbness was spreading through her, and she stood still and ghostlike, the abandoned bride amongst the drooping flowers.

In the hours that followed, Shelamzion wandered the courtyard. Watching silently as one of the maidservants pulled the heavy bolts across the door. Sitting beneath a stunted fig tree, arms wrapped around her body, shivering despite the heat of late morning. At last she gave into the maidservant's entreaties that she come indoors to rest. She ordered that a mattress be taken up to the roof, and lay down on it with little expectation of sleep.

Some hours later she awoke from the tangle of a dream. The sun was higher in the sky. It dazzled her vision, filling it with glaring stars. But it was noise, not light, that drew Shelamzion to her feet then sent her stumbling towards the low balustrade that surrounded the roof. A vast sound. Like a hundred wedding parties. She lifted a hand to her brow, still too dazzled to see beyond shape and shadow. But with sight lost, hearing became more acute. Above the bass shouts of men and the inhuman call of trumpets, she could hear the high-pitched screech of frightened birds. No, not birds. Shelamzion dropped her hand and stepped backwards, her eyes darting from side to side. Not birds. That was the sound of women screaming.

They were coming. Florus' men. A maniple or more, loosed on the ancient cobblestones of Jerusalem. Marching death. The engorged glory of Rome. Falling on the panicked crowds with the ferocity of avenging angels. Men and women were going down, like ears of corn before the stone-faced reapers of death. Most fled. But Jerusalem was an Eastern city, huddling in on itself, close and secretive, its streets unable to contain a panicked mob.

Finding themselves trapped by a congestion of bodies, some turned and ran back the way they had come. And the soldiers, their weapons glinting in the shadowless light, met them without mercy. Scalp prickling with horror, Shelamzion watched as an angry tide of red swept down from the palace of the Hasmoneans. A flood of humanity heading towards the very spot where she was standing. *Run*, screamed the panicked animal in her soul, but she did not move, mesmerized by the inevitability, the impossibility of death.

After a while, the piteous cries of the household slaves below penetrated her frozen senses. Numb with holding back her own screams, she tore herself away and slowly descended the stairs. Two maidservants were waiting for her. They were plump Benjamite women. Fairer than Shelamzion, with a copper sheen to their hair and hazel eyes. Those eyes were now staring at the newest mistress of the house with a kind of sullen terror, waiting for her to do something, convinced that she wouldn't.

Their frightened expressions pleaded, '*What can we do?*'

And her grim face replied, 'Nothing. There is nothing.'

A thundering noise outside shook the hinges on the courtyard door. The maidservants screamed and clung to each other. But Shelamzion kept her head, knowing that what they heard was only the sound of running feet, and what they had to fear was not soldiers who ran past, but those who paused to wonder what was on the other side of the door. Behind her the Benjamite women were calling out to God for deliverance in breaking voices.

'Go inside and fetch the knives.'

The voice that had spoken was so firm and calm that the maidservants looked round, half expecting an angel to have sprung from the earth. But it was only Simon's child-bride standing between them and doom.

'Go inside and fetch the knives.'

The Benjamite women looked at each other. But they had never been schooled to think for themselves, let alone disobey. And it was more natural to them to follow an external order than one that came from inside their own heads, so they hurried indoors to fetch the sharpest bread knives and the cleavers for cutting meat.

When they returned, they found Shelamzion standing closer to the shuddering door. *Was she mad?* They approached her nervously, noting her chalk-white face, her clenched fists.

'Lady?'

She glanced over her shoulder, then wordlessly selected a meat cleaver before turning back to the door. Her back was very straight and her shoulders set back. It was clear, even to the dull minds of the Benjamite women, that anyone entering the courtyard would not get far.

For a long time Shelamzion maintained her vigil, standing like a soldier, the last survivor of a battle, shocked and dazed, but clinging to his weapon for dear life, until the sounds beyond the door gradually grew fainter then died away altogether. Then slowly she lowered the cleaver. 'I think—' she began, meaning to say that they were safe now.

But a violent knocking on the door drowned her words. The maidservants began to weep and shake until Shelamzion shushed them with an irritated gesture of her hand. Instinct took her closer to the door, listening. The sounds on the other side were indistinct. Neither clearly friend nor foe. She stepped back, frowning. Then a wild urge impelled her to command, 'Open it.'

Having no other weapon than insolence in their armoury, the maidservants stood dumbly and did not move. Then, seeing they would not be budged, Shelamzion threw them a look of contempt, and despite her beating heart, went to the door and loosened the latches herself. Her hand trembled a little as she undid the final one. If she was wrong—but her hesitation was momentary, possessing as she did too strong a character to doubt herself for long. Deliberately, she curled her fingers around the handle and pulled the door open a crack.

The weight of something falling against it knocked it from her hand, and she jumped back as a wounded man fell through the gap and landed at her feet. There was an instant of shock. All three women sharing the same horror. Not simply because the imagined terrors beyond the door had now become real, but because this man was known to them.

'Simon?' The word left Shelamzion's lips more as question than statement. Could this be Simon, this bloodied, dishevelled creature, struggling in the dust just to get to his knees? His sword was at his side, and he leant on it heavily, pulling himself to his feet, rising up before their shocked countenances, like a vision of apocalypse. There was blood running in rivulets from a wound in his forehead and he seemed dazed. And, to their startled eyes, not quite real. With the open mouth of a wondering child, Shelamzion took a step forwards, extending her hand towards his wound. But he flinched from her, seeming to recover his wits in the process.

'Ready yourself. We must leave.'

She had been prepared for confusion, half expecting muttered explanations laced with concern or reassurance. But this cold order barked in her face struck like a blow. She might have wept. Instead, she answered with dignity, 'I have first to find my mother then we will go to Florus and secure my father's release.' Summoning all the strutting hubris of her youth, she made as if to walk past him.

'It is no use.'

She paused, looking up questioningly into his face.

'She went with your brothers to offer a bribe to Florus.'

The swiftness of this action sounded an ominous bell somewhere in Shelamzion's brain, but she lifted her chin, saying, 'Then I will go to the tribunal and find out what has befallen them. Let me pass.'

But he blocked her way. She looked him squarely in the face, defiantly.

'My parents would not like you to hinder me.' Her voice was firm. 'My brothers would not like it.'

He gave his answer, and though she saw his lips move, she did not hear him. It was as though a dark veil had suddenly been dropped over her head shutting out the world. There was no sound but the blood rushing in her ears. At last she repeated a word that seemed to be swelling across her tongue until it took shape.

'Dead?'

'Yes.'

She looked up, and his face was the whole world, a bleak, agonized place she did not recognise.

'How?' The word was so small, yet she barely managed to get it past her lips.

Simon rubbed the sweat from his brow then glanced over his shoulder. 'Not here. We must get away.'

Get away? She took a step backwards. 'Where? I can't leave.'

'We must.' Simon sheathed his sword. 'They will be looking for us.'

'No.' She turned away, pushed her hands against the sides of her head. Nothing made sense. At sunrise she had been adorned as a bride. Now, before the day had completed its full arc, here she was alone in the world. Her parents were dead. Her brothers were dead. She could not take it in. All she desired was to close her eyes and go to sleep as a child does. And when she awoke all of this would have faded as in a dream.

'If you have kinsmen it would do well with you to go to them.'

Simon's harsh voice made her blink. She had no kinsmen she could think of. But he was looking over her head at the maidservants. They did not answer him, but clung together, staring at him with empty, shipwrecked eyes. Simon wiped the blood from his brow. The wound, Shelamzion saw, was, after all, not deep. And now she could hear the sound of running feet and the ugly barking Latin of the legionaries beyond the courtyard walls. The maidservants heard it too. They turned, as one, running for the shelter of their master's house. Simon took a step after them, then paused.

'They will be safer together than at my side,' he said, and there was finality in his voice, as one who speaks to himself.

'I will stay with them,' Shelamzion insisted. Better to cling to this familiar rock, barren though it be, than to allow herself to be swept away by the chaos beyond the door. But Simon came angrily towards her.

'You are not safe. Florus will never allow an insult to have legs while there is still a chance to bury it.'

She did not believe him. Backing away, eyes searching his face, as though there might yet be proof of falsehood. He is wrong, she thought. Wrong, because she could not allow him to be right. Her mother was alive, her brothers … she had spoken to them only hours ago. There were too many. The Angel of Death could not have taken them all. She looked beseechingly into his face. 'My father is waiting.'

'No.'

There was no gentleness about him. She found her wrist in the manacle of his fingers—as though there was no indecency in the act, as though he was already her husband—then they were beyond the safe confines of the courtyard and abroad in a world grown monstrous. She froze, struggling for breath, in amongst a nightmare from which there was no waking.

Death screamed at her from all directions with lolling heads and broken limbs. Simon was pulling her forward. She took a small step then stopped. So silent. No groans or cries. The Roman killing machine was efficient. Yet she was surprised to discover that it was not blood or dismemberment that was most disturbing, but the utter emptiness of death. Even clothing, if well worn, holds something of the personality it once sheathed, the smell, the shape. Not so flesh. Void of its spark, she saw with mounting revulsion, that it stiffened into a grotesque parody of itself, as though all its previous animation had been illusory. The jerking dance of puppets.

Simon tugged at her arm again, and she forced herself to take another step. A black cloud of flies rose up, buzzing and disturbed, from one of the bodies. Her hand flew to cover her mouth and nose, and she stood for a moment, eyes closed, swallowing hard. Everything that was good and pure in her rebelled against the uncleanness of death. Unthinkable, only a few short hours ago, the daughter of Rabbi Judah ben Eliad stepping over corpses. But now Simon's lips were at her ear, shouting over the roaring inside her head.

'Unless you would join them, come!'

She did not look at him, nor acknowledge his words with the smallest utterance, but she lifted her foot and stepped over the stiffening legs of a fleshy man of middle age.

And now that the first step was taken, Simon led the way. She followed blindly, disturbed only by odd, disconnected thoughts of surprising clarity. The cedar-wood chest, opening to reveal her gown, scented with sprigs of spikenard … Her father coming into the bedroom then leaving without a word. Frozen out by her silence. All the tender words he might have said now were lost. Never to be known. The wounds these thoughts opened shielded her from the immediacy of her situation, so that she scarcely hesitated over each morbid pace, passing numbly over the bodies, as though merely avoiding an unpleasant excrescence overlooked by the dung-sweepers.

Only once did they encounter danger. A single Roman, separated somehow from his maniple, picking his way across the detritus of bodies and broken stalls that littered an open stretch of market square. He was young and fired up with the murderous power of his right arm. He let out a yell as soon as he spotted them.

'Curite vos canes!' Run dogs.

Shelamzion turned to obey, but Simon drew his sword, leaving her, like Eve standing before the forbidden fruit, knowing she should flee, but fascinated by the danger. And though she knew nothing of the dance of death, of how men throw themselves against the edges of mortality, she was filled with the unbidden knowledge that Simon was the superior fighter. The Roman was a skilled artisan, well-steeped in his technique. But the thrusts of his weapon were like precisely made pieces of mosaic, as though he were crafting death from a time-worn template. But Simon was an artist. In his hand the sword became a living thing. He dispatched the Roman with the grace of a Minoan acrobat, and did not even break sweat.

With no word exchanged between them, they left the still-twitching body of the Roman. But this time, when Simon reached for Shelamzion's arm, she shrank back, not only from the unutterable indecency of the act, but because, during the fight, she had seen something tortured and restless about his soul, and it set him apart from the other men she had known and made her wary.

They went on until the steep angles of the Women's Towers, flanking the great gate set in the city walls, filled her vision. Shelamzion stopped. 'Why are we here? Why have you brought me here?' The gate that led out of Jerusalem. Into the unknown. A stream of refugees was walking, leaden-footed, towards it; pilgrims caught up in the fighting, blank-eyed men and women looking neither to right nor left, clutching their feeble belongings in one hand and their pitiful, strangely-silent children in the other. Shelamzion looked wildly about. 'I must return to my father's house.'

'No.'

He offered no explanation. And if she had been older, she might have realized that there was shock and horror on his face too, but she was not yet seventeen and still looked at the world with the inward eye of a child.

'I must go home,' she insisted. 'You cannot hold me here.' And while she still had the strength to say it, she threw her final barb. 'You are not my husband. We are nothing to each other now.' And she would have taken to her heels and run, but for his words, which stopped her in her tracks.

'I am not your husband *yet*.'

She had taken several steps in the direction of the Temple, and she kept her back to him now, feeling her insides turning to stone. He was only offering to make good on the promise of the betrothal. In other circumstances she might have felt gratitude. But marry Simon. The very idea made her gorge rise. She clutched at her throat, feeling as though everything in the world had grown vile, and even the air was a choking noose around her neck. With slow, deliberate movements she turned to face him.

'I cannot talk of these things now,' she said haltingly. 'I must go … and put my affairs in order.'

His expression hardened. 'You can do nothing now. Florus has every soldier under his command under orders to kill the kin of bar Judah on sight. We must leave. Before they close the gate.' He turned and began walking rapidly towards the Women's Towers. She watched him in stunned silence, then, not knowing what else she might do, followed with slow, wooden steps.

By the time she caught up with him, Simon was already in line. She saw that his sword was gone and it gave her an unexpected wrench to see him defenceless. He turned to look at her and she thought to whisper some words of consolation. Instead, he spoke first, and his tone was rough. 'Say nothing. Be assured Florus has his spies amongst us.' She nodded silently.

Feeling cold, despite the stifling, late-afternoon heat, she wound her cloak tightly about her. Moving when the line moved, taking tiny leaden steps forward. As the day progressed she found her body growing increasingly heavy, while her head floated in a fevered haze, tortured by the flares and sparks of random thoughts. She had not known death. Not truly. Her grandparents had all been dead long ago. The last living child of the family, she had only glimpsed the monstrous void bereavement leaves on other people's faces.

Up ahead an old woman had broken into a staccato series of wails. The sullen-faced legionaries on the gate had ripped open her bundle and thrown her possessions in the dirt. She had fallen on all fours amongst the smashed crockery and torn linens, and was trying pitifully to gather them up in her arms. One of the legionaries openly seized a carved drinking vessel, which only made the old woman's wails grow louder.

Shelamzion watched with the passive horror of the helpless, knowing only a day ago she would have run to help an old woman in distress. Now, she stood, shackled by Rome, not daring to draw attention to herself. She glanced up at Simon. He made no comment, but Shelamzion saw that he was pale, his mouth set in a rigid line, his eyes constantly scanning the dark mouths of the streets and alleys. At that moment, had he offered her a single crumb of comfort she would have grasped at it greedily, and turned to him as her protector. But he kept himself apart, leaving her to her loneliness and the chaotic convolutions of her thoughts.

Her eyes travelled wearily over the debris-littered streets, the huddled families, the tattered hem of her wedding dress. *Can all this have come about as the consequence of a joke*, she wondered. *Father will be so angry with*—Then she cut off. No one would be angry at Menachem and Judas ever again. Menachem with his easy laugh that shook the curls of his beard. And Judas, always the timid one, looking to Menachem for cues how to behave. Gone. And all for a jest. And again it came back to her, who had first made the joke. Simon, sitting at her father's table, likening the procurator to a beggar. Menachem laughing and holding out his bowl to collect alms on Florus' behalf. How had she failed to see? Why had she not understood?Her eyes were fixed on Simon with such loathing that he stiffened and turned towards her.

'What is it?' He searched her face, thinking she had seen something.

'How was it my family met their deaths?' There was a lump in her throat, so though she framed the question calmly, coldly in her head, the words came out muffled and fretful when spoken aloud. Simon's eyes flashed for a moment with the most extraordinary pain then became hooded and secretive. 'Now is not the time.'

'I am not a child,' she said chokingly. 'Tell me.'

He compressed his lips, and she thought he would refuse, but then he said, 'They were betrayed.'

'Betrayed?' She could scarcely believe what she was hearing. 'By who? My father is a respected Pharisee. Who would dare?'

He looked at her oddly then. 'Pharisees are not universally loved. Especially by those who rank themselves nobility, or, worse still, by those who think themselves the pillars on which society and order stand.'

'You talk in riddles,' she snapped. 'I cannot understand you.'

He sighed and closed his eyes a moment. And when he opened them again he did not look at her, but stared off into the distance, as though he could not bear to meet her eyes. 'I went to the tribunal to offer my services. I had some small conceit that as governor of Acrabetene my opinion could lend weight to your father's case. However, Florus had everyone who was not there by direct summons hemmed behind a line of his own men. I had barely time to send my servant with a message to your brothers before we were penned in, helpless as cattle.'

'But my brothers came.'

'Yes. And they brought your mother with them.' Simon paused.

'Tell me,' Shelamzion hissed.

With reluctance, Simon continued. 'I believe your brothers meant to come in stealth. To find out what Florus would accept for a bribe then make haste to secure it. They could not know how ugly things had turned.'

'But surely,' Shelamzion interrupted despite herself, 'Surely Florus was persuaded that no true insult existed.'

Simon laughed bitterly. 'Rarely have I heard the city elders speak with more eloquence.'

'Then—'

'Florus is a little-minded man. And such men cannot imagine that there is a greater danger to the order of the world than a slight to their pride. He listened not to the humble entreaties of the noble and the wise, but insisted that the perpetrators of the jest be found. In his arrogance, he warned there would be blood shed amongst the people if he were thwarted, and even threatened the Temple with violence, saying he would set his troops to tear down the holy of holies—'

Shelamzion gasped even at the echo of such blasphemy. 'And my brothers? My mother?'

Simon's eyes filled with pain. 'They would have slipped away, I think. But Shimeon, cousin to the High Priest, and not an unambitious man, recognized Menachem. He let out a cry naming them as the culprits. Knowing all was lost, they drew their swords, but what match can two men be against a maniple of trained soldiers? Menachem fought bravely but he was cut down.' His words trailed off, and he drew the back of his hand across his brow. For a moment, Shelamzion thought he would not go on.

'And Judas?' she pressed.

Simon's top lip lengthened in a grim line. 'Judas would have given himself up. Seeing all was lost he threw down his sword … But the soldiers' hearts were filled with bloodlust and they cut him down where he stood.'

Shelamzion let out a low groan. But mixing with the wails and lamentations on all sides, it went unnoticed. With difficulty she said, 'My parents, you saw them die also?'

'When Florus loosed his troops, your mother ran with the crowd as I did.' He shook his head sadly. 'I tried to reach her. But no one who did not possess a sword escaped with their lives.'

Shelamzion took a moment to digest these words, and a sudden ray of hope lit her heart. 'Then you did not see my father die. He may yet live.'

Simon did not answer. He was looking directly ahead, watching the family at the head of the queue. The mother and father gesticulating. One of the soldiers, face like stone, dragging the eldest son to one side. The family kept following, trying to make the soldiers understand that the knife they had found was a shepherd's tool, not a Zealot's silent dagger. Pleas in Aramaic were dismissed in Latin. The mother was almost beside herself with anguish. Shelamzion took a step forward, but Simon gripped her arm.

'We cannot afford to draw attention to ourselves.'

'But the soldiers … they don't understand.'

'They choose not to.'

'You don't—'

But Simon turned, with an expression that would have silenced the jackal's bark. 'Open your cloak.'

'I—' Before she could draw breath he had pushed her cloak wide, his big hands coming forward to rend apart the skirts of her robe. The silk was fine. Rabbi Judah ben Eliad had spared no expense for the wedding of his only daughter. It tore noiselessly, while Shelamzion stood rooted to the spot, her bones fused with shock. Only her eyes moved across Simon's face, the pupils growing large as questions.

But now the second legionary was beckoning to them. Slowly, they made their way forward and stopped when he held his *pilum* across their paths.

'Names.'

'David ben Gamaliel,' Simon answered. 'And this is my sister, Leah.'

His hand was still gripping her upper arm, and she was glad of it. A trembling had seized her and she did not trust herself.

'From?'

'Hebron.'

'Hebron?' the legionary repeated. 'That's a long way when you've no baggage.'

'Alas,' Simon said coolly, 'What little we had was stolen when the … troubles arose.'

'What's this?' The first legionary joined them.

'Says he's going to Hebron. No baggage.'

'It was stolen,' Simon repeated.

The second legionary pushed his face right into Simon's. 'Do I know you?'

Simon drew back and Shelamzion felt a wave of panic.

'Please,' Simon's voice was very soft. 'My sister has been sorely used. I beg you do not tax her delicate state of mind still further by delaying our departure.' Without warning he reached out his free hand and pulled Shelamzion's cloak open, revealing the tattered ribbons of silk, brownish bloodstains, picked up from the street, creeping up from the hem.

Shelamzion said nothing. She was white with humiliation. *Sorely used.* How well she knew what the Romans would make of that. Bitterly she thought, *He is using me to make good his escape.* Then tears welled up in her eyes and splashed upon the dusty ground, tears she knew they would interpret as admission of her shame, but she could not help them. The second legionary was an older man. He frisked Simon roughly, then stepped back. 'Clean,' he said, throwing a look half of pity half of distaste towards Shelamzion. 'Let them through.'

Simon bowed, as though servility towards Rome was in his nature, and they moved on. But, when he would have steadied her grasp, she broke free and walked ahead.

The wall in which the gate was set was several feet thick. On the far side there was an arch of light through which Shelamzion could see the slope of green hills, fading under the purplish shadows of early evening. But closer than these was a thing that filled Shelamzion's vision so completely that it blotted out the hills and the sun and the light. A row of dark crosses. And upon each was nailed a sagging sack of flesh.

'No!' The word escaped her lips, a long, compressed note of pain, and echoed off the vaulted stone of the gateway.

'Hush.' Simon's breath was hot and harsh in her ear. 'I had hoped to spare you this. I thought Florus would be satisfied with displaying his trophies at the tribunal. But his bloodlust is insatiable.'

'Who are those men?' Her voice sounded very small and distant to her ears, and Simon's reply seemed to come from a long way off.

'Those are the men who opposed Florus at the tribunal.'

'Is my—' Shelamzion started to say 'father'. But she found she had forgotten the most basic functions of life. She could not form the word. In her wretchedness she tried to pull away, but she had forgotten how to walk. Her legs crumpled beneath her, and Simon had to catch her in his arms to prevent her from falling. There was a sound of galloping, growing louder and nearer, and she was mildly surprised to see that Simon did not seem to notice it. Then the sun sank suddenly, shockingly, like a curse upon Pharaoh, and the world began filling up with blackness.

'Shelamzion … *Shelamzion!*'

She blinked. The sun had not set at all, and Simon was holding her upright. She glanced to her right and saw that the legionaries still had their backs to them. She could not bring herself to look left. The shape of the crosses still burning behind her lids. Simon was speaking, low and urgently.

'Listen to me. We must go on.'

She started to shake her head, but he was insistent. 'Your family has gone. There is nothing for you here in Jerusalem.'

Still she shook her head with the blind incomprehension of a dumb beast, and Simon pressed his face close.

'We have very little time. Do you understand? You are the remnant … all that is left. Only you can carry their memories on for future generations. You must live.'

He had his hands under her elbows now, propelling her forward. 'There are legionaries beyond the gate, guarding the crosses. You must walk past them, as though your thoughts were only of getting to Hebron. And never look up.'

'No.' Her voice was so small, it barely parted her lips. 'I can't.'

'You can. I will be there at your side. If you cry out we will both be lost. Don't look up. Keep your eyes on the ground.' And all the time he was leading her towards the dying light and escape. She did as he said, keeping her eyes lowered and letting her ears fill up with unfamiliar sounds. The crunch of her sandals on the pebbly, unswept path. The low sighing she took to be the wind at first, then realized was the moaning of the refugees marching in single file up ahead. The edgy, muttered exchanges between legionaries.

The shadow of a cross fell over them, and she faltered, half ready to flee back the way she had come. Then Simon's voice was there in her ear, 'Keep walking.

Don't look up.' And she obeyed him because, in some childish recess of her mind, what she could not see could not exist. As long as her eyes were averted her father might be spared his fate.

But when they reached higher ground and could stop to take a breath, Shelamzion looked round and realized what Simon's words had deprived her of. The crosses stood around the city gate, strange, dead trees with dying men hanging from them instead of foliage. And those men were no more than small, black dots against the fading sky. Which one was her father? There was no way of telling. Her heart squeezed to a thin, hard point. He was gone and she had lost her chance to say goodbye. A lump formed in her throat and she felt suddenly that she could not take another step. Something was changing inside her.

She was a pillar of salt. She was Job, from whom God had taken all things. She was Eve cast from *Gan Eden* never to know paradise again. And all because of a jest. A joke started by Simon bar Gioras that had not even made her laugh.

'Come.' His hand was on her arm. 'We cannot stay here.'

Her eyes turned towards him ... and they were full of hate.

Chapter IX

*The family from which I am derived is not an ignoble one … I am of the royal blood; for the
children of Asamoneus, from whom that family was derived, had both the office of the high priest-
hood, and the dignity of a king, for a long time together.*

Josephus Flavius

Building work on the devastated Temple of Saturn was taking place at
astonishing speed. Following Quintus, Cornelius passed a gang of slaves
trying to manoeuvre a complicated pulley system into place under the
watchful eye of two engineers. And a little further on, a harassed-looking architect hurried past, longs rolls of papyrus sticking out from under his arm,
like the many limbs of an Eastern god. And it wasn't only this temple that was
feeling the Emperor's beneficent touch, Cornelius knew. All over Rome temples
and public buildings were being gilded with Flavian coin. Little wonder they were
calling Vespasian *Restitutor Aedium Sacrarum*.

His eyes narrowed. Yet how many spared a thought for the plundered Jewish
gold that underwrote all this conspicuous splendour? He glanced at Quintus,
wanting to share his thoughts, but Quintus, for once, seemed remote and uncommunicative. Indeed, so silent was he that Cornelius began to wonder if he was
suffering from the after-effects of another imprudent night spent reducing Festus'
wine cellar.

Cornelius followed the strangely silent Quintus down the Capitolinus then
on to the darker, narrower Argentarius. At the Carcer, Quintus walked by without
a second glance. But Cornelius found himself looking up at its bland facade and
wondering what Shelamzion was doing. How did she spend the lonely hours
between his visits? She was no longer chained. That was his doing. But what was
there to feed a sensitive, yearning mind in that stench-ridden hole? Perhaps he
would bring her something to read. Yes. Something by Paterculus … and Cato of
course. And Plautus for relief. She wouldn't have read those works, and it would
be refreshing to hear her opinions. Perhaps he might even begin to guide her
gently in the art of understanding poetical forms. And then if—

A cloud suddenly covered the sun and the world grew grey and unfamiliar.
Cornelius' steps slowed and he let a low groan escape his lips. O worst of indisci-

plines. He had allowed himself an indulgence he would have despised in others. To grow fond of a prisoner. To dream of awakening her mind to the world's marvels when she would never see or experience any of them. All his plans to elevate her soul were suddenly cut short by a vivid image of the executioner's callous hand.

What a fool he had been. Nothing could save her now. Only think if rumour of his indulgence got out. The barely withheld sniggers, the sly references at the dinner table to Pygmalion-like figures who fell in love with their own creations. No, no. He had gone too far. And now he must face up to his actions and find a way to disentangle himself.

Of course, Quintus had been his main confidant. If there had been any indiscretion in his manner surely Quintus would know. He opened his mouth, trying to find the most delicate way to frame his question, when something in the air made him pause. They had left the main street. How long ago? Instinct made him glance over his shoulder, half expecting to see the familiar money shops. Instead there were dirty, noisy booths attempting to sell their cheap wares as if they were the rarest treasures, and street harlots with stout limbs and painted faces, which cracked like badly glazed pots when they caught him looking.

'Quintus.' Cornelius hurried after his cousin's rapidly receding back. Quintus slowed, but did not stop, casting a half-angry look in Cornelius' direction.

'There's no time. We're late.'

'Quintus, really. I must protest.' Cornelius was painfully aware of the stiffness in his calves that made it impossible to keep up with Quintus' youthful legs. 'You drag me from my work without warning or explanation. You refuse to allow me a litter. And then you deny me the smallest hint about our destination. I insist that you tell me at once where we are headed or I shall be forced—'

'Shh,' said Quintus. 'We're here.'

'Here?' Cornelius looked up at the shabby tenement before them, then at his cousin. 'Is this some kind of jest?'

Quintus did not answer. His nose and mouth covered, he was already slipping through the low doorway. Cornelius stared for a moment, then followed. They climbed a worn staircase, pursued by a strong smell of urine and cabbages. And on every landing the mewling of hungry infants filled the air. Outside a door on the top landing a large, evil-looking Nubian was standing, his gaze facing the stairwell. Quintus walked towards him, despite his cousin's whispered entreaties.

'Quintus, please. Have you gone mad?'

Quintus said something in a low voice to the Nubian and the man stood aside. He opened the door and nodded at the two Romans to enter. They stepped into a surprisingly large room. It was austerely but stylishly furnished, the sideboard topped with marble, the *alabastra* Corinthian in style.

'Quintus,' Cornelius said slowly. 'Whose house is this?'

But even as he said it, the historian in him was minutely cataloguing the items in the room, which formed their own picture. The few striking pieces spoke of eloquence, not opulence. A nobleman fallen on hard times, perhaps? No. Not quite right. And those lamps. Squat, unpleasing. Lacking even the smallest adornment. A sign of poverty? But even the poorest man might scratch the image of a goddess on to soft clay. Unless … unless … such imagery were forbidden. Lifting one of the small lamps he now recognized as Herodian in style, Cornelius said in low, horrified tones, 'You have brought me to the house of the traitor.'

'Yet I hope you will not hold it entirely against me,' said a soft, penetrating voice. Cornelius whirled round. And there, having emerged from a side door into the room, was a tall man approaching his middle years. He had a full, sensuous mouth from which flashed a sickle-shaped smile aimed at Cornelius, and dark, hawkish eyes, which moved over the historian in careful scrutiny. 'Allow me to introduce myself.'

Flustered at his indiscretion, Cornelius interrupted. 'There is no need. I recognise you, Joseph ben Mattathias.'

A shadow crossed the man's face, but only for an instant, then he closed his eyes. And when he opened them again his expression had changed, as completely and effortlessly as a Greek player lifting a mask to his face. He gave a courteous bow. 'If you will do me the honour, I prefer now to be known as Flavius Josephus.'

'And your patron sanctions this'—Cornelius struggled for words—'this tribute you do him?'

'Cousin.' Quintus leaned forward. 'You are forgetting that it was Josephus who prophesied our Emperor's rise to glory.'

And what fool could have failed to see that coming, Cornelius thought. But he gave a stiff, little bow of consent and allowed himself to take the weight off his feet while Josephus called for wine.

When he returned Josephus seemed more congenial than ever. He took the seat opposite Cornelius and insisted on pouring the wine himself.

'You must forgive my poor hospitality. But, as I am certain your cousin will have explained, my presence in Rome is clandestine.'

'No,' said Cornelius with a sharp glance at Quintus. 'He has explained nothing.'

'Ah.' Josephus leaned back and interlaced his fingers. They were long and exquisitely manicured, Cornelius noticed, but unadorned by rings. He took a long, considering sip of his wine before continuing. 'I have been engaged until recently in accompanying the Emperor's son on his victorious tour of the east.'

'The experience must surely have been a painful one,' Cornelius said, taking a tentative sip from his cup. It was surprisingly good wine.

But if this strange Jew, who claimed the Emperor's favour, had been disturbed by the sight of watching his fellow countrymen paying the price of his betrayal he showed no outward sign. He ran his finger round the rim of his goblet. 'Rome has shown great civility towards this humble servant, and I deem it my duty to be useful to my master in any way I can.'

'It's thanks to Josephus that half the valuables in Galilee weren't spirited away by the Zealots,' Quintus interjected lazily. 'Titus keeps him busy cataloguing all the recovered treasures so that their ritual significance can be preserved for posterity.'

Cornelius avoided asking if it wasn't true that Titus now ate his meals off an altar table. Instead, he said, 'And now your usefulness extends to Rome.'

'I fear so,' Josephus agreed. 'Although my stay is to be a short one before I rejoin my master where he has taken up quarters in Berytus.'

'Yet you do not stay at court.'

'Regrettably, there are some things a man may learn more easily if he remains in the shadows. But please—' He held out a bronze dish filled with plump figs towards Cornelius. 'Won't you try some. Coming from Antioch, they are particularly fragrant at this time of year, don't you think?'

Cornelius took a handful. But the only scent he could detect was that of intrigue. What did the Emperor's son fear enough that he would send his spy to Rome even as he was being hailed the darling of the war? Did not all Rome thirst for heroes? He reached for his cup, but did not lift it, as a thought occurred to him.

In our greed do we not swallow our heroes whole then forget them. Our tongues already sticking out, eager to lap up the next willing candidate for our fickle love. And Titus has a brother here in Rome. Cornelius let his eyes focus on Josephus, who was listening politely to Quintus. O clever man, Cornelius thought. To come here was your idea. To sniff the way the wind is blowing amongst the common people. Are they for Titus? Or are they for Domition? You want to know. For your master's sake ... And for your own.

Quintus had said something that made Josephus laugh. He turned to Cornelius and there was a warmth suffused in his face that Cornelius had not seen before.

'You must forgive me,' he said. 'I have spent the last weeks with camel drivers and sailors. It is a joy to speak with people of breeding and education. Especially'—he held Cornelius' gaze—'with those of a scholarly persuasion.'

'I—I don't know what you mean.'

'But you are too modest. Was it not you who wrote the commentary on the Etruscan Wars?'

'You have read my work,' Cornelius said with forced lightness. He leaned towards the bronze bowl. The figs, like the wine, were excellent. Josephus watched him, then suddenly said,

'History being the rightful booty of the conquerors, they rarely give credence to the provocations and motives of the opposing side, and for that reason the vanquished find that added to their suffering is the annihilation of their past beneath the historian's obliterating ink. Yet before they can raise their voices in objection, they are forever silenced.'

Cornelius stared at him, astonished, the fig suspended halfway to his mouth. Josephus lowered his eyes. 'Perhaps I have misquoted you.'

'No. Indeed. You quote me with great elegance. May I ask what drew you to that particular passage?'

Josephus' eyes suddenly filled with an exquisite pain, but he merely said, 'In the circumstances it seemed most pertinent.'

Cornelius blushed. 'And you think this is the fate that awaits your people?'

'How can I think otherwise?'

'But this is how my cousin may reassure you,' Quintus suddenly announced. 'As I told you, he intends to write a history of the war.'

'Ah,' said Josephus sadly. 'Many have done that.'

'But not like this. He intends to write from the perspective of the enemy—' He caught himself and smiled apologetically. 'Not that you are the enemy, of course.'

Josephus looked between the cousins, shaking his head.

'It cannot be done. Rome would never allow it.'

'But I intend to use unimpeachable sources,' Cornelius broke in. 'When the characters of my history are shown to have lived and breathed the smoke of battle … when they show themselves to be creatures of flesh and blood, rather than the noble savages of the imagination. Then my readers will be forced to understand their world in new and marvellous ways.'

'Marvellous? You really think so?' Quintus said, helping himself to more wine. 'Yet now I think on it, doesn't your writing make banality a virtue and reduce heroism to the commonplace?'

'That, dear cousin,' Cornelius exclaimed, half choking on the fig he was chewing. 'That is the whole point. Heroes are marvellous because they are men and nothing more. If we are forever ascribing our victories to the gods and turning our enemies into demons, how can we ever find what is sacred and inviolable within ourselves?'

'What a delight to the Stoics you would be,' Josephus said coolly. '*To mankind, mankind is holy.*'

Cornelius, about to go on in the same vein, paused. Did the Jews understand the concept of the free will, that spark of divinity interred in the hearts of all men? Or were they simply little clay pieces used by their god to animate stories of celestial invention? Cornelius found he did not know.

'Naturally, I intended no offence,' he said cautiously.

The eyes of the Jew were fixed on him, like two pure droplets of night. 'And surely none is taken.' Josephus clapped his hands and gave his slave orders to bring more wine. Cornelius waited uncomfortably.

As Josephus poured the amber fluid into his guest's cup, a thought seemed to occur to him. 'You say that you intend to use the testimony of those whose misfortune it was to live through the tragedy of our times.'

Cornelius nodded eagerly.

'Yet,' Josephus continued, 'it is my hope that you do not intend to cast me in the role of witness.'

'Indeed no,' Cornelius beamed. The wine was a little stronger than he was used to. 'You have no need for fear on that account. I already have a most reliable source to work with. My cousin must surely have informed you. We hold in our prison the wife of the bandit king himself, Shelamzion bat Judah.'

'Simon's wife.' Josephus said the words softly.

'An unexpected gem,' Cornelius continued.

'You'd scarcely think it to see her,' Quintus put in with a laugh. Cornelius glanced at him with sudden irritation.

'She is a woman of great complexity. Her true nature lies well beneath the surface, I think.'

'That I do not doubt.' Josephus' eyes were so troubled that Cornelius asked at once, 'You do not agree?'

Josephus shrugged. 'That she has hidden depths, how could I disagree? But do not forget that depths are, by their very nature, dark, unpredictable places. You may discover things there you do not seek.'

Cornelius smiled uneasily. 'I feel you are offering me a warning.'

'I would not be so bold. It is only that you must recall that I have found myself at the mercy of these wily and dangerous minds. They may mislead the most stalwart soul into mischief. And I know this to my own cost. Did I not join their campaign in Galilee against my most sound judgement?'

Josephus fell silent a moment, as though lost in the bitterest regret. And Cornelius found a vein of pity opening in his breast. After all, to be forced to choose between one's countrymen and one's beliefs—The conflict had never resonated so strongly. To Cornelius the choice had always been between citizen and barbarian. *Civis* versus *barbarus*. Yet, were not loyalties forced upon a person as an accident of birth? To defend one's own people even against the wiser counsel of conscience was surely a noble thing. He felt humbled and a little abashed by his earlier hostility.

'You believe what is said then, that Gioras was a conniver and a schemer?'

Josephus' voice shook as he answered. 'A more tyrannical deceiver would be hard to find. The people of Jerusalem welcomed him in as their saviour. And in return he set himself over them as their king and devoted all his time to the plunder and ultimate destruction of our fair city.'

Tears appeared in Josephus' eyes, and shocked, Cornelius muttered almost to himself, 'And yet his wife remains loyal to him.'

Josephus gave a short, mirthless laugh. 'My people have long known that the worst schemers amongst us clothe themselves in the garb of the fairer sex. Can it be any coincidence that in Peraea dwells the Baaras plant that will yield to no man's hand. But a libation of menstrual blood will wither its roots, like poison.'

'But she is under sentence of death. What can she hope to gain?'

'The only thing the historian has to offer. Immortality. And you have offered her that, have you not?'

'O, but she—' Cornelius flushed. He had been about to say she had been reluctant, that he had forced the story out of her. But mightn't that be exactly what she had wanted him to think? He saw himself suddenly as decrepit Tithonus forever entranced by the youthful glamour of his nymph, and a wintry chill went through him. How had this happened? That he, a man of education, should fall for the full lips and clear eyes of youth, that winsome promise that lures the elderly down through the generations. It was scarcely credible. Perhaps it was true; the Jews were sorcerers and necromancers after all. Dazed, he raised his eyes and found his host watching him.

Jospehus bit down on that sensuous lower lip. 'Forgive me. But that is not all you promised her, is it?'

Cornelius blinked, like a child caught in a half-truth, before spluttering, 'No. I—That is to say, she exacted a … promise from me.' He glanced at Quintus with what he hoped was an expression that conveyed that the folly originated entirely with him, then went on bleakly, 'The nature of the promise was such that she would provide the detail for my history in return for information about her child. It seemed little enough to ask … '

His words faded. Josephus pressed his fingertips together.

'She knew then that the child lives.'

'I may have—Indeed she—' Cornelius coughed. 'I believe the idea was implanted by my own hand.'

Josephus lifted his wine to his lips and took a long, slow draught, his eyes never leaving Cornelius' face for an instant. But when at last he put down his cup, he was smiling. 'Well, what of it? It's a poor deed that denies the bond between mother and child.'

Cornelius felt an inexplicable rush of gratitude at his host's magnanimity, which was duly rewarded when Josephus went on, 'You will surely allow me the pleasure of helping you honour your promise.'

'That would be most kind, but—'

'It would be my pleasure.' Josephus arose and went to the sideboard, from where he produced several scrolls.

'My notes,' he explained, seeing Cornelius' curious expression. 'A few poor scribblings from the days when Rome still questioned … my loyalties.'

Ah yes, thought Cornelius. There was a time when Vespasian condemned you to the darkness in which he now holds Shelamzion. Perhaps you pity her for that shared history.

Josephus had laid out the scrolls on the low table between them. Cornelius leaned forward eagerly, hoping to catch a glimpse of this extraordinary man's thoughts. But they were written in an unfamiliar script and he could decipher nothing. Josephus ran his eyes along the lines of ink in that curious eastern manner that runs right to left.

'Yes,' he said after a few moments, then, 'Yes, as I thought.' He looked up and nodded gravely at the cousins. 'A boy thought to be the son of Simon was found in the last days of the war by a centurion. He was near death, and he took him to a nearby physician, thinking Titus might have use for the boy, and no doubt hoping for reward.'

Cornelius and Quintus exchanged glances. 'This much we know,' Quintus agreed. Josephus went back to his papyri, changing scrolls several times before exclaiming, 'Ah, I knew it!'

'Yes?'

'The physician reported the boy as having an extraordinarily robust constitution. Perhaps a legacy of his parentage. He is said to have recovered in a matter of weeks and was seen to be doing well.'

Cornelius released a tightness in his chest he had not known was there with a long expulsion of air. 'So the boy's whereabouts are known?'

'Alas no.' Josephus frowned, turning the scroll over and scrutinizing its reverse side. 'When the news first reached my ears, I naturally made enquiries. But Fate stood, blocking my every path. The physician had given the boy into the care of a centurion, called Aelius Celatus of the XII Fulminata. But a centurion by the name Aelius Celatus does not exist in the XII Fulminata.'

'O, but—' Quintus interrupted, but Josephus held up a hand to silence him.

'Believe me, friend, when I tell you that I have checked every permutation of name and circumstance. Had such a man existed he could not have escaped me. Besides, though my Latin is poor, it seems to me that the name is a deliberate attempt to mislead. Does it not mean, *He who seeks to learn the secrets of others*?'

The fingers of Cornelius' hand loosened their grip on his wine cup and he slumped backwards. 'Then there is no hope.'

'O no, I did not say that.' Josephus seemed surprised. 'One thing we do know is that the child is alive, and that he is being given shelter, almost certainly by someone who knows his true identity.'

'Someone who will surely keep that identity a secret at all costs.'

Josephus put his head back, as though amused by something Cornelius could not see. 'Secrets may be precious beyond gold. But who are the keepers of secrets but men.' He cocked his head to one side. 'And what man does not have his price?'

'I—' Cornelius floundered in the face of cynicism. 'I don't—'

'Indeed not.' Josephus' manner was all at once reassuring. 'What civilized man would? But if you would accept my counsel as one who would like to be your friend, you will question the wife of Simon with the utmost exactitude. She may know more than she admits.'

'I always thought her a woman of great integrity.'

'Of course. But there may be things that she knows without understanding that she knows them. Trust me when I say that my master would count it a great favour if you were to leave no stone unturned—What is it, boy?'

Cornelius jerked at the change in his host's tone. The large Nubian guard had entered silently, and now approached his master. He bent down and whispered something in Josephus' ear, who frowned and shook his head slightly. The Nubian straightened and left the room, his footfalls soft as a stalking cat. And, without knowing why, Cornelius found himself rubbing the tender flesh of his throat. But his host was on his feet.

'My friends, I must apologise. My duties call me elsewhere.'

Quintus stood up. 'We must not stand in your way.' He turned to Cornelius. 'Come, cousin.'

Cornelius blinked, like a man awakening from an intricate dream. 'Of course,' he said thickly. 'We have presumed too much upon your hospitality already.'

'Not in the least.' Josephus reached forward and took Cornelius' hand between his. 'I only regret this poor fare was the best I could offer. You will appreciate that my circumstances prevent a more blatant display.'

'Indeed,' Cornelius agreed. 'I can only hope that your journey has been a fruitful one.'

Josephus squeezed his hand. 'If coming here allows me to count you as a friend, I will consider myself well rewarded.'

'I—' Cornelius was flustered. 'You do me a great honour.'

'Not at all. I confess an interest in your work, as indeed does my patron. Besides, if I was not your most ardent admirer, would I have been so eager to make my presence known to you?'

Cornelius, swollen with the knowledge that his name was being whispered in the ear of the Emperor's son, felt a sudden pang of conscience.

'But how can you know if I am to be trusted?'

He regretted the question instantly, as Josephus' kindly expression dissolved, and, for the first time, he seemed to falter. His gaze grew distant, as a man's gaze will when the ghosts of the past suddenly rise before him. Then he blinked them away, and let his focus rest on his guest once more.

'Forgive me,' Cornelius said weakly. 'I meant only that in these times, the word of men has grown so fragile a thing that it shatters at the smallest provocation. Yet you seem willing to trust mine.'

'Really, cousin.' Quintus put his hand on Cornelius' shoulder. 'Can your curiosity never be satisfied? Will you insist upon knowing even the most hidden corners of a man's heart?'

But Josephus shook his head, saying softly, 'No, I will answer.' Then with his eyes on Cornelius, and his expression a mixture of pity and loathing, perhaps even envy, he said, 'I have known men like you before. And they could no more break the bond of their word than they could tear the hearts from their own breasts.'

Chapter X

Think too of Simon, son of Gioras. What crime did he not commit? What outrage was not done to free citizens by the men who gave him unlimited power? What friendship or kinship was there that did not increase the wantonness of their daily murders?
The War of the Jews, Book VI

She was the wife of Simon. Simon's wife. Simon, no kin of her kin. Simon, brother to a dead man. Simon, the convert's son, possessed of a wit so sharp it could kill. Simon the politician. Simon the leader. Simon the man.

She awoke, strangled by her own silent screams, and lay in the darkened room fighting for breath. As always, terror preceding memory. The flood of questions. Where? then Why? then How? Rapid images flicking though her consciousness, a maelstrom of memories, slow-turning tablets on which words gradually appeared.

The flight from Jerusalem. Swaying on the back of a mule. Sick from the rocking motion of the animal beneath her and the churning grief in her stomach. Watching Simon's back swaying ahead of her, all the time thinking, *I cannot marry this man. There must be a way to escape this. Surely there must be a way.*

'Halitzah,' she said at last, calling after him.

He tugged the reins of his mule back, drew alongside her. 'Halitzah?'

'Hillel teaches us,' she began, faltering under his burning gaze. 'He teaches us that it may be deemed as much a man's duty to leave his brother's widow alone as it is to marry her. Did not Naomi take the shoe of her near kinsman and spit upon the ground so that he might be freed from his duty of taking her as a wife? The ritual of Halitzah set them free.' Now that she said these words aloud she felt the powerful truth of them. The only bond between them was spilt blood. Not enough to bind them through eternity. She looked up at Simon with renewed hope, certain that he had regretted the rashness of his proposal and only wanted a way out.

'I have a distant cousin in Galilee,' she said eagerly. 'In the circumstances he will surely not turn me away.' And thinking she saw doubt whisper across his features, she pressed on. 'Have no fear on my account. I will be well taken care of—'
He was looking at her so coldly that she faltered.

'It is not on your account that I fear.' He spoke in a low, angry tone. 'But rather I fear for the memory of my brother. You were to carry on his name, if only through the poor substitute of myself. Yet you seem eager to cast us both aside, the living brother along with the dead.'

And when she stared at him, like a lost child, he kicked at his mule and rode ahead. She did not offer a way out again.

They followed the Ridge Road, losing themselves in an undulating sea of hills, two specks of dust in amongst the burning umbers and ochres, lying low, covering their tracks. In the crumbling village of Shilo, with no words of comfort or caress, Simon took her for his wife, calling on the village elders to stand witness. And they came, a dirty, ragged lot, who scratched themselves even as they intoned prayers in dead voices to a god they scarcely thought was listening.

Shelamzion, feeling the rough scratch of the peasant's veil Simon had purchased for her, drew it back and peeked out at the village. Shilo. Holy Shilo where the children of Israel had gathered to erect the Tabernacle. Where the tribes had gone to divide the land by lot. Where Chana had come to pray for a son and been granted one. Samuel, dark prophet who had inspired a Benjamite king to reach out and grasp the kingdom of Judah with his right hand and the kingdom of Israel with his left, and to bring them together in a single, thunderous clap. Shilo, mired in myth and mystery until the stones sang the Holy Name of God. Brought low. Rotting for centuries, the Tabernacle torn from its grasp, its roofs gaping to the stars, its stones sinking back into the earth, like tombs.

Shelamzion thought this as she circled Simon. Seven times, as Joshua had led his people seven times around the walls of Jericho. Seven times, like the great, branched candelabra in the Temple, like the seven golden gates that belonged to a mother goddess long forgotten. And her eyes were on the hills, as they caught fire, grazed by a sun that watched the world with the envious eye of slighted godhood.

'*Harei at li le'intu*. You are hereby my wife,' intoned Simon, and she scarcely heard him or felt her lips moving as she replied, 'I am your wife.'

The *huppah* he led her to was only a tent, animal skins stretched taut over staffs of age-blackened olive. But she crawled in gratefully, falling on her face, suppliant before the god of oblivion until Simon gripped her shoulders, digging his long fingers into her flesh, dragging her to her knees.

'No!'

She shrank from him. It was too soon. The scent of death still clinging to her. Simon's eyes burned in the darkness and she trembled before them. But when the assault came he struck at her with words, 'What do you think of it then, this world outside holy Jerusalem?'

'I—' Why was he doing this? Her parents were dead. Her brothers were dead. She stepped on sackcloth and breathed ashes. What did she think of the world?

'I don't like it.'

'Those men,' said Simon, sitting back on his heels, as though she had not spoken. 'Those peasants you despised. What were they in your eyes? Empty bellies? Sunken cheeks? Animals scraping at the land?'

'Suffering—' she broke in. 'I saw suffering … and pain.'

'You saw defeat.' He let her go, and now there was something hiding in his expression, as though it was he who wore the veil. 'You do not understand,' he said at last. 'How could you?'

The coldness of his words drenched her in fire. She tore the veil from her head and would have howled her rage directly at him, but for the agony which constricted her throat and hoarsened her words. 'You think I do not know … suffering?'

His eyes searched her face, brutal and pitiless, two altars of obsidian upon which he sacrificed the last little vestiges of her pride. 'You are suffering now, and think you are like them. But those men and women were born out of generations of suffering into generations of suffering. They suckled on their mothers' breasts while their fathers and brothers fell. Every power that turned in greed towards Israel has come to Shilo and tried to grind it into the dust.'

Without meaning to, she glanced towards the opening in the tent with its sliver of dusty, rocky earth showing through, and Simon caught her look and understood its message.

'No, they have not succeeded. Shilo is not yet dust. Out there are the true children of Israel, scourged and vilified, pushed beyond those limits men should endure, chosen above all others to inherit the world.'

The intensity of his words held her rigid, like a kid caught in the stare of a puffing serpent instinctively feeling the fatal consequence of one wrong move. But outside something spooked one of the mules and, rigid and terrified, it brayed at the moon. One of the men of Shilo cursed it, pausing outside their tent to fart ripely before moving on. And the ugly, tearing sound of it wrenched a strangled laugh from Shelamzion's compressed throat. 'Is he too one of the chosen?

'Chosen, yes. Because he will fight.'

'You think such men will stand up to the fury of Rome?'

The shadows in the tent had stolen Simon's features, but she heard his voice lengthen, like a smile. 'They will fight. And they will fight like the Hasmonean warriors, who threw the Greek from this land. Because soon they will have more to lose if they do not.'

The next day they crossed into the toparchy of Acrabatene. And Shelamzion began to understand something of Simon's words. Derelict figures at the roadside, their dirty hands outstretched, their red-rimmed eyes feverish, already focused on the wriggling horizon between this world and the next. They clutched at the travellers with flaccid, hopeless limbs that fell back to their sides, like the branches of blasted trees, as soon as the mules had passed them.

'Forced off their land,' Simon whispered. 'By greedy bureaucrats in the pay of wealthy landowners.'

'But why? The peasants are needed surely?'

'Not by rich Sadducees, who envy the profits of the vast, slave-run estates of their Latin cousins. Their method is to tax the peasant until he is forced to go begging to them for a loan, which they then give at exorbitant rates of interest. When he cannot pay that either, they throw him from his land. He, and his family, are replaced with slaves at a tenth of the cost.'

'But surely—' She was filled with revulsion and moral indignation. 'This must be stopped.'

He looked at her strangely. 'It will be—when the people are ready.'

It was not the city of Acrabatta that was Simon's home, but the smaller town of Gerasa south of the city. And, unlike the great Decapolis city that bore the same name, with its cosmopolitan, pagan population, Gerasa was a Jewish town, nestling in the hills, unadorned by idol or icon, unblemished by mythology. No battles were fought over it, no covenants revealed, no kings came from Gerasa, no gods were born there. For Shelamzion, steeped in the marvel and mythos of Jerusalem, it seemed a cold place. She shivered, and felt the loss of her father so badly that she would have welcomed even Simon's arm around her shoulders. But Simon rode on, his jaw set in a firm line, his eyes fixed on home.

And such a home it was. Set between two hills, overlooking the rooftops of the town, like the eye of a god, a tall, white structure, columned in the Greek style, two ancient terebinth trees shading the dusty path to its entrance. It was twice, no three times the size of the house of ben Eliad, and she had always known her family to be a wealthy one. They rode through a wide archway of pale limestone into an outer courtyard, where Simon dismounted with ease, leaving her to swing her stiff limbs clumsily to the ground unaided.

A door opened from the far side and a male slave came running. Shelamzion was astonished to see Simon bend to embrace the man, who brushed tears from his eyes and began to whisper trembling psalms of blessing. But before she could dwell on the strangeness of the scene, a woman appeared in the doorway. She was tall and straight-backed, but her unbound hair was grey and she wore a shift fashioned from a rough weave of goat's hair. Her face—Shelamzion saw with a shrinking heart—was the stern, uncompromising stone of Simon's. And, for all her red-rimmed eyes and the ash that streaked her forehead and cheeks, she walked towards her son, not in weakness, but as the queen of a defeated people might approach her general.

Simon waited until she was before him, then he inclined his head in greeting. 'Mother.' That was all. Even through her tiredness Shelamzion noted that there was no affection shown, no embrace. When his mother spoke her voice was low, and Shelamzion heard the long sibilants and soft diphthongs of the north in her Aramaic. 'They are saying that Jerusalem is awash with blood.'

Simon nodded grimly. 'News travels swiftly. It is so.'

Her face altered little. 'Whoso sheddeth man's blood, by man shall his blood be shed.' The quote might have suggested a will given up to the submission of piety, had it been delivered less coldly. Then, without changing expression or tone, she asked, 'Who is the woman who stands behind you?'

Simon started and half glanced round, as though he had forgotten they were not alone. 'This—' He almost sounded surprised. 'This is my wife.'

There was a silence. Not the warm silence of startled joy—*Your bride has come to dwell among us*—but the bone-chilling silence of crypts and graves. Shelamzion stood, head bowed, and despite the layers of dust and sweat that coated her head to toe, shivered as the shadow of Simon's mother fell across her. She raised her head to meet the other woman's eyes. But Simon's mother did not extend her hands in either greeting or warmth. And it was to Simon she spoke when she said, 'Surely not Saul's betrothed? You would not impose such cruelty upon me.'

'It is no cruelty, mother. It is the Law. And Saul would surely have wished it.'

Shelamzion saw the woman before her grow pale beneath the streaks of ash. She closed her eyes and spoke painfully through lips that barely moved. 'Saul's mouth is filled with earth, and my throat is parched from feasting on dust. Do you tell me now what he wishes?'

'It is the Law,' Simon repeated.

'The Law.' His mother pronounced the words like a curse. 'How devout your trip to Jerusalem has made you.'

Just then the male slave who had wept at Simon's return hurried back to his mistress' side. She glanced sidelong at him. 'Take my son and … his wife to the rooms that were prepared for Saul's homecoming.'

Simon took a half step forward. 'Mother, no—'

But she held up a hand and he checked his pace. 'You cannot pick and choose the parts of Saul's life you would take then discard the rest.' Her hand flicked dismissively towards Shelamzion. 'You have your bride. And truly her price must be beyond rubies that you would loot your brother's grave for her.' With that she turned and swept from the yard, strangely stately for all that her garments were of sackcloth and her hair was unbound.

Simon stood watching her, then he spoke to his wife without turning round. 'Forgive my mother. She loved Saul and her grief knows no bounds.'

Shelamzion gave a small, exhausted nod, hardly caring what his mother thought if only she might have a place to lay her head. A storm of dust was rising up behind her eyes, and through it the world swirled, dim and grainy.

She followed Simon indoors, through a complex of rooms to a large, palatial hall whose pillared coldness was relieved by many bright, colourful objects evidently put there by a woman's hand. Sandalwood chests, bowls of burnished bronze, and from the tall windows heavily embroidered drapes hung from poles of brass. Even the lyre-backed couches, so common amongst the wealthy of the time, were strewen with many brightly-woven cushions arranged along their backs, like scattered petals. Feeling diminished in the midst of such splendour, Shelamzion stuck close to Simon. But instead of leading her through one of the doors at the far end, he stopped in the centre of the mosaic floor and stood lost in his own thoughts. Shelamzion, weary beyond measure, waited through the dragging seconds before daring to ask, 'Will our room be readied soon?'

He stared down at her in surprise then drew his arm about him in a grand, sweeping gesture. 'This is our room.'

'Our room?' She looked about in confusion. Sure enough, amidst the sandalwood and silks was a bed. A wonderful bed. A bed bigger than the room old Sarai used to sleep in, piled high with soft rugs and fresh sheets of Ægyptian linen. She turned back to Simon, mouth gaping. But he was already turning towards the door at the far end of the room.

'I will leave you now.'

'Where are you going?' She was very young, and desperate that he should not leave her alone in this place of strangers and strangeness. But he shook his head and started for the door. 'I have things to attend to. You have nothing to fear. You will be well looked after.'

In fear and loneliness she called out to him, 'But you are my husband.'

He turned slowly then, his eyes full of darkness, his mouth set in a grim line. 'This is your bridal chamber,' he said flatly. 'It was prepared for your coming. But I was never the groom it awaited.' He turned, as a general might turn, and strode from the room, dismissing her as a general dismissing the lowliest of his foot soldiers.

The next day began her strange existence as Simon's wife. And her first mistake was to call to the household slaves and order them to bring her water to bathe in and fresh clothing. The two maids, a stern-faced woman and a round-faced girl, exchanged glances. At first Shelamzion thought that they had failed to understand what was asked of them, and was wracking her brains for a different manner in which to make her request, when the stern-faced one cleared her throat and said firmly, 'We are here because Simon asked us to attend you. We are not slaves to be ordered.'

The roots of Shelamzion's hair burned with confusion. 'I—' she began, then faltered. 'I do not—' Again her words stumbled, and the round-faced girl took pity on her.

'There are no slaves in the house of bar Gioras.'

No slaves! Shelamzion gawped with the unconscious insolence of a child. No slaves in a rich man's house. Might as well tell her there was no bread. Yet the memory of Simon listening to the prattling talk of old Sarai flashed through her head, and this time she said it in wonder: 'No slaves?'

As the weeks wore on she discovered many other strange things about the way the bar Gioras house was run. Slaves who were not slaves came and went as they pleased. They were unafraid to meet Simon's gaze, even going so far as to argue openly with his decisions. But it was clear that both mother and son were held in a deep, affectionate respect. And it was rare for their judgements to be overruled. In different circumstances Shelamzion might have been charmed by a household so eccentric to her experience. But grief and neglect overpowered her, and ignored by her husband and mother-in-law, there was no one she might turn to for consolation.

Since arriving in Gerasa, Simon seemed to have forgotten he had a wife. Indeed, it had been a relief at first. The thought of him finally touching her had made her body pulse with red rage. Yet as the weeks had gone on, she felt a creeping sense of pique that she was to be spurned, like an unclean thing. His duty to his brother performed in Shiloh, she had become an object without attraction or meaning.

With no clear understanding of her motivation she took to watching his movements. He had been receiving visitors, strange groups of men, often heavily armed, sometimes arriving during the night. Then Simon would lock himself away with them to talk for long, secretive hours, sometimes attended by his mother, but never his wife. Indeed it seemed she had no role to speak of. She was appointed no tasks, nor called on to help with the household. Her days were her own.

Every morning she awoke choked with horror. Her maids would attend her, chattering amongst themselves, never unkind, but never open with her either, treating her like the stranger she was. Then she was left to her own devices. When first she had approached the stern-faced maid, whom she now knew as Mari-amme, asking, *But what am I to do?* She had been met with blankness. *Do? You are the wife of Simon. You may do anything.* And even through the insensitivity of youth Shelamzion could hear this dry stick of a woman soften when she said *Simon*. They all loved Simon. That much was clear. And they envied and resented her position, even as they cherished and humoured her in his name. To them the wife of Simon might do anything. It was only within herself that she drifted, lost as an angel cast from the heavens.

The hills of Acrabatene offered her a refuge. In Jerusalem she could not go to the end of the street unaccompanied. But here she was left to plan her day, and her instincts took her to the lonely places and the high places of her ancestors. Searching for God on their windy heights. But God was not waiting when she got there. No bushes burned. No voices commanded her to turn towards Mount Gerizim. Not for her, an angel should descend, laying hands upon her, twining their bodies together, wrestling for her soul through the breathless hours of night. And she wandered blind and numb, longing for some familiar thing to relieve the ache of loss from her belly, until she would even have been glad to see her spindle and distaff.

Not even the breaking of bread brought relief. At home she would have helped serve the men then sat with the womenfolk to eat her meal, spicing her food as much with gossip and laughter as with herbs or salt. Always she had been a little envious of the table of men, with their passionate outbursts and their tense, sparring talk, more like gladiatorial combat than conversation. But here in Simon's house she was expected to sit with both her husband and his mother while they were served by slaves who were not slaves and to listen to conversations that were not conversations, but more like the talk of military tacticians planning a campaign.

' … I could raise ten thousand … '

'But how many could you be sure of?'

'Many, now Florus has quit Jerusalem … '

On the first night, when she had entered the open terrace where dinner was served, mother and son broke off their conversation to turn and look at her. She saw Simon's mother narrow her eyes and glance at her son before saying without warmth, 'Peace be with you.'

'Peace be with you.'

Awkwardly she approached the table, instinctively heading for the couch furthest from Simon until she saw the lines of his mother's face part, like the raw sides of a wound. Without having to be told she understood she had been about to take Saul's place. For an instant she considered sitting there in defiance. Let the house of Gioras see her contempt. Then the immense lethargy that had shadowed her since she had left Jerusalem took hold. She did not feel up for the fight. Head bowed, she slowly made her way to the top of the table and joined her husband where he sat upon a low couch. Simon's mother said nothing and the conversation continued as though she was not there.

And so was set the pattern of her meals. Food that tasted of ashes inside her mouth, and conversation that excluded her. Then one night Simon announced, 'I have received word. The Captain of the Temple has persuaded the priests to cancel the sacrifice to Caesar.'

His mother stopped with her goblet of wine halfway to her lips. 'There can be no going back after that. Surely they are preparing for war.'

War? Shelamzion felt her heart jolt, as though struck by lightning, and she glanced sharply at her husband. Simon seemed quite unperturbed by his mother's words. He reached for a dish of figs. 'They think they are ready now in Jerusalem. But later they will need strong leadership.'

'And that is how you see yourself? As a leader?'

'If the Lord wills it.'

'Pah!' Simon's mother slammed her cup down, spilling its contents. 'Do not speak to me of the Lord's will. Do you will it? Do you wish to lead them?'

Simon stared at the splatters of wine on the table for several moments before raising his eyes to his mother. 'I do.'

A peculiar expression crossed her face. 'Is this the road Saul would have chosen?'

The biting comparison as always. Shelamzion had noted these barbs before, aimed at the lesser son, the convert's child. And she had gleaned enough from the household gossip to understand that the second marriage of Simon's mother had not been a happy one.

Simon's father had been attracted to the proud beauty of a woman who would have nothing to do with him, and thereafter determined to have her. Ignoring the protests of their daughter, her parents gave their consent—he was a rich man, this suitor, and willing to convert. The bride price of a widow was not that of a blushing virgin, but not to be sniffed at—So Simon's father won the day, but he had not reckoned with the pitiless mind that animated the beauty he had fallen for, or how it would despise and diminish him as the years passed.

'Is this the road Saul would have chosen?' Simon's mother repeated the question.

'I am not Saul.'

'Too well I know that. He would have been content to live in the world as it is, with no thought to put himself above others. And he at least could trace his ancestors back to the time of Ezra. Men crave leaders, but they seldom thank those brave or foolish enough to grasp the sceptre. One day they may treat you as a saviour and the next, they might cast you down as the lowest tyrant. Think of Herod. And I do not mean that weak-willed fool who now sits on Chalcis' throne. But Herod the Great, Herod the madman, the monster. Do you think he did not start with visions of glory in his mind? And now, who can pronounce his name without a shudder—'

There was a silence, and Shelamzion felt the tension in Simon, like a sinew-strung bow pulled all the way back. He was close to snapping, and she sensed that, if he did, his power would conflagrate in a single self-destructive act, tipping the balance in favour of a future filled with nothing but the self-obsessed regrets and tantrums of those who miss greatness.

There was a faint whirr of air by her cheek. Simon had let out a long breath, his whole body had relaxed and he was smiling at his mother, as though he found her beautiful. 'As always your counsel is given with wisdom and dignity.'

His mother half inclined her head.

'But—' And there was a quivering note of danger beneath the calmness of his voice. 'Your advice is that of the heart. And on so grave a matter as destiny I would hear another's judgement.'

Shelamzion, who had been watching the scene unfold, as one absorbed in the drama of the Greeks, was astonished to find herself looking into the face of her husband. His eyes narrowed as he regarded her. 'My mother mentioned Herod Agrippa, who sits on Chalcis' throne, yet fashions himself as a king of Jews. Did you know that in the days following the massacre he was heard using his eloquence to persuade the people that the Almighty also belongs to the Romans, that without Him their empire could never have grown so vast, so powerful?'

Shelamzion regarded her husband warily. Part of her wanted to sit in stony silence, denying him even the wifely duty of simple courtesy. But another part of her mind was a parched wilderness aching for stimulation. She drew in breath, feeling Eve's helpless longing for the taste of knowledge in her mouth. 'If the king said that to persuade the Jews against war then he is in the gravest error.'

'How so?'

'Because every Jew knows God belongs to them.'

'And that is why we will win?'

'That is why the people will believe they will win.'

He did not answer, and she did not know if he thought on her words or dismissed them. A stolen glance at his mother revealed her tight-lipped and tense. Shelamzion considered saying more. But Simon suddenly got to his feet with unaccustomed violence. Both women regarded him in perplexity. 'Where are you going?' his mother demanded.

Simon looked at her tenderly, but his voice was low and harsh. 'I have received word that the Syrian Legate, Cestius Gallus, moves on Jerusalem with an army at his back. Tomorrow I leave to join the forces against him.'

Chapter XI

... as the Romans went up the slope to Beth-horon Simon, son of Gioras, fell upon them from behind, severely mauled their rearguard, and carried off numbers of their baggage-animals, which he then drove into the city.
The War of the Jews, Book II

Gaius Cestius Gallus to Nero *Claudius Caesar Germanicus, Imperator, and also to the Senate of Rome, I extend my greetings.*

Before all else I offer my submission before the Imperator and make sacrifice to the gods that his reign may be long and glorious.

Doubtless the news has already reached you of our defeat at Beth Horon. The facts of the case are as follows: As you are aware the Jews are a notoriously difficult race, requiring freedoms and advantages quite unheard of from other suppliant provinces, and they have a long history of insurrection and civil disobedience of which they seem uncommonly proud. Nonetheless, with good management, they can be brought to heel. I refer you to the excellent practices of Pontius Pilate and Lucceius Albinus.

It thus pains me to relate how Gessius Florus, now returned to Caesarea, mishandled his role as procurator. Far from dampening the flames of insurrection, he seems to have used every possible means to stoke the fire. The result has been an outbreak of unrest hitherto unseen even in this unstable region of the world, with eruptions of violence against Jewish populations occurring in Caesarea, Heshbon, Ptolemais, Ascalon and Tyre, to name but a few. With no foreseeable end to the escalation, and a dreadful massacre of the Jews of Alexandria by the Greek population, I felt the necessity of action, and set out from Antioch at the head of the XIIth legion. My numbers were considerably reinforced by the generosity of a number of vassal kings, most notably King Agrippa of Chalcis, who provided me with 3,000 foot and nearly 2,000 horse, and accompanied me in person. With this force we advanced towards Ptolemais, gathering considerable reinforcements from the cities, for it was not hard to find those able to transmute their greed into hatred of the Jews.

We subjugated Galilee in the accepted manner, and the troops were very satisfied with the quantities of loot they managed to acquire. Indeed, we met no serious opposition until we made our approach on Jerusalem. The population was swollen with many Jews, who had flocked there to celebrate their feast known as the Feast of Tabernacles. On learning of the imminence of a Roman army they disregarded their sacred seventh day's rest and came streaming out of the city to attack us with furious abandon. Such was their frenzy that they were able to breach our ranks, inflicting heavy casualties. Had it not been for our cavalry I have no doubt that all would have been lost that day.

Their frontal attack finally thwarted, many Jews returned to the city, and I deemed it wise to fall back towards Beth Horon. However, as we did so, we were attacked by Jews led by one Simon, son of Gioras, which means convert in the Aramaic tongue. He is a large man, taller than most, and it would not be ill fitting to say that he is little more than a youth in age. His men were fiercer than any we had hitherto encountered. They severely mauled our rear-guard and carried off considerable numbers of our baggage-animals into the city.

During the next days, attempts were made to reach a resolution. King Agrippa made an appeal for the cessation of hostilities, and when this failed we marched again on Jerusalem, burning the Bezetha district. But the insurgents retreated to the Inner City and the Temple, the walls there being much older and almost impregnable. Now the season was late, already past the 30th of Hyperberetaios, and I deemed it unsound to bed in for a long siege. I gave the order that we must travel light, and the mules and asses were slaughtered and even the wagon-horses, excepting those conveying missiles and artillery.

But our retreat was severely hampered. As soon as we reached the defiles of the descending road we were vigorously attacked, pelted with missiles from above, while our progress was cut off by a faction led by one known as Eleazar the Zealot. 'Zealot' is the name given to anyone ascribing to the fanatical beliefs that contact with 'foreigners' is polluting, and that the land of Judea should be cleansed of all gentile elements. Nor was it possible to retreat, as again Simon bar Gioras harassed us from behind, causing a most horrible carnage. And the screams of the wounded and dying were a horror to those of us in the vanguard. I am proud to relate that none of the men gave themselves up to despair or panic. But I fear their courage would have gone unrewarded had darkness not soon fallen and the Jews retreated.

We took refuge in Beth Horon, while the Jews waited in howling jubilation to attack us again at dawn. Knowing that our destruction was imminent I devised a plan to leave behind 400 of our most courageous men, posting them on roofs to call out the watchwords and to give the impression

*that the entire force had retired. We fled, knowing that the corpse flies were
already rising over our fallen comrades, and hotly pursued by our enemies
almost all the way to Antipatris, where we discarded all our machines of
war and finally outran them.*

*The situation in Judea is indeed more serious than previously thought.
I have named Simon and Eleazar for their particular ferocity, but it was
clear that there were many other unnamed commanders capable of similar
savagery. The Jews have made themselves into an entity to be reckoned
with, and I suggest that a force commensurate with that sent against the
Britannic Celts be dispatched to quell the insurrection without delay.*

*By all the gods I swear this report to be true and faithful. I salute you
and pray for your continued health and fortune.*

Slowly Shelamzion put the report of Cestius Gallus back down on the table.
It had arrived some days ago in the hands of an envoy sent by Simon. The envoy
was a thin, angular man, with lines on his young face and sad, brown eyes. He
went by the moniker Yeled—Boy—a slave so long that no one could remember
his name, least of all him. He went straight to Simon's mother with his message,
and soon the house was abuzz with talk.

By listening at doors Shelamzion learned that her husband had been victorious. And that Yeled had won his freedom by fighting alongside Simon. Indeed,
such was his valour that Simon had given him the task of bringing the news of
victory directly to his home, entrusting him with a captured report written by
Gallus. Yet all this she found out for herself. Now that Simon was gone the Gioras
household did little to hide its contempt. They sensed that she did not share in
their rejoicing and they drew back from her and did not include her in their
thoughts.

At last she went to his mother, standing before her, a wife who was not a wife,
and asking, 'Where is my husband?'

Simon's mother had been perusing a grainy parchment when her daughter-
in-law entered the room. She had it held close to her face, as though her eyes,
which Shelamzion was certain could wither spring blooms with their fire, found
it hard to distinguish a flowing line of ink. She lowered the parchment when
Shelamzion spoke, but did not look up. 'Your *husband*?' The word was drawn out,
mocking. 'Your husband is in Jerusalem.'

'Why?'

With an irritated gesture Simon's mother put down the parchment and
turned to her daughter-in-law. 'Because the High Priest wills it. They have torn
out the Eagle's tail feathers. Only now do they think what that means.'

Without thinking, Shelamzion protested, 'Simon knew well enough.'

Her mother-in-law arched an eyebrow. 'Spoken with the loyalty of a newly-
wed. Truly it is said that the unrestrained husband is sanctified by the wife.' She

gave a short, bitter laugh then turned and left the room. The parchment was left on the table, its contents quite deliberately unmentioned, as though they were a private matter, of no business to a woman who had to enquire after her own husband's whereabouts. Shelamzion lifted the parchment and examined Gallus' greeting. It was a pity Simon's mother had not stopped to enquire whether her daughter-in-law could read.

But the contents of the report disturbed her, painting a violently-hued picture of her husband that she did not fully recognise. For it was one thing to see him caught in the tangle of single combat, fighting for his life, and quite another to know that he was capable of leading men to kill or be killed in the charged heat of battle. She placed the report back on the table and stood looking down at it, her brow furrowed and her thoughts already far away. Simon? She didn't know him at all, this man who called himself her husband. Who is Simon? Her fingers drummed on the inlaid surface of the table. What nature of man have I married?

'L-lady.'

She turned sharply, found Yeled standing in the doorway. He still had the slave's way of not looking in the eyes of the person he addressed and his stutter was the result of having been beaten once too often by his master, or so the maids whispered. Still he was Simon's man. 'Yes?' she said coldly. 'What is it?'

Before she knew it she was running towards the ridge of hill behind the bar Gioras house. To any uninformed onlooker, she was a dutiful wife hurrying for a first glimpse of her husband returning. But inside she was a burning cauldron of conflicting, contradictory emotions that at one moment slowed her step and the next increased it. Simon was coming home, and what did that mean for her, a wife who was not a wife?

Breathless, she rounded the last curve of the path and found Simon's mother already there, wrapped in a shawl, staring out over the valley floor, like Jochebed searching for Moses. She did not turn as Shelamzion joined her, and they stood, side by side, watching the speck on the horizon growing larger. Two women waiting in silence, while the storm of their hopes and fears, their resentments and presentiments, swirled about them like the crackling leaves cast down at their feet.

When the speck drew near enough that it was no longer a moving shadow on the land, but a group of flesh and blood men coming towards them, Shelamzion turned to go. But her mother-in-law surprised her by speaking, though she did not look at Shelamzion, but let her words fly into the wind. 'Saul was a gentle and loving son,' she began. 'He never troubled me, not even when he was in my belly. And as a child he was a big, strong boy, the kind other boys like to fight. But he never struck the first blow. Not once. His physique was that of a Goliath, but his nature was that of a lamb.'

Shelamzion drew in breath to stem the flow of such painful admissions, but her mother-in-law had not finished.

'Simon.' Her eyes slid towards Shelamzion. 'When Simon slipped from my belly I thought I had given birth to a stone or a statue, so blue and still he was. I told them to take him away. But the midwife put him on my breast and he lay there, as though death had suckled him, until I could not bear it and took hold of him, intending to hurl him from me. Then, feeling the pinch of my fingers, he opened his eyes. And, even as his mouth grew wide with sobs, his eyes were not blind, like those of a newborn, but strangely knowing. I knew then his first battle had been fought, and I knew also that, now that he had tasted his first victory, he would forever be seeking his next.' She shrugged and suddenly looked old. 'You do not believe me.'

'I did not—'

Simon's mother raised her hand in dismissal and turned back towards the figure on the horse. 'What can you know? I see how you look at us, disdaining everything that is not part of the holy capital. Were you there when he would have thrown himself at a pack of dogs for tearing at a starving bitch? Were you there when he insulted our finest guests for daring to have slaves in their households? Always the next battle. Always the search for justice. And always Saul to save him, to pull him back, to intervene when my husband would have beaten him for his insolence.' A phantom memory blew across her face, momentarily raising the corners of her mouth in a half-remembered smile. 'Simon is like a storm, raining down anger on the unjust, whereas Saul was like the lap of the sea, a steady beat that draws the storm back in. Yet Saul is gone.' Her smile vanished. 'And who will draw Simon in now?' She did not wait for her daughter-in-law's answer, but turned and began making her way down the path.

Back in the courtyard an eerie silence had fallen. Shelamzion followed her mother-in-law to stand at the head of the assembled servants. Standing stiff-limbed and brooding, knowing that this was her place, yet at the same time filled with a sinking sensation that she had no right to be there. A moment later the clatter of horses' hooves shattered the silence in the courtyard and Simon appeared on horseback, flanked by two others. In the confusion that followed Shelamzion had a vague notion that one of Simon's companions was young and fair, the sun catching the russet tones in his hair, hinting at a link with a noble Hasmonean lineage. The second man was older, with grizzled beard and hair. Old to be a soldier, Shelamzion thought. Perhaps he was another freed slave.

But there was no time to ponder. Amid the jubilation someone had spotted the bandage on Simon's neck, from which a dark red stain was oozing. At once the women began a high, ululating cry, immediately silenced by a look from his mother. Without taking her eyes from her son, she gave a crisp order to one of the male servants.

'Bring my physic chest.'

But Simon would have none of it. 'Peace. I am only weary.' He dismounted in one fluid movement that was marred by a slight stagger as his feet touched solid earth.

'We must attend the wound,' his mother insisted.

'There is no time. We are betrayed.'

Betrayed?

The word echoed round the courtyard, growing in magnitude and alarm with every repetition, until finally Shelamzion, who had been standing frozen and apart, lifted her voice above the rest. 'What is this you are saying? Who has betrayed us?'

Simon blinked at her, as though he had forgotten who she was, then his countenance grew dark. 'The good nobles of Jerusalem, the followers of Ananus, the High Priest. They have set their armies against me.'

'No. Impossible.' Simon's mother's hand clutched at her breast. 'You were instrumental in Cestius Gallus' defeat. We received news of your victory—'

'And believe me, mother, when I tell you the deed afforded me no credit in their eyes once they were of a mind to turn on us.'

'Turn on us? But what would bring them to such a state?'

'There is no time.' Simon began to walk purposefully towards the vestibule. 'My men are camped beyond the town. And Annanus' men are less than a day's ride from here. We must flee while we can.'

'Then you should go alone.'

The words froze Simon mid-stride. Then he spun on his heel and faced his wife. 'What do you say?'

Such a look of barely controlled anger filled his face that she flinched, but repeated in a voice all could hear, 'You should go alone. Taking the women with you will only slow you and make you more vulnerable to attack.' Then she added recklessly, absurdly, 'A good general must not sacrifice himself for the sake of the weakest members of his party.'

A muscle danced in his cheek and fires danced behind his eyes, and when he opened his mouth she expected his words to be like a flame scorching through her. Instead, they were cool, like chips of ice. 'Either, wife, you are better lessoned in military tactics than I or perhaps I am not such a very good general.' He swung back towards the house, not waiting for her reply, and flinging orders over his shoulders, like alms to the needy. 'Fetch only what you can carry. Spare no thought for sentiment. Take that which will nourish you and keep you from freezing. Nothing more.'

'But, master—' an old man, known as Tobias the Elder, interrupted timidly. 'The books and papers of your father. We cannot leave them to our enemies.'

Simon shrugged, barely stopping to look round. 'The men who are after us are Jews. They will not spill ink when there is blood to be shed.' He strode on, leaving an aghast Tobias staring after him, his lower lip trembling.

Even when his life is in danger he is cold, Shelamzion thought. She let the flurry of bodies billow past her on either side. Then, slowly, feeling each footfall to be an individual act of defiance, she went to find Tobias.

She found him in his old master's chamber, weeping and hugging his scrolls to his chest. He did not look up as she entered, but said in a rebellious voice, 'I shall not go. I will die here protecting what my old master held most dear.'

'You will do no such thing.' Shelamzion held out a small cedar chest she had taken from her room. 'Place the scrolls in here and we will take them.'

'But the young master—'

'Did you not hear him? He bade us take that which would warm and sustain us.' She nodded at the scrolls. 'Surely you do not believe he would leave our spirits devoid of nourishment?' She pushed the chest into his arms. 'Be in the courtyard in less than five minutes.' She turned to make her exit, but his words halted her.

'It is true then; you are wise beyond your years.'

She turned towards him, and her eyes were those of a child, longing for praise, yet fearful of hearing it. Her lips parted, but then her name was called from the courtyard, and she jumped as though caught in a guilty act, and hurried from the room.

The flight from Gerasa was filled with pain. All the more so for Shelamzion, who saw the too-large, too-bright eyes on the colourless faces of those around her as a terrifying echo of her own flight from Jerusalem. Only Simon seemed calm. He rode in front, sending Yeled or the young nobleman, whom Shelamzion learned was a Sadducee by the name of Hyrcanus, down the line from time to time to check that no one fell behind, while all the time his eyes scanned the distance, searching.

At Yeled's last report he merely nodded. But Yeled did not leave his master's side. And Shelamzion riding on an ass next to Simon felt the young man's awkward need to know more. Without awareness that she did so, she felt a kinship with his slave past, the chains which had once bound him bound her also. To be shaped and shackled to the destinies of others without choice or consent was too close to her own predicament to go unrecognised. And that Yeled was now free of such constraints made her warm to him much as a freezing traveller will warm to the hint of a light flickering far off in the distance. The sense of defiance filled her again, and she said boldly, 'We are a large party. Should we be separated it would be best to know our destination.'

Yeled threw her no look of gratitude, but asked quickly, 'Is it to … to …to GGischala we are headed?'

And Hyrcanus added, 'John of Gischala would surely bid you welcome. Were you and he not childhood companions?'

'Which is the very reason our enemies would first seek us there. No, I will not put John at further risk than he is at present.' Simon pulled his horse's head up and fixed his eyes on the distance. 'No. We will go south.'

'To Jerusalem?'

The question came out in such a bolus of fear and hope that it drew Simon's gaze round to meet his wife's.

'No,' he said, and something in his searching glance made a dark colour stain her cheeks. She looked away, hearing him say,

'I am not strong enough to take Jerusalem. Not yet.'

But when she lifted her head, full of doubt and wonder, he had already turned back to Yeled.

'We will make our way past Hyrcania and Herodium and on into the wilderness.'

Yeled licked the salt from his lip before saying tentatively, 'The wilderness is a hard place to feed so many mouths. With the men you have brought we number near five thousand.'

But we will follow him, Shelamzion thought with a flash of anger. As our forefathers followed Moses into the wilderness so shall we follow Simon. Never knowing if he is led by the divine or by his own demons.

'You speak wisely,' Simon was saying to Yeled, with that special grace he reserved for simple men. 'We will not make the wilderness our home. The fortress of Masada is but a day's journey once we reach Ein Gedi.'

'But Masada is held by the Zealots.' The older man, with the grizzled beard, had spoken. She did not know his name yet.

Simon frowned. Then, to Shelamzion's surprise, instead of answering him directly he drew in breath and continued, his voice raised so that others might hear, 'The Zealots fought bravely at Beth Horon. But it was not justice they received at the hands of the High Priest's party, but death and banishment.' He paused long enough to let his gaze fall on the hastily assembled bundles carried on backs and under arms before adding, 'As have we. The Zealots hold Masada now, but have not enough men to oppose Jerusalem. We will bring them strength and youth. And it may be that they are willing to make an alliance.'

'An alliance with fanatics. That is how desperate we had become—' Shelamzion broke off. Cornelius' pen had not moved for several minutes, and even now he did not seem to notice that she had fallen silent, but sat lost in thought, leaning forward on his elbows, twirling the pen along the length of his fingers.

'*Archon*?' she ventured. Then again, louder, when he did not respond, '*Archon*, would you hear more?'

He started, then blinked, frowning at her, as though she had dared to throw wide a door to his private thoughts. Yet all the while he was watching her face with his old man's eyes, seeing how bewilderment had furrowed her brow and parted her lips. Soft lips. Trembling slightly. He felt a responding quiver deep inside him, and sat back, aghast. How had this happened? That he had grown fond of her he had readily admitted. Had resolved to discipline himself in matters of sentiment. But her beauty—too alien, too exotic—had held no sway over him. Or was that a part of her power? The mirage of innocence disguising undercurrents of a potent sensuality, set around her like a nimbus of heady, intoxicating scent. Yes, now he thought on it, he could almost smell her perfume filling his nostrils, muddying his thoughts and confusing his reason.

He dropped his pen and felt his breath quicken. Necromancers and deceivers these Jews, to a one. He forced himself to take a calming breath. No. No, that was unfair. Had not Flavius Josephus been the one to warn him? He must go carefully from now on. She called him *archon*. Well then, let him show her that he was lord and master of her fate. He saw her lips twitch, as though she was about to speak again, and brutally cut her off. 'Tell me what you know of an individual by the name of Flavius Josephus.'

What had he expected her answer to be? Feigned surprise, a fumbled attempt to dissemble? Certainly not the anger which fell at once across her countenance, like the blackest night. 'I knew him,' she said, clearly forcing the words through a tensed jaw. 'During the war. He went by another name in those days. But I am certain it is the same man, if man he can be called—'

'You would do well to remember that he is a respected member of the Flavian household these days,' Cornelius interrupted.

'Would I?' she asked, holding him in her steady gaze. 'You think I require further reminders of his treachery?'

Cornelius' cheeks grew hot. 'You forget yourself.'

'That I do not.' She glanced towards the bolted door, as if that alone served to remind her of her torment, then back at Cornelius. 'I have not forgotten, no. But I fear Flavius Josephus has tried with all his might to forget that once he was Joseph ben Mattathias, the Jew, who led the revolt in Galilee.'

There was the charged silence of stalemate for several seconds, then her shoulders slumped. She had gone too far. Letting her stupid pride raise its wild head through all the ugliness and degradation that had become her life. Thinking she was once more the proud wife of a man who would be king when in truth she was a fragment of broken potsherd buried in the ground. She took a deep breath and let the ragged nails on her fingers bite deep into her palms.

'I—spoke without thought. Your pardon.'

Cornelius was silent, liking her less for this forced contrition than he had during her passion. 'Tell me what you know of Flavius Josephus,' he said at last.

She sighed, not answering at first, but taking her seat on the low stool and wrapping her arms around herself. And when she spoke, it was in the bland singsong of a child reciting a lesson, while her eyes looked towards the fire and reflected their flames. 'I first learned of the man you call Josephus from my husband as we fled towards the fortress of Masada. He did not speak to me of these matters directly, but to his most trusted men. Often they looked at me askance, not daring to question his authority, but waiting for him to send me away. But he never did.' Her expression softened for a moment. 'He never did.'

'And this was the first time the name Josephus was mentioned in your presence?'

'Yes.' She glanced at Cornelius. 'I will use his Roman name though it was not used then.' She shook her head. 'There were so many names. So many of them strange. At first all my husband and his men talked about was Ananus, the old high priest, who had seized power in the days after Cestius Gallus' defeat. How he was bent on giving power to his friends and allies while ousting any who raised a voice in opposition.'

'Including your husband?'

'Aye.' Her chin came up. 'Simon, who attacked the Romans at Beth Horon, sending all but a handful flying in panic. Simon who kept not an item of the spoils of battle, but took them all to Jerusalem so that they might be put to best use.'

'You are certain the spoils were taken back to Jerusalem?' Cornelius felt an odd tickle of unease at the back of his throat. Was this the action of a bandit, a self-seeking thief and deceiver? But his question had brought Shelamzion's head round to face him.

'The spoils were taken back,' she said bitterly. 'And for his pains he was stripped of his rank and ousted from his command—' She broke off, outrage choking her throat. And for a moment the dull beat of Cornelius' fingertips drumming against the desk was the only sound to be heard.

'I do not understand,' he said at last. 'Why would Ananus oust one of his most successful generals?'

The spectre of a smile played on her lips before she answered. 'You are right, *Archon*. How little you understand. My husband always said that every Roman gives up his soul to become part of the great machine that is Rome. And in return he is given dominion over the world. Whereas we Jews are a nation of individuals, guarding our precious freedoms so jealously that we are apt to tear ourselves apart.

'When my husband entered Jerusalem it was not to a grateful monarch, keen to reward his valour, but to a swarm of petty-minded bigots, each filled with the determination to seize power for themselves, and willing to make alliances with all the demons of Sheol if it gave them an advantage—'

Again she broke off, a violent trembling having seized her. She closed her eyes and grew deathly pale. And Cornelius, almost without thinking, poured wine into his own cup, and hurrying round the desk held it to her lips. She swallowed a mouthful, then, opening her eyes, looked up at him over the rim of the cup with such helpless trust that Cornelius awoke to the fact that he had fallen under her spell once again. He yanked the cup away and set it down heavily upon the desk.

'I thought you faint,' he said, avoiding the puzzled eyes boring into his back.

'I—I felt weak,' she conceded. 'I am not as strong as I once was.'

He glanced back at her, certain she wanted to say more, and their eyes met for a brief, hopeless moment of clarity, then she turned her head back to the flames and went on in a bland, flat voice, 'It was on his return to Jerusalem, after the victory over Cestius Gallus, that my husband first met Josephus. He knew of him, of course. Josephus was of a noble family, distantly related to the honoured lineage of the Hasmoneans, a connection he never failed to exploit. Yet my husband had heard that he was a restless, wandering soul. First following the ways of the Sadducee then the Pharisee. He had even followed Banus, the hermit, into the desert to attempt the life of an ascetic. And now here he was in Jerusalem styling himself as a general.'

Cornelius raised an eyebrow. 'And naturally your husband mistrusted a man who dedicated his life in the pursuit of enlightenment?'

'My husband mistrusted him,' she answered, dark eyes flashing, 'because he was a man who changed loyalties as the wind changes direction in the month of Adar. He was known to have strong interests in Rome, and yet here he was claiming a lead in the rebellion.'

With a slight clumsiness that made Cornelius' heart lurch despite itself, she got to her feet and stared down at the fire.

'Simon always said,' she went on, 'that one need never fear men who are steadfast in their beliefs.'

'Even when those beliefs are of the vilest nature?'

She looked round, smiling. 'Even then. For a man who sticks to principle, no matter how misguided, must of necessity submit to rules of behaviour that govern his conduct. But a man of inconstant morals, whose conscience changes as others might change a soiled robe, is a worse enemy by far.'

Cornelius stared at his prisoner with wide open eyes.

'How so?'

Shelamzion shrugged. 'Because he is unpredictable. One day your enemy, the next your friend. And even as he swears allegiance to your cause his mind is ever moving, readying itself to hear the argument of another.'

'And Simon thought Josephus to be such a man?' He watched as she turned back to the fire. The blaze caught the edges of her hair in a corona of copper. He shifted uncomfortably in his seat. 'You do not answer.'

'Forgive me.' She seemed to be seeing things in the flames. Then she straightened and turned to face him. 'Yes, Simon thought Josephus to be such a man. But he was not the only such man in Jerusalem that day. Already Ananus and his followers were talking of new alliances with Rome.'

'Which your husband opposed?'

'It was too late!' Some of her earlier passion boiled up beneath the surface of her skin, flushing her face with dark blood. 'Simon understood that it was too late.' She spread her hands and took a pleading step forward. 'Think on it. Would you wound a sleeping lion then stroke it with caressing fingers?' She rested her fingertips on the edge of the table and leaned forward. 'Simon was like a wise fisherman, who feels the first breath of wind and knows that a storm is coming, while those around him jeer and mock, thinking to hold back the tempest with the force of their words.

'Time and again, he tried to make them understand that there could be no going back, but they would not listen. Ananus wanted rid of any voice who would oppose him. He ordered Simon's command be taken and sent armies to drive him from Acrabatene. And all the while Flavius Josephus, the new commander of the Galilean force, stood by hiding his poison in honeyed words that he dripped into Ananus' ear.'

She stood back, breathing hard, triumph animating her face. She had proved her point. Josephus was a traitor, not to be trusted. A smile of satisfaction playing about her lips, she looked to Cornelius for recognition. But the assistant governor's face was devoid of expression. He was like a tightly rolled scroll, unreadable. Her smile vanished. Had he not understood? Surely the meaning was clear? Blinking at him stupidly, she opened her mouth to ask what was wrong, but Cornelius cut her off, turning to the door and calling, 'Guard.'

The dour Cilician entered, and Cornelius indicated that the interview was over with a brief nod of his head. That was it. No farewell. No promise of a future meeting. All the niceties of their strange relationship dissolved at the whim of her captor. Too stunned to protest, Shelamzion let the guard lead her from the room, only turning her head in confusion to glance back at Cornelius before she was led out.

And Cornelius, sensing the bewildered face that sought him out, kept a stiff posture of indifference until he heard the door thud shut. Then he slumped forwards, resting his chin on his hands. So many words. Knotted nuance and meaning. The more she had talked, the more he had become oppressed with the need to sieve each sentence for falsehood or contradiction, until he could not bear to listen further. Then sending her away had seemed the only solution to end the noise in his head.

But now the silence felt reproachful. Slowly he raised his gaze to the fire. What scenes had danced before Shelamzion bat Judah's eyes when she looked into the flames? Truth? Lies? Her story seemed credible enough. Yet he could not entirely bring himself to doubt Josephus' sincerity either. All he wanted to do was write his history, yet here he was caught in the middle, not knowing who to trust. He looked into the orange flames and saw Shelamzion's liquid eyes looking back at him. But, at the same time, inside his head he heard Josephus' voice whispering, *How eagerly does a man's ear bend to the soft words of a temptress?*

He lifted his wine cup and breathed in the calming cardamom-scented vapours. Perhaps there was more *veritas* in *vino* than there was in the word of Jews.

Chapter XII

[Near the Dead sea is] A rock with a very large perimeter and lofty all the way along broken off on every side by deep ravines. ... On this the high priest Jonathan first built a fortress and named it Masada ...
The War of the Jews, Book VII

Alone in her cell, Shelamzion paced up and down, trying to stem the wild river of panic that was flowing through her brain. What had she done to offend the assistant governor? It had been weeks since he'd mentioned Simon or Jathniel, and she had been too afraid to rouse his ire by asking. Again and again, walking to their meetings heart pounding in her chest, hoping that this time if she answered his questions well enough she might be thrown some crumbs of hope. Leaving each encounter with empty hands and a heavy, plodding step.

Yet she had not given in to despair. Not while he was kind to her. And he had been kind, had he not? She glanced around her cell. It was clean and dry. The water jug always full, the blankets plentiful. And there were the luxuries, candles, books, dresses of a finer weave than any prisoner had a right to expect. Through the narrow window she could hear the clamour and clatter of ordinary people hurrying through the Forum, absorbed in their everyday lives, with no thought spared for a lonely prisoner shut up behind the monstrous walls of the Carcer. Or if there was, she realized with a grimace, it was with sneering gladness for her fate. And yet she had never thought Cornelius glad. Roman that he was, her gaoler even, he had never seemed eager to see her brought low. All the unexpected generosity, broth brought grudgingly by the *custos*, a lamb's-wool shawl to keep her warm, even the wine he had held to her lips to stop her from fainting. These small acts had whittled down her defences, gradually opening her up to the possibility of another being's humanity.

But just as she'd summoned the courage to reach out her hand he had withdrawn. Brutally cutting off her lifeline to the world outside. And why? Why had he done this? What had she done? Was it too much to hear of Simon's role in the uprising? Perhaps he was revolted by the detail of Jewish hatred for Rome. No, something else had sparked this cruel retreat. Some deadly seed of suspicion had been sown against her. Why else would he ignore all the carefully plotted details of her history to insist upon an irrelevance such as her knowledge of Flavius Josephus? *Josephus.* She froze mid-step, muscles tensing against the painful shock of clarity. How could she have been so blind? Josephus, the darling of all the turncoats might be here by now. In Rome. Why hadn't she had the wit to foresee this?

An emptiness, far worse than any lack of food, grasped her stomach, and she wrapped her arms around herself and moaned. O Simon, even now he is not finished with us.

Just before he left his home, Cornelius received an unexpected gift. A short book, in the Greek tongue, entitled *Herod's Rise To Power*. It was beautifully written in a clear, bold hand. And while there was no accompanying note, the inscription read, *A gift to the owner of a noble mind in recognition of his patience towards one who is sadly flawed.* The inference was clear. And, turning the scroll over in his hands, Cornelius could not help but experience a quivering sense of triumph. To be remembered by one so close to the Emperor's ear. Now there was a conquest. Who knew what might come of such exquisite exposure? An audience at the palace. Commissioned works. He placed a hand over his heart. Perhaps a call to write a portrait of Vespasian. A pity, he thought as he got into the hired litter, that the only person he could tell of this precious gift was Quintus. Quintus, who would have greeted the divine Muses with a sly wink and a goblet of wine.

Cornelius leant back on the cushions. Of course there was also the difficulty of how to acknowledge the manuscript. As subterfuge was of the essence a letter was out of the question. And the fact that Josephus was obviously a man of refined taste made the problem of offering a gift a thorny one. A base offering would be an insult, while an extravagant one might be misconstrued as a bribe. Then again, as one scholar to another—Cornelius tapped his fingertips together. Surely an extract from his history would be the most appropriate of tributes. But in thinking of his history, thoughts of dark eyes turned beseechingly in his direction came inevitably into his head. And suddenly all the pleasure of his day was gone.

Could a traitor's gift be trusted? Or was Josephus playing him for the vain fool he was? The flattery. The promises. A word in his master's ear, and all that might mean. The careful way he talked of *we scholars.* Spinning a beguiling web of lies, into which Cornelius was all too willingly crawling.

Outside, one of the slaves stumbled. The litter tilted and Cornelius was thrown indecorously backwards, his hands dragging at the curtains to prevent himself from being tipped out on to the street. Once righted, he barked an angry reprimand, and pulled the curtains shut. But not before he had noticed that the day's brightness had been superseded by a dull, sulphurous light that made the shadows stand out in harsh relief. At once depression began to gather in thunderheads behind his temples.

Shelamzion was waiting for him when he arrived in the cell of interrogation.

And, though this was exactly as he had ordered, the actuality of her presence aggravated him quite beyond reason. He forwent his normal greeting, choosing rather to turn his back on her and busy himself about the task of laying out the day's work. This time she made no attempt to attract his attention, yet her silence only provoked him further. Of course, he said to himself, now that he thought about it, there was nothing to actually say that Josephus was playing a game of manipulation. The son of Mattathias came from a noble family. That much wasn't in dispute. Whereas, what claim had his bandit queen to elevated credentials? Josephus offered him friendship. Broadly hinted at greater things to come. What was there to gain by siding with the wretched wife of a fallen rebel?

Satisfied with the reasonableness of his arguments he turned ready to face his prisoner. Then stopped. It was almost as though in that moment, when his back had been turned, he had somehow managed to forget her face, to transfigure it into an amorphous set of features viewed dimly from great distance. A face lost in a crowd. But now he stood in front of her, the full impact of her existence struck him with a ferocity he was ill prepared for. She was luminous. Her back, straight as a young general's. Her hair, drawn back in a long plait, leaving her face curiously vulnerable so that her eyes seemed huge, their dark depths liquid and changing, glittering with hurt and incomprehension. *Magnificent*, a voice in his ear whispered. *But it doesn't mean she's to be trusted.*

Just then, she made a slight movement with her head, tilting it to one side, as though she was listening to something. And he suddenly had the irrational fear that she was hearing his thoughts. With a dignity he did not feel, which translated itself into an angry rapping of his knuckles on the desk, he walked briskly back to his chair and sat down.

'If I remember correctly,' he began, annoyed at the shrillness of his voice. 'You were telling me how your husband and his entourage were fleeing the established government of the day.'

He saw her flinch at the jibe and half hoped she would grow passionate and fiery again, but the muscles in her throat danced as she swallowed down the insult, and in the voice of a prophetess forced unwillingly to commune with the dead she began.

'It was almost sunset when we reached the fortress of Masada—'

The dull embers of a winter sun were sinking behind the prominence of Herod's desert fortress, when Simon and his party emerged from the last of the salt-drenched land on to the rockier slopes at the foot of the mesa. Shelamzion looked up at the sweeping elevations of this strange rock in the desert and shivered. Masada. She glanced at Simon, and saw his eyes climb the great plateaued outcrops—so like some Greek Titan's staircase—then slowly he smiled. Impregnable. That was what he was thinking. And, as if she had spoken aloud, he turned towards her, saying, 'We will be safe here. It will give us time to plan what we must do next.'

Before she could answer, a small shower of pebbles fell from the path above them. They were not alone. Simon stiffened, and from behind there was a pawing of hooves and frightened cries from the women. Shelamzion saw Simon raise his arm for silence then let it fall as he addressed the air. 'Peace. If you be a man then show yourself.'

From out of the shadows a wiry, hollow-cheeked figure appeared. He looked at Simon with eyes that burned, like stars. And Shelamzion felt a tightening in her chest. So this was a Zealot.

'I am no demon.'

'That I see, Eleazar ben Yair.'

The man's eyes flicked across the waiting party then back to Simon. 'You know me then.'

'I know that when they killed Menahem the Zealot in Jerusalem his kinsman fled here. And I believe Eleazar ben Yair is not a man to send another to face his enemies.'

Ben Yair's eyes narrowed. 'Is that what you are then? My enemy.'

'No, brother, I am not.' Simon's words were soft as lamb's-wool. 'I am Simon bar Gioras, commander of the Acrabatean forces. And I too have been sorely treated by those calling themselves the government of Judea. You may be certain that Ananus is no friend to me.'

Ben Yair said nothing. Shelamzion saw Yeled glance nervously at Simon, and the imperceptible shake of Simon's head. They were flooded in red light. The sun was sinking fast and soon they would be left in darkness. Defenceless. Her grip tightened on the reins in her hands, and her mount shifted nervously, lifting its head uneasily and stamping the ground.

Slowly, his eyes never leaving ben Yair's, Simon dismounted. Again there was that slight clumsiness, the only sign of how much his wound pained him. He unstrapped his sword and handed it to Hyrcanus, whose handsome features stiffened a little, masking a reluctance to play the sword-bearer when Yeled, barely free of the stamp of slavery, sat mounted at his side. But of this Simon appeared to notice nothing. He simply turned and walked up the slope towards ben Yair with all the quiet confidence of a man who feels his destiny closer than his shadow. When they were face to face, Simon stopped. He glanced upwards, and Shelamzion felt her spine pull tight as she understood that glance was meant for his men.

There was nothing to see in the diminishing light. But Simon needed no further gesture to explain. The pressure of a hundred deadly shafts aimed at their heads cast a mantle of brittle silence over them. And in that silence came Simon's deep, cool voice, piercing the dusk, like a shaft of brilliant moonlight. 'You think me here in fear of Ananus and his armies. But you are wrong, friend. It is love of liberty that brings me to your side.' He took a step closer to the Zealot.

'Ananus is an old woman, who cannot see that the time for making peace with Rome is over. We have wounded the Eagle, you and I. And no one can gainsay it. But, if the Lion of Judah is to continue to walk the land freely, we must grow stronger. Rome will not forgive us our trespasses. And her armies will be a hundred times what that fool Gallus had under his command. Now is the time to forget the grievances of the past and to cleave together as the tribes did in the days of King Saul.' Simon paused and the only sound was far in the distance, the throaty rasping of a jackal's cry.

Ben Yair heard it too. He shifted uneasily and glanced in its direction before saying, 'You talk of kings. Here only the Lord has dominion over us.'

'I did not come here to be a king,' Simon said quietly. 'I came to help you lead your people on a righteous path.'

At this ben Yair's laughter broke over the gloaming light, a rough, snarling sound, as though he was kin to the jackal. He took a loping step towards Simon and his laughter died. 'A righteous path?' he echoed. Abruptly he turned and gestured up the burning slopes. 'The people who followed me here came from nothing. They dragged themselves out of the earth and made this their home because the Lord raised them up. They have nothing but what He provides, and they wish for nothing more than to obey His will. If I am their guide it is only with His blessing. They do not need the son of a convert to show them the path of righteousness.'

At the word *convert* Shelamzion saw Simon stiffen, and his right hand reach instinctively to where his sword hilt should be. He will never persuade him, she thought in terror. Ben Yair is a man who has fought for every mouthful of bread that has passed his lips. By his own admission he has clawed his way into power by transforming his desperation into religious zeal. And he will never relinquish the smallest grain of his influence while he sees himself as the mouthpiece of the Lord. What can Simon be to him, save a rich man's son come to steal his glory?

She saw Simon's hand fall away from his missing sword, the slow rise and fall of his shoulders as he shrugged.

'Forgive me,' he said coolly. 'I came in friendship thinking the number of my fighters would swell the ranks of your own. It may be that I have erred in my judgement. Perhaps Zealots are not men who can share in a dream of freedom.' He turned to go.

'We will die to defend this place,' ben Yair growled after him.

Simon stopped, looking back at ben Yair over his shoulder. 'Indeed. Perhaps there will come a time when the Romans so overrun the land that this barren rock is the last place where the light of freedom exists. It is good that you will be here to see the Romans finally extinguish it.'

Ben Yair did not answer, but raised his left hand slightly, as though in acknowledgement of some secret sign.

We will die, Shelamzion thought. Ben Yair will loose his arrows and the morning sun will find our corpses buried in the sand. And having spent so much time hardly caring if she lived through another day, the fact that she did not want to die came upon her with surprising sweetness, like the sharp taste of wild honey. She looked to Yeled, who clutched the hilt of his sword and whispered, 'Only let us d-die as men, Lord.' And a huge anger came over her that Simon would promise them sanctuary then lead them blindly into the waiting jaws of a trap.

Two men had appeared, stepping from the solid rock, to stand at either side of ben Yair. They had the powerful upper bodies and short, bowed legs of fishermen, but they carried bows on their backs, and at each of their belts was the curving glint of the Zealot's *sica* dagger. Simon turned slowly to face them. From the back he seemed careless of the danger, but Shelamzion knew him better. He would be smiling. But his eyes, black with concentration, would be searching every nuance of ben Yair's face. Only let him start to give the order to attack and the Zealot would feel Simon's hands about his throat before he drew his next breath.

But ben Yair did not give the order. He took a step towards Simon, and though he did not extend his hand, he spoke in a voice that carried across the desert and reached up towards the excoriated cascades of rock above his head. 'The men of Masada have a dream. They dream not of wealth nor freedom, but of surviving. A poor man's dream, Simon son of Gioras. Born from the dust of the earth. The same earth rich men, like you, crush beneath the heels of your boots.'

Shelamzion heard Simon raise his voice in protest, but ben Yair was not finished. 'You say we have a common enemy and that he will return stronger than before. That I won't deny. But it does not make us brothers. You may stay Simon, the proselyte's son, but you will keep to the lower camp. Your men are not welcome here. And your women will veil themselves modestly at all times.'

Humiliation scorched Shelamzion cheeks. Hours ago she had forgone the stuffiness of a veil to breathe the cool, clean air. Simon had not seemed to mind, and several of the maidservants had followed suit. Only his mother remained veiled and strangely silent, keeping to the rear of the party. And it had been so good to feel the rush of the wind and the pale, winter sunlight on her skin. But the Zealot's words spread, like a smear of mud, across the pristine joy of her actions. She drew her mantle tightly around her neck, keenly aware of her own physical presence.

On the slope, Simon turned to face ben Yair, then nodded grimly, as though he had been expecting something like this. 'My men will camp in Ein Gedi for now,' he agreed. 'And I will guarantee the modesty of my women.' He gave a deep bow. 'Your men need not go in fear of them.'

A dusty, yellow moon followed them up the serpentine path towards Masada's high plateau. Already exhausted from several days' flight, the climb was a harsh penance to pay for such gracelessly-given asylum. Soon the animals grew skittery on the loose shale of the path, and Simon ordered the riders to dismount and lead the beasts on foot. And thus they followed him, slipping and sliding on the shifting pebbles, cursing Herod for the magnificence of his schemes and his madman's compulsion to build wherever nature defied him. Pitying the poor men whose backs were broken hauling slabs of stone to fulfil a tyrant's dream.

Shelamzion turned her ankle on a loose stone and was forced to hobble behind Simon, her thoughts turning this way and that, trying to escape the fiery pain in her leg. How much longer? She glanced up and found the summit no closer. A curse on Herod, King of the Jews. Yet no true son of the Promised Land. That's what they said, wasn't it? His father, an Idumean convert. Never accepted. Always striving to prove himself. Poor man. Is that what drove him to his wild excess?

Stifling a groan as pain spiked up her ankle again, she found herself captivated by the strangeness of her thoughts. What a long, desperate way she had come to find herself pitying a tyrant. Perhaps it was this place, the audacity of a man who would defy the world. Perhaps Simon's mother was right. He had begun with a clear vision. Yet he could never reach it. Never be pure enough, never devout enough to wash away the sin of not belonging. She stumbled a little and let out a gasp. Simon glanced back in her direction, but she did not meet his eye. In that instant of pain her mind had cleared, and she saw now what she had not seen before. Simon bar Gioras. Simon the proselyte's son, reaching for his sword hilt as the Zealot taunted him with his impure lineage.

Masada was in darkness when finally they crested the eastern edge of the plateau. Torches were lit along the higher ground, marking out the Zealots' territory. Yet there was no welcome in them. They gleamed with menace, a hundred diabolical eyes watching their every move. Ben Yair pointed to the north. 'Take the lower camp.'

Their eyes turned as one towards Herod's famous hanging palace. A palace where no palace should be. Plunging from the cliff face, like a madman's suicidal leap. It made the hairs on Shelamzion's neck rise. How can we stay here, she wondered. In this unearthly place. So at odds with the righteous order of the world.

But ben Yair was speaking again. 'You'll forgive our poor hospitality,' he said with a cold gleam of humour. 'We were ill-prepared for guests.'

'Indeed,' Simon answered. 'How should we complain against our brothers? For as the Lord says, were we not strangers in the land of Ægyptus?'

The glint of humour in ben Yair's eyes died. It was clear to Shelamzion that he did not wish to be reminded of scripture by a proselyte's son. And equally clear to her that that was the very reason Simon chose to remind him. He hitched his thumbs into his belt and made a low, snarling comment that Shelamzion did not catch. But he made no further move to taunt Simon, pausing only to hawk spittle upon the ground before turning and loping away up the slope to his own people.

'A pretty nest of vipers you have made bedfellows with.' The voice was Simon's mother's.

'Do not berate vipers,' Simon answered softly, his eyes following ben Yair's retreating back. 'Low as they are, their ways are simple and honest. We have more to fear from those who come in the guise of lions, yet are hiding the hearts of jackals.'

Herod's palace reeked with the pagan scent of sin. Flickering torchlight. Sinewy shadows obscuring the corners of the rooms, filling their imaginations with the forbidden exotica of a mad king. They crossed the black and white mosaic floors in silence, their footsteps echoing. Simon, with Hyrcanus by his side, his mother behind, leading the gaggle of open-mouthed maidservants, and finally Shelamzion with old Tobias, half-forgotten, trailing at the rear.

Unlike the others, who seemed afraid to tear their eyes from Simon, Shelamzion looked about, deliberately, with no attempt to hide what she was doing, openly examining the cruel sensuality of the Herodian world. The high, frescoed walls, their patterns shifting and transforming in the smoky light, the soaring planes of the roof lost in depthless shadows, the swooping columns gathered against the plunging drop towards a land-locked sea. Every angle, every crevice screamed its strangeness. Yet Shelamzion walked to the middle of the room, slowly turning this way and that, thinking, *It's possible. We might make a home here.*

'What sanctuary is this?' Simon's mother voiced the fears of the others.

Simon stopped and looked back at them. His eyes were the eyes of a stranger, but there was also doubt on his face, as though he too was disturbed by the unexpected sorcery of the place, the giddying sense of having chanced upon the eye of the storm in a madman's troubled mind. And much to her surprise, Shelamzion found herself seizing upon that doubt, recognizing it for what it was, a chink in Simon's armour, a way through that unassailable poise that cowed and awed all those around him. This place, she thought. It weakens him. As though he recognizes something dark here. Some part of Herod's soul that is twin to his own. And she drew power from the knowledge that Simon doubted himself.

In Jerusalem she had been forever constrained by her role as dutiful daughter. In Acrabatene grief and guilt had crushed her spirit. But here, in Herod's palace, she was beginning to understand that she could finally be herself. And with something like the sensation of awakening, she perceived that Simon's weakness would only make her stronger.

'We cannot stay here,' Simon's mother said decisively. She was already turning back towards the way they had come. And Simon was nodding, slowly giving way to defeat, 'We will find another place.'

'No.' Shelamzion's voice had a new sharpness about it. The empty vault above her head stole the word and repeated it greedily. Then, as all eyes turned towards her, and the echoes died away, she spoke out in a wonderfully calm and elevated voice, 'This is no sanctuary. But it would be a wondrous place to win a war.'

Chapter XIII

For by wise counsel thou shalt make thy war: and in multitude of counsellors there is safety.
Proverbs 24:6

Cornelius looked up, HIS hand no longer travelling across the wax, his pen tapping idly against the side of the tablet. 'You wish me to understand that you encouraged your husband in his acts of defiance?'

Shelamzion gave a slight, dismissive shrug with one shoulder. 'I am but a simple woman.'

'O no. That you are not.' And Cornelius, warming to his theme, went on, 'You were his wife, albeit—' He paused delicately. 'A rejected one. You had a certain standing … an influence over him.'

A contemptuous curl of her lip showed what she thought of that. 'Anyone who thinks that they had influence over Simon is either a fool or a madman. The Almighty himself could not sway my husband once he had chosen his course.'

'Yet you pointed out the advantages of Masada as a military base. You shared his vision.'

'No.' She began to pace violently. 'I did not share his vision. Only one thing did we hold in common, our need for vengeance. And, even in that, we differed.'

'How so?'

She stopped pacing and spoke softly again, 'Simon wanted vengeance on the world. He wanted justice for the oppressed and punishment for those who would oppress in the name of their own glory—'

'And you wanted none of these?' Cornelius was taken aback.

Surprised, she turned to look at him. 'I did not think of these things. A million injustices did not matter to me then. All my thoughts were focused on the bitter pain in my breast and the vengeance I would wreak against the one who had put it there—Simon.'

Cornelius put down his pen and drummed his fingers on the desk.

'Yet you helped him. You opened his eyes to the possibilities of war.'

No muscle in her face twitched yet her expression altered beyond all recognition. Here was a side to the bandit queen he had never seen before. A coolness suffused her complexion making it seem like marble, and there was steel behind her eyes. 'I helped him to see that he could become a great leader, perhaps the greatest leader of them all.'

'But why?'

'Because the higher his star should rise, the greater his fall would surely be once I had betrayed him.'

Beneath the fluted capitals of the columned portico that encompassed the lowest tier of Herod's palace, Shelamzion stood looking out over the leonine hues of the landscape, watching shadow chasing light chasing shadow across the fissures and flaws in the rock down at the bottom of the world. Watching, yet not seeing. Her thoughts filled with the minutiae of the day. The maidservants would have to be found occupations to keep them out of mischief—Simon's mother no longer seemed up to the task, but kept to herself, praying in corners, coughing constantly, as though choked by the dry, desert air—their supplies must be organized and accounted for and she must discuss with Simon how they were to keep channels of communication open with the men stationed at Ein Gedi.

She leaned against a pillar, half-smiling to herself, knowing the tasks of the day should be daunting, yet feeling nothing but a wild exhilaration flooding her veins. There were no mirrors in Masada, but had there been Shelamzion would not have recognized the girl who stared out of them. Her cheeks were flushed and her eyes bright, like one succumbing to intoxication or fever. She was riddled with odd feelings and strange energies that did not seem to belong to the simple daughter of a Pharisee. It was as though a leopard had lain, slumbering, inside her. Now it awakened, stretching out its claws through her skin.

'Wife?'

She turned at the sound of her husband's voice, painting on a smile as false as a whore's. Simon stood in the doorway, regarding her with a slight but detectable wariness. The whirlwind turn of her character, which had seemed to throw dust into everyone's eyes, had not quite blinded him. He welcomed her newfound resourcefulness, yet did not fully trust it. She went to him openly.

'What news?'

Simon looked grim. 'They do not trust us, and they cannot provide for us.'

'How so?' Shelamzion was stopped in her tracks. Who had not heard of the abundance of fruit and grain Herod had squirreled away in the storerooms of Masada? Some even went so far as to say that the unique dryness of the air kept the provisions unblemished down through the seven decades that had passed since Herod's death, that even the fruits were still fresh. Shelamzion doubted this last, but she had been certain they might rely on plentiful supplies of grain. Simon was shaking his head.

'There is nothing. Ben Yair told me that it has all but rotted away.'

'He is a liar then.'

Simon flashed a quick, weary smile at his wife's passion. 'Alas, I saw what his children were eating with my own eyes.'

Shelamzion stood frowning a moment, then brightened. 'All the more reason for him to make an ally of you.'

'An easy task when he sees us only as more mouths to feed.'

'You must persuade him.'

Simon sighed and sat down on one of the benches of stone left by Herod's artisans. He traced the pattern of the mosaic with the toe of his boot.

'I have not been idle. He wishes me to accompany him on his next raid. To test my mettle, he says.'

'Which means?'

'Killing, I suppose. He will choose the victim, some petty merchant who has accepted Roman gold, or dirt-scratching farmer who fails to keep the Sabbath zealously.'

Half in genuine wonder, half with the desire to needle him, she asked, 'You are afraid?'

He jerked his shoulders irritably and shifted his glance to her face. 'Does it not make you wonder at the nature of our deity? Those closest to him are always the ones baying loudest for blood.'

She felt a shiver when he said that, but answered only, 'Will you do it?'

He cut his eyes away, staring into an unreadable future. 'What choice do I have?'

The first raid was counted a success. A Peraean merchant, bound for the great trading cities of the Decapolis, with their wealthy pagan populations, was ambushed in a rocky pass near Hebron. His rich cargo of spices—cumin, ginger, mustard seed, black pepper, and sweet-smelling pearls of bdellium—was seized and carried back to Masada.

Shelamzion watched as Simon took his leave from ben Yair. She could not hear the words, but she understood things were not well between them. Simon was stiff in his gestures and curt with his replies, turning at the first opportunity and striding towards his quarters, leaving the Zealot to watch him with down-turned lips and narrowed eyes. He saw Shelamzion waiting for him, but made no acknowledgement, pushing past her and descending the steps, as though she was the lowliest slave in his household. Except Simon did not keep slaves.

In the room set aside as Simon's chamber, Shelamzion stood on one side of her husband, his mother on the other, watching as he washed the black blood from his hands. He did it morosely, looking at neither woman. And at last Shelamzion asked, 'You killed him then, the merchant?'

'I did.'

His mother let out a gasp. 'My son—a murderer.'

'A soldier, mother.'

'What war is this? What great battle have you won? A merchant … his slaves.'

Simon froze and drips ran down his hands into the bloodied water. 'It was not my will that the slaves were killed.'

'Nor your doing that they lived.'

'What can it matter now? Ben Yair trusts you.'

Shelamzion had spoken too eagerly, and Simon and his mother turned to stare. She faced them undaunted. 'Do you think Nero sits in Rome waiting to see what we will do next? He sent a fool and an incompetent to break us last time. He will not make the same mistake twice.'

'My wife speaks the truth,' Simon said grimly. He shook his hands from the water and accepted a towel from his mother. 'The dreamers in Jerusalem think they are free. But when Rome strikes again, who will seize the day, but the man who commands an army strong enough to match them.'

'Pah!' Simon's mother was sceptical. 'Would Saul have counselled thus, an alliance with men like—' She broke off, a grimace of horror freezing her features. Shelamzion whirled round. Ben Yair was standing in the doorway.

'Men like me?'

Hyrcanus was at his side. 'I tried to stop him.'

Simon gave a little nod of assent.

'Eleazar ben Yair'—He glanced over ben Yair's shoulder—'and his friends are always welcome at my hearth.' He gave that short, mocking bow that Shelamzion had come to recognise as a sign that fury lurked just below his smiling expression. But he gestured amiably enough, and ben Yair stepped into the room, followed by a thin, elderly man wearing pious garb, the *phylactery* and the *talith*, the fringes of the latter coming down past his knees.

'My cousin,' ben Yair explained with a flick of his eyes towards the man. 'Hizkiah ben Zadock.'

At the sight of Shelamzion and her mother-in-law the man dropped his eyes. The two women backed away into the shadows. Taking Simon's lead, ben Yair and his cousin sat down on the rugs brought from Gerasa. Shelamzion noticed ben Yair's critical eye examine the sumptuous fusion of wools dyed in indigo, sage and rose madder. *He longs for beautiful things*, she thought. *Yet despises those who have them.* And she would have watched longer, but for the scolding glance of her mother-in-law. Bridling inwardly, she feigned meekness and followed the older woman from the room.

In accordance with custom, and not wishing to shame her son, Simon's mother ordered that a meal be prepared. Mother and daughter-in-law stood in thin-lipped silence watching their dwindling supplies dwindling further still. But when Shelamzion made as if to stop the last of their dates being added to a dish, her mother-in-law overruled her with a sharp rebuke. Shelamzion bowed her head obediently, all the time thinking how that sharp mouth would be stoppered with anguish when Simon was finally brought low by his own wife.

By the time she returned to the room where Simon entertained his guests, the atmosphere was subdued, the exchanges between the men coming in short, sombre bursts.

'So little?' Simon sounded shocked.

Ben Yair repeated the figure and Simon shook his head. 'A donkey perhaps. But an entire caravan—'

Ben Yair shrugged. 'Ananus is no fool. His men are everywhere blocking us from trading. Only the very brave—perhaps I should say the very foolish—are willing to trade with us. And they exact a high profit to make up for the risk.'

'But you have brothers still. In Jerusalem.'

'Few. And they are holed up in the Temple. Ananus has them surrounded.' Ben Yair accepted a cup of wine from Shelamzion.

'Then what do you propose to do?'

'There is nothing we can do.'

'The Lord will deliver us,' Hizkiah interjected piously. He averted his eyes from the cup Shelamzion held out, and after a moment she placed it on the ground before him. He reached for it gingerly, as though it might demonically transform, then added, 'We are tested for our faith.'

Simon's expression did not change, but he asked evenly, 'In the meantime what would you have us eat?'

'We have done well enough for ourselves,' ben Yair answered. But his eyes flicked hungrily towards a dish of roast wheat as he said this. Shelamzion seized the moment, kneeling down to offer it to him. And he snatched it from her hands with the incivility of the slowly starving. 'We will continue to take the spoils of the ungodly,' he continued through mouthfuls. 'They have forfeited their rights in the eyes of the Lord.'

'Then we must pray the Lord seeds our path with the impious before our bellies cleave to our backs,' Shelamzion broke in.

A shocked silence followed her words. More likely that the rocks should have spoken. Ben Yair stopped chewing and exchanged a glance with his cousin. 'Indeed,' he said finally, addressing Simon, as though the words had come directly from him. 'We must hope that the Lord will provide. For it seems He has first seen fit to provide us with extra mouths to feed.' He began to chew again with slow, sullen motions of his jaw, but it was clear that the matter was far from settled. And Hizkiah leaned forward, eyes darting, like a greedy jackal hoping for the scraps from a lion's kill, muttering a proverb under his breath, '*Better to live on a corner of the roof than share a house with a quarrelsome wife.*'

Shelamzion's throat was dry. She could not find the words to go on. And she let the sounds die on her lips as her eyes strayed enviously towards a flagon of wine atop Cornelius' desk. Once he would have offered her a cup as a matter of course. Now a hostile rift existed between them, a dark chasm of doubt through which she could find no path. Cornelius had his head bent forward. He was scratching out notes, striking lines through then scratching them anew, and did not appear to have noticed that she had stopped. Then, just when she was summoning the courage to ask for a sip of wine, he looked up, asking, 'How long?'

'Archon?'

Frowning, as though irritated that she could not read his thoughts, in much the same manner he appeared irritated whenever she guessed what he was thinking, he asked, 'How long before Simon won over the Zealots?'

'I—' She cleared her throat and glanced once again at the flagon. 'Never.'

'Never?'

She hated the habit he had adopted recently of repeating back her answers in the form of questions. As though everything she said concealed hidden meaning. She tried again. 'He did not convince the Zealots. Could not … convince them. They followed ben Yair in thinking that we could hide from Rome … They did not understand that we had to meet Rome with force and win our independence.'

'Yet you surely did not think it possible?'

She bridled a little at that. 'We were not without our victories. Did we not banish the Greek Seleucids two hundred years before? And do not think us ignorant. We knew of the Pisonian conspiracy. And how the queen of the Iceni had brought the Northern legions to their knees. Even the rumblings along the Parthian borders came to our ears.' She leaned forward. 'Rome seemed but a carcass, rotting from within. We saw our chance.'

Cornelius traced the rim of his cup with a finger. Struggling to maintain his facade of indifference, he failed to notice Shelamzion's eyes fixed on the cup. 'Even so, if Simon failed to persuade ben Yair then how did he come to lead the rebellion? Surely something happened.'

She dropped her gaze to the ground. 'Something did happen. In the months we hid there many things happened … that changed the course of what might have been.'

'I see.' Cornelius put down his cup, untouched. 'In your own words, can you describe the first of these events?'

'I—' She started to shake her head, then lifted it suddenly. 'Yes,' she said. 'Yes, I can give you your answer.'

At once his face brightened. Was this not what he had been hoping for? The bald facts. Evidence that would stand up to the scrutinizing eye of enquiry and reason. After all, he reminded himself, *ouden kripton ipo ton ilion*. Nothing remains hidden under the sun. If she was lying he would have her. Cornelius' fingers tightened around his pen and he bent his head over the soft wax. 'Begin.'

The silence of Masada closed around Shelamzion's head like the thick, dead waters of Lake Asphaltitus. Simon had not uttered a word for more than an hour, yet, desperate as she was to know what he was thinking, a childish sense of pride kept her in sullen imitation at his side.

In the days following her outburst before the zealots she had waited for Simon's wrath. What wife would interrupt the negotiations of men? Let him be angry then. Anger she could face. But it did not come, and she waited in vain, her newfound leopard's skin itching and burning with frustration. Yet she knew that Simon, too, had his frustrations. As the months passed the Zealots still refused to budge, certain that piety was shield enough against Roman cunning, and Simon's moods grew in frequency and darkness. Their supplies were almost exhausted and it was clear that they were reaching a crisis point. Something must change and soon. But whatever Simon's thoughts on the matter, it was clear that he had no intention of sharing them with his wife.

From time to time Shelamzion picked up a piece of sewing then set it down, unaltered. She stole sidelong glances at his face, but he was pale and unseeing until a noise on the stairs made them both jump. 'Ephraim.' Simon got to his feet and strode towards the man who had appeared in the doorway. Shelamzion recognized him as the older man who had ridden into the courtyard with Simon on their last day in Acrabatene. She had seen nothing of him since their arrival at Masada, but she recognized his grizzled beard and the keen intelligence that belied his wide-set eyes. He saw her curious look and bowed. But Simon was in no mood for ceremony, demanding, 'Is it true?'

There was little need for an answer. Ephraim's appearance was reply enough, covered as he was in the thick, red dust of a man who has ridden for several days without stopping, a man who has news he dare not keep to himself. 'Jotapata has … fallen.' He would have said more, but he began to cough, and Simon took him by the shoulders to steady him. 'Water,' he barked, and Shelamzion hurried forward with a jug.

Ephraim drank in greedy, slurping gasps, then poured the remainder over his head. At last, in a croaking voice on the point of breaking, he told them what he had seen.

'They mustered at Ptolemais under a new general … the Vth, the Xth and the XVth. People are saying your defeat of Cestius Gallus has driven them into a frenzy of hatred … they show no mercy … all Galilee … burning.'

Shelamzion's hands flew to her ears, as though she could hear a million voices screaming. But Simon's face was stone. 'Go on.'

Ephraim swallowed, his red-rimmed eyes moving restlessly. 'The general led them to Jotapata.'

'But Ananus—he had troops stationed there?'

Ephraim drew a dirty hand across his forehead. 'Under the command of Josephus, the son of Mattathias.' At a flicker in Simon's expression, he added, 'He is known to you?'

'His words persuaded Ananus to strip me of my command. In that way he is known to me.'

Ephraim's eyes stopped roving and he nodded grimly. 'The word is that Josephus mishandled his command from the start. Thinking to preserve the city's treasures above all else. Then gathering the people together to collect water so that the Romans found them easy targets for slaughter.'

'And when he saw that Jotapata would fall?'

Ephraim's brow drew down, and he pressed his lips together in distaste before continuing. 'He tried to persuade the citizens that it was in their interest that he escape and draw the Romans off with a diversionary campaign. And when they would have none of it he fled during the final hours of the siege, with forty others, to a cave beneath the city.'

Simon had resumed his seat, listening to Ephraim with his chin resting in the cup of his hand. Now he asked, 'What of John of Gischala? Did he come to the city's defence?'

'He sent word that he would come. But he had troubles of his own and did not reach them in time. Once the Romans had the city they put everyone—men and women—to the sword.'

'The children?' Shelamzion could not help herself. Ephraim started, as though he had forgotten she was there.

'No. Not the children. Though it would have been a kindness to kill them. Taken off as slaves.' Forgetting himself he spat on the floor and made the sign against evil. 'Better off dead.'

'And Josephus?' Simon asked.

Ephraim shook his head. 'I know nothing for certain. But rumour has it that, when he was taken from the pit two days later, only he and one other remained alive. All forty had pledged to perish rather than fall into Roman hands. But Josephus fixed the lots until he was left alone with one man, whom he persuaded to live by dint of claiming the Almighty had spoken to him through dreams.'

Shelamzion looked from Ephraim to Simon. 'Is it possible? Josephus has priestly training.'

Simon raised an eyebrow. 'It does not take a priest to divine that the Almighty's voice and Josephus' bear remarkable kinship.' He turned back to Ephraim. 'The Romans have him now?'

Ephraim nodded.

'That will be an end of him.'

Ephraim shot a glance at Shelamzion then wetted his bottom lip. 'I think not. They say he is off with the Roman general, gilding him with that silver tongue of his. I warrant it won't be long before Josephus is a free man again.'

Simon nodded. 'We will deal with him then.'

He said nothing more. And his silence was so deep that Ephraim took it for dismissal. But as he turned to go, Simon stopped him. 'This general, from whom all Jews run save for Josephus, do you know his name?'

Ephraim hung his head. He was silent, as though he thought it an ill omen to pronounce the name. And when the words finally came, they sent an echoing shudder down Shelamzion's back. 'Flavius Vespasianus.'

As soon as Ephraim was gone Simon fell once more into silent reverie. But Shelamzion, imbued with a sudden frantic energy, paced up and down, throwing glances of increasing agitation in her husband's direction. All Galilee alight and Simon sits dreaming. She opened her mouth to speak, but as she did so, Simon's mother swept into the room. Her hollow eyes went straight to her son. 'It is true then. Jotapata has fallen.'

'It is true.'

'And their commander, Josephus, a prisoner of the Romans.'

'No.'

'No?'

'I think he would prefer to describe himself as an honoured guest.'

Simon did not rise as was his custom in his mother's presence. He seemed dazed. And curiosity checking Shelamzion's step, she turned her head to watch him. He stayed seated, his back against the wall, one long leg swinging, his eyes half closed. *Shocked*, she thought. *He is afraid. He doesn't know what to do.*

Simon's mother, too, seemed exasperated by this strange torpor that had grasped her son. 'And John of Gischala?' she continued, voice rising. 'You sent him word? Surely he will come; he is your friend.'

Simon shrugged. 'John has troubles of his own.'

'But we are safe here, yes?'

'For the time being.'

The older woman threw a venomous glance towards her daughter-in-law. 'I don't understand. What is he saying?'

And Shelamzion, surprised to be addressed, answered simply, 'The legions are busy now plundering Galilee. But they will not stay in the north forever.'

'But here, in Masada, we are safe.'

'Very safe, yes.' A red fury was spreading beneath Shelamzion's skin. 'Safe to wait, like penned animals awaiting slaughter. Who do you think taught Herod his tricks of engineering? Did the Romans share the knowledge of how to build this fortress without keeping the knowledge of how to tear it down?' She was going too far, but she could not help herself. From the corner of her eye she saw that Simon's foot had stopped swinging. She should stop. Stop now before she said too much. But she was seized by the reckless torrent of her words and carried along in its flow. 'Might is the creed that every Roman mind respects. And power is the only thing they will yield to.' Her voice shook. 'We need an army. An army that will stand and fight.'

'Silence!' The older woman's face was a death mask. 'Dare you suggest such a thing? Do you think my son can defeat the Romans with a dozen men at his back? Or do you set your sights on ben Yair?'

'Ben Yair will never be persuaded,' Simon said quietly.

Triumph lighted his mother's face. She looked at Shelamzion with unguarded malice. And Shelamzion, filled with her own savage fury, turned to Simon intending to argue further. She found him on his feet, the torpor quite gone from his eyes. He looked down at his wife in wonder. 'The Lord worked in mysterious ways indeed when he chose to make you a woman,' he said. 'But my mother is right. Ananus controls the armies. And I cannot fight Rome with only a handful of men at my command.'

Shelamzion's shoulders slumped. 'Then you intend to die here.'

Her words made Simon smile, a slow kindling warmth spreading across his face, like a flame scorching parchment. 'I intend to live. I will raise an army. And my army will not run.'

She heard him, but even then she could not quite believe it. 'From where? Will you gather your army from the dust?'

His smile grew broader. 'In a manner of speaking. I propose to free the slaves.'

Her own gasp was echoed by that of her mother-in-law.

'It is not—' she found herself stuttering. 'Even if it were possible—'

'It is possible,' he answered calmly. 'It has been done before.'

'Uprisings, yes.' Simon's mother had found her voice. 'But who is to say slaves will follow you once you liberate them? How will you trust them?'

'Ah mother, once freed, an enslaved man is simply a man. And men must follow someone.'

'As you do?' she retorted. 'Who is it my son follows?'

Simon did not answer, but something shifted behind his eyes and his smile faded.

Some time later Shelamzion went looking for her husband and found him praying. She had never seen him pray before. She had taken it for granted that he must do so. No male Jew would let the arc of day pass without prayer. Yet always he had kept apart, as he kept apart from physical intimacy. *As though I am unclean*, she thought bitterly, and would have turned away, but something in the fringes of the prayer shawl that fell in spotless cascade from the delicate folds of silk seemed in such contrast with the strong, young frame beneath that she hesitated. Or perhaps it was some subtle reminder of her father in the way he held his arms outstretched, palms upwards, that opened new wounds in the shrivelled husk of her heart and made her weak and breathless so that she found it hard to look away.

'Elohai' neshamah' shenata'ta bi tehorah' hi
Atah' veratah' Atah' yetzartah', Atah' nefachtah' bi,
veatah' meshamrah' bekirbi' veatah' atid' litelah' … '

The liquid sounds of the Hebrew poured over the arid places of her spirit, and without thought she moved closer into their calming sphere. But her footfall had alerted Simon, and he broke off, throwing back his shawl and turning to face her, his expression thunderous, as though he thought the legions had come on him by stealth.

'I came—' she began. But she could no longer remember why she had come. They stared at each other until she blurted out, 'Can it be done? Can the Eagle be cast out of Judea?'

She expected him to puff up with male pride. To rain down vision and distraction to further plump the peacock feathers of his ego. Instead, he bowed his head and replied, 'I do not know.'

Forgetting herself, she came forward, gripped his arm. 'But surely—'

His glance fell questioningly to her hands and she withdrew them, afraid of what he would read into the gesture.

'You must believe we will win.'

He let the shawl slip from his shoulders, then folded it with gentle reverence before answering. 'The time has come. We must face our enemy. But would that the Lord had seen fit to send another.'

She was intrigued. 'You know him then, this general Rome has sent?'

He nodded. 'Yes, I know him. Is Vespasianus not famous for his part in the invasion of Britannia? And they say he fought dear for that godforsaken isle. But that is not why I fear him.'

'Then for what reason?'

'Only that he is a good man.'

She burst out laughing. 'But what reason is this for fear? Do they not say the same of you? So we will have two good men pitted against each other.' With a toss of her head she turned to go. But he caught her arm, and bending low spoke softly in her ear. 'Only remember that when two good men are pitted against each other, it makes it hard for the Almighty to choose.'

Chapter XIV

Nothing is easier than self-deceit. For what each man wishes, that he also believes to be true.
Demosthenes

The villa of Valerius Paulinus was poorly lit. In fact there burned but one lamp upon the desk behind which Paulinus sat. The lamp threw a watery pool of light into the vast darkness of the room, illuminating the unfurled scrolls upon the desk and the room's only other occupant; a man who stood silent and ill at ease, watching Paulinus studying his scrolls, yet not daring to speak.

At length Paulinus put down the scroll he had been reading and looked up. He was not a big man, not given to using his voice to magnificent effect. At this moment there was no sign of the energetic soldier he had been, except for the ramrod straightness of his back. A glance might have had him as a clerk, narrow-shouldered and bookish. His black, unblinking eyes were expressionless, though there were deep lines scored on his forehead, suggesting that he suffered from continual headaches. Yet such was his position as an agent of the imperium that he held the other man in complete and awe-filled silence. At length he spoke, and his voice was surprisingly mild

'Fabius Cornelius Grammaticus.'

Cornelius nodded, adding quickly, 'If in some unwitting way I have offended—'

'Step into the light.'

Cornelius stepped closer to the lamp, which had the effect of exposing the stark, frightened detail of his face while throwing an enigmatic veil of shadow over the features of the other man.

'Do you know why you have been brought here?'

'I—' Cornelius cleared his throat with difficulty. 'I do not.' He was dishevelled, having barely had time to throw a cloak over his sleeping-shift before he was torn from his bed by the two guards who had brought the summons.

Paulinus nodded and noted something down, then he put his pen on the desk and stared up at Cornelius, chin resting on the steeple of his hands.

'You know who I am?'

'Yes.' Cornelius felt a prickle of sweat lift the hairs of his scalp.

'My reputation precedes me. You will have heard that I am a friend and ally to the noble Vespasian?'

As Cornelius began to nod, Paulinus cut him off.

'Then you are mistaken. I am more … much more.' He pushed himself back in his seat abruptly. 'You are an educated man, Fabius Cornelius. Do you know how big the empire is?'

Cornelius blinked, understanding that he was not supposed to answer, and Paulinus went on, 'If the censuses are to be believed there are more than fifty million people living within our borders. Even as we speak, we are quelling the Pictish hordes in Caledonia and plundering the treasures of Illyricum and far off Petraea. Does that impress you?'

Cornelius swallowed. 'I do not—'

Again he was silenced by a look. Paulinus drummed the fingers of one hand upon the table. 'I tell you these things, not to impress you—You are a citizen after all. You know them very well—I tell you only so you will understand something about me.'

The room was cold. No fire burned in the grate and the windows were shuttered against the night. During the seemingly endless march through empty rooms to reach this one, Cornelius had noted only a few bare sticks of furniture, and not a single slave had scurried from his path. This was an empty house, opened on this night for a single purpose. Tomorrow it might be boarded up again and no man would be any the wiser as to what had taken place here, or to whom. Cornelius fought a powerful urge to shiver. Only guilty men shook in the face of authority. And he had done nothing. Was guilty of nothing. He could not get the image of the door at his back out of his mind. His world, his life lay beyond it. A few short steps. Yet whatever he might say or do in the following hours would determine whether he would walk through it again to the safety of familiar things. Paulinus was watching him closely.

'You have heard that I was a soldier. Vespasian's agent sent to mop up the rabble discharged by Vitellius; to make them swear obedience to the colours of a new emperor. And, doubtless, you have heard that I was awarded the procuratorship of Narbonesse Gaul for my pains and wonder what I am doing back in Rome. But what you have not heard is that these are the least of my duties. I go wherever I am commanded. No matter where, no matter how forsaken-by-the-gods a spot is, if it is the Emperor's pleasure to send me, I go. Because I , and I alone, am Caesar's eyes and ears.' He leaned forward suddenly, as though they were to be intimate, and his voice lowered accordingly. 'Believe me when I say that in the furthest barbarian-ruled outposts, a louse does not crawl upon the filthy head of a child without me knowing of it.'

And Cornelius, staring into the granite eyes of this man who styled himself Vespasian's right arm, believed it.

'What do you want of me?'

'You have come to my attention. I have heard of you … and of your work.'

'That is most gratifying.'

'Do not take it for a compliment.'

'Only it seems strange that you would trouble yourself over a simple historian.'

'As a historian you do not trouble me. Historians have their eyes forever turned backwards towards the dead. And, despite what those new Jews might think, the dead do not rise again to trouble us. No. You have come to my notice, not because you are a historian, but because you are an impatient man. You do not think so? Yet you don't deny that you sought your position as assistant governor in order to interview the prisoner, Shelamzion bat Judah?' He lifted one of the scrolls and ran his eyes along its contents. 'You do not deny that you have openly, even proudly boasted at dinner parties of bar Gioras' successes in conquering Idumaea, claiming that his army of slaves was but a beginning. That the wealthy and well-connected flocked to join him'—He paused to find the exact quote—'*Like Spartacus reborn. A leader of the impoverished and the dispossessed.*'

'If my loyalties are in question—'

'If your loyalties were in question you would be dead.'

Cornelius swallowed. 'But histories of the living are not unheard of. Xenophon himself wrote *A History Of My Times.*'

'Eulogies. Sophistry to promote the common good. You understand the process quite well. For all your protests, I think you are a dangerous man, Fabius Cornelius. You are not willing to let the flesh rot from the body of history before you begin to pick over its bones.'

'I assure you—'

'Do not give me your assurances. They fall from your lips too readily, and you may promise more than you are being asked to give.'

'Then tell me what you ask.'

'Very little. Only that you are careful.'

'You may trust to my discretion.'

'And were you discrete when you met with the Jewish traitor?'

'I—' Did Paulinus know he had met with Josephus or was he only guessing? Hesitation was lethal. 'We met as historians. He has honoured me with a scholarly interest in my work.'

'How diverse and intriguing you make the world of scholars seem. My life of soldiering is dull by comparison.' He smiled and Cornelius smiled back and gave a little bow. Paulinus' smile vanished.

'My agents intercepted this letter on its way to your house.' He lifted a papyrus from his desk and held it out. Cornelius took it, noting the broken seal and understanding the power of a man who need make no apology for breaking the seal on a private letter. But Paulinus was smiling again. 'Read it … aloud please.'

Cornelius read:

Josephus Flavius to his friend and teacher Fabius Cornelius Grammaticus

Before all else I pray for your health and make supplication for you before the One True God that you will always be well and prosperous. I, too, have reason to thank the Lord for his mercy. He straightaway saved me when our boat foundered off the coast of Phoenicia. We took shelter in the port of Sidon, and it was there I chanced across a man who claimed to know you. Laelius Kaetus was the name if memory serves me right. He was an admirer of your work and claimed your acquaintance, though I am not certain that he ever met you. He was much taken with your translation of Pytheas', 'On The Ocean', and boasted that he would recreate the voyage to the Pritanic isles, taking his young stepson with him, a boy of not more than two years of age. Naturally I warned him against the folly of such an adventure, advising him of the simple virtues of home life, but he seemed determined, quoting Socrates at me and calling himself 'a citizen of the world'. I can only hope that Virgil was indeed correct when he said, fortune favours the brave.

You must forgive this rambling from a poor and weary traveller. I meant only to offer this humble anecdote to entertain you. Until we meet again I pray for your good health.

Cornelius finished the letter and lifted his eyes to find those of Paulinus watching him. It was as though he had been handed a riddle and was expected to answer.

'It seems little enough.'

'That is the very reason it intrigues me. Who is Laelius Kaetus?'

'I do not know.' In that much at least Paulinus would detect no lie. Cornelius attempted levity. 'Even historians may have their sycophants.'

Paulinus looked at him gravely.

'You have met with Josephus. We know this. And you were wise not to lie about it.'

Cornelius felt his fingers dig into the fibrous texture of the papyrus, but he managed a faint acknowledgement. Paulinus continued, 'Would you say he was a man accomplished in discourse?'

'O, most certainly.'

'Then you will know Josephus uses words as other men use weapons. Words gave him command of the Galilean forces, and words gave him the mouth of a prophet when Vespasian held him prisoner. Words are his allies and he chooses them with great care.'

'Indeed, I am sure it is so.'

Paulinus' voice lowered dangerously. 'Do you think it likely therefore that he went to the trouble of sending you an anecdote simply to amuse you?'

Cornelius opened his mouth then closed it. In simple truth he agreed with Paulinus. No letter from Josephus, to a man he barely knew, would contain only one meaning. Yet the nature of those additional meanings was quite lost on him. But it was not possible to stand in the presence of an imperial agent and say nothing, so at last he ventured, 'I believe he may be warning me that he is returning to Rome with his master. And that we may expect to see them both very soon.'

'Any halfwit could detect as much.'

Cornelius lowered the letter to hide the fact that his hands were trembling. 'And your interpretation is?'

Paulinus stared at him peculiarly. 'I am without one … for the present. The best minds I have at my disposal have scrutinized the text, and the material has been tested for those hidden ciphers so favoured by the scribes of Ægypt. But we have found nothing. Nor is the ink false or the paper cunningly crafted … ' He went on, and Cornelius' gaze drifted once again to the page. For an instant he looked at it with a writer's eye. And now it struck him as odd that Josephus had chosen to write in Latin. After all, it was hardly the language of scholars. When they had met they had spoken in Greek. And it was clear that Josephus was not comfortable in the use of Latin. One of his verb endings was incorrect and he had used the Greek *K* when writing *Kaetus* rather than the more common Latinized *C*. Of course—

'Of course?' Paulinus repeated the words Cornelius scarcely knew he had spoken, and the assistant governor of the Carcer suddenly found his legs unsteady, as though he had been momentarily transported to the decks of that lurching vessel. Paulinus had leant forward. In the candlelight, his eyes were hawk-yellow, waiting. Cornelius swallowed. 'Of course I will do anything I can to help. If I might be allowed to keep the letter—'

'Indeed.' Paulinus sat back. 'It was my hope that as the recipient of the letter, you held the key to its unlocking.'

'I fear I am unable to help.'

'Ah, that may be. But perhaps if something were to occur to you, I might expect your call.'

'Most willingly.' Cornelius hardly kept the relief from his voice. Then Paulinus asked, 'Have you come to admire Gioras?'

Thrown off balance, Cornelius could but stutter, 'Admire?'

'Why not?'

'He … is a rebel. An enemy of Rome.'

'Quite. But there are those who might see him as something more. A freedom fighter perhaps. He cuts quite the heroic figure does he not? The lone wolf shaken from his lair by the powers that be, rejected by his own kind. At the head of an army dredged from the rabble. It's an old story. And not one we're averse to borrowing from when it comes to gilding our own heroes. Does not every politician, with an eye to Caesar's throne, declare himself a man of the people?'

'Yes. It is so.'

Paulinus smiled coldly. 'A hazard, is it not, when you delve too deep into the mind of your enemy. Let me tell you a story. During my time on campaign in Britannia, we had a legionary of the II Augusta taken by rebels of the Dumnomnii. He was a good man, well loved. And seeing the distress of this man's comrades at his capture, his commander decided to launch a rescue party. No easy task, for the Dumnomnii have a low, animal cunning that outwitted us for many months. Not to digress, we found the man eventually. He was hale and hearty. Still wielding a sword—But for the other side. They had no hope of winning, and he must have known it. But he had lived with the enemy so long that their ways had become beguiling to him.'

'Please,' Cornelius interrupted. 'I must insist. There has been nothing improper between the wife of Gioras and myself.'

Paulinus looked at him curiously. 'I did not for a moment consider it otherwise. It was the husband's influence I feared. His wife is merely a mouthpiece for his vanities.'

'Quite so,' Cornelius said hastily. Too hastily.

Without warning Paulinus got to his feet. 'Then my fears are misplaced.' He extended his arm towards the door and Cornelius bowed. But as Cornelius turned towards the happy sight of the portal through which he would make his escape, Paulinus stopped him with a question.

'What is it you hope to gain from your endeavours?'

Cornelius placed a hand on his breast. 'I want nothing for myself. Only the truth.'

'Then you want a great deal. I hope I may count myself amongst the first you seek when you find it.'

Breathless, stricken by the irrational fear that he was being watched, Cornelius arrived at the Carcer and demanded the prisoner, Shelamzion bat Judah, be brought to him at once. But by the time she arrived, hair dishevelled, eyes clouded with sleep, Cornelius was bent over his desk, scribbling furiously, like a madman.

'*Archon*?' There was a touching loveliness to her confusion that might have distracted Cornelius at another time. Instead, barely looking up, he pushed the letter into her hands.

'From our mutual friend, Josephus.'

She read it through, but though he waited eagerly, she was silent. He looked up.

'Well?'

Her face was chalk. 'You have found my son.' She said the words, but she didn't believe them. Her expression showed only fear.

'Come,' he said gently. 'He sends me proof.' He held out the torn papyrus that had been recipient to his scribblings. She took it, frowning, and read what he had written there. *Laelius Kaetus.* Then *Caetus. Laelius Caetus.* Many variants followed. But when she lifted her head there was only one name she spoke. 'Aelius Celatus.'

Cornelius nodded. That mysterious centurion who had shown pity to a dying infant in the court of the great Temple. For who else could the stepson in his company be? Aelius Celatus existed. She had begun to tremble, and he got to his feet and helped her to a stool set beneath the barred slit of a window so that she might breathe the freshness of the night. 'There now.' He spoke with the gentleness of a father and the concern of a lover. 'Mark my words, all will be well now.' Shining above her head the constellations of Castor and Pollux were brightly visible. A sign of good tidings if the astrologers were to be believed.

Chapter XV

Who is like unto the beast? who is able to make war with him?
Revelation 13:4

A new day. Shafts of dusty, yellow sunlight hanging, like cobwebs, across the drabness of her cell. And feeling them brush her cheek, she allowed her eyes to flutter open and looked, uncomprehending, on a golden day in spring. A light breeze squeezed through the narrow grate of a window, carrying the smell of new-baked bread and spices, and snippets of the careless calls citizens made to one another as they went about their business in the Forum. And hearing them, she was drawn to her feet with a sudden, unbounded enthusiasm for the world. And the feeling was so startling and alien that she took some time to recognise the sensation as happiness.

He was alive. Jathniel. No. No, she mustn't think that. There was no certainty. No proof. Only the skewed word of a traitor wrapped up in a letter to her enemy. But her enemy had also been her friend. That much she should not forget. And perhaps even a traitor may seek redemption in an honest tale. But such foolish thoughts. They made her head spin.

She got to her feet and made her morning prayers, giving thanks for this crumb of knowledge that made the sun burn brighter in the sky, and all the while adding earnest supplications that Jathniel be kept in safety and love wherever he might be.

The Pritanic Isles. With Cornelius' guidance she understood at once the corruption of Pytheas' Greek. Now she saw it as the same grey isle that Julius Caesar had set foot upon more than a hundred years before. The Britannic Isles. Britannia. Where tin was mined from the earth and the men decorated their skin as the Ægyptians decorated the coffins of the dead. A strange place. A wild place. But a place where there were still savage pockets of freedom, where the brute fist of Rome could not reach.

Beyond her window a wild, furious aria of birdsong broke out, and Shelamzion's heart lifted with it. Unbidden tears welled in her eyes and flooded from their insubstantial wells to splash upon the dusty floor. *Lord God, king of the universe, keep my son in the bosom of your care. Let some part of Simon continue in this world and let it not all have been in vain. Protect him in that desolate wilderness where You, in your wisdom, have chosen to send him, and keep him in the safety of your eternal Love …*

They stood side by side. Shelamzion and Cornelius. Their heads almost touching, their backs bent and their brows furrowed, going through the endless scrolls and wax tablets that were piled upon the desk. The frozen record of all that had passed between them. For the time being at least, it was almost as though the old bond of camaraderie still stood. Faint smiles at the misunderstandings that had arisen.

'A *nasiy* is a leader. You have written *nasos,* an island.'

'I thought you spoke figuratively.'

'Simon, an island? Yes. Perhaps it is best left.'

Frowns at the volume of work still to be completed.

'I have not told how the high priest, Ananus, was murdered—'

'No. No, it is here. Believing that Ananus planned to betray them to the Romans, the Idumaeans sent an army to Jerusalem. Gaining entry with help from the Zealot faction inside the city, whereupon they murdered Ananus and his most senior aide, Jeshua—'

'And threw out the bodies without benefit of burial.'

'Yes, I have it.'

'But what of their falling out with the Zealots? Have you made note of their return to Idumaea?'

'On that scroll there … No, the one in your hands.'

'Yet you have not written of Simon … when he learned of Ananus' death … of how hope came back to him for the first time since we arrived at Masada.'

Cornelius lifted a tablet and consulted it. 'You have told me that this meant Simon was able to leave the fortress and to pursue his ambition of conquering Idumaea—'

'Yes. Yes. But first we went back to the hill country, to Acrabatene, and made it our stronghold.' She began to rifle through the scrolls, her fingers becoming clumsy in their frantic haste. 'I have not explained how Simon took Herodium, the fortress bounded by four towers. They said it could not be done.' Two scrolls had wound themselves round each other and she almost ripped one in half trying to separate them. 'You do not know how it was that Jacob the Idumean became sympathetic to our cause—Recall he was witness to how the factions in Jerusalem fell to fighting amongst themselves—with Jacob's help we took the town of Hebron. And it was many weeks before we had to worry about filling the bellies of our army.' She paused, looking down at the scroll in her hands. 'Simon was alight with victory then. He knew that he did not need the Zealots on his side. His army

was strong. I wish you might have seen him, magnificent in his armour, addressing the thousands. And, from the lowest, cringing slave to the highest nobility
among our ranks, those who heard him became men that day. I think they would
have thrown themselves from the cliff tops if he had so ordered it. Even I, who
had shrivelled my soul with hatred, found it in my heart to admire him a little
when he spoke of freedom.'

'Then Simon was ready to take Jerusalem?'

'Yes. No. His friend, John of Gischala, had already taken the city. He had
made an unholy pact with the Zealots, and, together, they had control of the Temple. The city was in thrall to them.'

'But why did John not seek Simon's help? He was his friend.'

'So Simon still thought. But war makes strange bedfellows of men. I told you
this—'

She began a frenzied search through the scrolls, dropping half of them on the
floor then falling to her knees and crawling after them. Two hands fixed themselves around her wrists, and she looked up to find Cornelius also on his knees.

'You must tell me of Jerusalem. What made Simon make his stand?'

'Not yet. There is so much I must say. I have not told how John of Gischala
broke his alliance with the Zealots and tried to hold Jerusalem under his own
rule—'

Cornelius shook his head, and saw her face crumple. Unspoken between
them was the understanding that time was running out. Every second brought
Josephus and his master closer to Rome. And when Titus set foot in the capitol
once again this small reprieve would be over. Already there was talk of a Triumph. Some mention of an arch to commemorate the conquest of Judea. And in
this precious pocket of time overlooked by the gods, he must finish his history.
And she still hoped to find her son.

With difficulty he got to his feet and helped Shelamzion to hers. She was
quiet now and nodded her head when he said, 'You must tell me how Simon took
Jerusalem. How did he overcome John and the Zealots?'

She nodded again, distractedly. 'But first I must tell you what happened at
Adoreon … Adoreon changed everything.'

In Jerusalem all answers lay. Ananus had held it, John of Gischala and Eleazar
had taken it, and outside the Romans waited, breath baited, for the moment to
strike. Jerusalem was the golden key that unlocked the omphalos of the world,
and all eyes were turned towards it. But Simon, who always looked up when other
men looked down, Simon went south and began to collect an army from Idumaea. And he did so despite the objections of his wife.

'The Idumaeans are Jews,' Shelamzion protested. 'How can it benefit us to conquer them?'

He smiled at her sadly. 'Do you think if there was another way I would not choose it? You are a woman. And for all that you are a clever one, you do not understand what war is to men.'

'Doubtless you mean to tell me.'

Simon's eyes narrowed. 'War is not a game of words. The Idumaeans have not so easily forgotten their Edomite heritage. There are still those who bow down in the wooded groves before their serpent-faced god. Do not think they would hesitate to cast their lot in with Rome.'

'Lies. The Idumaeans sent an army in support of the Zealots in Jerusalem.'

'One faction sent them. Another did not. The inability to reach agreement is a Jewish disease.'

And so Simon had gone, as Moses had gone to slay the Midianites, or as Saul, who slew the Philistines. Or as David when the Lord ordered the slaughter of the Amalekites. He had gone as a king goes. And what king of Israel did not anoint himself in blood? And though Simon was wrong, and his wife understood war, for all she was a woman, she did not understand him, and so the rift between them grew, and at night her prayers called for vengeance.

'Lord God, King of the Universe, lay my curse upon Simon. May he be an abomination in your eyes. May you smite him as you smote the Assyrians for their arrogance. And may the issue of his loins shrivel and perish.'

But the Lord did not see fit to smite Simon, and between husband and wife grew a widening river of bloodied victory. Time after time Simon returned from battle, the bitter ashes of burned cities clinging to his hair and flesh, exhausted, his eyes full of wildness and hopelessness for what he had seen.

Once they met, when Shelamzion was out with her maids. Simon was walking with the broken steps of fatigue towards his tent, receiving reports and issuing orders as he went. Catching sight of his wife, he faltered, and for an instant their eyes met. She saw, with sudden clarity, that he had drunk from the cup of demons and now was paying the price. A word from her might have healed him then. She knew this. And it gave her satisfaction to pass by without acknowledgement.

But she was alone in this pleasure. To everyone else Simon was a hero. A man amongst men. A new David. A warrior king. As she helped Simon's physician, Ariel, with the wounded, she was forced to listen to the men sing his praises.

'He was there, all right. In the thick of it.'

'Not like some that shout orders from the lines.'

'He took out that big brute. Arms like tree trunks.'

'What of Jacob the Idumaean? Where was he?'

'Doing what Simon told him. Fleeing the scene. Yelling Simon was behind him with forty thousand men.'

'Forty thousand. We're barely twelve.'

'They don't know that. Idumaeans can't count past ten.'

'How come?'

'Idumaean sandals don't show the toes.'

'But what if Jacob has betrayed us?'

'Not a chance. Simon sent Hyrcanus, the Sadducee, disguised as his slave. One false word out of Jacob and—' The man slit his throat with a forefinger.

'He's touched by the Lord, Simon.'

'Like the Maccabees of old.'

'He's blessed. The Lord speaks to him … They say (the man's voice dropped) that he has taken a vow not to touch his wife until Jerusalem is taken.'

Simon … Simon … Simon …

There were times she was forced to squeeze her eyes tight shut to stem the molten flow of her anger. But the men, who saw only a woman moved to tears, whispered amongst themselves that the wife of Simon wept for their wounds.

Had it been an age when a wife might demand to know her husband's feelings, Shelamzion might have found a way to bridge the widening gulf that set the limits of her marriage. But Simon showed no inclination to divide his energies. His mind was set on Jerusalem, and all personal considerations had been set aside. Even his mother was gone, returned to her home in Gerasa. Simon had made it his stronghold and sent her there to be his eyes in the north. At least that was the official version. Secretly Shelamzion speculated that he was weary of being reminded that he was not Saul. Nonetheless, the order of things was changing.

When Simon was not there, she became his mouthpiece, often soothing the way for the obsessively ritualized Sadducees, who were scandalized by the broader thinking of the Pharisees. Or listening to the grievances of slaves whose new freedoms were so dear to them that they took the smallest criticisms for threat. There were times when Shelamzion wondered if Simon truly understood the rifts and divisions that undermined his singular vision of freedom. After all, men had been fighting since Cain killed Abel. And while talking of freeing men from slavery was a popular piece of poetry, few had tried it, and none had ever succeeded. And it was with this in mind that she decided to spy upon his council of war.

A gibbous moon, barely visible above the dark mantle of the giant bechaim trees, led Shelamzion down the dark paths to the grove where Simon met his most trusted men to hear their counsel. All the factions and divisions of Judea come together in a single lonely glade. But, before she could reach them, a young guard, Oreb by name, stepped out from the trees.

'Lady, you can go no further.'

She adopted an attitude of concern. 'Your wife is ill.'

At once fear flared in his eyes. The wife of Oreb was close to term and had yet to bring a living child into the world. He made as if to brush past her, then checked himself.

Simon—'

'I will explain all to Simon. Go now. He would wish it.'

His glance, which had flitted everywhere, now flicked to meet her eyes, holding her gaze suspiciously. Trapped in the instant, she thought wildly to shout that he must obey her, only to counter the notion with a desire to laugh and pretend that her words had all been in jest. But confusion proved her friend. Oreb seemed to take her silence for authority. He gave a bow, and disappeared among the trees. She waited, half afraid he would change his mind. But, when she had heard nothing for several minutes, she crept forward until she could make out the voices of Simon's council.

'I like it not,' Hyrcanus was saying. He spoke his Aramaic with the stressed syllables of someone more comfortable speaking Greek. He was a strange one, Shelamzion knew. Defying his father's decree to flee Jerusalem, taking up the rebel's sword instead to be with Simon, yet possessed of a strangely contradictory character, choosing to fight for the people yet showing no love of them.

'And what is it you do not like?' This from grizzled Ephraim, the cheesemaker from Jerusalem. A firm believer in the End of Days, and a man whose fighting skill showed no sign of his previous preoccupation with pressed curds.

'I do not like the south,' Hyrcanus continued. 'For every alliance we make, we uncover ten plots to betray us. Idumaeans are not to be trusted. Their ancestry makes them suspect.'

'Spoken like a Sadducee,' chimed in Zacchaeus, a fiery little Sicarius, who had joined Simon because he had been unable to tolerate ben Yair's unbroken patience atop Masada. He turned to Yeled. 'Hyrcanus means, what value can there be in trusting men without benefit of a great house behind them?'

'Y-yes. That's what he m-means,' agreed Yeled. Shelamzion noticed that he never looked at the others, but always offered his opinion to their feet.

'What use is it asking *his* opinion?' Ephraim wanted to know. 'Yeled always agrees with Zacchaeus. If Zacchaeus said that light was dark, Yeled would light a candle at noon.'

Yeled looked down, crushed.

'Yet Yeled knows truth when he hears it,' Zacchaeus countered. 'For Hyrcanus, truth must be weighed, like coin.'

Hyrcanus' eyes flashed, but before he could answer, Ariel the Essene spoke up.

'There is merit in what Hyrcanus says.' The others were silent. Ariel's was a voice they respected. A brittle stick of a man with a long, white beard, who had lived in the solitude of the desert communities among his brothers, until he had been nailed to a cross by Vespasian's invading troops. And, while he was there, he had lost his ascetic appetite for God and gained instead a thirst for blood, particularly Roman blood. In her dealings with him, Shelamzion had found him to be a solemn, reserved man, easier to respect than love. But his skill as a healer was unsurpassed. And many a soldier limped back to life after visiting Ariel's tent when they should otherwise have marched on into darkness. Ariel cleared his throat.

'I have no argument with the men of the south,' he said coolly. 'But it was not for Idumaea that I prayed to the Lord to spare me.'

'He speaks the truth,' agreed Ephraim, his gruff voice rising. 'What are we doing here? Trying to win over peasants who don't know a sword from a sickle. This isn't the place the Lord would have us.'

'He's right,' exclaimed Zacchaeus, getting to his feet in excitement. 'We have the men. We should march on Jerusalem.'

A murmur of dissent blew like an ill wind across the faces of the others. And encouraged, Zacchaeus turned to Simon, as though only just noticing that the son of Gioras had been strangely silent throughout the argument. He spoke defiantly. 'Would you have us sitting on our backsides when others are helping bring about the End of Days?'

In the shadows, Shelamzion caught her breath. Simon did not answer at once. He stretched out one long leg then bent the other beneath it. Then he looked up at Zacchaeus, neither smiling nor frowning, until Zaccahaus sat down and joined the circle again. When he was seated, Simon spoke, his eyes moving slowly across each man. 'What would you have me do? The Pharisee and the Sicarius want to move on Jerusalem.' There were grunts of approval and Simon waited until they had died down before continuing. 'Yet Vespasian is camped outside the walls. How many men would we lose against trained legionaries who have had months of preparation to await our coming?'

There was silence and Simon went on, 'And what if we could get inside? Ananus is gone. But John of Gischala and the Zealots still wage war against the citizens. That weak-willed Herod, appointed over us, has fled back to Tiberius. And his sister, Berenice, has gone with him. There is no voice of reason left in Jerusalem. Do you think Vespasian waits to lay siege because he is afraid to enter?' Simon met Ephraim's eyes and Ephraim looked away. 'Vespasian is no fool. He has heard of our apocalypse and it amuses him to see Jew murdering Jew for the honour of bringing it nearer. He is in no hurry. He is waiting. And if we charge in now, unprepared, you may be sure that the only days we will end are our own.'

Ariel and Hyrcanus exchanged glances, but it was Yeled who spoke.

'There's sense in s-staying here. An army w-won't feed itself. And in nearby Adoreon we might find supplies. I've h-heard my … m-m-master talk of its oil and honey.'

'We do not speak of masters here,' Simon said gently, but he was watching the others. Their faces were a mixture of anxiety and ill-concealed hope. The spoils of Hebron had been vast, but an army is a bottomless well, and all had known the bitter ache of waking with an empty belly and no prospect of filling it. Simon saw their hope, and his expression hardened. 'Adoreon it is. I will speak with the elders.' He began to get to his feet, and Shelamzion knew she must withdraw. But before either action was completed, by husband or wife, the trees parted and a new enemy poured in.

There was no time to think. Out of the dark recesses, the caverns of camouflaged light, emerging like pagan deities, like demons, they arose. The men of Adoreon. Their faces streaked green. Ghastly in the canopied light. Wild men, who came at their enemies with jaws stretching in a grimaced shriek of death. Their tall, steel-tipped spears gripped firm by their sides. Simon's party barely had time to grab their swords before they were upon them.

Pan, panic, pandemonium ruled. The God of Moses nowhere in sight. Shelamzion tried to slip into the shadows. But this was an ancient forest. It drew her in, hemming her between pillars of ancient, scaly wood, many times the width of a man. Frightened now, she tried to find her way back, but the forest had swallowed the path. In confusion she made demi-turns, until she did not know if she was escaping the battle or heading into the thick of it. A giant of the wood reared up in her vision, blocking her path, but something in its twisted girth was familiar. Uncertainly, she began to make her way around. But then came a shout, close to her ear, making her stiffen.

Two men, fighting just the other side of the great trunk. One of Simon's men—Josiah, wasn't it?—fighting a heavily armoured Adorean, and the side of his face and his sword arm were split open in several places and bleeding profusely. The blood looked black in the greening light.

The two men were tired, their feet fumbling leadenly among the writhing tree roots, the fallen boughs. The Adoreon's long sword was hampering him in the heavy undergrowth, but, weak with blood loss, Josiah could not find a way through the toughened metal cuirass or the thick, leather straps of his opponent's helmet. He caught a blow from the long sword on his own shorter blade, but it sent him staggering backwards. Then he feinted and caught the Adoreon on the leg, cursing as his sword bounced uselessly off the other man's greaves. Shelamzion pressed herself against the tree. But locked in their own private world of torment, neither man saw her.

Josiah feinted again, curving his sword outwards for a side blow then thrusting it up towards his enemy's straining neck. But the blow was never dealt. He stood there, his sword suspended, frozen, like some forgotten tale of heroes, skewered through the soft centre of his body. Dying on a cubit and a half of tempered steel. He made the strangest sound, neither a cry nor a moan, but a small exhalation; a rustle of leaves, a breath of wind. And his sword dropped to the forest floor with dull impact. The Adoreon staggered back, pulling his sword with him, then stood, dumbly, as Josiah's body fell prone before him. He seemed overwhelmed by what he had done, and Shelamzion saw, with sudden insight, that he was very young and that this was his first kill.

But still, he had a sword in his hand, and she took a slow, deliberate step backwards, meaning to slip away. The crack of a twig beneath her heel brought the Adoreon's bowed head snapping upwards and she froze, transfixed by the intensity of his gaze. He was young and strong and full of life, and Shelamzion understood that she could not outrun him. She waited through the painful seconds for death or worse. But he did not come after her. Instead holding her gaze in a kind of helpless, staring horror until a faint whine of ruptured air exploded beside him and the shaft of an iron-tipped arrow buried itself in his neck.

Shelamzion felt her legs go weak, and caught at the gnarled bark for support. From the thicket emerged Simon, armed with a horn bow, Zacchaeus at his side. He faltered at the sight of his wife, as though she were a demon conjured from the green sap. And she wanted to call out to him, but the anger in his face turned her to stone. Behind him the little Sicarius was upon the gasping youth, his curving knife cutting through the carotid artery with the efficiency of a Temple priest. The blood plumed in chaotic crimson feathers, spattering Zacchaeus' tunic. Blood that looked no different to that which had spilled from Josiah's body.

Chapter XVI

Professor Driver further identifies two other characters described in the Scrolls. The 'Man of Falsehood' fits Josephus's description of John of Gischala as a crafty and an unscrupulous intriguer, and the 'Lion of Wrath' may have identified Simon Gioras, whom Josephus describes as raging like a 'wounded beast'.

Rupert Furneaux, *The Roman Siege of Jerusalem*, The Habakkuk Commentary

He blamed her for the attack. Standing before her, as though she were a child, and he her father. Though he was dangerous in a way her father had never been dangerous. 'You have been with me many months now. A part of my house, my family. Chosen of two brothers and mistress of my affairs. Yet I think you know very little about me.'

She gave him no answer because he sought none. Simon went on.

'You never knew my father, may the Almighty curse his soul. He was a great man, at least in his own eyes, used to taking what, or even who, he wanted. Yet he was never happy. He was not awarded the respect he felt was his due. Behind his back my mother called him lord of everything and master of nothing. That this was her opinion he well knew, and he hated her for it. And because of this, he would never ask her advice or go to her for counsel, though she alone might have helped him. He did not appreciate clever women.'

Fascinated as she was, Shelamzion forced a little yawn of boredom, as if to say, what is this to me? Simon's expression hardened.

'Although I am told I am my father's son—so close in fact that there were times I think my mother could not bear to look upon me—I do not share my father's opinions. Least of all his mistrust of a clever brain in fair wrappings. My father would have called me a liberal fool. Yet I did not share his opinion … until today.'

'I choose to go where I will go.' The words burst out of her, unbidden. And suddenly, in one long-limbed stride, Simon was before her, towering, terrifying.

'Do you choose to endanger the lives of every man and woman who follows me? Did you choose to dismiss the guard, thinking it a game?' He took another step towards her and she backed away. 'No. From now on, you will choose to remain in the camp. I gave you maidservants, and you will choose to keep them near. You are a wife. You will start to act as one.'

What wife am I to you? Those were the words she meant to say. But her eyes suddenly filled with tears and she turned to hide them from him. And as she did so, Ephraim and Yeled burst through the doorway. They came to an embarrassed halt when they saw her, such strangeness to come across the wife of Simon in her husband's tent. But Simon, who did not need words to read a situation, followed them outside, leaving Shelamzion behind, like an unfinished thought.

When he returned he was still with Ephraim, but Yeled had been replaced by a thin, weary-looking individual with the dust of the road still clinging to his clothes. She did not know him, but instinctively she felt a cold mass of fear settle over her heart. To Ephraim, Simon was saying, 'We should have expected this. It has been too easy.'

'What has happened?' Shelamzion looked to Ephraim, but he shook his head. This was strange. She had become used to Simon's scorn, but Ephraim always had a quick smile to spare. Simon helped the stranger to rest against some cushions, then turned again to Ephraim. 'Tear down the camp. We march as soon as we are able.' To his wife he spoke briskly. 'This is Isaac ben Avrim. Care for him as a welcome guest.' He strode from the tent, Ephraim at his heels.

Shelamzion turned on ben Avrim. 'What news have you brought?'

He blinked, evidently unused to being questioned directly by a woman. But she was Simon's wife. So, tugging at an earlobe, he answered, 'I was taken prisoner after the fall of Gamala—'

Gamala. Shelamzion had heard tales of Gamala. Jews throwing their wives and children into a bottomless ravine rather than surrender them to the mercies of Rome. She bit her lips. Would there come a time when Simon would force her to her death then claim it for compassion? To hide her shudder she asked, 'How come you to be alive? Are you another Josephus ready to broker a deal with Romans to save your own skin?'

The man balked under the harshness of her words. And she was immediately ashamed, but she did not know how to make amends so stood silent as he explained.

'There was no saving the town. Titus broke through with some two hundred cavalry. And where the son was, the father followed not far behind. Vespasian's men turned the streets red with blood.

'But we fought, lady. Never think that we gave the Romans an easy time of it. What food was left in the town we gave to the combatants. Those that could not fight could not eat. That was our rule. They chased us up to the citadel. And up at that great height we should have been safe. But the Lord turned against us. And such a tempest came down from heaven that every arrow we let fly was deflected from its course. While every Roman shaft found a true mark.' Ben Avrim paused a moment and wiped his brow. A thick, crescent-shaped scar was revealed beneath his coarse hair.

'I was hit by an axe blade in the final wave. I remember nothing until a legionary dragged me to my feet, yelling, *This one's alive*. And I knew then all was over and done with. My family, my home … gone.'

'Yet you they kept alive?'

'And there were times, lady, I wished they had not. I was Vespasian's prisoner thereafter. Kicked from man to man, like a pig's-bladder ball in some infernal game of *harpastum*. Jeered at. Spat at. Told that my *filthy Jewish carcass* would be sold to the swine-dealers—O yes, lady, they know what is an abomination to us. But I took their insults and their blows, and I stayed alive. Because there is one thing they hate even more than a dead Jew. And that is a Jew who won't die. I stayed alive and I listened. And when the time came I made my escape—'

'Intending to join Simon?'

'No, lady. I did not know what a force Simon had become. It was to Jerusalem and John of Gischala I meant to go. And if he would not have me, I would have thrown my cap in with the High Priest's party. But when I heard whispers about the attack on Gerasa—'

Gerasa! A numbing chill spread down Shelamzion's limbs. 'Simon was a clever *strategos*, but Vespasian had outwitted him. He had seemed unmoved by Simon's gathering strength in the south, yet all the while he was planning to attack Simon's stronghold. Simon's home. The saying of the sages came back to her; *The tree with poisoned roots falls without an axe.*

But ben Avrim was swaying on his feet. And Shelamzion felt a rush of guilt for her poor hospitality. 'Sit here, please.' She led him to a pile of rugs in a corner of the tent, and ben Avrim collapsed on top and closed his eyes, like a man who has lost the last vestiges of his strength. Alarmed, Shelamzion poured a cup of wine then held it to his lips. 'Drink. You are with friends now.'

Ben Avrim's eyes fluttered, but they did not open. He took a spluttering sip from the cup then pushed it away. 'Do not trouble with me, lady.'

'Hush. You are no trouble.'

But he forced his eyes open and looked into hers. 'You must believe I speak the truth.'

'Of course. Of course.'

'I would not betray Simon.'

She put the wine cup down and stroked his forehead until he closed his eyes again and his breathing became rhythmical. 'No,' she whispered softly. 'You would not.'

The comforting smells of cassia and aloes, in the soothing balm applied to Cornelius' skin, took away the stinging in his cheeks left by the *tonsor*'s iron razor. He closed his eyes and tried not to listen to the whimpering of a newly-freed slave, who was having his brand removed in the other room. The *tonsores* was quiet, it being too early for the usual crowd of gossips and aesthetes to have arrived. But the *tonsor* himself was lively with tittle-tattle. He had been watching the preparations for the Triumph to mark Titus' victorious return to the capitol, and was eager for a chance to prattle about it.

'Brought back some booty with them, so I've heard. They say when Titus burned the Temple the whole treasury melted down between the cracks in the rocks. Not that it stopped our lads. They were up there the next day, prising the place apart stone by stone to get at it … '

It was nothing that Cornelius had not heard before, nor could the thought of an infinite line of frightened Jewish captives bring him joy, so he lay back with his eyes closed, allowing the *tonsor*'s chatter to wash over him, like a faint twitter of birdsong. There were more immediate matters pressing on his mind. An invitation had arrived. And though it was the first to formally address him as *historicus*, his pleasure was considerably diminished by the knowledge that the request came from Paulinus.

Nor was it lost on Cornelius that to couch Paulinus' invitation in terms of a request was something of a misrepresentation. After all, this was no supplication to his will. It was an order, plain and simple. Doubtless he should be on his knees thanking the gods that the man who styled himself 'Caesar's eyes and ears' had chosen papyrus rather than the Praetorian guard as his means of communication. Or perhaps it was not the gods he should be thanking.

Jolting upright in his chair, Cornelius came perilously close to severing his carotid artery along with his train of thought. As it was, the *tonsor*'s blade nicked the delicate flesh by his ear, opening up a thin seam of crimson. The *tonsor* gave a scalded leap backwards, a profusion of apologies welling from his throat. Cornelius waved him away distractedly, rising to his feet and snatching up a discarded towel to hold against his neck. Then, like some bloodied veteran of the battlefield, he headed for the door, needing the cool air to fan his overheated brain. No, it was not the gods that deserved his gratitude. Now that pain had parted the clouds in his mind his thoughts were heightened, and he saw with poignant clarity the reason for Paulinus' change of heart. Only one man possessed such an exceptional talent for transforming the most bitter enmity into an elixir of perfect fellowship. A man with a nature as veiled and secretive as an oracle's dusty lair. O Josephus. He whispered the words above the thrum of blood in his neck. *Fides Achate meus.* True and faithful friend.

Yet he arrived at the Carcer some time later, hot and out of sorts. He had walked too fast and a sheen of sweat now clung to his body, making his tunic stick unpleasantly to his skin. It was one thing to recognise the logic of Paulinus' change of heart, but quite another to believe in it. A feeling of being watched had trailed him all along the *Via Nova*. And once, a man, he was certain had been following at some distance, suddenly walked out of an alley directly across his path. He flinched visibly, but the man passed by, his bland pink features innocent of any hostile intent. Then again…Cornelius turned to watch his receding back—what spy did not possess more faces than the divine Janus?

Shelamzion was sitting at the desk when he opened the door to the cell. She was reading his latest draft and making corrections where necessary. Lately he had begun to allow her to do this in his absence, and after examining the neatness and thoroughness of her work, he often wondered why he hadn't allowed such a thing sooner. She smiled when she heard him come in. And that, too, was a thing that had only begun to happen lately. He stretched a false echo of the smile across his own lips and decided that his revelation at the *tonsores* was best left unmentioned.

She stood up to allow him her seat and he made a show of going through his papers.

'Where were we? … Yes … Gerasa. Simon's home. He led his army there to meet with Vespasian's forces.' He looked up and found that Shelamzion had stopped smiling. Taken aback, he lowered the scroll in his hands. 'What is wrong?'

'We were too late.'

Vile, caustic fumes of burnt-out fires reached Simon's army long before they saw Gerasa. As they drew nearer, a deadly hush fell over everyone. Not the smallest sound. Not even a whisper of prayer from Ephraim or Zacchaeus. And Shelamzion understood their awe. After the long months in Idumaea—The easy victories. The willingness of the people to fall under Simon's spell—They had half succumbed to their feeling of just cause. Half forgotten that these were Jews they conquered and already susceptible to the dream of freedom. Now as they crossed the scorched earth and heard the crash of charred beams falling in blackened homes, they knew the rude awakening of dreamers. Where were the people? The mothers, fathers, wives, brothers … the children. All left behind. And now not a sign.

Along with several others, Shelamzion lifted her hand to her nose to shield herself from the foul effusions that polluted the air, but Simon caught sight of what they were doing and wheeled his horse round to face them. He looked at each of them, his face a mask of anger, until instinctively they let their hands fall to their sides. And when they had done so, his voice rang out over them, 'Uncover your mouths and noses, and breathe deeply. For all this stink is like the putrid bowels of the earth, get to know it well. For this stench is our enemy. This stench is Rome.'

Then he wheeled his horse round and rode ahead.

They had been efficient, Vespasian's men. Led by Lucius Annius, they had gone about their task of destroying Simon's home with a ruthless, hate-filled proficiency. The confusing maze of little houses Shelamzion had passed through so numbly, as a new bride, had disappeared. Not simply burnt down, but their ruins pulverized into useless heaps of scorched, smashed stone. The well was fouled and the little synagogue, where Simon and Saul had gone for their schooling, lay smashed across the main path, like the broken body of a wise old man. Simon got down off his horse and walked towards it, hands clenched at his sides. On top of the wreckage lay the holy scrolls, crumpled and torn, a filthy heap of human ordure holding them in place.

From her place in line, Shelamzion could not see Simon's face. She did not need to. His rage was a living thing that was felt by every man and woman who watched him. He stood like that for a long time, then he turned sharply and addressed Yeled.

'Burn them.'

Yeled shook his head, less in disobedience than in shock, but Ariel the Essene laid a thin hand on his arm and whispered, 'Do it. Did not the Macabees of old cleanse the Temple with ashes?' Then Yeled stepped forward and pulled his flint from his cloak.

But before the first spark was struck, an old man, who was not one of their number, appeared. He had been hiding in the ruins of the synagogue, and now he called Simon's name.

'Does the son of Gioras not know me?'

Simon's face lit up. 'Tobias.'

Tobias. Shelamzion remembered this old man, who had wept at the thought of leaving the precious family scrolls belonging to Simon's father behind. What must he have felt to see the books of the Law ripped from the sanctity of the synagogue to lie torn and defiled on the ground? But if Simon shared these thoughts, he chose to ignore them. There was only one question on his lips.

'Where is my mother?'

But Tobias began to weep, covering his eyes with his hands. 'You do not know what you ask me. You do not know—'

Simon took a warning step towards him. 'Tell me.'

The old man's sobs increased, and before she knew it, Shelamzion had dismounted and pushed herself towards her husband. 'Will you kill him? Look, he can barely stand.'

She took Tobias by the elbow and led him to a spot where he might sit. Then she unhooked her water-skin from the ass she had been riding and held it to his lips. And Simon watched, without comment or interference, watched as his wife defied him again.

Once Tobias had drunk his fill he began to tell the harrowing tale of Gerasa's fall. Lucius Annius had arrived two days ago with a squadron of cavalry and ample numbers of infantry. He wasted no time. There were no demands, no negotiations. At his order, the Romans attacked. Anyone fit enough to hold a sword was slaughtered on the spot.

'And if they surrendered?' Hyrcanus wanted to know.

Tobias shook his head. 'There was no surrender. The Romans murdered them whether they held a weapon or threw it down.' He rubbed the knuckles of one old, gnarled paw over his eyes. 'They were only boys. Too young for fight or flight.'

'And the women?' called a voice. Then others,

'My wife's name is Abihail.'

'My little daughters … '

'What of my son … '

All round voices, kept silent too long, burst out in molten fear, threatening to erupt into a conflagration of panic, until Simon, who had been crouching by Tobias' side, stood up and silenced them with a look. And when they were silent he turned back to Tobias and asked, 'Where are the women and children?'

The old man sighed. 'Who can say? The lucky ones fled. But most were taken for slaves.' He shook his head. 'What difference does it make? They would be better off dead.'

'And my mother? Was she taken?'

Tobias stiffened, then lifted his rheumy eyes towards Simon. 'I told her to flee. I and many others. But she would not go. This was her home. She had been forced to leave it once, she said, and she would not leave it again.'

'Did they take her?' Shelamzion saw Simon's struggle to force the words through his clenched jaw. Tobias let his gaze fall to the ground. 'We could hear the screams from the townsfolk. She listened, then she bade her servants fly. And when they would not obey, she ordered them to do her will.'

'And did they?'

Tobias shrugged. 'Who ever disobeyed an order from the house of Gioras?'

Simon raised an eyebrow. 'Except you.'

'Me?' Tobias waved a hand at his withered legs. 'Am I one to fly? Better to ask the mountains to flee or the rivers to change their course. I stayed. Yes indeed. I stayed. Would that I had not.'

He fell silent, and something seemed to snap in Simon. He grabbed the old man by the shoulders and raised him to his feet. 'What fate befell my mother? Tell me before I run you through myself.' Tobias whimpered and there were gasps. This was a new wildness that no one had ever seen in their leader, and they were frightened by it. Shelamzion caught Ephraim's anxious look, and knew the time had come to act. Gently, yet firmly, she put her hands on Tobias' shoulders and eased him free of Simon's grip, all the while keeping her eyes locked with her husband's.

'Softly now,' she whispered in Tobias' ear. 'You are among friends. Tell us what you know.'

The old man sighed again, and it was a long and bitter exhalation. 'What is there to tell? They came, Lucius Annius' men, and they hammered on the gates and screamed to be let in.' He threw a reproachful glance at Simon. 'But she did not move, your mother. She stood in the courtyard and waited while they fetched a beam to smash through. And when they stood before her—the biggest of them sneering and speaking his pig Aramaic, saying that even an old whore could learn to dance a merry turn on the end of his cock—she did not speak. Not a word. She kept her eyes on him, then she pulled from her cloak an evil-looking dagger. Only the Lord knows where she got it from. But she kept looking at that big brute even when she—' Tobias stopped and thrust his fist against his breast.

The sudden brutality of this motion made Shelamzion gasp, and all around there were cries and shouts. But Simon stood still, bloodless to the lips. He looked at Tobias out of eyes like flints and asked, 'You were with her when she died?'

'To the last,' Tobias nodded. 'I laid her on the ground. And no one stopped me. Not even that filthy animal, who had the scars of a thousand battles ravaging his ugly face. He had her blood all over him, but he did not move. Did not try to wipe it off. And I knelt beside her while she said the *shema*. Then she called, *Saul, forgive me*. And she died. A great lady died.'

Simon had bent very low to hear Tobias' words and only Shelamzion heard him murmur under his breath, '*No word for me then*'. He straightened. 'My mother is dead. Yet you lived.'

'What choice did they give me? I pulled out my own dagger, but the big brute wrenched it from me saying, *No, old man. Live so that he might know what took place here.*' Softly Tobias began to weep. 'You see, he knew. Knew you were coming.'

Simon took a step back, as though he might escape Tobias' words. Might free himself from the horror of what he had done. He had left his mother behind to be his eyes and ears. He had ridden away arrogantly, heedlessly as the jaws of the trap snapped shut over her. Nothing could be changed. It was too late. Now the watching crowd began to edge away, understanding that this moment was not for them, and having yet to seek their own sorrows. And Simon stood, staring at the ground, until even Shelamzion could stomach his pain no longer, and led Tobias away.

The pleasant warmth of Sivan turned into the white, fiery days of Tammuz, and still they stayed at Gerasa. What was left of Gerasa. They had pitched tents and dug a new well. What food they had left was put under guard and carefully rationed. But these orders came from Shelamzion, not Simon, and were carried out in his name by each of his faithful generals. *Yet how much longer can this go on*, Shelamzion wondered, watching an argument between a woman and the soldiers who guarded the supplies. The woman was pointing angrily at her stomach, and Shelamzion felt a growl of sympathy from her own empty belly. Was this Simon's great vision? To stay on this barren site, with its blackened, ruined fields, until the flesh fell from them and their bones sank into the soil?

The essentially pagan nature of this thought frightened and angered her. But she was no longer the young girl who waited passively while others took the lead. Adoreon had changed her, as Masada had changed her. The soft curves of her youth had burned away. And she was like a creature fresh from the desert, feral, lean, and more than a match for the tidal power that was Simon. She turned decisively towards the path she knew Simon had taken. This must end.

But before she had taken more than a step Hyrcanus appeared, blocking her way. He bowed in his elaborate Sadducean manner, which always seemed more display than obeisance. Previously it had amused her. But today she was in no mood for courtly manners. 'If you seek Simon he will not see you.'

Hyrcanus glanced in the direction she had come from, and she saw a familiar tightening of his features. In recent days, he had become less adept at masking his frustration at his leader's inertia, or perhaps he no longer thought it worth the effort of hiding. That he thought his lineage superior to Simon's was an ill-concealed secret. And rumours had reached Shelamzion's ears to the effect that he was speaking openly of a need for a stronger hand than Simon's to be in command. With a stab of anxiety she wondered if she was about to face a direct challenge to her husband's authority. And what could she, one woman, do to prevent it? But Hyrcanus spoke courteously enough.

'Judah's daughter, I would speak with you.'

Shelamzion frowned, but nodded. 'Speak what you will.'

'The people are restless.'

'And the sun is hot and the Jews are the Lord's chosen.'

'They know Nero is dead.'

'What of it? The Romans have no lack of madmen to replace him.'

'Vespasian has returned to Caesarea. His orders dissolved with Nero's death. Some say he has gone back to take the throne for himself.'

Shelamzion shot Hyrcanus a frightened look. 'Do the people know?'

'Not yet. But they sense something is wrong. They want to know when Simon will act.'

'What would you have me do?'

'Persuade Simon.'

'Better that I grow wings and try to fly to the sun.'

Hyrcanus' expression did not flicker. 'If Simon will listen to anyone he will listen to you.'

'He will not listen.'

'Then the Almighty help us all.'

She gave him no definite answer, but she knew that in the gaps between words is laid the path to compromise. And so she found herself taking the familiar route behind the house of Gioras. She had walked it many times in her loneliness before the flight to Masada. It was too wild to have suffered Roman desecration, and she found comfort in the fragrant seas of broom and myrtle that grew freely on the steep slopes.

She discovered Simon standing alone, as she had stood alone so many times, staring out across the valley to where the narrow track opened up to meet the road to Jerusalem. She saw him in profile, the sun flaring against his skin, his back a soldier's back, ramrod straight despite the burdens it carried. And she knew then that there was no point in talking to him. His face had the closed look of grief that she recognised from her own dark days of despair. And young as she was, she understood that grief is a tyrannical master. Only the young, the strong and the free can escape it. And this they must do alone. Or not at all.

She thought to tiptoe away.

'Wait!' He came after her, encircling her forearms in his big hands. 'I saw something.'

'What is it?' His face frightened her. Ashen from nights without sleep. 'What did you see?'

'The Temple.'

'A dream?'

'Not a dream. A vision.'

'You saw Jerusalem.'

'I saw the Temple. Aeons from now. And it was split in two. Then two monsters rose up trying to devour each other and we Jews were caught in the middle.'

Shelamzion pulled herself free. 'It was just a dream.'

'Not just a dream.'

And now she was frightened. 'But what can it mean?'

Simon turned his head and looked towards the road that led to the south. 'We have twelve thousand men. Tomorrow, we march on Jerusalem.'

Chapter XVII

It hath been prophesied to me many years I should not die but in Jerusalem,
Henry IV, Part 2, Act 4, Scene 5, l.235

Blinded with the optimism of youth, it was all Shelamzion could do to conceal her joy at returning to Jerusalem. And conceal it she must with so many of Simon's party still mourning the loss of loved ones at Gerasa. But Jerusalem. It was her dream and her prayer. Over and over to her almighty, unknowable God. Only let me return … please … please … let me return. For in her mind the past was transformed. Gone was the horror and bloodshed, the helplessness in the face of evil, and all she remembered was the white dazzle of a city that rose from the mists each day, like the answer to a desperate prayer. Her prayer.

From time to time she glanced up at Simon and found him watching her. He seemed to be wondering what her thoughts were. But on each occasion she deliberately cut her eyes away to thwart him. But he did not speak and she rode on, finding the taste of this small victory bitter and unsatisfying. Time enough to wage battles of the mind when they reached the city.

But Jerusalem was a locked box, its gates barred and bolted against Jew and gentile alike. And Simon's messages of greeting to John of Gischala were met with stony silence. Simon took these rebuffs with a dogged patience, as though he hoped to wear down John's resistance. But the wait between each redrafted missive was unbearable to Shelamzion. And when Hyrcanus arrived to say that Simon had given orders that they were to maintain camp, her pent-up fury exploded in misdirected harshness.

'Delay again. We are half way through Heshvan. Must winter be upon us before we enter Jerusalem?'

'Simon says—'

'Simon says. Simon says. Have none of you a single thought but for what Simon says?'

Hyrcanus looked at her peculiarly, as though sizing up her resentment against his own, but he kept his own counsel. In time to come she would remember that look. But for now she simply threw up her hands, crying, 'O, get out of my sight.'

Yet she found strange allies to her cause. Before they had been forced to flee at the tail of Simon's army, not one of her maidservants had ever been beyond the province of Acrabatene. In obedience to Simon's will they had endured Masada, suffered Adoreon. But the thought of entering the holy city—even in the middle of a seditious war—filled them, especially the younger ones, with a trembling excitement. For the first time Shelamzion found herself the centre of their hopes and dreams, and was surprised to find comfort in being a woman amongst women. And so, when Hyrcanus came again with the news that there would be yet another delay, Shelamzion understood that now the time had come to act, but that she need not act alone.

She waited with a prickling impatience for Simon to call his men. And it was all she could do not to cry from relief when she heard the rousting cry. Yet it was puzzling to see Simon take so many men. Nearly every able soldier was scrambling to answer the call. Far too many for a delegation. Well, what of it? She turned away with a shrug. If her plans were made easier, it only showed that the Almighty took the side of the righteous. Yeled ran past, almost knocking her over in his eagerness to reach the lines. She watched him bitterly, thinking, *Run to Simon. All of you. Crawling on your bellies, like dogs. You'll run with your tails between your legs when Simon is brought low by a woman.*

Once in the tent, she called her maids, and announced her decision. 'Today, we go to Jerusalem.' This pronouncement was met with silence, exchanged glances, troubled shakes of the head. 'Is this Simon's will?' they ventured.

But Shelamzion would have none of it. 'It is my will. My husband makes for Jerusalem this day, and naturally it would be his wish that we go with him.'

'Would he not send word?'

'There is no need. The daughter of Rabbi ben Judah will always find a welcome in the *city of the high place*.' And this quote from scripture charmed and reassured them more quickly than any argument. Suddenly they were frantic to leave, running from tent to tent, anxious to gather their things.

'Leave them. Leave them,' Shelamzion cried. Wanting only to get away, afraid they would draw attention to themselves. 'Bring nothing. Tonight you will pour oil on your heads and dress in robes of silk.'

'Truly?' Ami, one of the younger maids dropped the blanket she had been folding. 'Even me?'

Shelamzion swallowed. The lie was getting out of control, but what choice did she have? 'Yes. Even you. Now, let that be, and hurry!'

Jerusalem is a city surrounded on west, south and east by deep ravines. Down through the ages all those bent on conquest—Philistia, Assyria, Babylon—came from the north. And it was to the north of the city that she had watched Simon lead his men. Let north be her guide too. She would lead her maids back along the ridge road, as though, to any watchful eyes, they fled from harm's way. But, knowing the geography of the area as she did, she would then cut eastwards down a little known track used by gravediggers, emerging in the Kidron Valley, that vast graveyard where it was said that the great and the good turned to dust alongside the bones of their more inglorious brothers.

She had some idea of following the aqueduct that bisected the valley and entering the city through one of the smaller gates on the east side. Of course, there would be the risk of patrols. But her plan was all the better for it. Let them be picked up, she reasoned. It would get her inside the walls of the city without the necessity of bribing a gatekeeper.

It was further than she had reckoned. Already past the sun's highest point when they found the track to the east. But such was her longing to see her home again that she scarcely noticed the blisters on her feet or the sweat on her brow. 'Hurry,' she called. 'Can't you tell? We're almost there.' But the numbing opiate of her joy did not extend to her maids. Two of the plumper ones had gone the rich red of carob blossoms, and panted out moans that grew increasingly loud the higher they were forced to climb. Pinch-faced Mariamme complained to anyone who would listen that they should never have left the camp without an escort. And even Ami glanced back anxiously from time to time, as though sensing the protective cloak of Simon's power diminishing. Shelamzion saw their doubts, and afraid that they would take flight and run back towards the camp, drove them on mercilessly. Pushing them up a stump-stubbled incline as bald as the shaved head of a Nazirite, all the while dazzling them with glittering promises of the citadel of God.

Gasping, wiping the sweat from her eyes, Shelamzion crested the slope and got her first clear view of the city. And yet, as she gazed down upon it, she felt a sudden lack of sensation. It was as though she had been promised Jerusalem, and had, instead, been fobbed off with a painted panel of wood. Nothing belonged to her in that city and she belonged to no one. It was beginning to dawn on her young mind that home exists only as a reflection in the eyes of those we love.

'Don't move.'

She gaped, but did not turn her head, knowing without seeing that this was no Roman who spoke. The Aramaic was too guttural, too redolent of his Jebusite ancestry. And when she looked up she knew she was looking at the thin, harsh face of a Zealot. He was not alone. His three companions, beards straggling, swords unsheathed, stood behind him. They had stony, hate-filled faces, as though every distorted idea they had formed about the world was carved eternally into their flesh. One, presumably their captain, brought the tip of his sword under Shelamzion's chin, forcing her head up.

'*Tim'ay?*' Whore?

She shook her head as violently as the sword would allow. It sank into her flesh and she felt a little bead of blood well up against the tip. And, although she knew it was the wrong thing to do, she held the gaze of the captain and answered, 'I am the wife of Simon bar Gioras. He has sent me to you as his messenger.'

'You lie.'

The sword point dug deeper into her flesh and one of the maids screamed. Shelamzion swallowed.

'Let the Almighty be my witness, I am here as Simon's messenger.'

The Zealot's eyes did not flicker. 'Simon does battle against Eleazar's troops this day. You are no messenger.' Then he spat on the ground, as though the taste of Simon's name in his mouth was an abomination.

Comprehension made the long muscles of Shelamzion's guts suddenly contract. The Zealots had turned against Simon. What a fool she had been not to foresee this. All the long months at Masada and yet never trusted. Ben Yair watching Simon's growing power with increasing alarm. And when Simon marched on Jerusalem—that jewelled fortress that was the key to the east—ben Yair had surely sent his messengers running with the wind beneath their feet to warn Eleazar. Warn him that Simon, the convert's son, was on his way. Simon, who did not wait for a messiah to rise up amongst them, but who conquered with a sword in one hand and a vision of freedom in the other. Simon, who was a greater threat to the Zealots than Roman oppression.

Shelamzion's eyes darted back and forth. She'd had some vague plan to reach the city fathers, to persuade the remains of Ananus the High Priest's party that Simon could be defeated. But she had miscalculated. The balance of power had shifted. She looked up into the eyes of the hard-faced Zealot before her and smiled. No matter. This was better.

They took them inside the city. Shelamzion and her maids. Bound, one behind the other, as though they were dangerous criminals, like beasts hobbled and bowed. At this treatment the maids began to weep hysterically. And Shelamzion turned on them, shocking maid and Zealot alike with the harshness of her rebuke.

She followed the Zealot leader towards one of the smaller posterns into the city, forcing herself not to shudder at the sight of four bodies, still clothed in stinking flesh, lying face down only yards from where they walked. From what she could tell they were all young. Two men and two women. They had met their end in violence. But whether they were trying to escape the city or hoping to gain access to it, she could not tell.

At the gate, the Zealot captain stopped and called out some words that were presumably a signal to his comrades. Slowly the gate opened, and two more Zealots, holding Roman weapons and wearing Roman armour, emerged. They eyed Shelamzion and her maids in surprise, and there was a quick, low exchange between the men. But in the end they passed through without interference. The Zealot leader grunted an order to bring them forward. A few more steps and Shelamzion found herself within the walls of Jerusalem at last. Suddenly the air seemed more breathable. Her face lit up with an inner light of pure joy, which faded as they crossed the vast, desolate space of the Temple's outer courtyard.

Lined along the tops of the high walls that surrounded the Court of the Women were scores of heavily-armed Zealots. They stood motionless. Watching. Immediately suspicious of anyone who drew near. Looking, for all their piety, like the forbidden statues adorning far-off pagan temples. While, down below, hunched, frightened figures, crept around the edges of the court, trying not to stand in the heaps and pools of filth that lay everywhere. Evidently, Shelamzion thought to herself, the Zealots' control of the city did not extend as far as the dung collectors. The Zealot captain was eyeing her curiously, waiting for her reaction. But Shelamzion stayed silent. In her short life she had learned one thing. Horror was still horror, whether or not you howled in its face. So she lifted her chin and let him lead her up the steps into the Court of the Women.

She was kept, with her maids, in the Leper's Chamber, a vast room set into the northwest corner of the courtyard. Their incarceration in a place designed to hold the unclean was not lost on her. As soon as the door thudded shut, she began to pace the stone floor, up and down, past the empty troughs of the ritual baths. As she paced she avoided the eyes of her maids. Not because she feared pinch-faced Mariamme's reproach, but because Ami was looking at her with round, hopeful eyes, as though she still believed that she would wear silks that night and adorn her head with oil.

It was dark before the door opened again. They had been given candles, but no food. Shelamzion hardly noticed, but one of the plumper maids had to be rebuked for constantly reminding everyone that they had been promised meat with their supper that night. By the dim light Shelamzion could see two men. She recognized the Zealot captain who had brought them here, and beside him was another, thickset man, with a fresh wound on his arm. Eleazar, she guessed, and the acid flux in her stomach began to boil. Everything depended on how the battle had turned out. If Simon had lost … her bargaining chip would be gone. Yet if he had been victorious, would he not have stormed the Temple intent on rescue? A little, dropping sensation of doubt made her ask for the first time what Simon would do when he found she was gone. She had flattered herself with thoughts of his disbelief, his rage. Perhaps, instead, he had simply washed his hands of her. Stalemate was her only chance, and she held her breath, waiting for Eleazar to speak.

But it was to his captain that Eleazar addressed his words. 'This is the woman?'

The captain nodded. 'We think they're camp followers.'

Shelamzion burned to the roots of her hair, which she had taken care to cover with a veil. But she made no comment. Living so long with ben Yair on Masada had taught her something of the way of Zealots. Eleazar was looking at her, and she felt his eyes taking in the weave of her overdress and the gold embroidery on her veil. She wanted to look him in the eye, to challenge him with her intelligence as she would have done Simon. Instead, she kept her arms at her sides and her eyes trained modestly down. Eleazar spoke again to his captain. 'This is no camp follower.'

'She says she is Simon's wife.'

'The half-Jew's wife out wandering while her husband does battle—'

Shelamzion dared to glance up. 'I am here as a messenger.'

He did not acknowledge that she had spoken, and she had not expected him to. Shorter than she, he spoke to the air over her shoulder. 'The convert's son has gone back to his camp to lick his wounds. Do you tell me he sends his wife to negotiate?'

'I came here—' Shelamzion began, then broke off. She stole a look in the direction of the maids. Somehow it was harder while they were listening. She met Mariamme's gaze and saw her eyes narrow suspiciously. Urgently, she turned back to the Zealot leader. 'I would talk with you alone.' For a moment she thought she would be ignored, then he turned to his captain, saying, 'I will take a walk with this woman across the courtyard. We may be seen by the men and need not fear rumour.'

He emphasized this last, and Shelamzion had the impression that an order had been given. She saw the captain's face crease in a frown, but he bowed his head, and stepped back. Eleazar strode past, and Shelamzion followed him out into the cool night air.

They walked round the great courtyard, which was the furthest she had ever been inside the Temple, Eleazar walking a little ahead. Of this she was glad. In the enclosed quarters of the Leper's Chamber she had quickly realized that the Zealot leader considered bathing to be a necessity of religion rather than a fact of life, and it was best not to draw breath too readily in his presence.

They had completed almost a full circuit before he spoke. 'You are here by the convert's will?'

She noticed that he did not sully his mouth with Simon's name. 'No.'

'No?' He did not stop, but she saw his step falter. She pressed on before her nerve failed. 'The enemies of Simon may have more in common with his wife than they might suppose.'

'Yet you *are* his wife.'

'In name only.' This admission cost her more than she had expected. 'A wife need have no loyalty to a man who killed her father, her brothers, who—' The catch in her voice prevented her from going on. Eleazar did not look back, but his hand stroked down the length of his beard. 'You come here to play the traitor?'

She drew in a breath and felt briefly the foul stink of the Zealot on her tongue and the dark stain spreading across her soul just before she answered,

'Yes.'

Chapter XVIII

A sudden break in the antiphonal chanting of the Levites had Shelamzion running for the door of her chamber. More likely the stones break loose and start to dance than the Levites stop singing in the Temple. She ran across the Court of the Women and bounded up the steps leading to the Nicanor Gate, knowing she could go no further, yet driven by her need to be part of things. At the top of the steps two Temple guards appeared and crossed their spears to prevent her from going further. By their brazen, mismatched armour she saw at once that they were not of the Temple's original force, but two Zealots. Men whose ancestors had prostrated themselves in the groves of the Great Mother, and now held themselves aloof from the contaminating touch of women. She held their gaze longer than wisdom dictated then wheeled round and walked angrily away. But not before she had seen Eleazar.

He was dressed in a rich man's robe pulled loosely over his soldier's garb. And by his stiffened posture she knew that he had seen her, but he made no acknowledgement, disappearing towards the Sanctuary without glancing back. The gesture was deliberately humiliating, and the sting of it was not lessened for knowing that this was the Zealot way. The way of pious men, whose God was so much in their likeness that the shape of a woman was a constant abomination. She bit down on her lip, feeling the salt tang of thirst upon her tongue. Since Vespasian's men had destroyed the great aqueduct that spanned the Kidron Valley, water was being rationed all across Jerusalem. Yet it seemed the wife of bar Gioras and her entourage merited less than most.

The cries of her maids drew her gaze towards the Chamber of the Nazarites. They were running towards her. Mariamme's expression closed and disapproving. Ami's open countenance full of anxious curiosity.

'Lady, what is it?'

'Nothing. Nothing. As always. Nothing.' She pushed past them, too angry to say more. But they followed, Mariamme's tongue barbed with complaint. 'There is no water.'

'Surely it was brought before the Tamid sacrifice?'

'The leavings of the piss-pot. No one can drink it.'

Shelamzion tugged at the collar of her shift, feeling the creep of her un-washed body. 'What would you have me do?'

'Talk with Eleazar.'

She might have laughed then, had she not wanted to weep. And she might have wept had she possessed more than salt for tears. Eleazar. What bitter lessons she had learnt with his Zealots as her teachers. Trust could not rival suspicion. Love could not outweigh hate. Their keening prayers were like war cries. And their devotion was tempered with a fierce, unpredictable edge that never balked at spilling blood. Little wonder that their friends were said to fear them more than their foes.

'Lady.' Ami's hand was upon her arm. 'Do not be downcast. Simon will come.'

But she shuddered at the sound of his name. In the first days, when she still believed in the Zealots' promise, she had gone to Eleazar and spilled the entrails of Simon's plans before him.

'The Feast of Dedication. Simon will make his move against you then.'

Eleazar had regarded her shrewdly. 'While you play the Jezebel in our midst?'

'Simon has the blood of my father, my brothers … the blood of Jerusalem on his hands. Is that not enough? … When will you make your move?'

'Soon … soon.'

'Do you fear my word? The Lord himself would not blame me for delivering Simon into your hands.'

'Do not blaspheme, woman. You will have your vengeance soon enough.'

But a day had passed, then another and another. And still the Zealots made no move to arms. Jerusalem was rotting from within, while the Zealots hid in the Temple. And Eleazar stayed in the Court of the Israelites, calling upon his silent God to tell him what to do.

Mariamme's petulant voice broke into her thoughts. 'Lady, the water.'

She turned angrily. 'Am I Samuel now that I should bring down rain and thunder—' But even as she spoke, the first cries reached her ears. Wild, hungry cries coming from the southerly side of the Temple. This was something new. She went quickly to one of the small side staircases that led to the upper eleva-tions of the court, mounting its steps two at a time. At the top she leaned out over the rampart and strained her eyes towards the Temple's outer wall. Men and women—mostly men—were pouring in through the double gate into the Royal Portico. They were following a militia of Zealots, who were dragging the strug-gling figure of a man between them. A trial. Yet on such a scale. Half of Jerusa-lem seemed bent on attending. And for what? To see lies, like lions, devouring the weak flesh of truth. Shelamzion's heart sank within her. And she would have turned away had she not heard one of the guards call out that the captive was Niger the Peraean.

Shelamzion was too far away to see his face, but she recognized the name as it was hurled through the air, like rotten fruit. This was a man much spoken of in Simon's circles. A hero of the battle against Cestius Gallus. A military man, known to dabble in the gentle art of reading, and who was rumoured to have a collection of manuscripts gathered from the furthest flung reaches of the civilized world. A man loyal to the party of the High Priest, who still sent extravagant donations to the sacrificial altar while the rest of Jerusalem was beginning to feel the pinch of bad harvests and months of war.

Shelamzion left the rampart and ran down the steps towards the Royal Portico. She could see Niger now, chained, twisting and writhing in the grip of four thickset Zealots. A sea of men and women flowing around him, some jeering, many looking on with taut, helpless faces. She began pushing forward, buffeted and elbowed by thin, desperate-looking men with empty bellies, men so eager to feast on excitement that they forgot the lessons of countless sages. The old justice of vengeance reared up in them again. And they chased their enemy wildly, crying, *Kill him! Cast him out!*

Niger, yelling and struggling in their midst, managed to free a hand, tore open the front of his shirt, revealing the screaming mouth of a battle scar across his breast. His words were lost in the riot of sound, but Shelamzion understood. He was trying to tell these zealous men, these fanatics of God that they were killing their heroes.

She would have tried to stop then. Sickened, only wanting to distance herself from the madness. But she had left it too late. Dusty, ill-smelling bodies buffeted against her, dragging her along against her will. 'Ami!' she cried, struggling to make herself heard. 'Help me!' And she would have been glad even for the pinched face of Mariamme, but the maids were nowhere in sight. She was swept along, through a forest of arms and legs until she was deposited within the great crescent-shaped Chamber of the Sanhedrin. The Hall of Justice. But looking round, Shelamzion could see that more than half the seventy-one seats were empty. No representative of the Sadducean persuasion was present. Of the Pharisees, only a few shrunken-looking men, huddled together, their nervous hands twisting the deep-blue tassels that edged their tunics. The rest were Zealots. Zealots in fine robes skinned from rich men's backs, their eyes like famished wolves. Lolling across the benches with the grand insolence of unaccustomed power.

A door opened, and Eleazar entered, a tall, red-haired man at his side. From a whispered conversation beside her Shelamzion understood this new man to be John of Gischala. Her heart skipped a beat. Simon had talked of him as a friend. Yet he too had thrown his lot in with the Zealots. For all he claimed to lead his own faction, his men had the same bloodlust behind their eyes. Shelamzion kept her eyes on John, wondering if he believed that he controlled them. But then Eleazar stood up to commence the trial. And the true perversion of justice began to unfold.

At a gesture from Eleazar a young Zealot, with a face like a fox, stood up and read out the charges in a flat, toneless voice. 'We accuse this man of infamy and treasonable acts against the state, leading to iniquitous dealings with the enemy, and with purpose ill-conceived against his fellow Jews in defiance of the overriding authority of Almighty God.'

No hand was raised. No voice of dissent called out to gainsay the accusation. The Zealots lounged on the luxury of silk cushions. The Pharisees looked down, twisting their blue tassels between their fingers. Niger seemed paralysed. Then a long line of witnesses was brought before the court, some frightened and whisper-mouthed, not daring to look at the defendant or his accusers, others smug and swaggering, eager for their chance to drag a rich man down. In the crowd, Shelamzion quickly understood that Niger was as much on trial for his wealth as any act of sedition he might have committed.

Many mouths, apart from her own, must have salivated at the sacrificial animals he continued to send to the Temple. What jealousies had been aroused by the succulent shape of his piety? What sudden longings whetted appetites and grievances alike? She looked round the crowd, seeing only greedy, eager faces. Eleazar seated on his marble throne, sprawled like a voluptuous tyrant, limbs limp, his face an incongruous, craggy outcrop above the swathes of silk. Beside him, John of Gischala, simply dressed, his expression shifting and uneasy.

Shelamzion saw him open his mouth to whisper some argument in Eleazar's ear. Saw Eleazar dismiss him with a flick of his hand, not even bothering to look up. And John's face darkening, yet he made no further attempt to interrupt. Out of fear? Out of respect for the court? A reserved man or a weak one? With a crawling pain of realization, Shelamzion understood that it did not matter. Either way Niger's fate was sealed. He had been plucked from the herd. Unblemished by poverty or desperation, he would be their sacrifice. And even as they swore allegiance to the One True God, they would throw this man headlong into the arms of fates and furies, the forgotten gods of Canaan.

What would her father have done in this place? She tried to call up the reassuring memory of his face. But the ghost was watery now. His features would not resolve into familiar lines, and it frightened her to see how quickly she was forgetting. And Simon, what would he have done? What was he doing to prevent this monstrous perversion of justice?

The air was thick with rumour. Simon was raging at the city walls, like a wounded beast. Simon was murdering anyone who tried to escape. Simon was planning to leave. His men were already in negotiations with the Romans. Rumour and counter-rumour. Even cloistered as she was, the dregs of the speculation filtered down to fill her ears. But trapped within the Temple's unyielding walls, she was without means of separating truth from falsehood. That there was wildness in Simon she knew for fact. But to consider an alliance with the Romans? Had her betrayal meant so much? Or was it all lies? She closed her eyes for a moment, trying to remember how she had come to this.

She was only a few short weeks off her nineteenth birthday, and already she had been witness to things that had caused men to fall to their knees and weep. Her mother and father were dead. Her brothers were dead. And what would they think of her, a daughter brought up in the ways of the sage Hillel, the ways of peace, turned traitor to her husband so that she might throw her lot in with madmen and fanatics? She stood a moment, immobilized by a diffuse sense of shame and loss, then she began to push her way through the wall of solid backs.

The place of the witnesses was only just ahead. She must speak out. She must reach the broad, marble steps and only then try to reach the minds of those men so close to God they had forgotten how to be human. But Eleazar's limp hand had given a lazy gesture, and already the guards were closing in on Niger. Just like that. No deliberation, no pronouncement of sentence. The Zealots had turned the sacred site of the Law into a Roman arena. A place where victims were dragged to their deaths before a jeering mob.

Niger was a brave man. A hero of the battle against Cestius Gallus. But as they began to drag him through the gates he feared for his soul. A great cry tore from him, and he pleaded no longer for his life, but for the dignity of burial. But not even that would the Zealots permit. Despair had spawned them. Lean, hungry men without mercy. And they showed none to Niger. They would throw him from the city walls and let the dogs and jackals devour him.

Shelamzion followed the mob blindly as they dragged him towards the Temple's outer gate. Niger cursing them with the vengeance of Rome, with famine and pestilence, battle and slaughter. And his voice breaking into sobs—with the curse of Cain against Abel. Jew against Jew. Brother turned against brother. Shelamzion was pushed against a pillar. And feeling its solid refuge against her back, she planted her feet firmly and let the swell of the mob flow past her, like an angry torrent. Bleakly, she watched them go, every last man and woman letting Eleazar's Zealots lead them down the path of destruction and ruin.

She heard her maids calling, and turned to leave. And as she did so, a hand took hold of her wrist and pulled her round. She gasped and found herself facing a haggard man with dark, pleading eyes and a Zealot's curved *sica* at his waist.

'Don't scream. It is not what you think.'

A *sicarius*, an assassin. Her lips parted and she would surely have screamed had there not been something in his face. Some lightning spark of memory that said, *I know this man.* He started to pull her towards the outer gate, and she looked round wildly, certain they would be stopped. But the excitement over Niger was not yet ended, and all heads were turned away. He drew her into a narrow alley cloistered in shadows, and she followed without protest, ducking under crumbling archways that looked as though they had been there since the city had been a Jebusite stronghold, picking their way through stinking, litter-strewn streets until he stopped outside a low doorway, then pushing it open the merest crack, pulled her inside.

The room was abandoned. Cold hearth, dirt floor, furniture all gone. A poor man's hovel stripped to the bone. They stood facing each other in the dim light.

'Do you know who I am?'

She shook her head. In the shadows she couldn't be sure.

'Yohanan. Son of Levi. Your father was my—'

She put her finger to his lips. 'It is enough. I know you.'

But his eyes were full of tears and the babble of his words was not so easily stemmed. 'I did not cast off the mantle of your father's teachings so easily.'

'I remember. Your family … killed in Caesarea.'

'And the procurator did nothing. The Zealots—They promised vengeance.'

She nodded sadly. Had not she been caught by the same bitter lure? 'My father wept to find you gone.'

'I think—Your father—He must have died cursing me.'

Her breast tightened and it cost her to speak, but she answered, 'My father followed the ways of Hillel. He cursed no one for following their true path.'

Yohanan looked as though he might argue. But just then there was a noise in the street, footsteps running past, and he drew her deeper into the shadows. When he spoke again it was in quick, hoarse gasps. 'I must get you away from this place.'

'Where?'

'Back to your husband.'

Simon! She could not take in the words, could not believe the evidence of her ears. She backed away, shaking her head. 'I will not go.'

'You must. You have seen what it is to be a Zealot in Jerusalem. And believe me when I tell you that you have seen but the smallest drop in a vast ocean of horror. Hatred and mistrust has become their creed. And they apply it indiscriminately.'

The floor was uneven beneath her feet. It made her stumble and she stumbled also in her words. 'They have known so much suffering. We should make allowances—'

'Suffering, yes,' he agreed. 'They know suffering. Have you ever seen a creature caught in a hunter's trap? In so much agony it attacks itself. Biting and tearing its limbs off to be free. Do you know what happens to such a creature?'

Shelamzion stood stock still, not daring even to breathe.

'It dies.'

Yohanan suddenly flung away from her, pacing like the trapped beast of his conjurings. 'I have seen the kind of freedom the Zealots offer. The freedom to love God through the shackles of their teachings. As though the infinite love of the Almighty was a thing to be held in a vice, forever tightened and squeezed, letting fewer and fewer men pass through.' He turned towards her, eyes burning in the darkness, breathing heavily. 'And when they grow tired of turning other men from God they fall to fighting amongst themselves. So that one Zealot is forever proclaiming that his way is the purer path, and denouncing the rest as heretics. I swear if we allow these madmen to win they will first eat up the rest of the world then turn on each other. And when the day of Judgement arrives there will be one, solitary man left in the world, as Adam was alone in the beginning. A single, bloated Zealot blown up with piety and the blood of the rest of mankind.'

He broke off suddenly and stood, used up by the ordeal of his words. Shelamzion did not … could not look at him. At last she whispered, 'You will tell this to Simon.'

'No.'

'No?'

'I cannot go with you. There are those who believe John of Gischala would break with Eleazar if enough men would back him.'

She felt a spark of hope. 'Then let me stay with you.'

Yohanan rubbed a weary hand down the side of his nose. 'You cannot stay here. Eleazar's men would hunt you down, and John is not the man to protect you. You must go to Simon. Tell him that we need him. Tell him there are those ready to join him if only he will come.'

'Then come with me.'

'That I cannot do. John is a weak man, but he is beginning to doubt the zealous way. He will need men who can strengthen his resolve when he makes his break.' He leant past her and pushed the door open a crack. 'The *Minha* prayer has begun. We will be safe if we go now.'

He held out his hand, yet she hung back. Wanting to say so much. To confess the reason she was here in this city. To ask for understanding if it was too much to ask for forgiveness, or for sufferance where even understanding might not extend. She drew in breath, but Yohanan had turned back to the door.

'We must go now.'

He caught her hand, then they were running, free in a city where the flame of freedom was a dying ember cooling in the winds of change.

They caught up with her about a mile from the camp, Simon's men out on patrol. They took her at once to Ephraim and Zacchaeus, who were their commanding officers. And the burden of her guilt was increased by the sight of their tears of gladness. She saw their exchanged looks that she had come alone without her maids. And her pangs of conscience made her babble assurances that they would not come to harm. For surely they would not. Eleazar would dismiss them as women, and serving women to boot. They were harmless, blameless. He would surely see that.

They left her in the tent she had shared with her maidservants, bowing as they went, kissing their fingers to her. And perhaps it was only her imagination when Zacchaeus said joyously, 'You have been returned to us even as the Lord returned Sarah,' that Ephraim added softly, 'For the Lord saw that she was a true wife to Abraham.'

She did not go to see Simon immediately. That she could not face. But called for water, clean, scalding water to wash away the dirt of Jerusalem, the dirt that Jerusalem had become. And she opened her cedar chest, choosing a shift of pale yellow and an overdress of a deeper shade, embroidered with the arrows and olive branches that honoured Simon's ancestral claim with the tribe of Mannasseh. With her fingers she massaged fragrant oil of cassia into her scalp. And trying not to think that it would have been Mariamme's job to dress her hair, she bound it in a loose plait that hung, like a thick, young vine from the swell of her shoulders. And when, finally, she had fastened two broad gold bands, emblazoned with the name of Gioras, on her wrists, there was nothing more to be done. She was ready.

Taking slow steps, like a queen walking to a place of execution, she walked the distance from her tent to the tent where Simon was waiting. There were many faces that turned towards her. With pity? With curiosity? But when she got there she found the guards dismissed. And what meaning could she read into it other than that she was entering the lion's den, and that no angel of the Lord should intervene when the lion tore her apart. Only let it be quick, she prayed. Do not give them the satisfaction of my screams. She drew a sharp, tight breath into her lungs, as though it would be her last, then walked quickly through the entrance.

Simon was sitting on a low, carved chair near the centre. She remembered the chair as a prize from their victory over Hebron. So many things she remembered now. All the tiny, forgotten details of her life suddenly in sharp relief, as though this was the day of reckoning and nothing must be overlooked. She went towards him, then seeing the obsidian gaze of his eyes, stopped and waited for him to make the first move. He said nothing. His face remained implacable, giving her no clue. Noises, hooping, hollering, energetic noises reached her from tents away. But here in Simon's tent all was silent. She saw that the fingers of one hand were curled round the hilt of his sword, and it unnerved her and infuriated her in equal measures. Did he expect her to throw herself at his feet, weeping and pleading for her life? She took a step nearer, saying, 'I am returned … Of my own free will.'

Silence.

Yet she owed him an explanation did she not? At least let her offer that.

'I did not mean—You must believe it was not my intention—' She took another step. 'If you will kill me there is none who would stand in your way. I am guilty and have betrayed you. Only know this. Eleazar has knowledge of your strategy, and it would go ill with you to try to take the city now.' At Eleazar's name Simon stood up. They were now only a pace apart.

'But you have friends. John of Gischala grows weary of the Zealots. He will make his move soon, and there are those who follow him who would follow you more gladly.' She had been speaking very fast on a single breath, and with the last air in her lungs she added, 'That—that is all I have to say. Except—except that I was wrong and … I am sorry.'

She stopped speaking and the silence in the tent pulled taut. And feeling death almost upon her, she closed her eyes, and held her face and shoulders tight against the killing blow—A blow that did not come.

Slowly, like a sleeper awakening from the deep stills of slumber, her eyes fluttered open, and met Simon's. There was an instant of terror when she understood he had been waiting for this—this moment of clarity between them when there could be no more secrets. Then he took hold of her dress and ripped it from her body.

Hours later she awoke, and the first thing she saw was the open tent flap, and beyond it a strip of indigo light punctured here and there with the prismatic glitter of distant stars. The world had changed. Not just the relentless mantle of night's falling, but the inner world. The world that was Shelamzion. She rolled over and looked at the strong, young body of her husband. He was lying at her side, naked, head pillowed in the crook of his elbow, fast asleep. And just the sight of him made her tremble. Remembering his lips cleaving to hers. The feel of his fingers parting her sex. And the joy of her sex opening, as though it were a deep, moist lily straining ever upwards towards an eternal light.

Then the weight of him, the lean, hard weight of a man who has lived by the sword and knows he will surely die by it. A man who has forgotten how to be gentle, who has done appalling things and things that appalled him. A man who has reached farther than those around him, and in doing so has found himself unreachable. A man so lonely and alone that nothing can save him, save perhaps for love—her love.

He opened his eyes and she was surprised to see that he was instantly alert, without the cloud of sleep that fuddles most beings on wakening. Then she knew that was how it would always be. He would always be surprising her. No matter how long they were together she would never truly know him, and that was part of his wonder and his beauty. The air between them seemed clean and new, cleansed of its tension. And it was strange how this man, whom she had blamed for every travail and ill that had befallen her, had changed not at all, but now was blameless in her eyes. She reached out and stroked his cheek.

'Why?'

'Why?'

'Why did you forgive me?'

He lifted a hand and teased her breast. 'I thought I would either kill you or bed you. Until the final moment, I did not know which it would be.'

He pushed himself up on his elbows and a dark stain was revealed between them. He frowned at it, as though it was a rebuke. 'For so long—I thought that you would rather have had Saul.'

She was quiet for a while, then she said, 'I was only very young and foolish. I thought you were to blame for my brothers' deaths. That stupid jest—'

His face darkened. 'You need not trouble yourself to bring those charges against me. The day does not pass that I do not condemn myself for the looseness of my tongue.'

'No.' Her fingers were on his lips—firm, cool lips. 'Jerusalem was a city of tinder awaiting the first spark. If not Menachem's jest then some other misconstrued remark or too-proud boast would have set the place ablaze. No one could have stopped it.'

'And yet—'

'No. I will not have it. Our true enemy is far off in Caesarea gathering force. And when it is ready it will roll across the land ruthless and indomitable, like a plague sent against Pharaoh, like a black cloud spreading darkness and desolation. And when it has passed, what will be left of our plans, our dreams?' In anguish she got up from the bed. Simon followed her with his eyes. 'Where are you going?'

'To make ready. We must redraft our plans. Or—'

Simon yawned. And now her temper flared. She picked up the nearest object, an embroidered cushion, and threw it at his head. He caught it in one hand and was on his feet before she had time to realise it. For a moment she thought he would strike her, then he lifted her up. To do what? To thrust her away. To crush her between his hands. Shock held her for an instant. Then the leopard—the leopard that was never far beneath her skin—stirred, and she leant forward and bit down on his ear.

They fell on the bed in a Gordian knot of limbs. Struggling, caught up in the violence of the bedclothes. Consumed by fire and madness. Moonlight and sweat glistening on the quivering rise of breasts, the taut thrust of buttocks. Secret openings darkly revealed. Deep breaths, blowing, like primal winds, through their strong young bodies. Flowing, like water over and through each other until, aroused and arousing, each lost themselves completely in the miraculous landscape of the other.

There was silence in the room when Shelamzion stopped speaking. Cornelius cleared his throat several times. Something had happened while his prisoner had been talking. Some uncalled-for rush of emotion had overtaken him, something he could not give name to, but which had left him lustrous of eye and flushed of cheek. Like a portly old Bacchus lost in his cups. He looked blearily at Shelamzion and realized that she was lost in her own thoughts. Love on that scale, even the memory of such love could not be easily brought to the surface without pain. Little wonder it is said *Iove ex alto periuria ridet amantum.* Jove laughs at the false oaths of lovers.

He coughed again and tapped his fingers on the desk. Shelamzion looked up slowly. '*Archon?*'

'You—You must tell me how you entered Jerusalem.'

'Ah, but we did not. Not immediately. Now that Eleazar knew of our plans we needed to meet him with force when we had hoped to use cunning. Simon went back to Idumaea to rouse more troops to his cause.'

'And you?'

'I went with him, of course. Only this time it was different.'

'Because you loved him?'

'Because now every battle was a torture to me. I had prayed for him to die. Now I wanted him to live.'

'It was only natural.'

'Does the Almighty listen to a woman's change of heart?'

'You loved him.'

'Yes. And by that time I was carrying his child.'

Chapter XIX

In a place where no one else is acting like a human being, you must act like a human being.
The sage Hillel

In something of a daze Cornelius mounted the steps to the villa of Valeria
Paulinus. It is no easy thing to enter the villa of man who has threatened
your life—however subtly—even as a dinner guest. Time had failed to heal
the weals of humiliation and fear that still smarted on Cornelius' back whenever he recalled their last encounter. And he felt his vulnerability all the more
keenly as his cloak was taken from him and his feet were washed by Paulinus'
slaves. Anxiously he searched their faces for signs of secret knowledge, but could
detect none.

He entered the dining room—now transformed with elegant couches and
a table groaning beneath its epicurean burden—and heard the soft, penetrating
voice of his host. And such is the pallor of memory compared with living actuality that the sight of Paulinus caused a door to fly open in Cornelius' brain
revealing the violent reds and purples of remembered indignity and despair.
Was it possible that Paulinus had discovered the hidden contents of the letter for
himself? Already on his way to intercept Simon's child? Cornelius stiffened, all
his instincts shrieking at him to turn and flee. But that was impossible under the
circumstances, and so, masking his reluctance with a show of solemnity, he made
his approach.

Paulinus was listening intently to the words of a man who had his back to
Cornelius. From time to time his grave, narrow profile dipped in agreement with
the words of the stranger. But as Cornelius drew level he lifted his head and Cornelius saw, by his expression, that he had been aware of his presence all along.

'Fabius Cornelius, we have been expecting you.'

At the mention of Cornelius' name the man who had held Paulinus' attention
turned round. He was younger than Cornelius had first guessed, with the short,
muscular figure of a soldier, and a slightly protruding belly that hinted of leaves-
of-absence spent too often in the company of Bacchus. 'Our assistant governor?'
He spoke in beautifully accented Greek. And despite Cornelius' insistence on
being known as a *historicus,* he did not correct the stranger. For in truth he was

no stranger at all, but familiar to all as the son of the Emperor Vespasian. Titus Flavius Vespasianus himself.

Titus studied Cornelius with a frank, open curiosity that bore no malice. 'My man, Josephus, speaks well of you. And if you are acquainted with him you will know that sincere praise falls from his lips as often as truth comes out of the mouth of whores. Is that not so, Paulinus?'

'Indeed it is the case,' Paulinus agreed.

'Though he's fond enough of we Romans,' Titus continued. 'Truth to tell, it's his fellow countrymen who most often feel the scourge of his pen. I rather think that if Caesar declared war on the Jews tomorrow, Josephus would be there demanding command of the legions.' He laughed loudly and Paulinus smiled politely.

'But why so dumbstruck?' Titus asked, clapping Cornelius on the shoulder. 'Josephus says you are a man of words. But you stand there without offering me a single gem.'

'I—I did not—'

'You did not expect to find me here as a guest of good Paulinus.'

Cornelius licked his lips. 'It is only that I was mistaken in my belief. I thought you still with the fleet.'

'But you are not mistaken. I am still adrift on Neptune's ceiling. It is quite certain.'

Cornelius blinked. 'I fear I do not—'

Titus laughed again, a laugh that was as refreshing and maddening as a solitary droplet of rain falling on parched earth. He swept an arm towards Paulinus. 'Our host is the master of appearances. You must consider me a conjuring of his invention. Rome expects a hero. Not a bedraggled wretch spent from too much battle and salt water. So he has spirited me away in order that I might find refreshment in the taste of good wine and the comfort of excellent friends. To-morrow he will present me to Rome as the lithesome, glad-eyed youth they have awaited.'

Cornelius looked to Paulinus, who merely smiled his polite and secret smile. Titus looked as though he was about to say more. But at that moment the din-ing-room slaves appeared and Cornelius was led to a space evidently reserved for him on the couch opposite.

As he reclined with more stiffness than grace, Cornelius was disappointed to find himself placed between a rather listless young man—introduced as Junius Fortunatus, a senator's son—and a well-known Stoic, called Kaeso, who had obviously been at great pains to advertise his philosophical leanings by coming dressed as shabbily as possible. Titus and Paulinus sat opposite and were joined by Josephus, who made a late and colourful entry, bowing in his Eastern man-ner and offering apologies in a voice so contrite it seemed almost mocking. He sat on the left side of Titus and acknowledged Cornelius with a gracious bow of the head. Cornelius returned the nod rather self-consciously. He was painfully aware of having stood before Caesar's son and yet having done nothing to present himself as a true adherent to Akademos. If he was to have the slightest hope of bringing his history into the conversation he must first present himself as a scholar in the minds of those around him. And with this in mind he made a comment on the charming arrangement of the dinner table to the listless young man at his side, adding, 'Are we not cautioned to be worthy so that the gods might invite us to dine?'

'Are we?' asked the young man without interest.

'Indeed.' Cornelius was a little taken aback. 'The *Ecologues* are abundantly clear on the subject.'

'The Ecologues?'

'Virgil's *Ecologues*.'

'O, Virgil. No one reads him nowadays.'

Cornelius threw a startled look at the Stoic, who shrugged his ill-shod shoulders. 'War, that's all the young want to hear about. Heroes and triumphs. Booty and conquests.' He looked venomously at Titus, who laughed good-naturedly and raised his cup. 'Ah, Kaeso, would that you had been at my side in Jerusalem. You would have cooled the passions of those Jews and taught them to disdain obsession and love indifference.'

'Then I can only assume they make better students than you ever did,' Kaeso answered tartly. He reached out a hand and took a most unrestrained fistful of truffles. 'You might otherwise have avoided the conflagration of an entire city.'

Cornelius gasped at the audacity of the Stoic, but Titus merely shrugged and turned to Josephus 'I'll give you my leave to answer the old goat, I think.'

Josephus' smile did not waver. He turned his midnight gaze on the Stoic and his voice was as soft and mesmerizing as any serpent's slither. 'Conflagration could not be avoided, I think. These were strange times. The world was changing and nothing was certain.'

'I beg to differ,' the listless young man interrupted. 'You had taken on the might of Rome. Your fate was surely sealed.'

Josephus lifted his wine cup and took a slow, meditative sip. 'And yet, Fortunatus, there was a prophecy that suggested that the ruler of the world would come from Judea.'

Cornelius glanced up sharply. He had heard of no such prophecy. But Kaeso said tartly, 'As you have provided so incontrovertible a motivation for the war, you must surely sympathise with those who were the architects of its design.'

Josephus' smile froze a little. He put his wine cup down and gazed into its depths. 'That I initially had sympathy with the agitators is no secret. As I said, these were strange, unsettling times. What might seem the most pristine truth one day was clearly shown to be falsehood by the next.' He paused, and drew a long, manicured finger around the rim of his cup. When he looked up his eyes were far away. 'Ours is a strange and mysterious deity. His ways are not to be questioned. That He sided with the Romans is evident. The destruction of Jerusalem's Temple—that too was His will. And it is certain that He perverted the judgement of the city fathers when they chose to escape the tyranny of John of Gischala and his Zealots by naming Simon bar Gioras as their saviour.'

'Come now, that is too harsh.' Titus was leaning back, holding out his goblet, into which a slave was pouring a perfect arc of wine. 'Gioras was a fine commander. It is not unreasonable that the people looked to him as their protector.'

Josephus shrugged. 'That he had low, barbarous cunning I do not deny. But a more wicked tyrant could scarcely have been imagined. Such was the vileness of his crimes it is a wonder the people did not think that Herod the Great was master of the city once more. And it must be said that Simon, like Herod, was not a true descendant of our esteemed ancestor Abraham, but the son of a convert—'

'Are the figs not to your taste?' Paulinus' quiet voice broke through Josephus' rising tones. There was a frozen pause in which Cornelius realized that all eyes were upon him, and that he was sitting in a stiffened attitude, his hand rigid above an earthenware dish, a plump yellow fig he did not remember lifting held in the cage of his fist, his fingers driven deep into the golden flesh. He closed his eyes, and in an instant the sound of Shelamzion's voice was in his head.

The camp was in tumult. Moments ago Zacchaeus had burst into Simon's tent, with so little of the usual formalities that there was scarcely time for Simon and Shelamzion to jump apart. They had been dining together, celebrating their return to the walls of Jerusalem, their army swollen with Idumaean recruits. Simon had been teasing his wife with a fig held just beyond reach of her lips. And Zacchaeus entered under cover of their laughter, and was almost upon them before either recognized the invasion of a third presence.

'Zacchaeus.' Simon got to his feet. He had dropped the fig, which now rolled from the table with a small but distinct plop as it hit the ground. Puzzled, Zacchaeus looked down at the fallen fruit. He seemed to sense a significance was attached to it, but found it beyond his ken to give it interpretation. He looked questioningly at his general. Simon coughed. 'What news?' he asked firmly.

'A delegation is coming.'

'From which direction?'

'From the city.'

Glances were exchanged. 'Are they John of Gischala's men?' Simon asked.

Zacchaeus rubbed a weather-beaten cheek. 'They are too far out for even the keenest eyes to tell. I have sent out an escort to bring them here at once.'

Simon clapped him on the shoulder. 'You have done well. Go then, bring this delegation to me.' And before Zacchaeus was out of the tent he turned to

Shelamzion. 'Have them bring a casket from the ones we took in Beersheba. I think the occasion calls for a fine Caecuban.'

She went smiling, knowing what he was thinking. Surely this was John, his old friendship with Simon remembered at last. And with John on their side the power of the Zealots would crumble, like the stone feet of the beast in the dream of Nebuchadnezzar.

But it was not John who came. The man who stood before Simon had green eyes set in a face prematurely lined, and a restless motion of his shoulders, as though there was something on his back he was forever trying to shrug off.

'I am James ben Sosas,' he announced as soon as he was led before Simon. 'I was in command of a faction of Idumaean foot soldiers in the city.'

'I know who you are,' Simon said coolly. 'What I wish to know is why you are here.'

And that much, at least, was simple. Fired up with the thought of defending Jerusalem against the unclean invasion of Rome, ben Sosas had led his men out of Idumaea. Simple men full of simple belief. They had followed Eleazar and John against Ananus' party, filled with righteous enthusiasm, only gradually beginning to question the direction that their blind faith was taking them.

'I had thought that wealth corrupted a man's morals,' ben Sosas said, the lines of his face deep as a scribe's scratches on wax. 'But I tell you this, Simon bar Gioras. If you would see the true nature of a human being then give him power. I have seen Zealots dragging good, God-fearing citizens into courts so corrupt that Herod the Great would have blushed to call them halls of justice. And this also I will say. No man, who had two gold pieces to his name, ever came out again. Indeed the juries were lucky to escape with their lives if they dared deviate from the predetermined verdicts.'

Simon took a sip of his wine. But it was clear from the fixed expression of his eyes that he had tasted nothing. 'And John, he did nothing to put an end to this?'

Ben Sosas shrugged. 'He broke with Eleazar. But, in doing so, he made allegiance with the Galileans. You know the sort, rough, coarse, northern men, who fall on the effects of the rich as starving wolves upon a bloated corpse. John holds the lower city and spends all his time now attacking the Zealots, who hide behind the Temple walls. '

'Then John might be persuaded to make an alliance.'

For answer ben Sosas reached into his sleeve and pulled out a small silver coin. He tossed it to Simon, who caught it then held it up to for all to see. Shelamzion leaned over his shoulder and found herself looking at a silver shekel, newly minted. On John's orders? Bearing the inscription *YEAR 3*. As though nothing had existed before the insurrection. As though all Israel's long, fertile history could be condensed into the tumultuous violence of the last three years. Simon turned the coin over, and the obverse face showed a seven-branched menorah flanked on either side by an olive branch. The words below read *l'goalit tzion*. For the redemption of Zion. And she drew in a sharp breath. It did not take the learned daughter of Rabbi Judah ben Eliad to understand the message encapsulated by this little coin. The two olive branches. The two prophets. The messiah of Aaron and the messiah of David. The anointed witnesses who would redeem the light of the nation. And John believed it. He believed in apocalypse. In disease and famine. In earth scorched black and rivers of blood. He believed the end of days was upon them. And to disagree was to become the enemy.

'John will not make an alliance,' she whispered.

Even so, ben Sosas heard her. 'It is true, John will make no alliance. But the party of Ananus is not dead. You were wronged once by it. But Matthias, the High Priest, now leads them. He sends me here to tell you that they beg deliverance from John and Eleazar. Only give the word and the gates will be flung wide to welcome the son of Gioras.'

'A sceptre shall arise out of Israel; he shall cleanse the Temple and destroy all the sons of tumult.'

In surprise, all heads turned towards the tent's entrance. Ariel was standing there. His Essene ways not yet given up, he had entered soundlessly, but his rich voice carried and his meaning was clearly perceived by all. There was silence. Shelamzion glanced at Simon's face. But already he was getting to his feet, not liking what he had heard.

'Such words do not befit me. I am a common soldier, not a messiah.'

Ariel bowed his grisly head. 'No.' But his eyes lifted, and they were filled with splendour. 'Not a messiah—a king.'

Cornelius' eyes opened and he was surprised to find himself at the table with the emperor's son, and only a moment seeming to have passed. Valerius Paulinus was proving to be a generous and entertaining host. From the groaning table arose an effusion of aromas, tantalizing as gaseous nymphs sent by Dionysus himself. Cornelius, who was schooled in restraint, found himself succumbing to a second helping of oysters, and he noticed from the corner of his eye that the listless young man, Fortunatus, had found the energy to slip a roast partridge into his napkin then discretely pass it to his body slave. Josephus, he observed, did not eat from the table, but was handed a series of dishes brought in by one of the household slaves. A concession to those strange laws of diet the Jews insisted upon. Yet what had he dined upon in the days when Vespasian still held him captive in chains?

Reaching for another oyster, Cornelius could not help but suspect that Josephus had managed to make peace with his god while saving his own skin. Or was that only Shelamzion's bitter opinion whispering viperously in his ear? Indeed, how had she overcome her distaste for unclean food? His hand, heading towards the oysters yet again, froze. Had not the *custos* complained that sometimes the food was left untouched? A soup containing perfectly acceptable mussels had been disdained. Were there other such times that she went without rather than break covenant with her exacting deity? The thought that a simple word from her—or a little more thought on his own part—might have saved unnecessary suffering filled him with a tumult of warring emotions. Foolish woman to starve herself in the midst of plenty. He wanted to punish her. He wanted to embrace her. For an instant the confusion of his feelings threatened to overwhelm him. He took a deep swallow from his wine cup to calm himself. What woman had ever held the reins of his spirit so cruelly, jerking him from high to low simply by the mechanism of appearing in his thoughts? Titus laughed loudly at something Fortunatus was saying and Cornelius' heart lurched. Now Titus was returned, how soon would his bandit queen's mysterious hold over him be severed forever?

Lowering his wine cup, he gazed dolorously over at his host. He had been afraid to come here. Yet it seemed inclusion was the pinnacle of his success. If Paulinus still distrusted Josephus he no longer showed it. Josephus was the man of the hour and Cornelius was surely benefiting from having chosen his friends wisely. Yet the victory felt hollow. He deposited his cup on the table with unintended force and Paulinus' shrewd eyes suddenly looked up. 'Perhaps, friend, you would give us the benefit of your opinion.'

Cornelius swallowed and shifted uncomfortably on his couch. 'My—my opinion?'

There was a pause, then Paulinus continued, 'Our young friend Fortunatus contends that Eastern minds have a rigid constancy about them that causes them to fall into arrogant self-righteousness no matter how the facts may stand in blatant opposition.'

The listless young man shrugged 'They say Jews and Ægyptians care for only two things. To make battles out of their religions and pilgrimages out of their wars.' He gazed defiantly at Josephus, then moving his look to Titus' face, quickly lowered his eyes and muttered, 'Present company excepted, naturally.'

'I have not found all Jews to be singular in their inclinations,' Titus said. 'Some are varied and ... most fragrant in their attitudes.'

Something in the softness of his expression took Cornelius unawares. He had heard the rumours, of course. Titus' dalliance with the Jewish queen, Berenice, was common gossip in every barber shop in Rome. That she was queen of that pauper kingdom, Chalcis, and not Judea made her no less suspect in a world where the lines between Jew and Judean were beginning to blur. Still it was faintly shocking to hear it from Titus' own lips. He felt Fortunatus move uncomfortably beside him.

'Berenice is of the Herodian line. I do not dispute that she is of noble blood. It is the common Jew I was referring to.'

'The common Jew,' Titus said quietly. 'I don't believe I ever came across such a creature.' He looked across at Cornelius. 'So, Assistant Governor, has your experience taught you that all Jews are alike?'

Cornelius felt Paulinus' eyes boring into him, but he kept his voice steady as he answered, 'Our friend Fortunatus makes a youthful error in thinking his enemy may be painted all in one colour. Men are not born equals. Such a concept would plainly be absurd to the educated mind. Why, then, should we assume that base instincts are received in equal measure? Society separates itself into a hierarchy from high to low. That is as Nature decrees.' And encouraged by the slow smile spreading across Titus' lips, he finished with a simple yet elegant epigram. 'Nobility is like oil burning brightly from a lamp. Yet mixed with water still it rises to the top.'

Titus' laugh was as refreshing and startling as ever. But it was to his host he turned. 'So you are right, Paulinus. The bandit queen has charms all her own. Our assistant governor seems quite smitten.'

Cornelius' mouth fell open. 'I do not deny I have a certain—scholarly interest in the war. The lady in question provides a unique historical perspective on the motivation of its leading general.' He looked anxiously at Josephus, hoping for the endorsement of a fellow scholar. But Josephus answered with an epigram of his own.

'When the bandit queen falls to her knees and prays for peace,
'her husband, Simon, lifts his sword and cries out, "War! War!"'.

The words fell, like drops, into Cornelius' cup. His eyes followed them into the swirling depths, and further into the private world of memory.

Not war, nor insurrection, nor pillage, nor bloodshed could destroy Shelamzion's joy at entering Jerusalem, not as a prisoner, not even as the daughter of a respected rabbi, but as Simon's wife. The people lined the dusty streets to watch Simon arriving at the head of his men. And he came not as a king would enter, on horseback or in a gilded litter hoisted on the bronzed shoulders of slaves, but on foot with the simplicity of a peasant and the humility of a prophet. Yet they greeted him as a king. '*Melech! Melech!*' Here is a king! And the trumpet swell of ram's horn and the impossible jewel brightness of the day made Shelamzion see Simon as those around her saw him. Yes. Here was a king. And she was his queen.

They were taken to the palace of the Hasmoneans, led down the long, cool corridors with their whorled mosaics and smoky lights by Matthias. The High Priest no less. He was not much like the high priests of old. The arrogance and superciliousness had been ripped out of him, and he had a wandering, deferential manner, clinging to Simon even as he purported to lead the way. Shelamzion found that she did not much like him, but it was a small price to pay for the joy of the day.

A feast was held in their honour—no easy thing in a city that had been ruled by a Zealot's hand—And, knowing this, she prepared with extra care, choosing to wear a silk gown of sapling green, trimmed in red. The darting, geometric embroidery, so typical of the north, gave her a pang. This was done by a hand such as Mariamme's or Ami's, and she closed her eyes and whispered through clenched teeth, 'Let them be found. If there is justice upon this earth then let them be safe and well.'

'Wife?'

Turning guiltily, she found Simon framed in the arch of the doorway. He was dressed in blue, the priestly blue that no woman would dare to garb herself in. He looked down at her, smiling. 'I have come for my wife. But instead I find a great and noble lady.'

Her brow arched. 'And who then is your wife?'

'A good and virtuous woman.'

'Indeed?' Deliberately she turned her back on him. 'Rumour has it that she is a wanton.'

His hand was on her neck and she shivered then went on hoarsely, 'It is said that she will perform acts no virtuous woman would perform for her husband.' And then she said no more because his mouth was over hers.

At the feasting Shelamzion sat with the women, smiling to hear them vying to announce that they had been first to call Simon their saviour. And all the while she had to fight the perverse urge to laugh at them then shout, *It is me he has chosen, the one who doubted him most of all!*

And, when it was at last all over, the revellers making their way drunkenly to bed, Shelamzion and Simon crept up to the vast marble balcony that overlooked the city, and stood watching dawn breaking above the Temple Mount. And Shelamzion found it strange and stirring to look down upon Jerusalem and to know that the future rested on the shoulders of the man at her side.

'Can it be done?' She asked not because she doubted, but because she wanted to hear him speak. His answer surprised her.

'I gravely doubt it.'

Tilting her face towards him, she looked for jest in his expression, but there was none to be found. 'You do not mean it.'

He turned to face her and brushed a curl from her cheek. 'What is this? Such blind faith from my greatest apostate?'

Her cheeks burned. 'I have learnt better.'

'No, never say that. You heard them tonight, calling me saviour. And even old Ariel would count me as a king. My mother spoke true when she said men raise leaders up as gods then cast them down as false idols.'

'But not you.' Her hand reached out and touched his face. 'They cannot knock you down because you will never see yourself as a god. If ever there was a man of the people it is Simon bar Gioras.'

He smiled, and his smile was a light in her heart. 'And you will always be there to remind me that I am a man.'

'Always.' Then to tease him she added, 'And if I am not—' His look of anguish surprised her, and she grasped his hand and quickly drew it to her belly. 'Then another will keep you in mind of your earthly place.'

He gaped at her. Simon suddenly speechless in the face of the most natural thing in the world. And she laughed and pushed him away. 'If you will not save the city for the sake of your wife then you must do it for your son.'

He did not offer her promises or take back his doubts. Instead, sinking to his knees, he grasped her waist in his big hands and laid his head against her softly swelling abdomen. And she stood stroking his black hair, feeling there was nothing their love could not accomplish, while at her back the rising sun struck Jerusalem and the city burst into flames in the conflagration of a new day.

'You can't save her, you know.'

Cornelius' head snapped up. He was taken aback to find that his chin had been resting on his chest and that the wreathe of roses he'd been wearing had slipped over one eye. On the table his wine cup, which had been full a moment ago, had mysteriously emptied itself, and he had the vague impression that it was Paulinus who had spoken to him. He felt an overpowering urge to correct him. 'She is innocent!' he cried. Then because both Paulinus and Titus were staring at him peculiarly, 'What crime has she committed save for falling in love with a man during inauspicious times?' It was a bold statement, and he felt a sobering wash of anxiety flood his veins, but it was too late to retract. There was a silence, and Titus' flushed face grew grave. 'How truly you speak, friend.' His look drew everyone in. 'Gentlemen, here we sit at good Paulinus' table, numbering between the Muses and the Graces. Let us drink then to a woman who would bring both graciousness and wisdom were she here with us tonight.' He lifted his cup, and Cornelius, moved almost to tears, followed suit.

'Shela—'

'Berenice!' the cry went up. And there was only just enough time for Cornelius to turn his tribute into a cough before the foolishness of his error was noted. He made a display of dabbing at his mouth with a napkin to allow himself time to recover. Berenice. Of course, Berenice. It was not to him Paulinus addressed his words, but to Titus and his infatuation with the Jewish queen. He dropped his napkin, with what he hoped was an air of carelessness, but when he dared to raise his eyes Paulinus was watching him intently. Cornelius felt his mouth go dry, and he opened it and closed it several times trying to think of something to say. At last he cast a piteous glance in Josephus' direction, who, seeming to understand, leant forward, sucking his bottom lip as though wanting to ask something but unsure how to begin. At last, when everyone's attention was on him, he said, 'My dear old friend, I am afraid you have bad news for me.'

Cornelius was bewildered. 'I fear I do not—'

'Indeed.' A body slave held out a dish to Josephus and he plucked a small bunch of black grapes from it before returning to Cornelius. 'We have not seen each other in many weeks. Yet you sit opposite me these last hours with no mention of the offering I sent to you.'

And now Cornelius understood. He beamed gratefully at his co-scholar. '*The Rise of Herod*. You must forgive the slow wit of an old man for not mentioning it sooner.'

Josephus shook his head sadly. 'Yet I fear it did not please you.'

'No, no.' Cornelius was eager to make amends. 'Indeed you mistake me. I enjoyed it in no small measure. You combine the composure of the most detached intellect with passionate involvement. The dullest reader would admire your talent for transforming the mundane into the epic, which is, believe me, a skill few writers recognise and fewer still possess.' Feeling on surer ground, he turned to Titus. 'I hope our friend here has not been too modest in sharing his work.'

Titus, who was negotiating his wine cup to his lips none too steadily, nodded without looking up. 'I have read his scribblings, be assured.' He raised his head and winked at Cornelius. 'And I'll admit he has some small talent for a story.'

Josephus laughed then miss-swallowed the grape he had been eating. His laughter became a choking cough, which raised much merriment round the table. Even Paulinus smiled. And Cornelius, feeling reckless, added, 'By your reaction I would deduce that Roman criticism has too strong a flavour for the Jewish palate.'

There was a pause, then Fortunatus almost fell from his seat and old Kaeso held his sides as though they were fit to burst. Wiping tears from his eyes, Titus reached across and patted Josephus on the back, barking at a slave to bring some water. Gradually Josephus stopped coughing and the flush on his cheeks died away.

'What a talent was near lost to Rome,' Kaeso remarked dryly. And Titus, still patting his companion affectionately on the back, replied, 'Indeed. For, with this worthy friend gone, who would finish the history of the Jewish war?'

The muscles of Cornelius' face were still stretched with anticipated mirth, and they did not fully respond to the incredulity in his voice as he repeated, 'He— He is writing a history of the Jewish war?'

Titus nodded vigorously. 'The blood will scarce have dried on the battlefield before the ink is wet on the parchment. History as it happens. Who else could have come up with such a bold plan?' He squeezed Josephus' shoulder, but Josephus seemed disinclined to look up. Cornelius stared at him with burning eyes, while Josephus' head remained modestly bowed.

'Interesting,' Kaeso said softly. 'How differently the *Punic War* might have been had it been penned by Hannibal.'

Josephus looked up sharply. 'Yet Hannibal lacked the flexibility of intellect to appreciate his enemy's motives ... to recognise when they could not have acted otherwise.'

'You refer, of course, to the burning of the Temple,' Paulinus suggested.

Josephus stiffened, and his eyes flicked towards Cornelius, but did not rest there. 'I have the capacity to recognise that it was God's will,' he said evenly. 'There had been portents telling of a voice, as of a host, coming from the Sanctuary, crying *We are departing hence.* God had abandoned us—'

'Perhaps he ran in fear from Jove and Mars,' Fortunatus interrupted. 'A fiery death is a horror ... even to divinity.'

Josephus laughed, though his eyes were filled with hate. 'That is, of course, one interpretation. When you read my history perhaps I will persuade you of another.'

'And will you also persuade us that you have first-hand knowledge of the motivation and purposes of those you betrayed?' Cornelius asked in a shaking voice. He was going too far, attacking Josephus openly, but a huge anger seized him and he pointed a trembling finger across the table. 'Can you claim to offer unbiased assessment of those men who would now call you traitor? Or will you be forced to steal the ideas of others when you come to write that which you so blithely call—*your history!*' A chasm of silence opened up. And teetering on the edge of it, Cornelius had just time to see Titus' puzzled countenance turn towards his favourite, and Josephus' faint, dismissive shrug, before the profusion of wine coursing in his veins began to make the room spin. Suddenly it was impossible to breathe and he grasped at the table's edge. 'I—' He struggled to focus on his host. 'I fear I ... have outstayed my welcome. Forgive me, but I must take my leave.'

Paulinus bowed his head, and it was a measure of Cornelius' desperation that he felt no twinge that his farewell was accomplished with no element of regretful protest from the party.

Outside, Cornelius stumbled down the broad steps in front of the villa to await his litter. That he had disgraced himself before his superiors, that he had spoken openly and recklessly before Vespasian's self-confessed spymaster seemed to matter little. All he could think about was his history, now lost to the viperous grasp of a traitor. A man clever enough to recognise vanity in another and to know its worth as a weapon. All that talk of 'we scholars', the keen yet humble interest in Cornelius' work. And how he, Cornelius Flavius Grammaticus, lapped it up, the easy flattery, the cloying plaudits. Eyes focusing so far into the glittering future that he did not notice how his history was being taken from beneath his nose. With a groan, Cornelius leaned his forehead against the coolness of a pillar and closed his eyes.

A noise behind him made him stiffen. He opened his eyes painfully and found Kaeso standing there. The Stoic looked at him with neither pity nor contempt. 'You do not like history?'

Cornelius blinked then said an emphatic, 'No!'

'Strange. I would have taken you for a scholarly soul.'

Cornelius said nothing, and Kaeso shrugged and turned to look at the sky. It was still light, the inky darkness only just beginning to suffuse the fading blue. And for a while they stood there, with Kaeso looking at the sky and Cornelius looking at Kaeso. And when Kaeso spoke again it was almost to himself. 'There will be a Triumph, you know.'

Cornelius nodded, though Kaeso was not looking at him. Kaeso rubbed the stubble of his chin, but his eyes were unblinking. 'A triumph,' he repeated. 'They have burned the great temple of the East and they think they have rid themselves of the Jewish god.'

'You don't believe it?' Cornelius was curious despite himself. The Stoic turned to meet his gaze and his expression was grave. 'A god does not die because his temple has been destroyed. Did Zeus die when his temple was burned by the Persian horde? Did Artemis vanish after Herostratus' villainous act?' Kaeso's eyes stole back to the heavens. 'The Jewish god is out in the world now, and who can say what will happen?'

Chapter XX

John and Simon were strong in numbers and equipment, Eleazar in position. There were continual skirmishes, surprises, and incendiary fires, and a vast quantity of corn was burnt.
Tacitus, *Historiae*, Book I

Seated behind his desk within the Carcer, head sunk in his hands, Cornelius waited through minutes long as eternities. He had arrived indecently early, unable to contain his desolation until the proper hour, and demanded that Shelamzion be brought at once. She came owl-eyed and anxious. And she was barely seated before he began to pour out his wrath towards her fellow countryman. While he stormed and blustered she made no attempt to interrupt or gainsay him. Not even when he was finally spent and retreated behind the fleshy bars of his fingers. She remained silent. Yet he sensed she was watching him. At last he permitted himself a long, low groan. 'I cannot go on.'

'You do not know that.'

He slammed his fists down on the desk. 'My history is gone. Did you not understand what I told you? Your friend Josephus has stolen my idea.'

'Josephus is no friend of mine.'

Cornelius dismissed this comment with a shrug of his shoulders. 'Not your friend. Certainly not mine. Everything I have worked for—Everything I have striven to—' He could not continue. His head sank towards the desk. 'Gone.'

'Archon?'

He could not lift his head, could not bear to look at a woman who must now be regarding him with scorn. Nonetheless, he gave a faint acknowledgement to her query, and she went on, 'In my cell, I hear things from the window. People calling to each other as they cross the Forum.'

'Are they calling the glories of Rome's newest historian?'

'They talk of a Triumph … You must tell me. Will it be soon?'

He shrugged. 'Titus is returned. It cannot be long—' He broke off, unable to stomach the thought of where his words were leading him. He raised his head a little, but still avoided Shelamzion's eye.

'*Archon*, what news of my son?'

It was the question he had been dreading. His rant against Josephus had been partly motivated by the need to avoid the inevitable. But now she had asked it. *What news of my son?* As the silence drew out between them she began to wring her hands. 'Tell me. There is something. I can see by your face.'

Cornelius closed his eyes and drew in a sharp breath. 'The news—All the information I had of your son came from a single man, a Jew—'

'No! No, it cannot be.' She would not let him speak the name aloud. 'You are lying.' Her hands flew to her temples and she began pacing up and down, murmuring wildly to herself. 'You are angry with me. Yes. Yes. That explains everything. You are saying these things to frighten me—'

'Lady—'

But she would not let him speak. 'I should not have asked. The time is not right.'

'You must listen—'

'Tomorrow.' Her eyes were very bright. 'We will talk of this tomorrow. And then—'

'Flavius Josephus is the singular source of all my information concerning your son.' He shouted the words, hurling them, like rocks, wanting to break down her denial. She fell silent, her back turned to him. And though she did not argue, neither did she show any sign of having heard. 'Lady, do you understand me?'

'I understand.' Her reply was so low he barely heard it, yet it tore sorely at his heart. Wanting to explain, he went on quickly with an intensity that verged on desperation. 'You can trust nothing I have divulged to you. The sympathetic centurion, Aelius Celatus, the depositions of the legionaries. Most of all the mysterious *Laelius Kaetus* hauling his stepson all the way to the Brittanic Isles—All are doubtless pieces in Josephus' curious puzzle.' He sighed. 'As indeed are we.'

Shelamzion turned slowly to face him, eyes still downcast. 'Then I have been his dupe. Even here.' She raised her gaze slowly to meet his. 'But why? He has his freedom. What threat am I?'

'You threaten him only in that you know him. He is Rome's darling, and he cannot afford truth to sully the pristine quality of his lies. All this time I have been his creature, his eyes and ears inside this cell.'

'Then all I have said, all I have told you—You believed none of it.'

Cornelius' felt his jaw working, but all his eloquence had fled. At last he said, 'Who am I to decide that one voice speaks the truth while another lies—' He meant to go on, but she was staring at him so coldly that he faltered then grew silent.

She drew herself up. And he realized he had not seen that gesture of imperious defiance since their first encounter. It was her shield, her only protection against Rome, and now she used it against him. Feeling that something was being torn from him, he got to his feet. 'Lady—'

But she only demanded, 'Why now?'

He understood what she was asking and wished he did not. 'Now that Titus is back in Rome Josephus is untouchable. I do not believe he deliberately engineered mention of his history, but it was no great concern to him that his intentions should be thus revealed.' He hurried to the front of the desk, but did not dare draw nearer. She was like a column of ice, and he—a representative of the mightiest nation on earth—could only stand before her mumbling what they both already knew. 'Josephus is careless of his secrets because he believes you are discredited and your days left on earth … too few to matter.'

She nodded bleakly. 'Then all my hopes are shattered.'

Cornelius watched her turn away, shoulders hunched, and thought she would begin to weep. Instead she murmured, 'I am to blame. I have listened to false prophets. And look how they have brought me low.'

And there was so much defeat in her voice that Cornelius grew frightened. 'Do not give in to despair. Not yet.' But she only hunched further over the dull axis of her pain until hopelessness and blind instinct made him cry, 'Shelamzion!'

Her name, so strange upon his lips, drew her slowly round to face him. She stood wordlessly, an expression of puzzlement scintillating in the black depths of her eyes. And Cornelius, finding her name to be a key which had unlocked a Pandora's box of suppressed feeling, could only blurt out, 'My dear, I gave you hope once. Let me do so again.'

'How can this be?'

'Let me save you.' He saw her draw back and plunged ahead before she could deny him. 'I am not a young man, but neither am I a poor one. I have a small villa far from here in Calabria. We would be safe there.'

'And would you have me walk out of here on your arm?'

'I have thought of that.' He glanced at the door, as though just recalling it, and lowered his voice. 'Truth to tell, I believe I have been thinking of it since I first laid eyes upon you.' He felt a rush of exuberance and would have liked to have taken her hands in his, but she was looking at him so oddly that his courage failed. Instead he went on rapidly, 'We shall say that, overcome with grief, you took your own life.'

'They will want to see the body.'

'This is Rome. Every morning sees the *cohortes urbanae* clearing bodies from the alleyways. A few hundred sesterces in the right hands will provide us with the evidence we need. Remember you are not well known here. I will have some official identify the death as the wife of Simon, then the body will be spirited away to the common pit before suspicion is aroused. They will call me an overzealous fool, and I will resign, naturally. You will be hidden in my villa and we will depart for Calabria at once.' She was silent so long that he felt compelled to add, 'I do you no dishonour by this proposal. I mean to make you my wife.'

'My husband is not yet dead,' she said sharply, then seeing his crestfallen look, added more gently, 'It is a good plan. A noble one. But, *archon*, be certain that Josephus is already aware of it. By your own admission you have been his creature and you will have betrayed yourself in a thousand unknowing ways in each moment you have spent in his company.'

He felt a surge of hopeless anger. 'You will not do it?'

'I will not.'

'Then you do not want to live.'

And now she, too, was angry. 'Who has shown me what befalls those who tamper with the seals of fate? I will die, *archon*. The Lord has decreed it. But I will not have your life on my conscience too.'

Cornelius opened his mouth then closed it again. How had it happened that their situations were now reversed? The captive suddenly granting life to the captor. It was against reason. It shook the cool foundations of his Hellenized logic; the lamb does not grant life to the lion. He found he was looking at her yet did not see her. And unable to bear his gaze, she turned away. Then he, moving like an old man, walked slowly back to his desk and sat down.

For some minutes her face was hidden to him, and only the rapid rise and fall of her shoulders told of the battle she fought with her demons. At last she gave a long, shuddering breath, and when she turned to face him her expression was composed.

'Come, we are wasting time.'

He looked at her without comprehension, and she gave a nod to the pens lying upon the desk. 'You will need one in order to write.'

Cornelius found his fingers curling around a slim length of reed. 'But what am I to write?'

'Your history. I had described Simon's defeat at the Temple, had I not—'

'But this is preposterous.'

'Preposterous? Why? Because Josephus has received royal sanction to write his own version of events?'

'Yes. And any attempt to offer a variant will be deemed ridiculous at best, or, worse, it will be seen as seditious. Surely you—'

Without warning, she strode to the desk, and grabbing the first papyrus to hand, began tearing it to pieces.

'Lady!' Cornelius struggled to his feet. 'What madness is this?'

'Madness? Why, none at all.' She gave a shrill laugh. 'What use are these jottings now? Should we preserve truth when the world would rather read a toadying defence of Empire? No, better to destroy these and help prolong a traitor's life.' Her hand reached out for another scroll.

'No!' He thrust himself forward, hands stretching protectively over the crumpled papyri. It was little defence. There were dozens of scrolls and she was a madwoman. They faced each other over an infinite moment where anything could happen until Cornelius whispered, 'What do you ask of me?' For an instant he thought she would ignore him, that she would go on destroying all those months of meticulous work. But slowly she put down the shreds of papyrus, and breathing heavily so that her words were forced out in torn rags, she said, 'Finish what you began.'

He could not take his eyes from her. 'I cannot.'

'Not now. Not yet. Did you not teach me that a battle's history is written by the last man standing? Hide your manuscript. Time will be its guardian and secrecy its friend.'

Cornelius' fingers tightened round the pen, then slackened. 'But even if men were one day to read it. Who will dare believe it?'

She bit her lips. 'I do not know. Perhaps there will come a time when a braver breed of men walks upon the earth. Men who dream of freedom as the greatest good.' Her expression grew wistful. 'Surely in this strange, contradictory world the Lord intended that such a time would come to pass.'

Cornelius lifted his pen then shook his head. 'What could I write that Josephus will not already have told?' Despite his best efforts the question trembled on a note of suppressed eagerness, which she seized on, leaning her hands on the desk and stretching over it so that their faces came close to touching.

'You ask what you will write. Let me ask this. Did Josephus come into Jerusalem in those last days? Was it he who suffered and bled behind its walls?' She thrust out her hand. 'Only close your eyes and I will take you there. I will show you what really happened, the things Josephus cannot know. Do not forget, he is Caesar's puppet, and doomed to write the sycophant's honeyed words. But you—' She leant forward and he could smell the hot exhalations of her mouth. 'You can change everything. I do not care if I am to be a forgotten line in history. But how can you, of all men, sit there and leave Josephus the final word?' Her lips were so close, her eyes as big as stars, as she searched his face. 'Will you, my last hope, condemn Simon to become a monster in the eternity of men's memories?'

Even after she had stopped speaking he could not find his voice. Could not look at her without thinking of the moment when this woman, whom he knew as no other, who had stood before him speaking with the calm voice of a seer or trembling on a precipice of emotion, who had made him angry and defensive and confused and sometimes happier than he had known was possible—This woman, whom he had grown to love, would soon be crushed from existence beneath the relentless wheel of Roman justice and there was nothing, not the smallest thing he could do to prevent it. There were tears in his eyes as he bowed his head and reached out to dip the reed pen into the inkpot.

The hands of the little boy were grubby with all the grime of Jerusalem's streets. Any true queen would have recoiled at the sight of them, much less the touch. But Shelamzion was not a true queen. She was a rabbi's daughter, who had lived beyond her years and seen too much to sit in her palace, gorgeously adorned and serene, while people on the streets went hungry.

And hungry they were. Three years of war had changed the Judean land-scape forever. Jerusalem, the mighty city, now sat like the blind eye of a cease-less storm. And, radiating out from all sides were devastated fields and ruined orchards; the peasants who had worked them and nurtured them down through countless generations long fled or murdered in the name of something they did not understand. And Shelamzion, listening to the reports that came from as far as Capernaum and Caesarea, knew that she was living on borrowed time. Each day brought fewer caravans into the city, and those that came had fewer things to sell. She had seen the gaunt faces of mothers handing over their jewels, while one, two—three if they pleaded—scoops of grain went into their pitiful sacks. At their feet, children scrabbled in the dust and the dung, looking for fallen grains as though they were treasures. Shelamzion had watched and then she had turned and gone to seek Simon.

'We must feed the people.'

He looked up from the map he had been studying and smiled, but there were dark shadows smudging his skin, and his eyes were troubled. 'We have an army to feed.'

'This city has been ruled by three generations of the Herodian line. Even with the last one gone there is grain enough to feed its populace for a generation.'

'And most of it controlled by John and Eleazar.' He got up and went to her, laying his big hands on her swollen belly. 'Do you not think it is my heart's desire to break the deadlock? They have the Temple. Solomon built a place of worship. But Herod used his madman's powers to create a fortress. The Lord knows I have tried to force my way in these last months.'

'Yet the Zealots took it.'

'The Zealots had surprise on their side. The same trick cannot be played twice. And all they need do is wait.'

'But if John and Eleazar cannot be beaten—' She pushed him away and began to pace, chin resting on the span of her knuckles. 'You must make peace with them.'

'Peace cannot be made with madmen and fanatics.'

'But they must see that Rome is almost at the door.'

Simon sat down heavily. 'What is Rome to them when they daily expect the Lord to part the heavens on a new age. Have you not seen the half-crazed proph-ets they send to infiltrate the markets and the bazaars? All day long screaming that judgement is coming for non-believers and glory and wealth for the rest.'

'They are not believed.'

'The people are frightened and weary. They *want* to believe.'

'Then feed them.'

He had not wanted her to go. The people had seen her standing at his side, attired in rich cotton—more expensive than silk—a diadem of Ægyptian-worked gold encircling her head. A queen in their eyes, a symbol of hope. How then could she walk amongst them, untouched? But she had laughed at him, pulling the gold bracelets from her wrists and the ropes of precious stones from her throat then flinging them down on the table.

'If the wife of Simon cannot walk freely amongst the people we have lost before we have begun.'

And now, here on the dusty streets, amongst the poorest of Jerusalem, Shelamzion found the beginnings of a strange kind of happiness. The happiness that comes with giving freely of oneself without expectation or precondition. A small boy, grubby with all the grime of poverty, snatched the loaf from her hands and ran away. Yeled, who had insisted on bringing a small guard to protect her, made as if to give chase, but Shelamzion called him back. 'He is just a child.' Yeled scowled. It was well known that, like many ex-slaves, he had a special contempt for the poor.

'He treated you with disrespect.'

'Come now.' She held out her basket to make light of it. 'Should we punish the one who has lessened my burden?' And as the day wore on she was more than glad to have her burden lessened. Her shoulders ached from the lifting of basket after basket, and the child in her stomach grew restless and uneasy. She felt its disquiet in the strain of her back and the swelling of her feet. But the people fought for the privilege of taking the bread directly from her hands, though they did it gently and respectfully. And she did not chide them, except when they began to call her a *saint* and a *mother to the people.* Then the faint echo of idolatry creeping into their words frightened her and she would not have it. But when they called Simon a saint she made no protest.

A hush fell across the crowd. And busy with the organizing of the baskets, Shelamzion did not understand at first, until she turned and caught sight of him coming towards her. Simon. Sweeping through the crowd, with the people falling back on either side, eager to be near him, yet also overawed and a little afraid. She understood how they felt. To see Simon was to burn. And she burned for him now despite her swollen belly and her aching back.

He joined her, and without saying a word, took the basket from her hands and began to distribute the loaves. And watching him she saw that there was nothing of the *politicus* about him. No gleaming show put on purely to dazzle. Only a complicated man with the knack of being simple. And this was the Simon she loved, master of all men because he put himself above none. As he reached for another basket, their hands accidentally touched, and she felt the searching reach of his fingers curl around hers for an instant. Then he was gone, turned away to pass a loaf down to a haggard-looking woman with a listless baby at her breast. And Shelamzion followed him with her eyes, knowing with a sudden, startling clarity that this was the happiest moment of her life.

A cry, like a knife, cut through the air, and Ephraim was running towards them like a man possessed. Simon put down the basket he was holding, and in that one gesture his whole manner was altered from benevolent patron to steely commander of an army. His glance parted the crowd and Ephraim ran breathlessly forward, halting before Simon to give his salute. But it was clear that he was winded by his flight. Not a young man when he had joined the rebel forces, the years of war had aged him. Shelamzion watched anxiously as he struggled to catch his breath. And it was not until Simon leant forward and whispered urgently, 'Speak, friend,' that he managed to gasp, 'The Zealots—They have broken with John. They are at war—'

Simon's body relaxed. 'That may well be in our favour.'

'No!' The older man clutched at his chest in an effort to force the words out. 'There is no time … They are burning the grain stores.'

In the shocked seconds that followed Shelamzion felt a deep well of agony rise up from her abdomen. She clutched at her belly, and gave a low, anguished moan, squeezing her eyes tight against the pain. For a moment she could think of nothing but the pain, then there were hands on her shoulders guiding her upright. When she opened her eyes again Simon was anxiously searching her face.

'The child?'

'It is too soon.' In an age where men distanced themselves from the act that had brought them into the world, Simon's concern distracted her and allowed her to regain her poise. She repeated the words with more assurance this time. 'It is too soon.' For a moment she thought that he did not believe her. Then he frowned. 'I must leave you now.'

'Yes. Yes. Go.'

The pain had vanished as miraculously as it had appeared. And, at first, she had no difficulty keeping up with Yeled as they made their way back to the palace. Yeled was tight-lipped and watchful and she was grateful for his reticence. With Simon gone she had little taste for talk. And, besides, the sun had grown so hot. It sent out a vicious, slanting light that mercilessly swept the stepped limestone of the streets, scorching away the shadows.

Shelamzion's pace began to slow. It was hard to look ahead, but impossible to look down at the reflected glare. The first cries of the battle reached their ears, followed by a dull explosion and a shower of sparks that appeared fleetingly above the Temple precinct. Feeling that she was suffocating, she pulled the thin veil from her head. Yeled glanced back in surprise, but he was still a slave at heart and it was easy to silence him with a look.

They pressed on, aware of the danger, aware that the streets were emptying as citizens ran to barricade themselves in. More than once the guards under Yeled's command had to force their way through throngs of men and women trying to escape in the opposite direction. It was pitiful to see their drawn, anxious faces, and Shelamzion began to regret her decision to disdain the use of a litter. In a litter she might have drawn the curtains and rested her aching head on smooth pillows. But even when her feet throbbed and her belly dragged the wife of Simon must be seen to walk through the streets, back straight, expression serene. She knew the sight of her returning calmly to her home was a comfort and a consolation to all who saw. But when the graceful towers of the palace came into view she felt an immense rush of relief, just before the second wave of pain made her legs go weak.

It was much worse this time. A living agony, ancient and nameless, assaulting her with such violence that she could not believe that this was her child's herald into the world. She stumbled forward blindly, heedless of everything but the immensity of her suffering.

'Lady?' Yeled was at her side. She sensed the quivering motions of his hands as he fought with himself. The serf who dare not touch his mistress.

'What must I d-do?'

Stop being such a slave. Did Simon free you to become a snivelling simpleton? These were the words she wanted to cry out, but her jaw was locked against the pain. Instead she turned tormented eyes upwards that said only, *Help me.*

Then Yeled forgot he was a slave and remembered he was a man. He took hold of her elbows and let her rest against him, asking, 'Shall I send for a litter?'

She shook her head, and gasped, 'No. It is only a little further. Only help so that I am not seen to stumble.'

They made it back to the palace without further incident. Again the pain eased and she was able to walk, supported against Yeled's small, wiry frame. Once in her chambers she fell upon the bed almost weeping with exhaustion. She was aware of Yeled staring down at her. 'I will fetch the midwife.'

'No.' She struggled to sit up. 'It is too soon.' But another wave took her breath away and this time Yeled shook his head. 'Simon would wish it.' He turned to go, and finding herself alone and terrified she whimpered, 'Don't leave me.'

He glanced back, and in his glance was the memory of all the long years of his own suffering mingled with hers. His hand reached out for the door. 'Patience. I will not be long.'

The sounds of the battle were growing louder. She lay, alternately sweating and shivering, trying to make sense of it all. But there was no sense to be had. Eleazar and John were fighting, heedless of how Rome was closing in. And at the very time Jerusalem needed to be whole, they wounded and tore at Her with endless schisms and fractures. Simon was right. There could be no persuading men whose eyes were bright with the world's destruction.

'Si—mon!' She moaned the word through gritted teeth, stretching out her body in an effort to accommodate the immensity of her pain. 'Forgive me.' She was losing the child. That much she understood. Even in her ignorance and inexperience the rush of water between her legs felt like an ill omen. She clutched the edge of the bed, head turned towards the chamber's stately windows. Their eastern outlook showed a sky whorled with smoke. And already the charred, faintly appetizing smell of burning grain had begun to drift across the city. Shelamzion felt her heart turn to lead. If Simon failed—If all the grain was lost—Another spasm took her, and this time her howl of despair was not only for herself.

'In here. Quickly.' Voices beyond the door. She had waited in an agony for them, but now they were here she was shocked by their nearness. As Yeled entered, leading an unfamiliar woman in heavy veils, she tried to pull the sheets over herself.

'No point to that,' said the woman in a voice that was somehow familiar. 'I need to examine you.' She walked over and sat down beside Shelamzion. And though she was thickly veiled Shelamzion said at once, 'I know you.'

The woman ignored her, asking, 'How long since your last pain?'

'Not long. Moments only.'

'And before?'

Shelamzion shuddered, and before she could answer another spasm took her breath away. When she could focus again Yeled had crossed the room to stand next to the midwife. 'We must leave now. It isn't safe.'

'And where will you take a woman in the throes of birth?'

'No!' Shelamzion cried, heaving herself up to a sitting position. 'It is too soon. You must make it stop.'

'And shall I command the sun to halt in the heavens also?' the woman enquired. She turned back to Yeled. 'Stay or leave. It is nothing to me. But this woman can go nowhere.' She turned her back deliberately and Yeled stared at it in confusion. 'SSimon has sent word. We are to retreat.' As if to lend credence to his words there was another dull explosion from the Temple precinct and a flash of carmine struck a brief, gaudy note against the sky. Yeled threw an anxious glance in its direction then leaned forward, searching out Shelamzion's face. 'What m-must I do?'

But it was the midwife who answered. 'Stand guard outside the door and neither enter yourself nor let another pass.' And when Yeled looked as though he might argue she turned on him, literally pushing him from the room with her rough, reddened hands.

With Yeled gone the midwife returned to the bed and began an examination of her charge's condition. And Shelamzion, who had parted her legs only for her husband, found the energy to marvel that she should care so little about the blatant gaze of a stranger. She half smiled, intending to share the joke. But the midwife was frowning. 'Your last flow, when?'

Shelamzion's smile vanished. 'Early in Kislev.'

'Kislev? You are certain.'

'There can be no doubt.'

The midwife's frown deepened and the fingers of one hand twitched as she made her calculation. 'Seven months.'

Shelamzion let her head loll miserably on the pillows. 'My child is lost,' she said bleakly. But to her surprise the midwife stood up and began to search through the small sack she had brought with her. 'All is not lost.'

'Then—you can make this stop.'

'No. Too late for that.' She pulled a jar from the sack, examined its contents and seemed satisfied. 'The child will be born. But strange as it seems, a child born in the seventh month sometimes has more vigour than the one born in the eighth.'

'How so?' Hope was raw in her voice. But the midwife gave an irritated jerk of her shoulders.

'Do I make the laws which govern men? If you want philosophy let me fetch a rabbi.'

'I am sorry,' Shelamzion said humbly. 'It is only that I am afraid.'

The midwife stopped examining the jar and let it rest in her lap. 'You are strong,' she said slowly. 'You will suffer. But you will live. Be thankful that you are loved enough that a man has given you this gift.'

And Shelamzion, so attuned to an age that attributed all blessings to the Lord, noted the slip in the midwife's words and was made curious by it. 'Have you no children of your own?' she asked. The midwife stiffened. But whatever her answer was to be, it was lost in her charge's howls of pain as the fibrous muscles of Shelamzion's belly pulled tight in another contraction.

And so the pattern of the hours was set. Shelamzion's world reduced to two simple states; pain and the absence of pain. The midwife applied a plaster of birthwort and oil to the birth canal. And afterwards the contractions came thick and fast, bathing her skin with a sheen of sweat, her organs each screaming with a measured note of their own. These were the times she begged for release, even if it was to be in death. But the midwife only shrugged her shoulders, saying, 'If you have breath enough to pray, pray for the child.'

Then came the blessed times when the spasms vanished and she could rest and breathe for a while. But the midwife grew more anxious, pressing her fingers between Shelamzion's legs and shaking her head. 'Too small ... still too small.'

Shelamzion did not care. She only wanted to lie back and close her eyes, letting sleep overcome her in drowsy waves. But this also the midwife would not permit. 'Stay awake. You must be ready when the time comes.'

'So tired ... just a little rest.'

'No. The child is trapped. You must do all you can to help him out.'

Help him? She looked at the midwife in a daze. Her belly was soft, her strength gone. What could she do but lie here, a flaccid receptacle with no will or desire. She turned her head to the windows. Outside the sky was deepening to evening. There seemed no cessation in the battle. The bitter smell of charring was stronger and a pall of smoke had begun to creep into the room. The midwife began to cough, and Shelamzion managed to set her own troubles aside for a moment to wonder how stuffy and unpleasant it must be under that thick veil.

'Will you not show me your face?' she asked suddenly. 'We are two women alone.' And as she said it, it occurred to her that the woman had never given her name, and now a feeling of unease made her command imperiously, 'Show yourself to me.'

The midwife, busy in her task of arranging herbs at the foot of the bed, now stood and looked silently down at Shelamzion. There was something so familiar in the obstinacy of the posture that even as she lifted her hands to remove the veil, Shelamzion whispered, 'Mariamme.'

The pinch-faced maid, who had tended Shelamzion so grudgingly, her eyes softening only when Simon was in the room, now stood in the birthing chamber. She was just as Shelamzion remembered and at the same time she was nothing of the woman who had been left behind. Her narrow face bore the marks of suffering, two scars running across each cheek, but in her eyes was a terrible kind of gentleness that had never been there before. From her pillows, Shelamzion gaped, murmuring, 'Zealots?'

A shadow passed over Mariamme's face and she dropped her gaze to the floor. 'They were cruel, those men of God. They called us whores and worse. They seemed to find excitement in saying those things to us. It drove them mad. It made them do horrible—'

'Ami,' Shelamzion broke in. 'She is with you?'

Mariamme did not answer and in her silence was everything. Shelamzion began to weep. And now Mariamme found the words to go on. 'It was harder on some than on others. But Ami is beyond pain now. You should not weep for her. She held you at no fault.'

'I hold myself at fault.'

'You do yourself a disservice.'

'I never thought to hear those words from you.'

Mariamme placed her veil on a stool and pushed a hand through her hair. 'I was—gladdened by the news that you had returned to Simon. They say you are devoted to him now.'

'I do not deserve his good opinion of me.'

The midwife did not answer, but something of the old Mariamme shone through in the arching of an eyebrow, and overcome with emotions too difficult to disentangle Shelamzion blurted, 'You are home now and the best of everything shall be yours—'

Mariamme shook her head. 'No. This is not my home. Let me send word to those maids who wish to return. Some have found new lives, but there are those who would be glad to know that there is still a welcome for them at the house of Simon.'

'But not you?'

'Not me.' Mariamme's thin lips pulled back in a shy smile. 'I have found my home amongst those who call themselves the Poor.'

'The Nazarenes?'

'No, lady. Do not look at me like that. They are honest, devout people, who put themselves above no one.'

'No indeed,' Shelamzion agreed. 'Only above the Pharisees and Sadducees and the Essenes.'

Mariamme lifted a soaked cloth and began to dab Shelamzion's brow. 'They have seen the Messiah.'

'With their own eyes?'

'Through the eyes of their leader. His own father witnessed the Messiah healing the sick in Peraea.'

'And the son has inherited the sight of the parent. A miracle indeed.'

'Do not mock me, lady. You do not believe. Yet look at me; I am not what I was before.'

'No, you are not,' Shelamzion said, solemn now and a little wondering.

But there was no more time for talk because the pains came quick and relentless. And soon her screams hung in the air and mingled with the smoke, and she tore at the bedclothes and cursed all men and all maleness for bringing her to this state. And when she could catch her breath she whimpered for her baby and Mariamme was always there to assure her that, of all the early-borns, a child that comes in the seventh month stands the best chance.

She listened in a haze of fear and pain, feeling the minutes grind by like eternities, yet somehow hours went by unnoticed. Once the door opened and she heard a man's voice, and much as she hated all men she wanted none other by her side. But Mariamme stood firm. Veiled again, she wedged herself in the doorway and faced Jerusalem's mightiest general, saying in low, urgent tones, 'It is not good. The pains come, but the baby does not move.'

'Let me see her.' Simon's tall form peered over Mariamme into the gloomy murk of the room. Shelamzion raised her head weakly and might have found the strength to speak, but Mariamme would have none of it. 'Has the Lord put children in the loins of men now that they should dally about the birth chamber?' She stood with her hands on her hips and Shelamzion saw the big, strong man that was her husband suddenly weaken in the face of women's mystery. He bowed his head, looking clumsy and awkward in the light of the doorway until Mariamme pushed him gently but firmly from the room.

'Get up!'

Painfully, Shelamzion opened her eyes, surprised to find she had shut them. Mariamme was crouching by the bed. 'Come, you must stand.'

'I cannot.'

'You must. There is no one here to help me, but we must try this now. Come.' She placed a hand behind Shelamzion's shoulders and helped her to her feet. Shelamzion groaned and clutched at her belly, feeling not pain, but worse, the fear of pain. Her shift was sweat-soaked and her hair falling in loose, drenched tendrils that clung to her face and shoulders. She followed Mariamme meekly to a thin pillar, allowing her to place her hands around it at chest height.

'Bend your knees.'

She obeyed. She could have scarcely have stood upright. But when Mariamme stood behind her and began to press down on her stomach she protested and tried to pull away. Mariamme took a step back and studied her charge quizzically. Then without a word she went to her bag and brought back a length of rope. Shelamzion's eyes followed the rope and she shook her head feebly. But Mariamme stretched it taut, saying, 'The other midwives are all in hiding, and I cannot hold you alone.' She bound Shelamzion's hands to the pillar then pushed down on her belly.

'Stop! You are killing me.'

'You must bear down. The child is stuck.'

'The child is dead.'

'No.' Mariamme was kneeling on the cold tiles of the floor. 'No. Not the child of Simon.'

A spasm that would have split creation wrenched her sides; she could not breathe.

'Bear down. I feel the head.'

And with those words hope entered the world. When the next pain came she bore down, sobbing and calling out meaningless snatches of terror and desperate longing. 'Lord God, king of the universe … save my child … Let the seven months of his beginning be his amulet and his protector … You, who chose seven words to begin the Law … and … set the seven seas to gird the world. And the seven heavenly bodies and—' A cry tore out of her in an agonized, inhuman voice, and moments later her child's head broke free into the world.

In the minutes that followed she collapsed against the pillar, feeling the tiny body slither out. The silence she had banished with screams now rushed back into the room. She tried to ask if her child was alive, but her lips would not obey the command to move. Down on her knees, working with knife and wool to cut and tie the cord, Mariamme was too absorbed to speak. Or was she afraid of what she had to say? Shelamzion's eyes closed and fresh tears began to leak out beneath the lids.

'Lady, will you not look.'

'There is no need. My child is dead.'

There was a cry. A small, mewling cry of utter helplessness. Shelamzion opened her eyes, and through the fractured light of her tears, saw a tiny, bloodied bundle clutched in Mariamme's arms. And when Mariamme whispered, 'Your son,' she only nodded because now words were unnecessary.

She could not take her eyes from her child. Could not believe that this tiny living being was the work of her own body. There was a rush of something so fierce and precious from her heart that she did not care when the pains came again to expel the afterbirth or when Mariamme cut free her bonds, and led her back to the bed. With her son curled against her breast the dark clouds of pain shrank away, and she hardly noticed when Mariamme knelt between her thighs and began to pack her womb with boiled linens.

Simon came into the room. He approached the bed, his eyes full of hope and wariness, as though he had been given news he did not dare to believe. She watched him half amused that he should approach her so reverently when she was lying there like some shipwrecked thing left behind by the tide.

'Softly now. You approach a queen.'

He did not return her smile. But knelt down beside her, laying one hand upon her head and cupping his other hand around his son.

'And never has a queen had a more precious jewel upon her breast.' Then his smile came, slow and beautiful.

'One child,' she whispered, awed. 'Yet everything—changed somehow?'

'Everything is changed.'

She noticed there were black smudges of soot on his forehead and cheeks. They etched the lines that had grown ever deeper over the last few months. She reached out and clutched his arm. 'The battle—'

He heard the fear in her voice. 'No. No. We are victorious. What grain is left is in our hands now.'

'Is it enough?'

'If we are careful.' He spoke reassuringly, but his shoulders slumped and his eyes were red with smoke and fatigue. She forced herself up on her elbows, though the effort cost her. 'What is it? There is something else?'

He rubbed the back of his neck and closed his eyes for a moment. And when he opened them a moment later everything was laid before her.

'Zacchaeus is dead.'

Her hand flew to her mouth. 'No, it cannot be.'

Simon sighed. 'I would not have told you. But you are not a woman from whom things can be hidden.'

Her elbows gave way and she slumped back on her pillows. 'How?'

'There was panic in the streets. In the confusion Zacchaeus saw a mob of men and women running towards the fire, and knew the flames to be tempered with Zealot arrows. He tried to stop them—' Simon paused. A muscle danced in his cheek , drawing his lip upwards, as though in a snarl. 'But the good citizens paid no heed. They trampled him to death. We would not have recognized him, but for the Zealot's dagger Yeled found on his body.'

He looked towards his son, though his eyes did not seem to see him. 'Yeled has taken it badly. I did not know that there was such love between those two. When Ephraim would have comforted him, he answered bitterly, saying Zacchaeus would have been better off with his Zealot brothers; at least he would have been alive.' His black eyes met her scandalized expression. 'Yes indeed. Even Yeled thinks he would be better off without me.'

'No,' she whispered. 'He is but grieving. Zacchaeus was a good man. Misguided at first perhaps, but his death was an honourable one.'

Simon's eyes rolled heavenwards. 'Lord spare us another honourable death.' He fell into a morose silence.

Impulsively, she said, 'Let us escape this place. Why should we stay here? Jerusalem is becoming a trap. And when the Romans reach us our chances will be gone.'

He stroked her cheek. 'And what will happen to you, my queen?'

She pushed his hand away crossly. 'Is this a queen you see before you? You have a son now. I want no greater gift than to know that he is forever safe and protected.'

'If we do not win this war there will be no place in the world a Jew may walk safe and protected.' Then he frowned. 'No. Let us not talk like this. I will put my grief aside today. Yesterday I was alone and almost without hope for the future. But today I have a son.' He lifted the child gently from her breast and carried him to the window. She watched him standing there in silence, looking down at the smoking remains of the battle, his son cradled against him, and saw that he was filled with pride and hope and longing. Knowing that she was the cause of this in him, she felt a great rush of relief wash through her. And when it ebbed away she was exhausted and her eyelids heavy. Yet before the sweetness of sleep claimed her she saw him bend forward to kiss his son's forehead and thought he murmured, '*Re'shiyth chadash*.' Here is a new beginning.

Chapter XXI

Let God arise, let his enemies be scattered: Let them also that hate him flee before him. As smoke is driven away, so drive them away: As wax melteth before the fire, so let the wicked perish at the presence of God.

Psalm 68

She came, as always, with the unhurried dignity of a queen, and Cornelius never tired of marvelling that here was a woman whom the gods had tried to break so many times, yet she stood shielded by the armour of her grace and poise. She was studying his face, and before there was time for an exchange of greetings she asked, 'What has happened?'

He met her eyes solemnly, feeling bleakness settle over his heart. And he was forced to breathe in deeply several times before finding the strength to announce, 'Your husband is here. They brought him an hour ago.'

'Simon! Where is he?'

'Held in the Tullianum.'

'The dungeon?' There was accusation on her face, though her tone did not change.

'It is Titus' orders.' And knowing how little she would think of that, he added quickly, 'I have no choice but to obey.'

Used to the acidity of her wit, which so often left him breathless in argument, he found her silence more oppressive than any rebuke. But then, as he watched the colours of her emotions rising and fading beneath her skin, he understood that he was very far from her thoughts.

'My dear, I—I should not have broken the news so bluntly.'

She met his eyes with an effort. 'All this time,' she said slowly, 'I knew. Yet I did not believe.'

'It is true,' Cornelius said softly. 'He does not yet know you are here. Word of your capture came late to Titus, and it seems that Josephus has been at pains to keep your presence as little known as possible.'

She said nothing, but her face was an eloquent question. Cornelius made a helpless gesture. 'His purpose? I cannot say.' Then he could not help himself from adding bitterly. 'Josephus is preparing a copy of his history as a gift for the

205

emperor. He will not care to remind his patron that there is a source, who can contradict his version of events.'

She was still looking at him, but there was a blank hopelessness in her expression that wounded him to the heart. And though it cost him, he forced himself to say. 'You have only to give the word and I will take you to Simon.'

He did not know what he expected her to do. To scream. To weep with gratitude. To fall to her knees and clutch his hand to her lips. Any one of those reactions might have seemed fitting to the circumstances, might even have gone some way to appease the little demon of envy that tore at his heart. Yet she did none of those things. She stood perfectly still for a moment, a look of the most abject horror on her face, then she backed away from him shaking her head.

One of the first acts of the Roman Emperor Tiberius Claudius Caesar Augustus Germanicus had been to appoint his friend, Herod Agrippa, —grandson of that specimen of wickedness, Herod the Great— king of Judea. But having witnessed how madness ran through Rome's imperial family, like a river of blood, Agrippa sought to protect his new interests in the most concrete of ways. He ordered that the extensions of Jerusalem be fortified with a wall more than twenty cubits high. But the divine Claudius intervened. The wall was never finished and Herod Agrippa died mysteriously before thousands of onlookers at games given in the Emperor's honour. Everyone agreed that he had been struck down by God, but there were many in private who asked the question, 'Which god?'

Now that Simon ruled the upper city the wall had been completed. Great blocks of stone many cubits thick had been levered painstakingly into position. And Simon himself had helped manoeuvre the great lifting towers, taking his place amongst the sweating labourers to turn the capstans that worked the pulleys. From the Temple walls the Zealots had watched listlessly, unable to see why stone should be necessary when they were encircled with righteousness. But Simon had kept on building and now the wall stood firm, crowned with saw-toothed battlements and soaring watch towers.

Shelamzion stood on the walkway of this wall looking northwards towards Mount Scopus. And what she saw filled her with stone cold dread. Roman legionaries—thousands of them—pouring over the ridge of hills. An army of ants marching relentlessly down the Antipatris road towards them. No longer headed by Flavius Vespasianus, or Vespasian as he styled himself now that he was emperor of the civilized world. His eldest son, Titus, whom the world knew as his father's scourge, now led the army of ants marching on Jerusalem.

The ants were growing bigger as Shelamzion watched. Burnished armour catching in the pure light. Backs weighed down with eighty pounds of equipment apiece. Flint-hard men, come to destroy a nation, not out of passion or the scorching influence of holy ideal, but for orders. *Orders for orders sake*, she thought bitterly. That was the Roman way. *Severitas* and *Disciplina*; the Roman virtue and the Roman god.

There were others standing on the wall beside her, and so she kept her face impassive. But inside her belly twisted into knots and her heart pounded, like a frightened bird. She turned to Simon, whispering under her breath, 'How many?'

'Thirty thousand. And Ephraim's men say Titus can rely on another two legions joining him.'

Her eyes grew dark with disbelief. 'We are barely fifteen. How many can John count on?'

'Six, perhaps seven thousand. And Eleazar has less than three.'

Her eyes slid back to the army of ants. 'Is it possible that John and Eleazar stay blind to this?'

'Worse, I fear. A blind man may at least flail at his enemy and inflict some damage. John and Eleazar stand, like men in a dream, singing the Lord's praises, while Rome's fist closes around us.'

'What can we do? I cannot believe—'

But Simon was not listening. He was leaning out over the parapet, his eyes trained on the approaching army. And following his line of sight, Shelamzion understood what had captured his attention. The main body of men had stopped. From what she could tell they were making camp. No doubt the blatancy with which they went about their tasks was intended as a deliberate insult to the watching Jews. But it was not this that Simon was studying. A contingent of men, considerably forward of the rest, had left the main body.

They were on horseback, riding out, as though intending to inspect the large octagonal tower that served to watch over the north-westerly approaches to the city. And with an audacity that bordered on contempt, their leader flaunted a cloak of the imperial hue. Tyrian purple. Only one man could sport those colours in Judea. 'Titus.' Shelamzion heard the name as a hiss of breath from Simon's lips, then he was gone, plunging down the stairs towards the Women's Gate. She ran after him. 'Simon, wait!' But he did not wait. Halfway down he met Hyrcanus. The younger man's face was flushed with excitement. 'Titus. I saw him less than half a league—'

Simon put his hand on his shoulder. 'Muster the men.'

'We can take him,' Hyrcanus insisted. There was an unguarded defiance in his stance.

Simon shook his head, 'We need more men.'

'There are enough here. The chance may be lost if we do not act now.'

Simon paused and looked squarely into Hyrcanus' face. 'Muster the men.'

For a moment Shelamzion thought Hyrcanus would dare to argue, then he wheeled round and headed back the way he had come.

At the bottom of the stairs Ephraim and Ariel were waiting. Simon lifted a hand. 'Peace, I have seen it.'

'Do we go?' Ephraim asked.

Ariel ran his fingers down his long beard. 'It could be a trap.'

Simon disagreed. 'I am not much of a man for seeing the pattern of the past in the shape of the present. But it seems to me that here is a moment in history that we have seen before.'

'How so?' Shelamzion was at his side. She no longer played the submissive wife in front of the old guard and they no longer expected her to. Simon gave his answer simply and quickly.

'Two hundred years ago, when Judas the Maccabee saw the Greek army marching towards him, he knew his men were outnumbered four to one. Odds like that cannot be fought with courage and skill alone. They rely on moments of fortune. Judas saw his luck turn when the leader of the Greeks rode out before his troops. He took his chance and cut him down. Perhaps such a chance presents itself again.'

Ariel, for all his renunciation of orders, was scandalized. 'Are you so much the Sadducee that you cannot see the Lord's work anywhere in the world?'

Simon gave him a weary smile. 'No, not that, old friend. These moments of fortune are surely given us by the Lord's hand. And it is up to us to use them rightly.'

At that moment Yeled came running up with a score of men at his back. 'Is … is it true?' Then, seeing Simon: 'Ephraim sent word. There is a *hundred* on its way here.'

'Good.' Simon's next words were cut off by the creak of the gate being opened. And seeing the nervous agitation of the waiting men, he walked to the front of the line to give orders. 'Hold steady. Time enough when he's in our sights.'

Shelamzion had seen enough, and knowing that this was a battle that would be better viewed from above, she turned and started up the stairs again. She heard Simon say *Steady* once more. Then there was a rush of air. She pivoted round and saw ten or more horsemen charging through the gate. There was barely time to register their faces, and it was instinct alone that helped her recognise the narrow features of Hezekiah, son of Matthias, the current High Priest, and also that the man leading them—in express contravention to Simon's orders—was Hyrcanus.

There was an instant of confusion, then she heard Simon utter an oath.

'The Almighty curse him.'

She had never heard Simon speak that way before. Nor had the men and women about him. The excited cries that had been kicked up at the heels of Hyrcanus' horses now faded away, and all eyes turned to Simon. He threw himself on the back of the mount Ariel had brought forward for him, swinging an arm in a great arc towards the gate. 'Forward! We must save what we can.'

Shelamzion watched the outcome from the walkway. Looking down, as she had done so many times, like an impotent god watching the panoply of human disaster. Hyrcanus' men had cut Titus off with only a handful of legionaries round him. But he had too small a force to take his prey. Hard at his heels came Simon, his hard body flying like an arrow shot from heaven into their midst. His men fanning out, making the divide between Titus and the larger body of legionaries wider still. Shelamzion's fingers dug into the stone parapet and she stretched her body over the edge, feeling the juddering impact of each blow that connected with Simon's sword. For an instant she saw that Simon had been wrong. Hyrcanus, full of youthful impetuosity, had won the day. Vespasian's son was cornered. Enemies before and enemies behind. Without even a cuirass or helmet to protect him he would be cut down in moments.

She held her breath, feeling her senses magnify over the rippling air. There was a moment when Hyrcanus was so close that he must have heard the quickening of Titus' breath. Then Hyrcanus swung his sword upwards in a crescent of white light, and for an instant it hung there, balanced on the pivot of history. About to change the world.

A second sword appeared, the black iron in the blade casting a transverse shadow across the white. And it cut down the white in an arc almost too fast to follow. Then even Shelamzion echoed the cry of negation that rang out from Simon's men, cut short on an in-breath of confusion as all saw that it was Simon who had dealt the blow.

Time stagnated. It is not possible on a field of battle, but everyone stood still. Only Simon was animate, his free arm wheeling backwards in a gesture that held everyone else off. The muscles in Shelamzion's face lengthened in shock. How could this be? Simon refusing to kill Titus. Then Titus—no fool—saw that Simon was caught up in the act of holding back his men, and seized his chance. He charged forward, scattering the Jews. Tearing through their lines with all the gall and hubris of a prince of Rome. Two of his men fell behind and were dragged to their deaths, but Titus broke through the Jewish line, like some newborn Achilles, believing himself divinely favoured when it was the earthly act of a single man that had spared him.

Later that same day Shelamzion, walking like an avenging angel, made her way through the marble-lined corridors of the palace to the broad, columned room where Simon had gone after the battle. In her arms, her son was pressed against her, his gappy mouth making hopeful jabs at her breast. He was ten months old and growing too big to need suckle, but this was her first child. And with no other to demand share of her affection, she found it difficult to wean him from his dependence upon her. But not today. Today she must deal with greater matters first. She swept past the guards outside the room, who made only a cursory attempt to stop her, then seeing the look on her face, drew back.

Simon had his back to the door when she entered. He was alone, bent over a table in the middle of the room examining some scrolls. And though she saw his shoulders stiffen when he heard her footsteps, he did not turn round. She had only one question.

'Why?'

He lifted another scroll and laid it deliberately on top of the one he had been reading.

'You know why.'

'No, I do not.' She marched round to face him. Did he think she would stand there and address the back of his head? 'I do not understand. And neither does anyone else.' She might have stopped, now that she saw him. The blood and dust of battle slashed across his face, like wounds. His tunic was torn, and she could see a thin line of encrusted blood severing the flesh. But she could not stop. Too much was at stake. She adjusted her son on her hip to give herself time to talk calmly, but the words erupted hotly from her tongue. 'Have you heard what the people are saying?'

'It does not matter what they say. I did what had to be done.'

'To let Titus go.'

He lifted his eyes—those eyes that might have belonged to a prophet—and she said on a note of despair, 'You let him go.'

He looked at her coldly. 'Would you have had me cut him down? Should I have sent his head back to that snake-oil merchant, Josephus, to take back to his masters in Rome?'

His voice was hypnotic. She swayed slightly to its rhythm, and even the child in her arms lifted his head from his mother's breast and stared at his father. From somewhere she found the strength to say, 'Yes. May I find forgiveness. I would have had you do that. For otherwise we are ruined. They are saying you are a traitor. They are calling you … a coward.'

She had thought to shock him, but he merely shrugged. 'They are angry for now. When they are calm they will understand my reasons.'

If it were not for the child in her arms she would have torn the hairs from her head. 'How can they, when I do not?'

His eyes were on his son, who had gone back to nuzzling his mother's breast. 'Jathniel is hungry.'

Jathniel, the gift of God. What man but Simon would have allowed her to choose the name of their first child? She had hardly believed him when he made the offer.

'But I thought—Would you not wish it to be Saul?'

He shrugged. 'Time enough to call the second one Saul.'

'But if it should be a girl?'

'Then we will have to find her an understanding husband.'

Simon, who broke all the rules. But never carelessly. Never wantonly. She expelled the breath from her body in a slow, deliberate sigh then went to sit on one of the stools around the room. When her robe was adjusted and Jathniel settled hard against the subtle yield of her nipple, she looked over at

Simon once more, saying simply, 'Tell me, that I might understand.'

In the early evening as the shadows began to soften towards the walls of the Temple, Shelamzion gave her son into the care of a nurse. She went to her room and put on a pale shift with silver embroidery. On her head she placed a diadem, ornamented with sapphires. Then, taking Yeled and Ephraim with her, she climbed the city wall and prepared to address the people. Ephraim was nervous. He whispered in her ear, 'It would be better with me if we had found Hyrcanus.' Hyrcanus had vanished as soon as the skirmish was over. Shelamzion kept her eyes on the growing crowd below, instinctively knowing that it would be dangerous to look away. 'Hyrcanus will find his own way back. And with his tail between his legs no doubt. Best we put things right before Simon's party is as split as John's.'

Brave words. But the mood of the crowd was ugly. One woman pushed out in front of the rest. She stared up brazenly at Shelamzion, then spat upon the ground. The deed acted as a catalyst. The inchoate grumblings grew more animated and Simon's name began to be tossed upwards, louder and louder until it became a savage vent for their frustrations.

'Simon! Bring him to us.'

Yeled and Ephraim reached for their swords, but Shelamzion shook her head. A burly man with the arms of a blacksmith climbed the first few steps towards Shelamzion.

'Let Simon show himself. Where is he?'

'Dead.'

She did not raise her voice, barely having guessed what she would say to them. But the word did its trick. The sound of it died, but its meaning grew, spreading wide over the crowd until they were silenced and frightened by it. Shelamzion watched. They exchanged glances. Women covered their faces. And in the moment before she judged they would begin a new kind of clamour, she spoke into their silence, and her words carried in the dryness of the air.

'Think well what it would mean if my answer were true.'

Now they were confused, and she went on swiftly before they had time to gather their thoughts.

'Think well, you who called him to protect this city. Do you call him traitor now? Do you call him coward? *Melech!* Here is a king! Those were your words. And does a king explain himself?'

Many were won over, but there still bullish faces. She went on, knowing a single mistake would destroy everything.

'No, a king does not explain himself. But Simon would have you understand. Simon would explain his reasons to you—'

'Let him then!' a voice cried.

'Shall I drag him here to do your will?' she mocked. 'Shall I call the man who saved us all this day to do the bidding of a pedlar or a lamp-seller?'

'How did he save us?'

It was the piping voice of a child, but it was what she needed. And so she told them, explaining to them as Simon had explained to her, but with her woman's touch, her understanding as a mother. 'Will you kill Vespasian's son? What is to be gained by that? Do you think it is like the Greek legends; Vespasian will come, as the Trojan king did, kissing Simon's hands and begging for the body of his child?' She raised her voice so that none might miss it. 'Myths! Have we Jews not always despised myths?

'If Simon could have captured Titus then we might have seen Rome come to negotiate. But if Titus had been killed, not four legions would be outside our walls, but ten times that number—' She was exaggerating, but forty was a number they understood. Forty days and forty nights of rain. Forty years in the desert. It was engrained into them. Like the dirt beneath their nails. Like the scorching air they dragged into their lungs. Like the promise of heaven they believed was divinely theirs.

She went on talking, but her point was made. It happened slowly at first. She could not be certain it was happening at all. In ones then twos the crowd was trickling away. She allowed herself the luxury of growing dull, repeating the same phrases and covering the same ground until there was nothing new or momentous to keep them there. They drifted away, a dewy cloud burned off in the midday heat. But she waited until the last dirty ragamuffin had vanished off to seek out better things. Only then did she allow herself a shuddering sigh of relief and let her head to drop into her hands. From behind she heard Yeled say, 'The Lord bless Simon.'

And Ephraim answer, 'Aye. And the Lord bless Simon's wife.'

Cornelius lifted the flaming torch down from its bracket, his hand hesitating on the handle just long enough to betray his own doubts over the action. But it was no more than that. A hesitation only. Then he was walking quickly down through the labyrinthine corridors that fed into the gloomiest and furthest reaches of the Carcer. As he walked the torch grew smoky in the thick air. There was a nauseating stench, a crawling odour that clung to his skin and his lips, filling his nostrils with the scent of the tomb.

Several times Cornelius felt his resolve break and made up his mind to go back. Yet somehow his feet kept walking. Through the corridors, down two flights of steps, slippery with—he would not allow himself to dwell on what they might be slippery with—across a rough, earthen floor. Here he met the guard and dismissed them. They went quietly enough, their pockets already chinking with coin from Cornelius' purse. *'Simon is to know nothing of his wife's presence. Titus' orders.' He slipped them enough silver to bury any burgeoning curiosity, and had noted how they exchanged glances. A sign surely that this was not the first time they had heard these orders, nor the first silver that had bought their silence.*

He waited until their footsteps died away, knowing himself to be almost at the gaping mouth of hell itself. And though he understood that it was at least twelve feet deep, and that the tallest of men are little over half that size, he had to fight to take those last few steps towards its edge.

What had he expected? The Jewish army, elite troops, poised and ready to spring? There was a miserable tangle of about half a dozen men, naked to their filthy loin cloths, lice-ridden and broken, their skins a patchwork of scars and open sores. They writhed together at the bottom of the pit, like snakes in a basket. And the torch, fighting with them for air in that stinking atmosphere, sent demonic shadows leaping so that no man's face was distinct.

'Bar—' Cornelius began, then broke off, choking in the putrid atmosphere. He raised a hand to cover his nose and mouth. The action was a painful reminder—Had he ever, in his arrogance and ignorance, imagined that such degradation should be Shelamzion's lot? He forced himself to try again. 'Bar Gioras. Show yourself.'

For an instant, there was no discernible difference in the movement of the men crawling away from the light, then he heard a trembling voice murmur, 'C-come. We are not b-beaten yet.'

A man staggered to his feet, helping another up at the same time. Cornelius held the torch aloft, playing the guttering light across their features. They were both filthy, their hair and beards tangled and crawling. Cornelius could see purple bruises on both their faces, and one had a split severing his bottom lip. They should have been alike. Romulus and Remus caught in the belly of hell. But they were not alike. Cornelius saw at once that these men were not the same. There was defiance in both their eyes, but in one it was the cheap trick of the street conjurer. In the other it was barely visible, lost in the complex character of a man who beheld the world in new ways, and who walked alone because of it.

As Cornelius looked into the eyes of this man he saw not just defiance, but a strange, shifting amalgam of thoughts and feelings. Pride, yes. And anger too. But there was no fear. This man had a secret. And he looked at this Roman—as all Romans—contemptuously. And perhaps even pityingly, because they had not broken him. Even in here. And that is the secret of all great men, that they are sometimes less, but very often more than just men. Because to kill them is not to kill the idea they bring into the world. And this was Simon's secret. Or, at least, part of it. For Cornelius knew he had others. He believed his wife and child were alive and free.

In the pit the man narrowed his eyes, puzzled in the face of Cornelius' silence. But Cornelius was lost in his own thoughts, hearing again his offer to take Shelamzion to see her husband. For an instant her face had brightened. Then a shadow had fallen across it, and she had backed away from him, a look of horror distorting her features. 'No,' she had whispered. 'Do not ask me.'

And when he would know why, she had said simply, 'Can you imagine what it will do to him to see me here? And when he asks of his son, do you think it is possible to lie to Simon?'

Had he thought it possible, Cornelius wondered. He certainly did so no longer. One look was enough to dispel the idea that deceit could be used to influence this man. Was that why Josephus hated and feared him so? Far below he saw Simon open his mouth, as though to speak. And this Cornelius could not bear. He turned abruptly and stumbled away, full of horror and wonder that he should feel more like a condemned man than the one left behind in the abominable darkness of the pit.

Chapter XXII

Titus, who had been assigned to the war against the Jews, undertook to win them over by certain representations and promises; but, as they would not yield, he now proceeded to wage war upon them. The first battles he fought were indecisive; then he got the upper hand and proceeded to besiege Jerusalem.

Cassius Dio, *Roman History*, Book LXV

The mood in Jerusalem was strange. Shelamzion walked the streets with Jathniel in her arms and Yeled at her side, and saw the strangeness in the faces of the people. They were listless, yet prone to excitability. The smallest disturbance made them agitated and liable to fight amongst themselves. Those who still had basics to trade—food, clothing, miracle cures, talismans and charms—went about their business with an eager mania in their eyes. Those who had nothing wandered the streets by day, standing in long lines for the bread Shelamzion brought them.

At night, they gathered in the crumbling archways and the filthy corners of alleys in the poorer districts, and stayed there praying for miracles. Surely the God who stayed Avraham's hand, who wrestled with Yitzchak, who had spoken in Moses' ear, must now come amongst them in their hour of need. With their fears grew superstitions, and they became adept at reading signs in the ordinary events of their lives. They took to finding messiahs amongst themselves, who one after another disappointed and proved false.

On the twenty-third day of the month of Nisan, Shelamzion climbed the steep, narrow staircase that led to the top of the Psephinus Tower. At the top, half hidden by the battlements, she had a view of the northwest. The distance showed the Mediterranean, like a sheet of light. And by turning her head in the opposite direction she could see the mountains of Nabataea wriggling in the heat. But it was not for the view she had come. At least not today. For a while now the Romans had been occupied with the task of fortifying their camps, and there had been some respite in the fighting … at least beyond the city walls.

But John of Gischala was now adding to the thorns in Simon's side. For a small window of time it seemed that John was wavering, even lending aid to Simon's raiding parties once or twice. Perhaps if there had been a definitive victory that had seen the Romans fleeing, or if Titus had been taken alive, he might have come to Simon as an ally. But no such success watered the roots of their allegiance. And when John saw an opportunity to seize Eleazar's power base, becoming master of the Antonia Fortress and the Temple, he turned his head from Simon so that once again they were enemies. But his victory was short lived. Word followed swiftly; the Romans were surrounding the city. The siege was underway.

So Shelamzion climbed the tower known as Psephinus to see for herself. And what she saw made her heart thud hard against its bony cage. The camps were completed and the four legions had spread out to encircle the city walls. And that was not all. She stared, eyes smarting with disbelief. Where was the ancient sylva that covered the slopes and valleys? So many times, standing on the white, hot walls of the Temple, looking down into its green coolness. Now, nothing. A bleak, treeless wilderness as far as the eye could see. Even as she fought against it she understood what had happened. Titus had pursued the Jews then watched them melt away into the shadows.

And with that peculiarly Roman penchant for exaggerated gestures, he had ordered every living thing to be torn up. No oak nor olive nor twisted vine. No figs or carobs or perfumed cypresses. Not even the great, stately terebinths whose shade was a blessing to the traveller. Cut down. One and all. The hard light bouncing back from the uncovered earth caused tears to pour from her eyes, and she wiped them away with quick, fierce movements of her hands. They had known it was happening even as they fought amongst themselves. How had they let it get this far?

Yeled was at her side.

'Simon wants you—Josephus is com-com-coming.'

She joined Simon on the wall near the Western Gate. On either side of them was a long line of archers, their eyes trained on the approaching figure. Shelamzion turned to Simon. 'What does this mean?'

Simon shook his head. 'Where Josephus is concerned the only thing certain is that nothing may be divined with certainty.'

When he was at the distance of a stone's throw, Josephus stopped and made a bow. This was the first time Shelamzion had seen him and she was struck by the thought that here was a man who looked like a Jew, but who had the aura of a Roman. He did not wait to be invited to speak, but made his proposition directly to Simon. And yet Shelamzion sensed he had already taken her in, in every detail.

Josephus, the son of Mattathias, spoke in clear, measured tones.

'My master, Titus Flavius, has sent me as his emissary. You will understand the decision was not an easy one.'

'Naturally,' Simon replied. 'In times of war even an emperor's son may be forced to make use of base materials.'

There was a titter of laughter from the archers, but Josephus showed no signs of being put out. He had endured worse. His flesh still bore the bite marks of iron chains around the wrists and ankles. 'I have come to negotiate terms.'

'Terms,' Simon repeated. 'Your master cannot break down the door so he sends you to fetch the key.'

'No indeed.' An iciness crept into Josephus' voice. 'My master has only to raise his hand and Jerusalem will be broken down until not a stone stands in its memory. I am sent here today because he does not wish to see the ruin of our beautiful and ancient city.'

'Nor the ruin of his profits,' Simon replied.

Josephus stood silent some moments, then he shook his head, as though shaking off a veil. 'I see you are a plain speaker,' he said slowly. 'Well then, let us speak plainly. You are surrounded. The army that laid great Carthage's glory to rest—not to mention a hundred other rebellious nations—stands outside your walls. Have you any idea what that army has done to the entire world? There is nowhere left to run. Where will you go if you pursue this madness? Jerusalem will become your tomb.'

Suddenly. Surprisingly. He turned to Shelamzion. 'Dear lady, persuade your husband to listen to reason. If not for your sake then for the sake of your child.' Shelamzion fought to control herself, but Josephus was a man adept at reading a situation, even from a distance. 'You did not think to keep it from us, did you? All Rome knows that a son has been born to a king of Jews.'

'I am no king,' Simon insisted.

'No?' Josephus looked surprised. 'Yet they cried it in the streets. *Melech.* Here is a king. What are we to make of that?'

'Make what you will. You are the one with the talent for politics.'

'You flatter me. I am but a poor messenger—'

'Then say what you must and have done.'

Josephus paused. It was clear he liked neither the interruption nor the duty of carrying another's words. His stance became rigid and his voice mechanical as he spoke. 'Surrender. Throw yourself on Titus' mercy and you will find him generous in victory.'

'As you found his father?'

'You are a man of intelligence and cunning, Simon bar Gioras. You have fought well as a soldier. Nor is your renown in dispute. But you cannot win this war. Were you not welcomed by the High Priest as a man who would put an end to the people's sufferings? There are many behind Jerusalem's walls who clamour for peace. Will you stand there and deny them their chance?'

Simon's eyes were fixed on Josephus as a man's eyes might fix on a snake he would like to kill. But Shelamzion looked down the line of archers and saw a cloud of unease settle over them. Shoulders twitched. Glances were exchanged.

'I come before you,' Josephus continued, 'proof of Rome's largesse. Only think how they will greet a man who holds the heart of the people in his hand. And once they have their victory let us not forget that Judea will be in need of a king—' He took a step forward, as though he had forgotten death pointed at him. 'You are their king, Simon. With Rome's help you will have all the honour and legitimacy of a pure bloodline. And who then will remember you as half a Jew?'

In the silence that followed, detail grew large. Shelamzion saw whirlpools of dust blow across Josephus' feet. One of the archers coughed and all his comrades turned to look. A brown-necked raven flew overhead, cawing at the sun before it wheeled off into the blue. Only then did Simon speak. Shelamzion felt her heart jump, as though she had never heard the sound of his voice before. And perhaps it was true there was something in it that had not been there before. It was to Josephus he addressed his words. And he spoke softly.

'You must forgive my ignorance, but I have forgotten where your allegiance lies these days. Do you call yourself Sadducee or Pharisee?' Josephus did not answer and Simon went on. 'No matter. You are still a Jew, are you not, Joseph ben Mattathias?'

Josephus was rigid, his stance full of hate. Simon shrugged.

'What pain it must cause you to know that you were within an arrow's reach of these walls while Passover was celebrated in the Temple.' Simon tilted his head, as though suddenly curious. 'What, still no word for me, Joseph? You have spent too long in pagan company. Perhaps you no longer recall what Passover means to us—'

'I remember,' Josephus growled. 'No Jew forgets our flight from Ægyptus.'

'Yet surely you have forgotten.' Simon's voice was low, dangerous. 'No Jew who remembers our time of bondage would now seek our slavery to Rome—'

When they were back in their rooms Simon ordered food then did not eat it. And a little later he ordered wine, but did not drink it. Shelamzion sat with Jathniel on her lap and watched him patiently, lovingly. When he had paced from one end of the room to the other for the hundredth time, had lifted his wine cup then put it down untouched yet again, she said finally, 'Simon, you take less pleasure in victory than you do in defeat.'

He turned to her. 'Do you call that victory?'

'If only for the Romans, my love. You have doubled the efficiency of their emissaries. I'll wager Josephus returned twice as quick as he arrived.'

'You think it funny to see that traitorous brute humiliated.'

She looked at him defiantly. 'Yes. Why not? The Almighty help us, there is little enough joy in our lives. Let us laugh where we can.'

He dropped to one knee at her side. 'But not now. This is not a time for laughing. I must send you away.'

'Dear God.' She got to her feet, putting Jathniel down. 'What are you saying?'

'Only that, for all his wretched deceit, Josephus is right. Jerusalem is a tomb. You must escape while you can.'

She started to laugh, then seeing he was serious, broke off. 'And is it a garden outside? Where do you suppose Titus will escort the wife of Simon?'

'Titus has never seen you.'

'But Josephus—'

Simon stood up and began to pace again. 'Josephus saw a women in silks and a diadem. His eyes were dazzled. You will disguise yourself as a pilgrim. A widow with her son. Now Passover is done there will be enough of them clamouring to flee the city.'

'And where am I to go?'

'Galilee. And then perhaps to Alexandria. I have a distant cousin there—'

'I will not leave you.'

'And I say you will.'

She meant to argue. But the door was suddenly thrown open. Simon reached for his sword, but it was only old Ariel, breathless and leaning heavily on his staff. He blinked several times, as though it was a miracle to find them.

'Praise the Almighty. The rumour is that the wife of Simon and his child had already gone.'

Simon's hand relaxed. 'So they must.'

'No. No.' He stepped inside the room, shutting the door behind him. 'They must not.'

Simon's expression hardened. 'The decision is made.'

'Rather should you cut out my eyes than I allow them obey your will.'

This was an outburst strange in an Essene. Frightened, Shelamzion cried, 'You talk in riddles. What has happened?'

The old man gave Jathniel an uncomfortable glance, but she shook her head. 'He is too young to understand. Speak freely.'

Ariel spread his hands. 'A group of pilgrims mistook the sound of battle as their chance. They fled out of the postern before the word was given—'

Shelamzion felt coldness drain through her veins. She glanced at Simon. 'They were taken?'

'Almost at once. But that is not the worst of it. Some arrogant fool, who had dressed himself as a pilgrim—one of the gold merchants, I think—got into an argument. We could not hear the words, but we saw what happened next.' Ariel paused a moment to rub a sheen of sweat from his top lip. 'The legionary's sword was unsheathed. And, with no word of warning, he slit the man from hip to hip.'

'Dear God,' Shelamzion whispered. 'Say that it ended there.'

Ariel held her stricken gaze then slowly shook his head. 'It seems the merchant had swallowed his own wares. The legionary found a rope of pearls. And, once his comrades saw with their own eyes, they no longer had men and women seeking refuge before them, only sacks of gold waiting to be cut open.'

Shelamzion felt her legs go weak. 'How is it that the cup of men's ills so easily overflows?' She reached out a hand for Jathniel. But, understanding nothing of the danger, he ran past her, eager to catch the dust motes trapped in the columns of slanting sunlight.

She looked to Simon, thinking, Why did I not bow to his will this once? I might have given him a few precious seconds of hope before it was snatched away. Simon had taken a seat on a nearby stool. His large frame bowed forward so that his face was hidden. But she saw the fingers of one hand clutched at his throat and knew that he was feeling the noose tightening about them.

Over the coming days she kept her worries to herself, knowing that Simon was occupied with more pressing matters. Titus had organized his men in the building of huge ramps. Ramps that began on the slopes of the Gihon Valley and climbed upwards towards Jerusalem's walls near the tomb of the last Hasmonean king. And despite the bravery of Simon's men, and the many small victories won, still the ramps crept closer.

One night she awoke, limbs stiff, blinking in the dimness of a new day, feeling the tense ache of her body, hands still grasping the bedclothes in fistfuls, as though to ward off a momentous struggle. Stiffly, she turned her head towards Simon. He was deeply asleep, lying on his stomach, head pillowed in his arms. How much she wanted to reach out and touch him, to partake of that great strength that was his even in sleep. But she did not dare. Sleep had become a precious commodity in Jerusalem's troubled confines. Not to be trifled with. She rolled her head back and lay looking up at the ceiling, trying to prevent her mind from travelling down familiar grooves of worry. But it would not be disciplined. Instead running ahead, throwing up unbearable moments that must be relived until Jathniel stirred and cried out from his crib. Then she sat up and dragged her fingers through her hair. The light was rosy, not yet charged with heat. But it was early to be getting up. She slipped out of bed and went to the crib. Jathniel's eyes were closed and he was sleeping peacefully again.

As she turned back to the bed she saw Simon was awake, his dark eyes watching her. Yet neither of them spoke, wanting the stillness of the moment to last. And she thought how good it would be when all this was over. And they might go back to the house in Gerasa—no longer hateful in her mind—and rebuild it. The white house nestled in the lap of hills. And there they might raise their children, for Jathniel was surely the first of many. To live and work under the hot Judean sun was all she wanted now. To live simply and grow old with Simon. Days in the sun. And evenings spent together, sitting between the cool pillars that lined the front porch, watching the long fingers of twilight stretching east across Mount Gerezim, like the eternal, protecting hand of God.

She smiled without knowing she was smiling. And it was not until Simon's lips parted that she understood that he was about to ask her what she was thinking. She drew in breath, ready to answer. But the question never came. There was an explosion. A violent release of energy that shook the walls and sent her running to the window. Simon was close behind.

'What's happening?'

Before he could answer there was a second explosion. More dreadful than the first. Its dull, percussive echo went on and on, and through it they could hear the cries of the people, as though the first explosion had merely stunned them and now they were giving full vent to their fear. Jathniel began to cry, and Shelamzion went quickly to his crib and picked him up. Simon was throwing on a robe. He ducked his head towards the door. 'Upstairs. Come quickly!'

She followed him awkwardly, balancing Jathniel on one hip, and joined him on the flat plane of the roof. Simon was already at the western edge, his whole body straining towards the tomb of the Hasmonean king, and she drew to a stop at his side, trying to share his view. And there it was, spread out before her, Titus' army fully mobilized. Infantry poised in meticulous rows. Artillery flanking either side. And at the forefront, eclipsing all other danger—three monstrous siege engines positioned at the terminus of each ramp. The ramps were not finished. But now it became obvious that they did not need to be. Shelamzion's heart plummeted as she saw, suspended from the side of each engine, the massive rams that swung beyond the end of each ramp, as though flying on the feathers of angels, smashing their titanic heads again and again against the naked stone of Jerusalem.

'I thought we had more time,' Simon whispered hoarsely.

The sentries on the walls were loosing a flight of flaming arrows at the towers—Only two ways to destroy a siege engine: capsize it or burn it—but Titus had grown canny in his dealings with the Jews. His artillery was well positioned and the air was thick with deadly trajectories and the sound of men's screams. Simon took a step backwards. 'I must go down to my men.' He turned and made towards the stairs. She followed, Jathniel clutched in her arms once more.

'I will send word that the people should gather in the Tyropoeon Valley. They will be protected there,' she called after him. 'We will move as much of the grain as we can manage. And the wounded—we must make sure they are brought to safety.'

She was speaking swiftly, trying to delay the moment when he would walk through the door and be gone from her. But when he lifted his sword and turned to face her, the words died on her lips. So flimsy were the things she had to offer in the light of what he must face. Instead she whispered helplessly, 'What else can I do?'

He reached down and touched her cheek with that fleeting tenderness that was the mark of their relationship. 'Pray that the days of miracles are not yet over.'

Chapter XXIII

When I shall send upon them the evil arrows of famine, which shall be for their destruction, and which I will send to destroy you: and I will increase the famine upon you, and will break your staff of bread:

Ezekiel 5:16

In ancient times Jerusalem was protected by three walls. The first, and oldest, was begun by David, who slew Goliath. In later times a second wall was built to surround an area known as the Tyropoeon Valley, home of Ephraim the cheesemaker and his fellow mongers of pressed curds. The outer wall was the newest, its foundation stones laid by Agrippa to protect the 'new city' and finished by Simon son of Gioras. Three walls standing against the might of the world, one inside the other, like the layers of an improbable, impenetrable onion.

On the fifteenth day the outer wall gave way.

Shelamzion was standing in profile to Cornelius, her eyes trained on the light coming from the window. She spoke simply and without emotion, allowing Cornelius the time to scribe without need for pause. But now and then he caught a glimpse of a bitten lip or a spasmodic shudder that shook her shoulders, and he wisely kept his own counsel, making much of sharpening his pen or arranging his papers.

'There should have been plenty of time to organise everyone,' she continued. 'But we are Jews. We lack the Roman discipline. They did not understand, most of them. Even then. They packed sacred objects when they should have packed food. They wasted time. Husbands arguing with wives. Children getting lost in the streets then search parties sent after them. They would not listen.' She paused and bit her lip. 'How do you make thirty thousand people understand they are going to die?' She turned towards Cornelius, eyes sad and bleak. 'You see, Jerusalem was their wellspring, their cradle. Poor, foolish people. They thought the city gave them life when all the time it was the other way about.'

She fell silent, and Cornelius was beginning to wonder if she would speak again when she turned back to the window and continued her flat monologue as though there had been no interruption. 'I fled with Jathniel in my arms. I went through the streets so they would see me. The wife of Simon fleeing. And then they were afraid—' A violent knock on the door interrupted her words. Shelamzion and Cornelius exchanged glances. But it was only the *custos* come to pass Cornelius a note. He bowed obsequiously to the assistant governor before he left, and threw Shelamzion a glance mixed with venom and wariness in equal measures.

'He thinks me a witch still,' Shelamzion said, smiling.

'Are you?' Such a short time ago and the question would have been anything but jest. She looked back towards the window, and Cornelius was glad of it. It gave him time to read the note, which was no more than he had been expecting. Bar Gioras was to be made ready for the mob. Titus must have a worthy opponent to march in his Triumph. Not some lice-infected skeleton.

'If I were a witch,' Shelamzion said softly, breaking into his thoughts, 'I would not be here. I would fly away.'

'With us all turned to worms, no doubt.' He squirreled the note away beneath the scrolls on his desk.

'It would be fitting. A bookworm amongst his scrolls.' She turned and gave the papyri a playful flick, not noticing Cornelius' protecting hand over the one that concealed the note.

'A rapacious worm to consume all this,' he added quickly, nodding at the scrolls that covered the desk and littered the floor. But the moment was lost. She sighed and looked up at the light again, resuming her discourse.

'We gathered in the Tyropoeon Valley, an older part of the city. Better defended. With an ancient wall, higher and thicker than the wall Titus was struggling to break through. We thought we would be safe there. Even when Titus captured one of our soldiers and crucified him on Mount Scopus for all to see, still we thought we were safe. And when the first wall fell we did not falter because we believed in the strength of Jerusalem's defences. But, three days later, the second wall fell—'

Word that the second wall was crumbling reached Shelamzion's ears while she was dealing with the objections of a certain Yehoshua bar Ragesh. A tanner, known to run a good business buying animals rejected for sacrifice. He was a square, bullish man with dirty fingernails and he faced Shelamzion with a mixture of deference and defiance.

'No disrespect to your husband, lady. But they can't board here.' He cocked a thumb at a pitiful family of refugees. A couple and their three daughters, pilgrims from Galilee, come for the Passover. Now they were caught in the midst of the tempest thrown up as the great powers of the world creaked and shifted. The tanner rubbed his hands. 'Now if only they'd been boys I might have put them to use. But I'm a poor man. Barely enough to feed my own family. Cursed as I am with daughters.' He met Shelamzion's eye then let his own slide away shiftily. 'No disrespect.' He rubbed a dirty toe on the ground, making it dirtier still.

Shelamzion closed her eyes for a moment, aware that a crowd had gathered to watch. The day was hot and the threads of her temper were beginning to fray. By her side was Ariel, but he was staring at the ground silently, his monastic background self-evident in his ability to shut out the world. Even her own guard was listening, waiting to see how she would resolve the crisis, and she had not the beginnings of an idea. This was the hundredth such conversation she'd had this morning and the dazzle of her diplomacy was wearing thin. At that moment bar Ragesh added almost whiningly, 'You take the bread from my children's mouths. How am I to be compensated?'

Without warning, Shelamzion tore the diadem from her head and threw it at bar Ragesh's feet. 'Will that be sufficient to your need?'

The action had been shocking. Bar Ragesh actually took a step backwards. And the diadem, the prize of proud and beautiful Jewish queens, lay fouled in the dust, like a whore's discarded trinket, until Shelamzion commanded, 'Take it!'

Clumsy as an ox, his small eyes darting from side to side, bar Ragesh bent down and grabbed the precious circlet. He held it wonderingly in both hands, as though he suspected a trick or witchery would snatch it from him. Then he jerked a shoulder at the little party of Galileans. 'This way.'

They followed him, hollow-eyed and shuffling, through the low, smoky doorway of his dwelling, and Shelamzion watched them go with the numbness that follows violent actions. At her side Ariel's narrow, ascetic face was troubled. 'Was that wise, lady? You have given him more gold than he would have earned in a lifetime.'

She shook her head. 'He will learn its value when he tries to eat it.'

They would have moved off, ready to start with the next destitute family, but the sound of shouts held them in their tracks. There were men, clad in the light armour of skirmishers, fighting their way through the crowded streets. Shelamzion's guard immediately made as if to close round her. But she shooed them away.

'Wait! What are they saying?'

One of the guards—a tall, lean Alexandrian Jew, sent to Jerusalem for his education—stood frowning, then his eyes grew wide.

'Lady, the second wall—It's giving way.'

There was uproar. The violence of human terror had been unleashed. Shelamzion tried to call for order, but her voice was lost in the pounding closeness of the battle. Suddenly she was running just to keep her feet. Her guard was swept away. The air filled with the sound of women screaming. And beneath their screams were the curses of men, men who had stood against the encroaching tide of the dispossessed and now found themselves swept along, empty-handed, into their beggared ranks.

Somewhere in the churning chaos Shelamzion heard Ariel's voice, but she could not locate him. Her eyes filled with the sight of an old woman being sucked under by the blind savagery of men and women running for their lives. But when she tried to go forward to help, she was slammed against a wall, her head colliding sickeningly with the rough-hewn sandstone.

When the flash of pain receded there was a violent ringing trapped inside her skull. She stumbled forward. But everything had changed. People still ran. But their screams were muted. Somehow in this arid, dusty city she had slipped underwater. Even the pounding of the siege engines had become distant. Irrelevant. She understood that her dress was torn and her hair had come unbound. But the understanding brought no particular sense of urgency. Shock had stripped away the natural lining of her fear. And, detached, she made her way through the swarming surge of the crowd towards the Gennath Gate, curiously protected by the envelope of disconnection that saves men in battles. Even in the chaos there were those who noticed the strangely serene women who walked amongst them, and later it became part of the legend of Simon's wife.

She reached the Gennath Gate and there her energy deserted her. Alone and trembling she stood, the ringing in her head drowning out thought or action, so that when a hairy paw took hold of her arm she scarcely reacted. A face, big as a moon, peered into hers. 'Lady, are you well?'

'Yehoshua bar Ragesh,' she said slowly. Her voice was barely audible above the ringing. 'Where are the pilgrims I gave into your care?'

'Lost. Lost as my wife and daughters are. I can find them nowhere.'

Such swift retribution. Coming in a story or a play it might have been considered overly fantastical. But here on the brink of disaster tragedy had lost its power to surprise. Or so it seemed to Shelamzion. She merely nodded, saying, 'We will look for them.' But her voice shook as she said this and she cupped her head in her hands.

'No, lady.' Bar Ragesh's voice sounded far away. 'I will take you to safety, then I will search alone.'

And the last thing she remembered was him lifting her in his powerful tanner's arms. But this was not truly the last thing. Because the irony of a selfish man acting selflessly was not lost on her. For small acts of kindness had begun to take on the shape of miracles as the world disintegrated towards amorphous cruelty.

She was in the palace of the Hasmoneans, lying on a silken bed. That much she knew. She also knew when Jathniel crawled in beside her, his little hands clutching at the loose tresses of her hair in a way that brought her pain and comfort in equal measures. She knew when it was day and when it was night. And that Ariel sometimes peered into her face with grave, concerned eyes. She understood that the fighting was fierce, and that the second wall was lost. But she understood these things as though she had heard them or read them in some half-forgotten book with no meaning or relevance to her present situation. The ringing in her ears had faded, but was replaced by a scorching headache that tinged her vision with blood and coated her tongue with bronze. Then only sleep brought reprieve, and she clung to it, as a madman clings to the shreds of his reason, until the day came when she awoke and the pain was gone.

She sat up slowly. Instinctively she knew that Jathniel was not there and that she was alone, but still she looked round, searching the corners of the room and calling out his name. Her voice. So thin and cracked. Like a whisper of wind through rushes. There was some watered wine by her bed and she drank. Warm, slightly salty. It tickled her thirst rather than quenching it. 'Jathniel?' Who was looking after him? She got to her feet on limbs that did not seem quite connected to the ground. What was unsettling her so? The pounding in her head had gone. Why then the strangeness? She waited, listening to the silence. Then all at once she understood. The siege engines had stopped. Fear propelled her across the room. She snatched up an overdress from a chest and pulled it over her shift. One thought giving her the strength to act. Where was Jathniel?

Bursting from her chambers, she looked round wildly, half expecting to find the corridors abandoned and echoing, the sound of Roman boots blundering through the great halls below. But no such sight greeted her eyes. There were people everywhere: men, women, children. Huddled along the walls and collected in the corners, like grains of windblown sand. Some of the men were soldiers. She could see their bloodied clothing, the dirty bandages that bound flaccid limbs and lolling heads. Mostly asleep. What time was it? Shelamzion hesitated. The light was soft and shadowless. Early. In her panic she had not stopped to think. But now a little girl awoke and looked up at her with the huge sadness of a child. Then the adults began to stir. And it seemed she was a miracle to them, so eagerly did they gather round, reaching out to touch her and praising the Lord for her recovery. She stood tall amongst them, touched by their generosity, but only wanting to get away so that she might find her son. It was a relief to see Ephraim coming towards her.

He pushed his way through the throng and stood before her, joyfully. 'The Almighty be praised for sparing you.'

'Old friend,' she answered fondly. 'It surely takes more than the Roman army to kill the wife of Simon.'

'I will take you to him. You cannot know. He has cursed every physician in the city to the tenth generation as quacks and boobies for not rousing you. Even Ariel did not escape his wrath.' He turned to lead the way.

'But my son—'

He glanced over his shoulder, smiling at her concern. 'Fret not, lady. He is well cared for. He has made himself the darling of every soul beneath this roof. Surely we would willingly die for his smallest desire.'

His words were comforting. Yet the mantle of her unease was not so easily thrown off. Still hammering in her breast was the vertiginous terror a mother feels when her child is missing. *If I lost him,* she thought. *If I lost him—*To distract herself she followed Ephraim away from the clutch of eager hands, asking, 'What has happened? Are we still at war?'

He gave her a look as if to say, *Did you think miracles took place while you slept?* But he answered faithfully and simply. 'Titus has changed tactics. His men have been fighting day and night to win the first two walls. But he knows the inner wall is made of sterner stuff.'

'He is gathering strength then.'

'More than that. He is using time itself as a weapon. Yesterday he paraded one legion after another in full dress uniform on the Bezetha Mound. He paid his soldiers as the people looked on. Then they roasted goats below the walls so that the smell wafted over the city.'

Shelamzion felt the walls of her stomach contract on emptiness. 'He knows of the food shortages then.'

'He has spies.'

'He has Josephus.' The effort of talking had cost her, and she leaned against a pillar.

'Lady?' Ephraim was concerned. 'You must rest. I will call for Ariel.'

'No.' She forced herself upright. 'My husband, I must see him.'

Ephraim frowned, but it was not for him to argue with the wife of Simon. 'He is in the upper hall. John and Eleazar are with him.'

'John and Eleazar?' Suddenly her mind was clear. 'What has brought this about?'

Ephraim sighed. 'You know well that Titus has been building platforms about the city so that he might push his siege engines closer to the walls.'

A nod.

'And that Simon has harried them repeatedly to no good effect.'

She nodded again.

'What you cannot know is that John of Gischala had a more cunning plan. While Simon fought in the open, John had his men digging a tunnel near the Antonia.'

'Towards the siege platforms?'

'You have the measure of it, lady.' They started to walk, and Ephraim continued. 'As soon as John received word that the siege engines had been brought up, he had the props fired. The tunnels collapsed with such a thunderous crash that there were prophets out in the street proclaiming the voice of the Lord had called out *Netzah,* victory, when they fell.'

'And Simon? He cannot have let this pass unmarked.'

'Indeed not, lady. Two days later we were out attacking the remaining two platforms. Titus has little to show for his efforts beyond matchwood and cinders.'

Shelamzion stopped in her tracks. For all her tiredness, excitement was beginning to bubble in her breast. 'But this is a great day. What is left to Titus but retreat?'

Ephraim had taken a step ahead. He turned back now, shaking his grizzled head. 'No Roman general will so easily take his leave. No doubt we will be tested further.' But he could not disguise the hope shining from his old face. 'Yet I cannot help but think, if we can only find a way through this time of hunger then surely the Lord will see fit to deliver us as He did of old.'

Ephraim left her at the door of the small hall where Simon was, and knowing that he was giving an audience, she should have waited until he summoned her. But this she could not do. Days she had hovered on the borders between life and death. And days before that he had gone to defend the second wall. So she felt compelled to enter the chamber, yet when she saw him it was with the eyes of a stranger. He was taller than she remembered, all his features larger and sharper. She saw the scars of war, livid on his forearms and one on his cheek. She saw that his hair was still black as pitch, but that his shoulders stooped a little.

He had heard her footsteps, and turned, with the half-doubting expression of a man who does not dare to believe what is in plain sight.

'May the Lord be praised.'

Did he say those words or did she read them on his face? No matter. He was before her now, enfolding her in his arms, as though only the hot exhalation of her breath against his skin could convince him she was more than illusion. 'I would have torn down heaven if you had been taken from me,' he whispered. And she did not answer or make protest because she believed him.

There was a dry rasping sound as someone cleared their throat. Shelamzion sprang back, remembering that Simon was not alone. She was suddenly and uncomfortably aware of her unbound hair, the crumpled, unornamented overdress, her bare, dusty feet. Two men looked towards her, though only one dared to hold her gaze. John of Gischala. Thinking of him ordering his sappers to confound Titus' plans made her look at him afresh. He was gaunter than ever, but less hesitant than when she had last seen him at the trial of Niger the Peraean. Eleazar, captain of the Zealots, was with him, still too pious to meet a woman's eye, yet less sure of himself, eyes darting from the floor to John then back again. Shelamzion looked to Simon.

'I will go now.'

'No.' He rested a hand on her shoulder. 'Stay. I have been too long without your counsel.'

John's eyes narrowed curiously and Eleazar's head snapped up, as though he could not quite believe what he was hearing. But neither protested when Simon led his wife to join him on the carved chairs where once the heads of the Herodian household sat.

There was silence. Shelamzion guessed John had asked for this audience, and custom dictated that he speak first. Eleazar kept flicking looks between John and the floor. Simon waited, his expression revealing nothing. At last John took a deep breath. 'So it has come to this.' He paused again, as though waiting for Simon to speak. But Simon gave the merest flicker of assent with his eyes, then waited for John to go on. A muscle danced in John's cheek, and Shelamzion saw him clench his jaw to still it. At length he said, 'There are Romans gathered outside the walls. For all they are licking their wounds they are still there, and I cannot feed my men.'

'Have you conjured no miracle from heaven yet?' Simon asked coolly. The barb was deliberate and John flinched from it. 'You blaspheme,' he muttered.

'If by blaspheming you mean that I do not listen to the ravings of madmen then I blaspheme.' His eyes were fixed on Eleazar. The Zealot lifted red-rimmed eyes.

'Careful, son of Gioras. These are the Last Days.'

'Of that I have no doubt,' Simon snapped. 'You predicted apocalypse and then you did everything in your power to make it manifest. Only look how you burned our grain stores. What greater gift could you offer Titus? Go to him with your demands. He will surely make you citizens.'

An angry fire swept Eleazar's face. He got to his feet, jaw jutting forward aggressively. 'We are the Almighty's avenging arm. Good men have died for less than has already passed here.'

'Make your threats,' Simon said coldly. 'Let me hear how you are a liar as well as a madman.'

Holding herself against overt reaction, Shelamzion threw Simon a questioning glance. Surely this was an insult too far. Eleazar's eyes bulged. His hand flew to the curved dagger in his belt, impeded only by John's restraining arm. The contempt in Simon's voice did not waver by the smallest degree as he added, 'Do not posture here, Zealot. You came because you have need of me.'

'There is need on both sides,' John interjected softly.

'Not quite.' Simon's eyes still held Eleazar's. 'There is value to be found in having more men. Show me the value in having an army fighting on empty stomachs.'

'As you say,' John agreed. 'Where the staff of bread exists there is life—'

'And power,' Eleazar growled.

John spread his hands, like a priest. 'There is no need for this. We are brothers here.'

'Do brothers hold back bread? Do they make us crawl on our knees to them?'

'If I do,' Simon said, 'then you crawl for nothing. There is no bread I can give you.'

John and Eleazar exchanged looks. 'You have what remains of the grain,' John said at last.

'I have the grain stores,' Simon replied. 'And fifty thousand refugees to feed.'

'Will you feed the mob while my men go hungry?' John's voice was low, disbelieving.

'I must.'

'He must,' Eleazar sneered. 'He means to keep the grain for himself and damnation to the rest of us. What did we expect? He is as much a Jew as that Herod who wrote his name across us in blood.'

Now Simon was on his feet. And fearing there would be bloodshed, Shelamzion cried out, 'Let them fight to eat.'

A stone-dropped silence filled the room. Simon and John turned to her. Even Eleazar let his gaze sweep the floor at her feet. Shelamzion drew in a long breath, knowing that everything rested on her ability to persuade these men of iron to listen to the soft words of a woman. 'It is simple,' she said, knowing it was anything but. 'Without grain to feed everyone, there will be only one law. If a man fights he will be given bread. His family must eat, so he will fight.'

'An abomination,' Eleazar cried. He took a deliberate step away from Shelamzion, though he stood furthest from her. 'Truly women have the tongues of serpents.'

'And if he cannot fight?' John asked. 'Or will not?'

'But it will not come to that,' Shelamzion insisted. 'Titus will retreat. He must.'

'And if he is not so persuaded?' Eleazar demanded.

'Then it will little matter as his belly will be filled with Roman steel,' answered Simon. He sat down heavily, his gaze fixed on his wife's face. But she turned away, unable to meet his eye.

Cornelius put down his pen. Something in the finality of the sound made Shelamzion glance back at him over her shoulder, pleadingly. 'Can you think it was with gladness that we took this decision?'

'Yet you did take it.'

'Was there choice?' She pivoted round to face him. 'What chance was there for life if we had thrown open the gates and admitted Titus. On his command a forest of crosses had grown up on the slopes round the city. No, we had the measure of that gentle prince.'

'You cannot have hoped for victory.'

She opened her mouth, pausing as new thoughts altered her words. 'We pinned our hopes on his retreat. We did not think in terms of victory or defeat. Only that something must change ... If we could only survive long enough then things would change in our favour. Many still believed the prophets who wandered the streets proclaiming that miracles would split the heavens—'

'Even when Titus began to build the wall?'

She did not answer at once, but a shadow, like an eclipse, fell across her face.

Chapter XXIV

I will make them eat the flesh of their sons and daughters, and they will eat one another's flesh during the stress of the siege imposed on them by the enemies who seek their lives.

Jeremiah 19:9

All Romans are thieves, Shelamzion thought. Murderers and thieves. She was standing on the ramparts of the great inner wall, its gargantuan marble blocks seeming solid as eternity beneath her feet. Shrouded in the tattered mantle of an alms-seeker she had come, secretly, invisibly, needing to see with her own eyes how Titus was destroying the world. Lifting a hand to shade her eyes, she surveyed the strange, new forest that was sprouting from the barren flanks of the hills. A forest where all the trees stood in perfect imitation of each other, their height, shape and angle mirrored on every side. And from each tree hung a single, withered fruit; the body of a dead Jew. *Let them be dead*, Shelamzion prayed. *Only let them be dead.* Doubt made her insides twist.

Down below, the legionaries were working, intently as dung beetles, engrossed in their task, and she thought it again. They are thieves. Not even their gods are their own. Everywhere they go, plundering the mysteries of other nations. Stealing the secrets of soldiering from Alexander. Then tearing open the soaring marvels of Ægyptus, and Greece so they might be engineers—

Her eyes moved purposefully up the sides of the ravine, along the spiny back of the mountain ridges and down again. And everywhere she looked there were towers and ditches and palisades. She had refused to believe it. But now there could be no doubt. John had tunnelled, and Simon had fought with fire and sword, to bring the siege platforms down. But Titus, with that supreme Roman impertinence, had found a new way to trap his enemies. He was building a wall. A wall that would circumvallate Jerusalem in strange parody of the city walls, holding within that which was designed to hold without. A cage, she thought. Around the holiest place in the civilized world, where men and women, pagans and Jews, paupers and kings flock as one to make sacrifice. He is caging it, as though freedom itself can be caged.

The fierceness of these thoughts was too much for her. Legs trembling a little, she reached out to grasp the ramparts. A tell-tale grumbling in her stomach had begun, and she schooled herself harshly to ignore it. Too many ragged bundles of withered sticks lay on the streets and rooftops of Jerusalem for Shelamzion to allow pity for herself. She had stepped over them on her way here, all the time recalling the words that had condemned them, words from her own lips—*If a man fights he will be given bread*. But what of those who could not fight? What of those who took bread, but did not share?

And now she knew why she had defied her hunger to come here. Desperation had driven her. The need to find a way out. Or rather, a way in. A way to bring food into the city. But there was none. Titus was sealing up every entrance. Knowing that inside the days were mounting up, one on top of the other, like empty chasms, while the ravenous beast of hunger tore Jerusalem apart.

Defeated, she turned and made her way back towards the sandstone steps. There were guards on either side, but they made no salute or acknowledgement. The woman who passed them was wrapped in a beggar's cloak, her face veiled. They thought her mad to waste her energy climbing a hundred stone steps to admire the view. But who were they to stop her? And besides, no one wasted energy on greetings any more. That was one of the first things Shelamzion had noticed as the food stocks dwindled, the people grew taciturn and the greetings stopped.

At the bottom of the stairs she turned on to the avenue known locally as Solomon's Purse, a name garnered from the conspicuous wealth of those who lived there. Most had fled in the early days of the siege. Those who remained were discovering how little nourishment is to be found in a carved ruby or a fine pearl. Shelamzion walked down the avenue with deliberate slowness, knowing it would not do to be seen to have strength. Famine had Jerusalem by the throat.

So quickly. Shelamzion had never imagined that starvation could take hold in so brief a time. But *Abaddon*, the ancient name of hunger, had the freedom of the city, swelling bellies, like two-day-old corpses, and gnawing through living flesh to reveal the bony extrusions of ribs and skulls. And, if the more grisly stories were to be believed, men and women had fallen prey to the foulest practices, eating unspeakable things. Soups made from the boiled leather of belts and sandals. Whole families murdered for the sake of a rumour claiming they possessed a crumb of bread. And, most hideous of all, she had heard of a mother driven to madness by hunger, feasting on the body of her child. This last filled Shelamzion with such profound horror that she refused to countenance its truth. But late at night she would stand with her stomach groaning, looking down into Jathniel's crib, knowing he had cried himself to sleep for lack of food, wondering if a time would come when—She did not dare to finish the thought.

Her fingers found the handle of the little side door she had left unlocked, and she entered the palace gardens unnoticed. Gardens? The name was a dry joke. Before her lay the brittle skeleton of a lemon tree, and she stopped, staring wistfully up into the stripped branches, her nostrils filling with the pale aroma of plundered fruits. But it was worse to indulge the ghosts of plenty than to ignore them, so, with heavy heart, she turned to go. A hand grasped her ankle. Crying out in terror she wrenched her foot free, certain of a furious assault. But it was only an old crone collapsed from hunger.

Looking down, Shelamzion felt a tingling revulsion for this inhuman thing at her feet, limbs tangled like the brittle, terracotta-pipe legs of a Persian puppet figure, head too heavy for the bird's neck to lift, slumped instead on to the bony cavern of a chest. She rolled that head now against the sharp-edged cavity of her shoulder, looking up at Shelamzion with eyes that seemed impossibly animated in her otherwise dead face.

'Don't go.'

Her voice, no voice at all, but a husk of something once living, nonetheless restored the balance of her humanity. Shelamzion fell to her knees. 'Let me help—' She lifted one of the crone's hands in her own, meaning to chafe it. But it felt dry, like kindling, and she was suddenly afraid the brittle fingers would snap. The woman swallowed with difficulty. 'Simon's wife—'

Shelamzion stiffened. To be recognized, even through her veil. But the woman wasn't finished. 'Like an angel … bringing bread to us.'

Striking her like a blow, the words made Shelamzion squeeze her eyes tight shut for a moment. When she opened them again the crone was looking into the distance, her expression filmy and unfocused. '*Lacmā*,' she murmured. Bread.

The finality of the sound sent Shelamzion fumbling for a crust hidden in her sleeve. She thrust it into the woman's hand. 'Here—Take it. Take it!' The crone did not seem to understand. Her fingers twitched round the crust, but made no move to lift it. With trembling hands Shelamzion tore off one end and pressed it to the woman's lips. 'Eat!' A convulsive motion in the woman's throat showed that she was trying to swallow, but her mouth was a dusty bowl.

'No … no … no.' Shelamzion sprang up. 'I will fetch water.' But the crone's fingers plucked feebly at her hem. And Shelamzion crouched down beside her, shouting frantically over her shoulder, 'Water! In the Lord's name, bring water.'

There was the sound of voices, a scuffle of feet, and Ariel was hurrying towards her.

'Bring water. Quickly!' Agitation made her commands sharp. But Ariel did not move. His grave eyes turned slowly towards the old woman, and Shelamzion put out her hand in a gesture of reassurance. At her touch the body fell forward, emptied of its little morsel of life.

They stayed there for half the span of an hour, Shelamzion and Ariel, laying out the body, wanting to restore some tiny measure of dignity to this unmarked and unmourned life. But, as Shelamzion leant forward to draw the eyelids down, she saw something that made her heartbeat quicken. The crone's face had softened in death, the lines of suffering less pronounced now that the sufferer was gone. And Shelamzion saw with a hideous kind of clarity that here was no crone with her eyes set towards the grave, but a woman in her first bloom of youth.

Agog with horror, she leaned closer, trying to read some meaning or message in the absurdity of this miracle. How young was she? Marriageable age. Younger. There was no way of telling. No way to read the story that had led to this final tragic conclusion. But, as the minutes marched mutely away from pain, the face relaxed further into innocence, until Shelamzion might have been sitting next to a bride, dreaming of her wedding night, or a child slumbering next to its mother. And this she could not bear. Seeing her pain grow shapeless and without purpose, Ariel insisted they return indoors. She let him help her to her feet without protest. But not until she lifted the crust from the dusty ground.

John of Gischala came alone to see Simon. He came at night, unannounced, escorted by Ephraim and Yeled, to the chamber where Simon and Shelamzion were waiting. There was no formality between them this time. They sat at a table lit by smoking lamps, laden with wax tablets, where moments before Shelamzion had been scrawling a complex cabbala of figures in her desperation to find the formula for dividing grain sufficient to feed ten thousand amongst more than seven times that number.

Simon stood up when John entered, a trace of his old, sardonic smile playing about his lips. 'It is a poor table you come to, where we offer you wax instead of wine.'

'Mayhap wax is more choice than wine when it comes from a friend.'

'Is that what we are now, friends?' The question was put severely. But Shelamzion was surprised to hear a note of longing in her husband's voice. *How very tired he must be,* she thought. *He longs for older, simpler times.* But the time now was anything but simple. John frowned and shifted uneasily. 'Whatever I have been in the past, I am here as a friend now.' He paused, glancing, not at Shelamzion, but at Ephraim and Yeled. Shrugging when Simon made no move to dismiss them, then continuing in a low, urgent voice. 'You know why I am here.'

Simon sat down again, shaking his head. 'I possess no art for divining the thoughts of another.'

'What arts are needed? The situation is obvious. You must flee.'

An exchange of looks between Ephraim and Yeled told the room of their thoughts. Shelamzion glanced at Simon, but he was amused. 'So my men are to be rewarded with the sight of my heels.'

'Better that than the sight of your body twisting on a cross.'

The light from the lamps flickered, sending flames of light followed by flames of darkness across Simon's face. The gilding on the burnished statues flashed. And the figures in the murals shivered with an illusory breath of animation. When Simon spoke again all amusement had gone from his voice. 'Do you take me for the kind of man who would leave others to fight his battles?'

A sudden movement by John set the lamps choking and guttering. 'There are no more battles. All that lies ahead is degradation and defeat. Nothing will stop Titus now.'

'You stopped him.'

'When I undermined his ramps? A victory barely worth its name. He is building towards the Antonia now. And the siege engines you destroyed are replaced. No, brother.' John leaned urgently across the table. 'Titus is more myth than man. I've heard it said that he is kin to the Greek Hydra. And you may be sure for every head we cut off he will grow two more.'

'Titus is a man,' Simon said calmly. 'And men can be defeated.'

'But not here. Not now. Have you walked the streets? Every rooftop, every stinking alley, choked with skeletons that breathe their last while crying out for a crumb of bread.'

Did he look at Shelamzion, or did she imagine it? She felt herself flinch inside. She had been thinking of bread, the hot, sweet bread of her childhood. Taken for granted then. Now the everlasting symbol of a time of perfect goodness. Had the longing shown on her face?

'And what of you?' Ephraim asked. 'Will you also flee?'

John turned slowly so that the shadows slid across his face and pooled in his eyes. 'I am tainted with the Zealot stink. Nor will I be washed clean of it so easily. Simon, on the other hand, is always Simon. If he flees now, the people here will not judge him. And once he is beyond these walls, free Jews everywhere will flock to his side to save Jerusalem.'

A bitter brew of pity and scepticism tightened the muscles in Simon's face momentarily, then he smiled and shook his head. 'Those Jews who are beyond these walls look to what is happening here with horror. I have no doubt if I went to them they would nod their heads and speak of our noble cause. But when the time came to put rhetoric aside and open purses it would be a different tale. We are doomed. In their eyes, spent goods. And they will not send good after bad. No, my friend. Now is not the time to run. If the inner wall collapses, perhaps then—'

'Can you think it so easy to pick and choose the hour of your departure?' John interrupted angrily. 'The prison Titus is building for us will not yield to your command. And it is almost complete. Truly is it said that a man who makes bargains with fate is either touched by the Lord or touched by the moon—'

In a rough, unexpected movement Simon got to his feet, thrusting the chair behind him. 'We are done.'

John's mouth was still moulded around his unspoken words. It hung loosely, while his eyes darted from Ephraim to Yeled then back to Simon. 'You cannot—'

'We have enjoyed your counsel,' Simon continued, as though no interruption had occurred. 'Leave us now that we might reflect upon it.'

The slackness of John's face disappeared and his features settled into thin lines. He gave a small nod, though more to himself than the company. 'May the Almighty guide your decision,' he said at last. He turned to leave. But before he did so, he threw a long, searching glance at Shelamzion. Though whether it was to communicate some pleading message or simply to satisfy his curiosity she could not tell.

There was a tense, unnatural silence once John was gone. Shelamzion could hear his footsteps fading into the distance, but could not bring herself to meet the gaze of Ephraim or Yeled. Still looking towards the door, Simon sat down heavily. With clumsy hands he lifted one of the tablets. 'Do we stand here, like dumb beasts, when there is work to be done?'

Shelamzion looked up. Spasms of barely controlled emotion jumped around Ephraim's mouth and eyes, and a strange, unsettled expression was distorting Yeled's features. He opened his mouth, but looked towards Ephraim first before speaking. 'There is truth in what John has s-said.'

Simon looked at him sharply, disbelievingly. But Ephraim joined his voice to the argument. 'Yeled is right. It pains us all to hear this. And the Almighty knows I have prayed for a miracle. But in your own words, those of us who stay are doomed.'

Simon thrust the tablet away. 'Am I to be advised by old women now? I brought you here for war. Instead you cluck at me, like toothless old hens.'

Shamed, Yeled hung his head. But Ephraim had been born a free man and stood ridicule from no one. 'Son of Gioras,' he said sternly, 'I have followed you as a man follows a king. And I have done it in the old manner that we Jews have of picking one amongst ourselves as worthy of our love and devotion.' By his sides Ephraim's hands clenched repeatedly into fists, and Shelamzion thought, *It is hard for him. To talk like this.* But Ephraim had opened his mouth, like a prophet of old, and the words would not be silenced. 'You are quick to see cowardice. Yet was it cowardice for John to come here? He would be murdered by his own men if word of the deed were to reach their ears. And Yeled? Can you think it an easy thing for him to stand against you? For all he is a free man his heart has long been your slave. And I? Should I speak out? An old man, a Pharisee, the son of a cheesemaker. What am I? Only your right hand in battle. And in politics have I not held my tongue to allow yours free rein? Not one weak or cowardly act have I committed in your service. Therefore if I stand before you, calling myself John's man in this, and telling you to go—then Simon bar Gioras, go you must.'

One of the lamps on the table guttered, sending up a wreathe of oily smoke. Simon stared at it, as though the sight of a dying lamp was something extraordinary. 'And you believe this would be Ariel's opinion also?' he asked.

Breathing hard, Yeled screwed up his face, as if wanting to express the huge complexity of his thoughts. But all he said was, 'Y-yes.'

Tensely, knowing that any remark she might make must not come too soon, Shelamzion watched Simon's face for a sign. He breathed in and out slowly, lips twitching slightly against the fury of his thoughts, then suddenly he began to laugh. Not joyously. Not with relief. But harshly, coldly. A scream in the darkness or a madman's bark. Shelamzion felt her scalp prickling. Yeled and Ephraim were transfixed. They waited in silence until the laughter died, then Simon filled the void with his voice, that deep, compelling voice that had commanded thousands.

'How long have I ruled in the kingdom of the blind?'

A muscle danced in Ephraim's cheek, and he looked as if he would answer, but the fury of Simon's words cut him short. 'Are John's promises so honeyed that you cannot smell the stench of deceit beneath them?'

'John was once your f-friend,' Yeled broke in.

'A friend who burned the grain stores. A friend who gave the order that saw Zacchaeus fall in battle. Did not Eleazar think him a friend? John turned on him. How long should I be gone before you found the worth of John's friendship? We face harsh times, and John relies upon our desperation to sway us. A friend who has betrayed us once will do so again. Need I remind you of that darling of the Romans who clamours at our walls for peace? If you would know the workings of John's mind you have only to remember Josephus.'

Shocked, Ephraim began, 'You surely do not mean to compare—' But an explosion of sound, as Simon brought the palm of his hand down on the table, ended all argument.

'Enough. I will hear no more. This conference is ended.'

Not one lamp had failed yet the room grew darker. This was something new. Something they had not foreseen. He had acknowledged their freedom then thrown it back in their faces. Yeled and Ephraim blinked, like men newly awakened to the knowledge that this was the price of putting their faith in one man. And Shelamzion breathed faster, knowing more powerful men than Simon had died for showing their tyrannical side. This was a knife edge. A pendulum swing between life and certain death.

Yeled looked sorrowful. But the fingers of Ephraim's sword hand twitched convulsively. And Simon, sitting very still, watched those fingers with the look of a man hoping in his secret soul for an excuse to fight. Ephraim's fingers made a fist one last time, so tight that his arm trembled. Then a shudder went through him and his shoulders slumped in defeat. He reached out a hand towards Yeled. 'Come,' he said gently. 'We are not wanted here.'

Simon bent his head over the wax tablets as Ephraim and Yeled took their leave. But the moment the door completed its closing arc he was on his feet and pacing the room. His energy was boundless, but unfocused. His hands made agitated half gestures to an unseen audience, while his eyes remained distant and unseeing.

Feeling emptied, Shelamzion sank down on to a cushion-laden bench, stretching her arms out between her knees and letting the curve of her spine slump down towards them. Her strength was gone. The tragedy of what had just taken place was not lost on her, but now that they were alone, the lacerating voice of hunger had awoken in her belly and it was hard to think about anything else. Was it worse to lose all hope of food, she wondered idly, or to be in this permanent state of never quite receiving enough. It was said that there were Bedouins who could torture men lost in the desert by tantalizing them with single sips of water until they died of thirst. Was that what life had become? Single, tortuous sips. She blinked, realizing that her mind was wandering. And, looking up, found Simon standing before her.

'You chose a fine moment to decide to become a woman.' The words were thrown angrily, clumsily. They caused her pain, but equally she knew how her silence had hurt him. Hunger had made them brittle, without subtlety. And now she hurled his words back at him: 'And you chose a fine moment to play the king.'

'Isn't that what everyone wants me to be? A king.'

She looked at him, her heart breaking. 'It is the only time I have seen you behave like a king, and I have never seen you less like one.'

His face became a mask. 'Even you—'

With an effort she straightened in her seat. 'Must there be sides? I am so tired. Today I saw a woman grow younger after she had died. And tonight I witnessed old and trusted comrades turn against each other. Such is our age of miracles. And now you would have me produce one to say that you are right even when I know you to be wrong.'

Abruptly he turned from her, and she regretted her words. What monsters hunger makes of us. She pulled herself to her feet to follow him. 'Simon.' He was staring down into the shadowed well of the courtyard. What could she say? *It is our fault. We have made you like this. Raising you up. All the time demanding that your will be done because only you had the courage to see the way ahead. And we have bent our heads and knees so often that you cannot tell us from the grains of sand beneath your feet … But now there is only a small chance of escaping this hell. And you must listen.*

She took a determined step towards him. 'Simon.' She said it more forcibly, expecting him to turn. He ignored her, hunching his shoulders forward, and she realized he was looking at something below. Drawing nearer, she saw figures in the courtyard. Lack of light made them featureless, but their raised voices and angry gestures were enough. 'Simon?' But already he was flinging past her towards the door that led from their chamber, throwing himself down the staircase, sword drawn at his side. Foolishly, Shelamzion ran after him, calling, 'Wait!' But he was gone. And by the time she reached the last step he was confronting three men.

Moonlight revealed two of the men to be Yeled and Ephraim. But Shelamzion barely acknowledged any sense of relief. Her eyes were on the man struggling between them, a tall man, more dishevelled than she remembered, but his fine, aquiline features essentially unchanged. She formed the word in a whisper, as though to say it louder was an invocation of something terrible. 'Hyrcanus.'

Simon blinked, as though the sound of his wife's voice had woken him from a dream. 'Let him go,' he ordered, and Yeled and Ephraim grimly obeyed. Hyrcanus fell to the ground then crawled on his belly towards Simon, arms outstretched.

'Forgive me. Or, if you cannot forgive me, then kill me. Here! Do it with the sword you gave me.' He pulled the blade from his belt and held it aloft, head still bowed.

'Get up,' Simon said with distaste. 'Men do not crawl to me.'

Then Hyrcanus got to his feet, yet still with many cringing gestures, until Simon lost patience. 'You took the trouble to seek me out. Now look me in the eye and tell me why you have come.'

Hyrcanus pushed the tangled hair from his face, eyes shifting wildly.

'I have news. News that will save Jerusalem.'

Chapter XXV

Which death is preferable to every other? The unexpected.
Julius Caesar

The play was a poor one. A shoddy reworking of Menander's *Heros*, in which the subtle comedy of the original was largely lost amongst a confused melee of slapstick antics and senseless debauch. Cornelius hadn't wanted to come, such frivolities seeming almost obscene in the light of the coming Triumph. But Quintus had insisted. 'Looks bad, dear cousin, if the family don't show.'

'What of your gift?' Cornelius gave a fleeting glance to the upper arcades, where a marble likeness of the Emperor now stood. 'Rumour has it that Vespasian is delighted.'

'Publicly, of course,' Quintus agreed. 'But privately he knows, as well as we do, that not so long ago it bore the head of Vitellius.'

On stage, a stuttering Daos was proclaiming his devotion to the heroine of the piece, while his partner, Gatos, wielded a huge, gilded phallus in graphic demonstration of where love's course was leading. The crowd roared and Cornelius shuddered.

Quintus shifted uncomfortably on his seat—more for effect than distress; the seats within the semi-circular *orchestra* were strewn with a luxury of cushions—.

'O, I quite forgot. You're wrong.'

'Wrong?' Cornelius turned his head from the play with relief.

'About the Triumph. Your little Jewess won't be the main attraction.'

'What do you mean?'

'Josephus has spoken against it.'

A scuffle had broken out in one of the upper tiers. The audience abandoned the play to watch. In his relief, Cornelius scarcely noticed. He forced himself to ask in as casual a tone as he could muster, 'Why?'

'Why? Because he is Josephus.' Quintus reached for some wine. 'Who can understand why he does anything?'

'You must know more.'

'Must I?' Quintus blinked slowly, the simple act of raising his eyelids already a burden. 'I tell you, I know almost nothing. It all comes second hand. Apparently Josephus advised Titus to put her in the rear along with the other women captives. Seems to think she'll take the shine from Simon. Odd really. She's no great beauty from what you've said. But I suppose oriental taste is different.'

Such eloquence clearly exhausting him. Quintus sank back on the cushions. Cornelius watched him for a moment then turned to face the players, his eyes stiff and blank as the marble head of Vespasian. At last he asked, 'And after the Triumph?'

His cousin was so long in replying that Cornelius turned to him curiously. 'You know something.'

Quintus' expression. Such an awkward fit for those insouciant features. In his surprise Cornelius scarcely recognized the shape of pity in their new arrangement. Then Quintus began to speak. And Cornelius listened, with the shouts of the audience fading behind him. As though his head had been plunged deep under the foaming waters of the Tiber.

In a daze Cornelius arrived at the Carcer. Outside its sullen facade a crowd had gathered. Jeers assailing his ears as he approached. Directed at him? No. Not these good people of Rome. These artists and artisans. These farmers and freemen. They recognized authority when they saw it, shuffling back with plebeian deference, clearing him a path. Cornelius walked between them indifferently. And not without some awareness of his indifference. Such a short time ago he had needed their respect to make the air more breathable. Now they were irrelevant. As he himself had become an irrelevance. A bit player in a masterpiece far beyond his reckoning. He mounted the stairs wearily. *Actus ultimus orsus est.* The final act begins.

Shelamzion was waiting for him, huddled in a corner of the room, hands over her face. And knowing what he now knew, he stood helplessly, watching until she became aware of him and spoke through the weave of her fingers.

'It is not for me. Only it is so loud. Simon must hear.'

'No,' he soothed. 'The walls of the Tullianum are too thick for that.'

She lowered her hands. 'That is the first lie you have ever told me.'

His fiercely flushing cheeks spoke more eloquently than any confession. 'Do not judge me too harshly—' he began, then found he could not go on. She was on her feet, searching his face.

'What has happened?'

So easy. Just tell her. Was he not the most virulent champion of Veritas? But he pulled away and slunk to his desk, like a whipped dog. 'It is not so simple.' She was looking at him expectantly, and he sought refuge in vexation. 'You have grown short-sighted within these four walls. Life outside is complex. I cannot give an explanation for every change, every nuance—'

She nodded, still searching his face, as though it would reveal its secrets. 'Tell me one thing then.'

'Yes.'

'What is to be the manner of my death?'

Chagrined that her intuition should so easily outwit his artifice, he stammered, 'You—cannot want to know.'

'Can it be worse than the thousand ways that come to me in my dreams?'

It surely could not. And so in the flat voice of a man who is appalled by his own actions, he admitted, 'I do not know the precise hour of your death, but I have been given an insight into its manner.'

A flutter in her throat. A dilation of the pupils. That was all. 'Go on.'

Cornelius' mouth was dry. 'I do not—'

'Tell me.'

He reached for the wine jug. Found it empty. Confound it! He cursed the boy who should have filled it. He cursed the *custos* for forgetting to remind the boy. He cursed ignorance and lack of manners and the decay of modern society. And he went on cursing, in a manner not at all like himself, until his temples throbbed and he gagged on the sour emanations of his own bile. Then he stopped, heavy, ragged breaths swelling his chest, and bowed his head like a guilty man.

'*Archon.*' Her voice was soft yet determined. 'Go on.'

'You will not be with Simon during the Triumph.'

She nodded. 'For that I am grateful.'

Grateful? Was gratitude the word to use here? He went on thickly. 'Afterwards there will be celebrations. But a certain chosen few will be invited to a dinner party hosted by Titus.' There was a tremor in his voice, and he fought to control it. 'The centrepiece of the festivities will be a play.'

'A play?'

Such a mundane question, yet more pertinent than any other she might have asked. He felt a trickle of sweat follow the path of his backbone before he answered, 'Seneca's *Phaedra.*' Then he added bitterly, 'A second-rate playwright. Now that he is dead he has become the critic's darling.'

Frowning, she asked, 'And after the play?'

It was the question he had been dreading. 'There will be no afterwards—' The words ground against the soft lining of his throat. 'For you.'

She glanced away, puzzling over what he had said, then back again, none the wiser. 'For me?'

'You—you are familiar with the drama's theme?'

'I know it in the Greek.'

'Of course.' He smiled weakly. 'As you have observed, we Romans are thieves. The version by Seneca is clumsy, misogynistic. Lacking Euripides' delicacy, but the plot is essentially the same. A woman's weakness in matters of the heart. Rejection and dishonour the inevitable outcome. And then—' His voice dropped away.

'And then?'

Still she did not understand. Why should she? Who else but Rome could take the sublime beauty of literature and transform it into a butcher's bloody slab? He breathed deeply. 'Tales such as these follow a pattern. The inescapable moral must be satisfied. Phaedra has fallen from grace. To placate the audience, she must—there is no avoiding it—she has to … '

'Die.' The word he could not say fell from Shelamzion's lips, like a bead of blood. 'I remember the original. She plunges a sword into her breast, does she not?'

How could he tell her? His voice came out in a hoarse whisper. 'My dear. In Rome there is no boundary between the real and the imagined.'

There was a long silence. Her gaze dropping to the floor then lifting several times, as though she expected him to reassure her that her assumptions were wrong. He said nothing. And at last she asked very softly, 'Am I expected to learn my lines then?'

'No.' Cornelius felt his heart trying to wrench itself from its moorings, but he made a valiant effort to speak calmly. 'An actor will play the part. The use of masks provides a dramatic device allowing the actor to be switched with the condemned. You will only be required for Phaedra's—final moments.' He got to his feet, tears in his eyes. 'My dear—' He moved towards her clumsily, then stopped. Pale. Her skin had taken on the deathly hue of marble. He reached a hand towards her, but she was so still, so preternaturally distant that he had the prickling sensation that he was looking at a face staring back up at him from the dark waters of a well. He let his hand fall. 'Shelamzion?'

She did not move, but the focus of her eyes came back to him. A brief smile, then she shrugged. 'So be it.'

An explosive anger burned in his veins. 'Can you be so cold? Is the thought of your death nothing?'

She looked at him in surprise, and he knew he was being unjust. Should he not rejoice that she accepted death so easily? But he could not. He could not. 'Please.' He was a child again, trying to change the abiding world of adults. 'There must be some way—'

She lifted a finger and laid it on his lips. '*Archon*, my son is gone. In a little while Simon, too, will be lost. What should I live for?'

He wanted to say, *For me. Live for me.* Instead, he walked brokenly back to his desk and sat down. Curling his fingers around the reed pen, he avoided her gaze, saying in the cracked voice of an old man, 'Hyrcanus returned to Simon claiming there was a way to save Jerusalem from Titus … '

As Shelamzion walked through the dim hallways with Ariel, she said, 'Now Hyrcanus has returned, he says there is a way to save us all.'

243

Ariel did not answer, and Shelamzion looked up into the narrow face of the Essene, trying to read his expression. 'You do not believe him?'

Ariel shrugged. 'If Hyrcanus were to claim that night follows day, I would not go to bed until I had seen it with my own eyes.'

'You are harsh. Simon trusts him.'

'If Simon trusted him, he would not ask me to bear witness to what he has to say.'

They entered the hall where Simon and the others were waiting. The lamps had been renewed and they cast a fresh, hopeful light across the company. Simon was seated. The others stood. As they took their places Hyrcanus shot Ariel a quick, searching glance. But the Essene's face betrayed nothing and Hyrcanus hunched his shoulders and looked away. 'I have wronged you.'

'You might have spared yourself the need of telling me,' Ariel replied coolly.

Hyrcanus bit his lip. 'I am deserving of your censure. While you all stayed true to your purpose I allowed my heart to rule my head. And yet when I spied Titus … so close.' He looked beseechingly towards Simon. 'At the time action seemed right. In thinking this you can scarcely think me alone—'

'Hardly,' Ephraim interrupted sourly. 'For it is surely with those like-minds that you have sought shelter until now. How do we know that it is love of us that brings you crawling back?'

'Enough.' Simon straightened in his seat and silence fell over the company. 'We are too much a people who let our past deeds set the mould of the future. What Hyrcanus has done he has done. And no words will bring about its undoing. All that matters is that he stands here offering a way to save us. And with Rome's hand clenched around us, like a fist, let us hope in the Almighty's name that this is the sign Ariel and Ephraim have been praying for.'

Disgust brought Ephraim round to face Shelamzion. 'If he comes from the Almighty he comes only as that snake which first entered *Gan Eden* to tempt men to their folly.'

The words were muttered, but Hyrcanus coloured a fiery red and tears welled in his eyes. The sight of those tears stabbed at Shelamzion. But knowing that a woman's tenderness would not be welcome here she looked instead to Simon, giving the barest nod towards Hyrcanus. Simon made no sign that he saw the gesture, but there was gentleness in his voice as he said, 'You were our friend once. Tell us now if you are to be our saviour.'

The tale Hyrcanus told was a strange one …

Much later Shelamzion stood at her window looking out over the chequered roofs of the city, while behind her Simon lay on their bed staring up at the ceiling. Beyond the door the everyday noises of human life filtered through. Shrunken refugees filling the bedchambers and the halls, the rooftops and the palisades. They had nothing to say, but they were never silent. At last she asked, 'Can it be true?'

She heard Simon's weight shift and knew he was looking at her.

'That Idumaea is raising another army? We must pray it is true.'

'And yet—'

'Our hopes lie with this Ishmael ben Onias Hyrcanus talks of?'

The shadows were shifting and folding beneath the rising light. Falling back, revealing Jerusalem's wounds.

'Have you forgotten that the house of Onias stood against us when we entered Idumaea?'

Simon made an irritated noise and she heard the sound of him swinging his long legs off the bed.

'So it was then. The siege has changed things.'

She turned from the window, struck by the inflexible note in his voice.

'You believe Hyrcanus?'

'Don't you?'

'I—' She paused, aware that she did and unsure as to the source of their conflict. With an awkward smile she spread her hands. 'I fear I have lost hope in hope.'

He came to her and embraced her. 'Despair has made cynics of us all. But I tell you this. I believe Hyrcanus. The information on the uprising came to him through chance overhearing. That crawling snake, Matthias, who dares to call himself High Priest held this knowledge from him because he guessed it must then come to my ears.'

With every taut, wearied nerve in her body she wanted to believe him, but still she asked, 'And you fear no betrayal?'

He leaned past her, and she followed his gaze beyond the window. 'You looked out here, while it was still dark. Will you look again?'

She averted her eyes. 'No.'

'No, wife? Will you not gaze upon holy Jerusalem? They call me king here. Look, there are my subjects upon the rooftops.'

'They lay the dead out on the roofs.'

He turned, his face both mocking and despairing. 'And if Hyrcanus is false and no help is coming, who else will I rule but a kingdom of the dead? Hyrcanus might have used his knowledge of the uprising to gain powerful friends in any party he chose. Instead he risked all to come here. No, we will believe him for now, and wait to see what the future brings.'

She thought of the mighty walls of the city parting before Titus, as the waves of the Red Sea had parted, and of the Roman soldiers swarming through, like one of Pharaoh's plagues. She shook her head. 'What can the future hold for us?'

Simon drew in a deep breath and his face softened. 'Perhaps the chance to build a new Jerusalem.' And as he said it he leaned on the sill of the window so that his fingers pushed through the shadowed bars of darkness and emerged out into the light.

Ben Onias was a stocky, middle-aged man, who had a sense of down-to-earth solidity about him that went beyond the obvious fact that he was not starving. His salute to Simon was soldierly, yet courteous enough to include his wife and do her honour. It was true, he said, the house of ben Onias had sat about long enough scratching their arses—Pardon my rough ways, lady. But things are changing— The patriarch had died recently of an ague. Natural circumstances or poison chalice? He wouldn't hazard a guess. But the way it was now, new blood was at the top. And that blood saw the way the wind was blowing and knew it was time to act. Some said it was the End of Days? Well it wasn't for a simple man to say. But Idumaeans were Jews, proud as any others, and they recognized a call from the Almighty when it came.

The plan was straightforward enough. The Idumaean army, near twenty thousand men once amassed, would march on Jerusalem. Titus' main camp was to be attacked from the rear once they reached the Valley of Thorns. And before either of the smaller camps could be called to reinforce Roman numbers, Simon's men would force their way through the siege wall, cutting off Titus' flanks.

Simon's eyes flicked towards his commanders.

'It could be done,' Ephraim said slowly.

'The casualties would be high,' Ariel added. 'On both sides.'

Ephraim shrugged. 'Romans are shopkeepers at heart. They will weigh up the worth of the treasures inside these walls against the cost of losing so many men and find the answer wanting.'

'Z-zacchaeus would w-want a fight,' Yeled said, startling everyone with his forgotten presence. And his words pricked at Shelamzion's conscience. It was obvious that Yeled was still missing the little Sicarius. Yet how long since Zacchaeus had come into her mind? Chased away by hunger's snapping jaws and the theatre of plenty that daily appeared to torment her whenever her eyelids drooped. *And when did I last think of Yeled's grief? Simon is right. Hunger makes monsters of us all.*

She turned to her husband, wanting to read his face, but he was looking at ben Onias 'You ask my help, yet you did not seek me out.'

Shelamzion was watching the older man's face carefully. No blush, no guilty aversion of the eyes. He looked at Simon squarely and his words were plain. 'Idumaea is not so close to the holy city. And the Romans have locked you away, like a whorish daughter. Pardon again, lady. But it was nearly my life to get in here. And your husband's position is not well understood beyond these walls. What Jew, knowing no better, would not first seek counsel from the High Priest?'

'True enough,' Simon agreed. 'In the days when High Priests were not bought and traded like oxen by greedy, corrupted men. But what counsel did Matthias offer you?'

And now Shelamzion saw shame surfacing along ben Onias' sturdy jawline. He cut his eyes away and shook his head. 'Matthias told me to go home and forget all that I'd seen or heard. He said there was still peace to be had, and better a degraded peace with the Romans than Jerusalem razed to the ground on the whim of fanatics.' He raised his eyes slowly, but it was Hyrcanus he sought out. 'I tell you plainly my hand felt the grip of the dagger against my thigh, and I might have plunged it into his cowardly heart there and then had this young man not chanced upon us and demanded to know what was going on.'

Hyrcanus, who had been keeping to the edges of the debate, stepped forward. 'They thought to keep ben Onias from me. It is only because I returned at an unexpected hour that I heard raised voices—' Breaking off, he looked beseechingly at Simon. 'Never when I sought refuge with the High Priest party did I expect … did I ever possibly conceive—'

'Spit it out, man,' growled Ephraim. But it was ben Onias who grimaced then answered. 'Matthias plans to have his sons murder Simon and his child. Then to take their heads to Titus as the price of Jerusalem's freedom.'

'So much the party of peace,' Ariel whispered. 'May the Almighty bring the plagues of Ægyptus down upon their heads.'

A choking cry escaped Shelamzion's lips, and she could be still no longer. 'Simon,' she croaked. 'Jathniel—'

Some men would have turned to her with loving reassurance and some men would have thundered their rage until the foundations trembled beneath their feet. But Simon only sat, like stone. Like the ageless rock upon which Abraham would have sacrificed his only son. And his silence was more powerful than any rage thrown by a Caligula or a Herod. It had an uncanny, eldritch quality to it that made mouths, which had opened in protest, snap shut, and hands, which had flown in anger to their sword hilts, fall away, limp and empty. And when, at last, he spoke, it was as though the earth shook. Yet he uttered only four words.

'Bring them to me.'

The deaths of Matthias ben Boethus and three of his sons were ruthlessly carried out. Simon gave orders that the youngest—who had ridden with Hyrcanus against Titus—was to be given a chance at life in recognition of his defiance of his father's party. And needing no second warning he fled. Some said to the Romans. But it mattered little. Simon already had the fish he wanted to fry.

The three sons were brought in, bound hand and foot, and placed at Simon's feet. Then Matthias ben Boethus, High Priest, was dragged in. A squealing pig of a man. Once fat—power swelling ego and body alike—the days of famine had eaten him away so that now he was a thin man grotesquely robed in sagging folds of flesh.

'Simon!' he cried, his voice high and shrieking. 'Have you forgotten who opened the city gates to you? You are in my debt.'

Simon looked at him coolly. 'My debts were cancelled when you thought to murder my son.'

'Lies!' the High Priest exclaimed, looking wildly round the room. 'Who tells you this? A traitor, trying to flatter his way back into your favour. Or that Idumaean dog, ben Onias—'

'The house of Onias has proven its worth to me.'

'And you would listen to a Jew who cannot trace his ancestry back two generations over your High Priest—' He broke off as the convert's son fixed him with a cold stare. Simon stood up. 'Where is my son?'

Stepping forward, Shelamzion led Jathniel by the hand. Although there was no danger, her heart was thumping, and she gripped the little fingers entwined in hers, as though she were holding him out over a precipice. There was silence. Matthias glanced at his sons on the floor. Simon took Jathniel by the shoulders and thrust him forward. 'Look at my child and tell me what I have heard is not the truth.'

But Matthias would not look up. 'Lies,' he whimpered again.

'Yet you cannot look at my child.' Simon unsheathed his sword, and Matthias threw himself to his knees. 'I confess. If it is confession you want then I confess. Only spare my children, whose only crime has been to follow their father—'

'Yet they are not children. They are men with minds of their own. Your youngest child knows the price of peace with the Romans. And him I have spared.' Simon pulled back the head of the eldest son, a ruddy-complexioned lad, whose eyes were glassy with terror. Matthias began to weep, huge ugly sobs shaking the pendulous folds of his flesh. 'Then kill me first. Let the father die before the sons, as is the nature of things.'

Simon paused. And, frozen where she was, Shelamzion could hear nothing but the hoarse breathing of the men around her. Then Simon blinked, as though coming back from a far off place, and spoke slowly. Almost to himself. 'The Idumaeans look to us. And we must give them no cause to suspect weakness. The time for mercy is over.' He lifted his sword, and Shelamzion felt a tug at her sleeve. Ariel.

'Do not let the boy see this.'

Her eyes widened. Then she snatched up her son and ran from the room. Ariel followed. The chamber they entered was long, its walls made of sandstone blocks so thick they had ruptured the spines and spleens of the slaves who had dragged them into place. But still they could not dampen the sound of Matthias and his sons' screaming or the hideous, charged silence that followed. After a moment, white-faced, Shelamzion turned to Ariel.

'He had to do it.'

Ariel nodded. But they could not meet each other's eye. And a moment later she heard him murmuring the familiar words of the sage Hillel. *Ma d'alach seni l'chavercha la ta'avid.* That which is hateful to you, do not do to others …

Chapter XXVI

And now the blood red days began. While the Roman camp ostentatiously made no move, —the soldiers given leave to roast their pigs and goats with deliberate malice— a desperate frenzy of activity had seized Jerusalem. For the first time if you were not for Simon you were against him. With ruthless authority he purged the party of peace. A certain priest, Ananias ben Masbalus, was next to be executed, followed by Aristaeus, the scribe of the Sanhedrim, then fifteen more. Looters and black-marketeers were sent squealing to their deaths alongside men of rank and position. Their bodies were displayed along the city walls or lobbed down into the watching Roman ranks. And least pity of all was extended to Simon's men.

One Judas, an officer, and veteran of the Idumaean campaign, began to voice doubts. He was found trying to defect to the Romans with ten of his men and brought before Simon. He pleaded for his life, and Ariel spoke for him. 'He is young. Despair sometimes weighs heavier on those who cannot remember happier times.'

But Ishmael ben Onias was at Simon's shoulder—transformed from Idumaean emissary to chief amongst Simon's counsellors. He whispered something, and Simon listened, frowning, then shook his head. 'Take them away.'

Stunned, Ariel stammered, 'Burial. At least you will allow that—' He met stone.

'Our Idumaean brothers must know that we give no quarter to traitors. Their bodies will be thrown from the walls at sunrise.'

Then ben Onias leant his thick body forward, whispering, 'If you'll forgive a suggestion. Let their names be announced beforehand so that the people might know your justice is impartial.'

And Simon closed his eyes. 'So be it.'

Watching from the side-lines, Shelamzion felt an impotent horror descending upon her. No longer the eye of the storm, Simon was the storm itself. A wild, uncontrollable force driven by hunger and desperation.

She had said, 'What if you are wrong? All this bloodshed. How can this be leading to a better world?'

But he stood straight and inflexible, and she felt a deep sadness filling her as she understood that he had shut her out. He was a column of rock, hard and unbending. Lost to her, like the high places of old, with their stone altars to their jealous god. She did not know this man. And, between the deep lines of worry gouged into his gaunt face, there was little sign that he knew her. Only for Jathniel did those hard lines sometimes soften. Then she saw the man she loved, and knew that he could be reached. *I will try,* she thought. *I will make him hear me. And together we will find another way.* But there was no time. During the night the north wall of the Antonia Fortress collapsed.

It had withstood the brutal force of the battering rams. Nor could Titus' engineers undermine its impregnable design. But the architect's vision had all been directed towards an external enemy. No provision had been allowed for an attack from within. And in the end John of Gischala was the unwitting author of its downfall. John's trick of tunnelling beneath the foundations to launch surprise attacks on the siege engines had backfired. The mighty stones crumbled and Titus' army poured through.

But here was triumph for the Jews. A second wall. Quickly erected, and not so strong as the first. Ranks of Jewish soldiers lined up behind. And every legionary knowing that to scale it was to find death on a point of cold steel.

The Jews heard Titus exhorting his men to arms. Were they cowards, he asked. Had they not idled here, filling their bellies, while famine and pestilence did their work within the city walls? Now was the time to act. Had they forgotten that the soul of a fallen soldier is set amongst the stars, whilst the faint-hearted vanish into darkness underground and sink deep into oblivion …

The next day Shelamzion was changing the dressing on a wounded man when she heard running footsteps. She froze, hands hovering over the wound she was about to cleanse. A young officer called Mordecai ran in, flanked by two guards. He gazed round wildly for a moment, then found Shelamzion in the confusion of the wounded.

'Come. Quickly!' He made as if to grab her arm, and she shook him off.

'Is the wife of Simon to be dragged by the nose, like oxen?' She spoke imperiously because she saw the fear in his eyes and it made her afraid.

'Lady,' he fell back a step, but would budge no further. 'The Romans have broken through. Simon orders you and his son to the Temple.'

'But the wounded?'

'No time. Lady. They are coming—'

And coming they were. Pouring through the tunnel dug by John's sappers. Shelamzion found herself jostling for space with dozens of frightened women and children in the Temple courtyards. She fought to face them calmly. But it was no easy task. Skittish with fear they would stay neither still nor quiet long enough to listen to reason. Amongst them Shelamzion spied a ragged prophet plying his trade. And wherever he went the chaos and upheaval increased. She had her guard bring him to her, and saw that he was a skeletal, pock-marked individual with an ugly mess of scar tissue criss-crossing his back, where a lash had once been laid.

Wild-eyed, he stood before Shelamzion, and recognized her. But she was first to speak.

'What do you tell the women when you go amongst them?'

'The truth, lady. Expect no less of me.'

'I expect nothing of you. You are unknown to me. Only tell me what you are saying to those poor, frightened creatures.'

Some of his wildness evaporated, and he looked at Shelamzion with undisguised disdain. 'There is no mercy for those who side with the violators of the covenant.'

The blood drained from Shelamzion's lips. 'Do you dare—' she said hoarsely. But the prophet was unrepentant. 'Do I dare, lady? Does your husband dare to take the side of man over the side of the Lord?'

'Simon is a man of the people. He cares about the people.'

The prophet sucked in his hollow cheeks. 'An earthly kingdom is what Simon cares about.' He spat the words venomously. 'He turns his back on the Lord and defiles his Temple with soldiers and unclean women.' He went on to list the many abominations Simon had committed in the eyes of the Law until Shelamzion's fear was replaced with a cold, hard resolution, and she called for her guards to remove him from her presence. The guards were young. Of the tribe of Manasseh and filled with the superstitions of their homeland. It was no easy thing for them to lay hands on a prophet. 'You would have us lock him away?' they asked, deliberately misunderstanding.

'No.' In this she would stand firm. 'Take him beyond the Temple compound and leave him there. The Romans are heathens. Doubtless they have greater need of his wisdom.'

It was a harsh punishment and the prophet knew it. He blanched, suddenly looking less certain of himself. But when he felt the firm grip of the guards on his shoulders he understood that he had lost. And now Shelamzion became his especial target. As they dragged him away, he screamed out abuse, raising his voice so that the frightened women turned towards him, and heard him shout, 'Belial and his whore shall be destroyed. And all the angels of his dominion, and all the men of his forces shall be destroyed forever—'

Shelamzion stood, with her back to the women, watching the prophet's writhing figure growing smaller. She was white to the lips, except for two burning spots of red on her cheeks, and there were tears in her eyes. But it was not shame that made her weep. Rather it was the knowledge that this was the first time she had directly ordered a man to his death.

The parched days of summer passed. The last hours of Tammuz melted into the searing month of Av. And still the Jews held out. When Titus' men killed the sleeping sentries it was Simon's troops who fought, like madmen, to keep him from reaching the Temple's spacious courtyards. Ishmael ben Onias fought with them, and it was soon noted that he had the courage of a lion and the luck of demons. Shelamzion heard the men recounting how legionaries turned and fled rather than face ben Onias' sword. Even Yeled grudgingly admitted that he was 'kin to Zacchaeus' in his skill. And all the time they looked to the south for signs of the Idumaean army. But the horizons remained empty as cloudless skies, and fresh lines of worry began to etch themselves on Simon's face.

'Ben Onias, no one doubts your courage. But we cannot hold out much longer—'

The Idumaean was wiping blood from his sword. 'A Roman force has attacked our men south of Etam. No more than a skirmish. But they are delayed.'

'And why did I not hear of this before?'

Ben Onias looked up grimly. 'Begging your pardon. But the news has only just reached me. Five messengers were sent, but only one got through. And he barely lived long enough to tell the tale.'

'The men are losing courage.'

'The men are hungry.'

Beneath a canopy of glaring summer sunlight, whose rays fell thick as rain, Shelamzion crossed the great central courtyard of Herod's palace, and went to seek out Simon. She found him in Ariel's charge, having a wound on his thigh dressed. The Essene was applying a sour-smelling wash of *acetum* to the infected area that made Simon wince as it was applied.

'Hold still,' Ariel commanded. His loyalty to Simon was without measure. But in matters of medicine he was master. 'Better a little pain now than the horror of infection.'

'I should let you loose on the Roman wounded,' Simon said sourly. 'Then truly they would call me the Scourge with reason.'

They had not heard Shelamzion come in, and she stood a moment watching them. Ariel in particular. Noting, with a pang, how white his beard was becoming. She drew breath, saying softly, 'Simon, we must speak.'

In his wife's face Simon saw something that made him turn to Ariel and say in a voice that brooked no argument, 'That will do.'

As soon as the door thudded shut, Shelamzion looked to her husband, saying, 'You cannot cancel the rite of Tamid.'

Simon's eyes were expressionless. He got up slowly and tested his wounded leg. 'My men are hungry.'

'Your men are Jews.'

'I have no choice.'

No choice? Disbelief rose in her throat, like a physical sickness. 'If the people do not see a lamb sacrificed in the Temple each day they will give up hope. God will abandon us.'

'There is enough blood spilt on the battlefield to satisfy the Lord's need for a thousand lambs.'

She knew he blasphemed because he was exhausted and in pain. And worse than that, he was trapped with no word of hope yet from the army of Idumaea. But still she whispered, 'Your men will not eat God's lamb.'

He looked at her bleakly. 'There are those amongst them who would eat their own fallen brothers. Do not flatter yourself that men's morals rise higher than their stomachs.'

The mighty Antonia Fortress was gone. Levelled by the indomitable force of Rome's fury. As a child, standing on the roof of her parent's home. Shelamzion had shuddered to see its long shadow fall across the Temple. Now she shuddered to see it gone. Without its monolithic protection they were exposed. And yet—

'The Almighty has surely heard our prayers,' Ephraim said. He sounded hoarse with relief. And Shelamzion looked to the ruins of the Antonia, which was proving too narrow an opening to allow Titus to mount his attack, then back to Ephraim. And there was such hope shining on his old face that she wished that she might reach out to pat his scrawny shoulders, as Simon would have done.

But it was not long before Titus was erecting platforms again, intending to scale the walls he could not push down. Simon ordered that the northern and western colonnades be destroyed. And seeing the anguish on his wife's face, he said, 'It must be done. If Titus' men scale the wall we cannot leave them an easy landing.'

Hyrcanus understood her misgivings. 'The Temple, Simon. The body of everything we hold most sacred.'

But ben Onias' brows drew down and he said flatly, 'If a body becomes diseased, its limbs must be cut off to save the rest. There is no choice.'

And liking the medical imagery Ariel also spoke in favour. And so it was done.

A crowd gathered to see how Simon would incise the wounded limbs of the Temple. Shelamzion stood at her husband's side, dressed in the vestments of a queen. The dress she wore had belonged to Mariamme, tragic wife to Herod the Great, and a smaller woman than Shelamzion in every respect. Yet hunger made it hang from Shelamzion's frame in gapes and folds, and she was forced to tie a silk sash tightly beneath her breasts to disguise her thinness.

Standing next to Simon she gave every appearance of composure. But inside she did not feel calm. She felt nothing but her hunger and a flat lack of emotion that left her pale and glazed of eye. Simon, too, appeared calm to any who did not know him well. But his tension was manifest to his wife in the controlled modulation of his voice and the quick, darting motion of his eyes.

It was a hard thing to watch. Simon gave the order and two men came forward bearing torches. There was a hiss of disapproval from the crowd, but Simon's men held steady. Watching the crowd behind her mask of queenly indifference, Shelamzion saw that they were hollow-eyed and defeated. More so since the daily sacrifice had been stopped. Or did she imagine it? There was no doubting their despair as the flames licked along the great colonnades. *O Jerusalem, if I forget thee, let my right hand forget her cunning. If I do not remember thee, let my tongue cleave to the roof of my mouth*—To watch the Temple falling beneath the blows of its own sons felt worse than striking the face of a dear and respected parent.

And perhaps it was in the face of this baleful horror that one Jonathan, a man of Simon's, decided to take matters into his own hands. He was a small man, even for those malnourished times, lacking either the wiry strength of Ephraim or the stocky solidity of ben Onias. His limbs were puny, and his head seemed too large for the narrow plinth of his neck. But his heart was that of a lion, and he had the kind of hot-headed nerve of a man who has fought against the odds all his life.

With no warning he broke free from the crowd and mounted the wall, yelling down to the bemused sea of Roman faces a challenge to the bravest and the best of them to engage in single combat. There was laughter in the Roman ranks. Yet Shelamzion heard striations of unease in their mockery. What danger could there be in killing this dwarfish freak, yet what honour?

Jonathan's abuse redoubled. And, at last, a heavy lout from one of the cavalry squadrons stepped out. Jonathan whooped gratitude to his One True God, and leapt down to meet his adversary. The Jews surged forward, Simon and Shelamzion in the lead, taking the stone staircases to the wall's height two at a time. Those who made it to the top shouting down a commentary of what was happening.

'He's a brute, that Roman.'

' … swinging with it. Jonathan only just rolled out of the way in time.'

'Jonathan's hit. He's bleeding from the shoulder. He's lost. He's—'

'No, look he's up. He's up—'

Turning towards Simon, Shelamzion saw in his face, gripped in concentration, a gravity that was mirrored in her own lurching heart. Something extraordinary was happening. This was more than the race of a foolhardy man to his own death. Here was the echo of history. A tiny shepherd boy and a Philistine giant made flesh again. A simulacrum of the moment Israel's future had teetered before impossible odds a thousand years before. A yell went up from the crowd. He was down. The Roman cavalryman was down. Drawn by the magnetism of the moment, Shelamzion took a step forward. Was it possible? Could another miracle be worked this day?

It was real. There was the big cavalryman's corpse on the ground, while Jonathan swooped and plunged, waving his dripping sword at the watching troops. There was laughter and shouts of encouragement from the Jews on the wall. Then

Simon held up his right hand, and the cheering Jews fell silent. He stood surveying the battlefield, as though not quite sure what it meant.

'Have we won?' someone asked uneasily.

Simon's eyes were on his champion. 'Jonathan,' he bellowed, 'get out of there.'

The little Jew turned at the sound of his master's voice. He bowed and took a jaunty step towards the wall, and as he did so an arrow, shot from the Roman side, pierced him through the chest. Jonathan stopped. He looked down at the arrow, as though confused, lifting a hand to finger its length. And only then did he lift his eyes to the aghast audience, muttering words too faint to hear, his legs buckling, his body falling prone across his vanquished foe.

There was silence. The Jews struck dumb by the appalling unfairness of it all. The Romans stunned for an instant by their own savagery and betrayal of custom. Then they started to howl and bellow their triumph. And, at Simon's side, Shelamzion stood stiff and frozen, knowing that their shouts were not for the victory of killing one small Jew. But for the knowledge that they had broken the unwritten rules of war, yet remained unscathed. The gods applauded brutality that day. And the legionaries hallooed a new era where the weight of many would always crush out the spark of few.

In disgust, Simon turned to leave, and knowing it her duty, Shelamzion made as if to follow. Yet she managed not the dignity of Simon's departure. Unable to help herself, she gave a final glance to where Titus sat. But her eyes were not for that future king of the world. They rested on her fellow countryman. Sitting on a dappled mare and wrapped in the red cloak of Rome, Josephus still retained that enigmatic air that set him at odds with the world. He did not join in the cheering, but sat, clear and still, watching something. Shelamzion's eyes narrowed. What held his attention now that Simon had left the stage?

The steps of the prison beneath Herod's palace were narrow, roughly cut, and led down into darkness. Using every ounce of control to prevent the revulsion she was feeling showing on her face, Shelamzion followed the guard downwards. The task was not made easier for the greasy residue that covered the stairs. Trying not to think what it might be, Shelamzion lifted her skirts and willed herself to hurry. She was carefully dressed, a cream-coloured shift beneath her saffron overdress. At her throat a necklace of topaz and opals, and encasing her wrists the gold bracelets with the lion-headed emblem of Gioras. Warm colours, borrowed from the brightness of the sun, to sustain her in her descent into the underworld.

The guard stopped at the foot of the stairs and jerked his head at a door of oak and iron. Shelamzion looked into his face. There was something insolent about his expression. He sensed her need to get away. She snatched the torch from him, saying in her most commanding voice, 'Open it and wait outside.'

'She has light, lady.'

'Then she will have more when I enter.' With a look that brooked no compromise, Shelamzion stepped aside, letting the guard fumble with the lock.

'There, lady.' A note of respect had entered his voice.

'Good, now leave me.'

For an instant Shelamzion stood on the threshold, her appalled senses taking in the clammy pressure of stagnant air and the dismal, smoky light of an oil lamp, which served only to add to the foulness of the atmosphere. Then her eyes, making the inevitable adjustment, found the outline of a straw pallet, a gourd of clay, and, lastly, the narrow, stooped back of a woman standing motionless in the corner of the room, arms outstretched in prayer. Not knowing how to interrupt, Shelamzion waited in silence until the woman lowered her arms, asking suddenly, 'Is he dead?'

Caught off guard, Shelamzion answered without thinking, 'Your son was at Titus' side this very day.'

'They told me he was dead.'

'It is not so. I may offer you that much comfort.'

The woman turned slowly, a grimace of disbelief pulling back her lips. 'You think it a comfort to be that creature's mother?'

And Shelamzion, finding herself staring into the embittered gaze, could only whisper, 'Yet you *are* his mother.'

There was a bleak laugh. 'Do we choose what issues from our wombs?' Her eyes narrowed. She was studying the fine quality of Shelamzion's dress, which had taken on antique hues in the dull light. 'Why have you come?'

But Shelamzion did not answer. She was thinking, Has it come to this? Are we truly so afraid that we must lock up old women?

The mother of Josephus sighed, as though she hadn't expected an answer. With a hand that trembled visibly, she pushed back a wisp of hair from her fore-head. 'If not to boast of my son's death then is it mine you seek? No.' She looked deeply into Shelamzion's face. 'They wouldn't send you for that.'

'I came of my own free will.'

'Ah, then you came for something.'

Shelamzion lowered the torch, glad to let the shadows steal away her features.

'Yesterday your son had a moment when he might have gazed upon my husband in triumph. Yet his eyes were on another. I could not tell who, though I sensed the motive to be ill. I come here, today, to understand.'

'Oh.' The older woman fell silent. Physically she was not like her child, tiny in stature, her beauty still visible in the fragile imprint of the bones beneath the withered flesh. She made Shelamzion think of the high cheekbones and sharp chins of Ægyptian corpses sometimes indecently exposed by shifting desert sands. But when the mother of Josephus spoke it was with the icy tones of the aristocracy to which she belonged. 'So now it occurs to you to understand Joseph.' She gave a short, arid laugh. 'Why come to me? Do you not think I have spent bitter years contemplating the enigma that claims origin in my loins?'

She walked to the bed and sat down, neither needing nor seeking Shelamzion's permission. Shelamzion was left standing, suppliant before the queen of hell. She swallowed, knowing it a mistake to give in to her emotions, and tried again. 'You are too modest, lady. If anyone might help my husband it is surely you.'

Her words amused Josephus' mother. 'Have I reason to help the convert's son?'

'Have you reason not to? It would convince Simon of your loyalty.' Leaning forward she offered, 'And I would see to it that you were housed in accommodation fitting to your station, with your maids returned. You have my word.'

The amusement left the other woman's face. She withdrew into herself and her eyes darted with internal debate. But when she spoke it was with every nuance of her exalted lineage. 'And whose word do you offer me? Or is it that you think me kin to the camel drivers or the cheesemakers to be so impressed by a silken dress and a necklet of shining stones?' The words were designed to hurt, and Shelamzion felt their sting. Nonetheless she controlled herself, saying, 'Ill-use has made your tongue sharp. But I know you do not approve your son's course. Only help me now, and I swear Simon will extend his friendship freely.'

'The friendship of a brigand and a thief.' Exaggerated disgust curled the corners of her mouth. And ignoring the anger in Shelamzion's face she added, 'Did you think to profit from my sorrow? Know this—as you stand there glorying in your plundered finery—whatever my son has done, he is still of a great bloodline. What is it that Simon offers the world?'

'Men like Simon are the hope of Israel.'

'They are its scourge.' Josephus' mother made an angry, violent motion with her hands. Then holding them up in horror, as though she did not recognise such excess as her own, she went on in a voice too flatly modulated to be anything but the seal on immense anger, 'The worst sin of men like Simon is that they put themselves above the Almighty.'

'You cannot mean that—'

'Can't I? Do you think it random chance that sees the good and the great born into the best families? Surely the dullest wit must comprehend the celestial order that He-who-is-all-glorious intended. Simon would tear that down. He would plunge us into chaos.'

'Simon sees the good in men. He freed the slaves—'

'By whose command?' Josephus' mother countered. The scrawny chest beneath her robe was visibly struggling to contain her breath. 'Is it the Law that slaves should be freed? Did the patriarchs think to liberate their bondsmen so that they might place a yoke around their own necks? From Sadducee to maddened prophet, I know of no man who proclaims freedom for slaves.'

Shelamzion met her eyes coldly. 'Were we not led from bondage in the great Ægyptus by a man like that?' But her hope of shaming the mother of Flavius Josephus was disappointed. The older woman got to her feet with the strength of generations behind her.

'You dare to lecture me in the meaning of freedom,' she hissed, her face a sickly yellow in the wan light. She was close now. Close enough for Shelamzion to feel the arid breath scorch her cheek. She took a step back, but Josephus' mother followed, asking venomously, 'Is a child free to disobey its parents? Is a woman free to cuckold her husband? Even the High Priest must obey the constraints of his position. Freedom comes from the order of things.' She pointed a finger at the younger woman. 'Is oppression by the pagan horde something new? For centuries they have come. Philistines, Assyrians, Babylonians, Selucids. Wave after wave. And who understood better than we Sadducees that survival is not to be won on the edge of a sword?

'The idolaters will always come, and there will always be more of them. Freedom is not some gaudy trinket to be fought over. It is a delicate balance maintained by intelligence and tact. Through diplomacy and prudence we keep our covenant as the chosen people. Not by trampling on the world's order in the name of some fabulous dream of liberty that has never—and will never—*exist!*'

She paused, winded and wounded by the ugly hopelessness of her words. And Shelamzion thought, *You are wrong. And I was wrong to come here.* But she said only,

'I will leave you now. But I will ensure that you are moved to more comfortable accommodation, and that your maids are restored to you.'

The mother of Josephus did not answer. She was seated again, head drooping like a withered flower, hands clutching feebly at the thin folds of her blanket. Shelamzion turned to go, but as she did so the older woman said unexpectedly, 'Beware the fatted calf.'

Shelamzion stopped. 'Your pardon, lady?'

Josephus' mother looked at her with burning eyes. 'I know my son. And I give you warning.'

'I do not understand—'

But though she was pressed, she would say no more.

In the days that followed Shelamzion forgot the warning from Josephus' mother. And though she kept her promise and had the old lady moved to a form of house arrest with her maids in attendance, the withered figure receded in her mind as grander, more vivid, events started to unfold.

The levelling of the Antonia Fortress having proved a disappointment, a frustrated Titus ordered fresh assaults on the wall that kept him from the Temple's outer courts. Days reverberated to the thunder of siege engines and nights were pierced by the howls of the wounded or the smaller, more poignant sounds of final breaths carrying their owners into oblivion. Shelamzion felt as though she did everything at an exhausted run.

Even the kisses she laid on Jathniel's forehead or that secret place well-loved of mothers, the nape of the neck, were fleeting, firefly caresses. Burning for an instant then gone. There were days when the hem of her skirt was stiff with blood, and weariness sat between her shoulders like a stone.

Yet in a strange way she would look back on these times as the last truly happy moments of her life. Despite the hunger she was still young and strong, and full of purpose. She had found love and had multiplied it. And now, as the eleventh hour struck, the Lord of all Creation was unrolling his plan to confound the universe and save his chosen citadel. And always Simon was at the centre of things.

Charging at the head of his men, across the flattened perspective of the outer courtyard. Ready to fend off the Roman ladders that were appearing, like the black legs of spiders, over the outer wall. Without breaking stride, turning to look over his shoulder, sword raised above his head, like Moses smiting the Amalekites, like David facing down the Philistine horde. A shaft of sunlight glancing off the upthrust blade shooting out sparks of divine light. Lifting his eyes for an instant to catch sight of her—He did, didn't he? Catch sight of her—So sure, straining forward from an open window, to be closer to him, if only by an inch.

Then roaring. The great lion of Judah setting the earth to tremble. And his men roaring back with a wildness that told the world that they were ready to die yet longing to live. Victory or eternity: how should it matter? If Simon was there to lead them they would follow.

Chapter XXVII

And the fourth angel poured out his vial upon the sun; and power was given unto him to scorch
men with fire. And men were scorched with great heat …

Revelation 16:8–9

Asleep, Shelamzion felt intrusive fingers of light fumbling in her consciousness. She rolled on to her back, struggling to ignore them. But awareness of the struggle only brought waking more readily to the surface. And she opened her eyes feeling the leaden drag of exhaustion in her limbs, and a confused awareness that hanging above her, like a sentient moon, was Cornelius' anxious face only inches from her own. He straightened when he understood that she was awake, and she saw he was holding something in his hands. Closer examination showed it to be a robe of vestal white. It was threaded through with golden letters from the Hebrew alphabet, beautifully worked, though their arrangement was apparently meaningless. *A dress fit for a Jewish queen,* she thought sleepily. Though no Jew had fashioned it. Then she was awake, as vividly as if she had plunged her head straight into a pool of ice-cold water. With her heart pounding, she looked into Cornelius' face, asking in a small, tight voice, 'Is it time?'

The tears in Cornelius' eyes spoke for him, but he answered hoarsely, 'It is time.' He held out the robe. 'You are to wear this. Soon two women will come to bathe you and dress your hair.'

'But Simon. He must not—' She got to her feet, almost swaying under the pounding rush of blood pumping through her heart. 'I must not be seen.'

Cornelius gave a weary nod. 'It is decreed that you will lead the women. But you will be too far back to be glimpsed by Simon.'

'I praise the Almighty for that.'

Cornelius swallowed. 'You will be chained. I cannot prevent it.'

She managed a faint curl of her lips. 'Are they afraid I will fly away?'

Cornelius smiled back. Then suddenly there seemed nothing more to say. Yet she knew this to be a ridiculous fiction, because lifetimes would scarcely be enough to exchange all the words they had yet to say to each other. His sad, brown eyes were looking into her face, and she thought him on the verge of saying something. But, as his lips parted, there was a sharp rap on the door, and her heart plummeted, like the last grain of sand dropping to the bottom of an hourglass.

Without thinking, she reached out and grasped his hand. 'Cornelius—'

He did not speak, but she felt the hard pressure of his fingers clasp round her own.

'Will I see you again?'

There was another sharp rap at the door. Panic dilated their pupils. Quickly, Cornelius bent forward and kissed the palm of her hand. An action that would have been unthinkable less than a day ago, yet she did not flinch. He spoke rapidly: 'We will see each other at the dinner party given by Titus. It will soon be over then. And I promise'—he raised his eyes—'It will be swiftly done. You will not suffer.' Then he wrenched himself back, calling in a gruff, angry voice, 'Enter.'

The door opened, and there stood the *custos*, two hard-faced slave women at his back. The *custos'* cheeks were rosy. He had partaken of the celebratory wine that had already begun to flow freely in the streets in advance of the Triumph. But his eyes were hard and glittering. He looked at Cornelius and Shelamzion with the undisguised malice of the lower orders who chance happily upon an indiscretion by their betters. But there was nothing to confirm his suspicions beyond the woman's white face—natural enough in the circumstances—and the man's hands clenched against the force of some emotion that the *custos'* illiterate development prevented him from reading.

He gave a short, impudent bow, saying, 'She's to be handed over to the Praetorians in one hour. And you are to join your esteemed cousin, Fabius Quintus, at the Forum Romanum immediately.' He looked up, hoping to have provoked an extravagant outburst. But the woman's eyes were glazed as potsherds. And the assistant governor of the Carcer stood with a face grimmer than any gorgon god, before pushing roughly past the *custos* and marching swiftly out through the door. He did not glance back, though the eyes of the bandit queen followed him until he disappeared.

The end was coming. From the walkway above the Court of Women, looking northwards towards the ruins of the Antonia Fortress, Shelamzion watched it approach, her sweating hand clasped around the hand of her little boy. A low balustrade prevented him from seeing what she was seeing, and he tugged at her sleeve wanting to be lifted up. 'No!' She spoke harshly to cover the black despair that rooted her to the spot.

Romans, a vast sea of them. A red flood that no exalted staff could part, swarming across the outer court. And the Jews going down in bloody, senseless chaos. On the ground, armoured limbs, heads, even clothes hacked off so that obscenity was added to their shining corpses. Sound, rising up, thick as walls, miles high. Fear and fury. And Death's shriek echoing off the ancient stones. Cries of war mixed in with the whimpers of the devastated and the dying. Men calling for their mothers. Mothers weeping for their sons.

And to Shelamzion, standing in the jaws of this maelstrom, it seemed that the whole world was screaming in terror. No, not quite the whole world. Idumaea was silent. Not the smallest whisper had come from their army, and now John and Simon fought alone.

In the days leading up to this pitched battle, as the Romans began to fill up the charred and blackened outer court, Simon lost patience with ben Onias, and sent two scouts out to bring back word of the Idumaeans' approach. They were caught before they had taken ten steps beyond Jerusalem's boundaries. And that day Simon, silent and grim, had watched as their broken yet living bodies were nailed to crosses. The youngest of the two was a boy named Micha the Swift. He was fifteen years old and the fastest runner in Jerusalem. They crucified him upside down.

Micha's mother had come then, terrible in her sorrow. Spitting curses at Simon, accusing him of murdering her child. And Simon had sat, as a stone sits, eternal and unmoved. Even when she struck him with her nails, leaving a thread of blood along his cheek. Even when Yeled and Hyrcanus dragged her sobbing, collapsing figure from the room, he remained silent, waiting until the great door of the hall fell closed, and only then allowing his gaze to fall slowly to the floor. Waiting nearby, Shelamzion understood without having to be told. *He blames himself.*

'Imma!'

Shelamzion blinked herself back into the horror of the here and now. Jathniel, no longer tugging at her skirt, but pointing upwards, his chubby finger tracing a remote arc high in the heavens. A firebrand, thrown by one of the legionaries. Tumbling through an impossible trajectory. Like the star of morning falling from grace. Shelamzion followed its path with her eyes. So small. Like a soul escaping the churning carnage below. And these thoughts were all she had time to think before the brand fell through the golden aperture of an upper chamber. And moments later the room burst into flames.

Light dazzled. Sound hurt. Even an inhalation of fresh air was dizzying, laced as it was with the acrid smell of animals, unwashed bodies, dung's foetid aroma, and the pungent scent of perfume that wreathed the bodies of every woman in Rome, from prostitute to patrician. Bewildered, and confused by her bewilderment, Shelamzion stumbled. Rough male hands righted her. But they did not seek to hurt her. She understood that the Praetorians would not beat her out here in the streets. Not for decorum's sake. After all, what Roman would flinch to see a Jewish captive being thrashed? But today, in their emperor's moment of triumph, everything must glitter with the Midas touch of victory. Once again she was a queen, dressed in silks, a diadem of gold upon her head. A queen. Pressing her fists into her belly, forcing her spine to straighten and her chin to lift. She thought, *They have dressed me as a puppet to prance in their parade. Let them feast their eyes on a queen of Israel then.*

But thoughts are not deeds. As the triumphal arch came in sight, its travertine marble a wonder in the hot sunlight, she felt the swooping plunge of her spirits. Was all Rome made so large in order that man might feel so small? Every building screamed of the agonies of those who had been forced to bend shoulder and knee in its construction. Shelamzion's breast tightened. What had made Simon believe he could fight this colossus of blood and stone?

The crowds were out in force now. She could hear their roar beyond the arch, so loud that the men of her escort were forced to shout to make themselves understood.

'Over there,' one called to his companion, pointing to where the snaking line of the procession stood in awkward anticipation.

Hands pressing roughly against her back, pushing her past the procession's head. First the Senate. Her impression was of fat balding men, plumped up with the importance of the Tyrian stripe ostentatiously displayed on their immaculate togas. Then trumpeters, gorgeously attired, curling instruments held loosely at their sides. They paid her no attention, and, in turn, were of no interest to the Jewish queen, whose eyes had alighted on the line of *fercula* waiting beyond them.

Huge, each one needing more than a dozen men to hold it aloft, laden with the wealth of a plundered nation. So much wealth. Shelamzion's eyes widened. It was the madness of dreams to see riches splayed out in a vast, scintillating convolution. But there was no mistake. Precious jewels with all the colours of tapestries, and tapestries shining like precious jewels. Gold to whet the appetite of Croesus, and silver running like a torrent between ice floes of ivory and pearl. And all this as nothing to the sight of the Temple treasures—the golden Table of the Presence and the great, seven-branched menorah—lewdly displayed, cheapened in the strong sunlight. Like trinkets for an unworthy god.

A jolt between her shoulders. She had stopped without realizing it. The pace picked up. Painted eyes of Roman gods following her progress. Two bulls, astonishing in their whiteness, attended by a gaggle of Camilli. When they caught sight of the captive queen in her finery they stared for a moment then began nudging each other and giggling in high-pitched boys' voices. One of the guards made a crude remark that would have had Shelamzion blushing to the roots of her hair but a day ago. Now it washed over, unnoticed.

It was all too much. Walking past marvels and miracles, lost in their dazzle.

The smells, the sounds. Too alien. Too exotic. And all filled with the implicit promise of death. So strange. To know this day was her last, yet not to sink down before it. To walk when she was told to walk and to stand when she was told to stand. Her head felt empty, the spirit already weightless. And each step she took was nothing more than the mechanical corollary of a well-oiled machine performing its function to the bitter end.

They passed huge travelling stages, three or four storeys high. And upon each one was a ghastly tableau of the siege. Shelamzion averted her eyes, yet she saw enough to understand that war could be turned into art. Indeed, by the blatant rivalry that existed between the tableaux, as they vied with each other to portray annihilation in ever more scandalous detail, it was also evident that art could be turned into war.

Heartsick, Shelamzion walked for several paces with her eyes squeezed shut. But somehow it was more frightening to be alone in the darkness than to face strangeness head on, and so she opened her eyes and saw him standing there, no more than ten paces away, as though he had never been gone. Simon. Just the same, yet impossibly changed. Thin. The hard leanness that had characterized him, even when starving, melted away. His shoulders stooped. A scrollwork of cuts and bruises clearly visible on his arms and legs. They had dressed him in a pristine tunic, but it hung awkwardly on him, the gathered folds only emphasizing the thinness of his body.

For the moment he was at peace. His guards had lost interest in him. Bored with the hot, sticky wait for orders they had left off taunting the prisoner and were sharing bawdy titbits of gossip with the actors of one of the tableaux. The prisoner wasn't going to run off. And if he did, all the more fun for them. But he had not run. Instead, he had lifted his head and looked up into the caeruleus blue of the sky, as though communing with something unseen. Shelamzion lit up with a flutter of irrational hope. *What does he know? Are we to be saved?*

Then, close by, a legionary uttered an epithet and spat on the ground. And somehow the brute vulgarity of the act brought Shelamzion crashing down into the filth and corruption of Rome's streets, where gods had the vices of men and men worshipped gods of vice. Hope faded. No miracle would be performed that day. No angel of the Lord was coming. No fire would rain down from heaven. And Simon was just a man letting the sun touch his face on this last of all days, when everyone had abandoned him.

And it struck her suddenly that she would die in more ways than one on this day. And the uncontrollable terror of that thought parted her lips and moulded them round two gliding syllables, Si—mon! Forget selflessness. Forget promises. Forget the intricate deceit that would have him believing that his wife and son walked in freedom. All she wanted was to have him look into her eyes and know that he was not alone.

'Simon!'

Her cry dissolved in the liquous swell of sound in which every voice in Rome was raised. Yet she kept her eyes upon him, willing him to look round. He did not. But the man next to him turned his head. A battered, disfigured-looking individual who she did not recognize, until she saw the burning acknowledgement in his eyes—and then came the sickening awareness that she knew this man. Yeled. The name formed in her consciousness even as she saw the urgent shake of his head. Pleading with her. Communicating in a single gesture that she must not break a vow he couldn't possibly have known she had taken. An immense anger overcame her. To ask this now. What right had he to demand it? What right had the world to expect it? Yet—her heart sank—by the same token, what right had she to refuse? She was *int'ta Shimeon*. Simon's wife. And if they were to be in this world only a little longer then she must give him this blessed ignorance as her parting gift.

Stiffly—only a few more steps and it would be over—she walked on. Glancing back but once. Defiantly. Hoping to trick fate into allowing Simon to catch sight of her, awe and surprise lighting his eyes. But Simon was still looking up into the infinite blue of the sky, and the only change was Yeled's hand, which was now resting gently on his shoulder.

A white, bright, blinding wall of heat struck Shelamzion full in the face. Toppling her backwards, arms flailing awkwardly to protect Jathniel, who was behind her. She tried to escape it by turning back the way she had come. Hopeless. A surge of bodies plunging towards them. Men and women scrambling down the stairwell, orange tongues of flame licking at their backs. No escape that way either. In her arms Jathniel's frightened cries cut off in choking gasps.

Wildly, she cast about, knowing that she had moved too slowly. The fire had caught up with them, crossing the Hall of the Israelites then sweeping down through the outer chambers, cutting them off. All her fault. She had waited when all that was sense and rational screamed at her to run.

But it was hard to make her body obey what her eyes did not believe. The Temple—glorious symbol of what made the Jews unique amongst the great nations of the day—burning. Its beams of precious cedar and perfumed cypress igniting ecstatically in the midst of hellish clouds, which rose like inverted waterfalls, flooding the skies. She had stood, slack-jawed and staring, ignoring the screams from down below, waiting for the One True God, revered and feared to the bursting seams of the empire, to extinguish this abomination.

And the longer it went on, the less she could make sense of it. Nothing seemed real. The Jews had broken ranks and were running back towards the blazing Sanctuary. They fell prostrate before it, pierced by *pilum* and arrow. Old men, young men, all going down in a bloody tempest so that the ground became slick even as the walls burned. And the sight of it set a raw, sharp-toothed fear gnawing against Shelamzion's ribs. She lifted Jathniel into her arms and started urgently across the walkway towards the stairwell and escape.

As she stumbled forward her eyes lighted on a desperate huddle of women and children clinging to the roof of a colonnade in the outer court. A wild-haired prophet stood amongst them—Surely not the one she had expelled?—Too distant to be sure. She saw him raising his arms, evoking the blackening skies, calling for deliverance. Would it come because this ragged little man demanded it? He was stretching out his hands, as though he expected to reach up and pull the Almighty down from heaven, while below legionaries, fuelled with bloodlust and death, crept towards the columns with burning brands.

Shelamzion released Jathniel and began to lead him down the steep descent of the staircase. But the fire was catching up. Heat-charged air sizzling the back of their necks. Panic making the voluted incline sway beneath their feet. Picking up her tension, Jathniel began a frightened, high-pitched mewling. It was echoed by the shrill terror coming from the direction of the outer court. The cries of women. The chilling screams of children. It drove Shelamzion, half-running, half-falling, downstairs towards a barrier of heat so intense that it glowed with the precious metals liquefied in its core.

With one hand she gripped Jathniel tight about the shoulders. He gasped out in pain. Ignoring him. Clawing with her free hand to find safety away from the hypnotic dance of flames. Her fingers connecting with the ashlar blocks of the stairwell, finding them hot to the touch. No choice. Stay here. Men and women still pushing their way down the stairs. 'Go back! Go back!' she pleaded with them. One or two glanced in her direction; most marched doggedly on. Reaching the curtain of flame, then trying to turn about. But now there was no room. The pressure of bodies from behind forcing forward the ones who had stopped agog before the furnace.

Panic broke out. Mouths moving hugely, but no single voice able to penetrate the collective clamour of fear. There were screams. Someone had been pushed into the fire. For an instant the voices were silenced in shock. But the momentum had been set. People were still pouring in from the upper gallery. More bodies began to slide towards the inferno. Flesh began to blister and crisp.

Against the wall, Shelamzion gasped at the seared air, powerless in the face of the engulfing chaos. The heat had dried the moist membranes of her eyes so that she could not shut them, and the sheer intensity held her head in a vice pointed towards the bright heart of the fire.

Her hands still grasped her son, and she struggled with what she understood were dying breaths to hold on to him; to shield him. And that small connection with life held her back from the grim abyss, even when she witnessed men and women blazing, like incandescent angels. Understanding with some remote corner of her mind that this was the beginning of something new. The shape of hell was changing, transforming into a smoking horror of brimstone and fire that would burn forevermore in the secret and fearful parts of men's minds.

There was a dull explosion. A crash of timbers. Air rushed in, and instantly the fire grew more powerful. Shelamzion felt life ebbing out of her. Sinking to her knees, willing herself to hold Jathniel. But her fingers growing weak, their grip loosening. The edges of the world turning black. Then, miraculously, the flames dying away. The air becoming breathable again, her thickened blood beginning to flow.

Shelamzion struggled up. The path before her was clear. The great Gateway of the Music that opened on to the Court of Women was gone. Its polished cedar doors ashes now. The men and women trapped on the staircase began pouring through, though clearly they were burned by the hot cinders beneath their feet. Shelamzion watched, unable to bring herself to leave the safety of the wall. The fire still raged ahead of them as well as behind. She could see its orange glow on the far side of the courtyard. Where did it end? And death was not only clothed in fire.

'Lady, come with us.' A young, soot-smeared face peered into Shelamzion's. She shook her head, not knowing him. 'Ishmael, lady. The son of Barzel.'

The smith? Yes, of course. Still she did not move.

'You must come.'

'Not yet. Soon.'

His wife was with him. She tugged his sleeve anxiously. He looked at Shelamzion. 'Come with us.'

She smiled, but shook her head. The smith's wife tugged at her husband again, and he frowned, eyes darting with inestimable calculations. Then he sighed. 'I will find Simon and give him word of you.'

'Thank you.' But he had already turned away, arm about his wife's shoulders.

Shelamzion watched as the smith and his wife crossed the courtyard, seeing how they very nearly made it to the Hall of the Israelites, and safety, before two brute-faced legionaries appeared. It was very quick, almost too quick. One moment the smith and his wife were living creatures full of purpose and perception, then they were two pieces of gutted meat, the red juiciness of their lives spilling out across the pristine stone. The sight brought saliva to Shelamzion's undernourished throat; then she clapped a hand over her mouth and retched.

A noise from behind made her whirl round. A man falling slowly towards them, his neck pierced by an arrow. Death was coming downstairs. Shelamzion clutched Jathniel's shoulders, paralysed by the knowledge that she could go neither forward nor back. Jathniel was quiet. She became aware of him, saucer-eyed, a finger worrying his lower lip, and her heart twisted. *My baby. Not my baby.* The incantation was as old as motherhood itself.

Then she was running, primal instincts keeping her low. Dodging behind pillars, her body curled protectively about her son. She knew that she was sobbing, but that it was the reflexive ululation of pain, some expression of what was human in her, while her animal nature, low and cunning, tore and clawed its way towards survival.

Up ahead was the Gate of the Women. There was still a chance that no Roman soldier had got so far. Only make it through then down the three steps into the Court of Israel, and then what—Into the city with its warren of alleys and backstreets. Lose herself in a dark cellar or the corner of a neglected hovel. Time enough for that later. She slowed her pace a little. The closer she came, the more evident it became that she was not alone in her plans. The welcoming rectangles of light, through which freedom lay, were obscured by the dark mass of bodies frantically trying to push their way through.

Shelamzion continued to make her way towards the gate, but she had lost her purpose. She felt suddenly the weight of Jathniel in her arms, and glanced about looking for a new direction. To her right were priests atop the flaming sanctuary. The flames so high now. How would they ever be put out? The priests were hurling the golden spikes from the roof at the encroaching legionaries, turning the holiest place on God's earth into a weapon. To her left there were men and women emerging from the flaming chambers with arms full of gold and fine cloth. Shelamzion felt hysterical laughter rising in her throat. Did they hope to bargain with the Angel of Death? How much life did a bolt of silk buy?

A pain next to her ear, so sharp for an instant she did not feel it. Confused, she turned to meet the glazed eyes of a legionary; a boy younger than herself. There had been no challenge, no confrontation. He had cut her with less regard than a farmer drawing his scythe through ears of wheat. Absurdity upon absurdity. The need to laugh again. Perhaps there was something to be said for the Dionysiac rites of Rome that raised up madness as a new reality.

Her ear was filling with blood, and she was suddenly vividly aware that the fire had lost all decorum and was raging out of control. There were new structures in the blaze. Archways and columned bridges rising up to link crenulated towers of flame so that the Temple, blazing and unbearable as any burning bush, was rebuilt even as it was consumed. And she knew all this in the helical twisting of a second that stretched out relentlessly even as the legionary raised his sword for the killing blow.

The dark curtain of her eyelids, closing then slowly opening. Repeated. Faster this time. The legionary lying dead at her feet. Arms empty. The crushing loss. A whimper. 'Jathniel.' And a man, soot-stained and smeared with blood, standing before her, Jathniel clinging to his legs. For a moment she couldn't breathe. Then she fell into his arms with the simplicity of a child for whom all terrors can be righted in the sight of a beloved face. Simon.

Chapter XXVIII

… [Titus] always acted as his emperor's partner and even his guardian. He celebrated a Triumph with his father and they shared the censorship jointly.

Suetonius, Lives of the Caesars

A metallic note. Caught up and repeated. Trumpeted into the quivering air from flaring shells of bronze and sounding brass. A hiccough of motion. Then again, more decisive. Shelamzion found herself taking first one step then another and another. The triumphal procession of Titus Flavius Vespasianus Caesar, Pontifex Maximus, Pater Patriae, and his victorious firstborn son, had stirred into life.

From behind, one of the captive women let out a keening sob. And Shelamzion faltered in her step, struck by a wave of guilt and self-reproach. *I should have offered some word of comfort while there was still time,* she thought miserably. But she had not anticipated how eager and excited the women would be at her arrival. As though she had come as a conquering potentate to demand their freedom.

She did not have to be told that the magnificent pageantry of their garments disguised the physical abuses they had suffered. And it had shaken her badly to see how very young they all were, with hope not quite dead in their eyes. *Lady, are you come for us?* their faces seemed to say. So when the guards had lifted the iron chains to fasten about her neck and wrists, she had felt the weight of failure added to their heavy links.

As the sobbing increased, she fought hard to see some pattern in what was happening. Something that could be said to these frightened girls to show them that there was meaning and purpose to all they had been through. Lifting her eyes, she tried to read a vital clue in the heavens. But, if they had spoken to Simon, they remained empty as glass to his wife. And feeling the cheap melodrama of communing with nothing, she let her eyes drop to the ground. Too late now to look for omens or grand design. Too late.

As they emerged from the Porta Triumphalis, out by the Theatrum Marcelli, the pressure of noise from the roaring crowd was so strong, it had a taste. Bloody, like copper. Shelamzion could feel its zing against her tongue. It made her bowels twist with fright, and she fought to master it.

Lifting up her head, despite the heavy iron that bound her neck, she stared ahead with an expressionless dignity that was a mask for her despair. Then, on either side, the mob's roar rose in oceans of hatred. Wave after wave crashing down on the captives' heads so that it became impossible not to feel a crushing loneliness even in the midst of the largest gathering of souls the world had ever seen.

The sun grew hotter. Shelamzion trudged on, trying to narrow her thoughts to the mechanics of moving forward. But the world would not be locked out. It broke through time and again. The glaring light. A shouted jeer from the crowd. And the realization that she was wondering about tomorrow on a day when all tomorrows would end. Was Simon thinking of tomorrow? No. He had looked as though he had made his peace with this world. And as hard as she could, Shelamzion tried to welcome the thought of death.

But despite her brave words to Cornelius, she could not embrace its chilly presence. Cornelius—He must be in the crowd now, heartsick at what he saw. A good man. No, he deserved better. A righteous man, that was the word. Simon would find it strange that she could call a Roman righteous. They should have met. What explosions might have occurred. The thought comforted her somewhat, and she tried to reconcile herself to the knowledge that she would be with Simon and Jathniel by the day's end. Yet the idea remained shadowy and insubstantial. Like the memory of a memory. Not quite real. And with a spine-tingling clarity that twisted, knife-sharp, in her heart she understood that, despite everything, she wanted to live.

Into the frigid darkness of a sewer a hundred cubits below the surface of the Temple Mount Simon led his wife and child. They were waiting now, joined by Yeled and Ephraim, while above their heads fire ate up the world. After a while, Shelamzion reached up and drew her forefinger tentatively along her cheek towards her ear. The blood from the legionary's cut had dried, forming a thin crust over the wound. But with nothing to dress it, it would bleed again, probably forming a scar. Shelamzion found that she did not care. Such vanities belonged to another life.

She could feel Jathniel's hot fingers digging into her neck. And in this cold and sunless place she was glad of their warmth. Looking round the barely visible faces of the men, thinking, *How has it come to this? Chased down here, like rats.* Then Yeled echoed her thoughts, saying aloud, but with disbelief coating his words, 'Y- yesterday the Sanctuary. Today the s-sewer. Is … is … is it possible?'

Ephraim gave an irritated jerk of his shoulders. 'Is it the first time the Almighty has chosen irony to educate men? We all remember the lesson of Job.' But his old voice trembled, and he glanced almost nervously towards Simon. 'I saw priests jumping from the rooftops into the flames,' he added after a moment. 'That is not nothing.'

Yeled agreed. 'Men must believe something to die by fire. Y-you cannot deny that the Almighty called them.' He looked at Simon and his voice died.

Shelamzion listened to them, feeling cold. And it was more than simply the pressing gloom or the dampness of the stones upon which they sat. She was experiencing a deep, psychological shock in an age that had no terminology to describe such a state. From its earliest days prophets had been proclaiming apocalypse from Jerusalem's lofty heights. But she had now been a part of the conflagration. And nothing made sense any more. The world had ended, yet here she was, still alive. And how else could she interpret such maddening contradiction, except as goose-pimpling coldness? Was Simon cold?

She looked to where he sat, a little apart, long legs drawn up, eyes fixed on the dripping putrescence that covered the walls. He seemed so remote that Shelamzion wondered if he had even heard what the others said. But he spoke suddenly, without looking up.

'I saw men jump into the fire,' he said slowly. 'I saw them die.'

And there was such finality in his voice that Yeled looked stricken, and Ephraim's lips trembled. And he had to breathe out heavily several times before saying in a gruff voice, 'We must check the other tunnels for survivors. As soon as we are rested Yeled and I will go. Has there been word from Ariel or Hyrcanus?'

Numbly, Shelamzion shook her head.

'I-I saw ben Onias near the Coponius Gate when I was running towards the fire,' Yeled offered. Simon looked up. 'The Coponius Gate. You are certain?'

'Y-yes.'

'He was ordered to give assistance to the Galileans. What business had he there?'

Shelamzion felt a spark of hope so unexpected it made her mouth water. 'The Idumaeans,' she whispered. 'All is not lost.'

And later she would wonder at the cruelty that dashed their hope even as it trembled before them, foetal and misshapen. There was the crash of footsteps. The men drew their swords, then the voice of ben Onias was heard. 'Peace. It is only rest we seek.'

'As well,' Simon answered. 'For you will find little else here.' But he was on his feet, and there was something of irony glittering behind his eyes. The glitter faded when ben Onias stepped into the light of the torches, Hyrcanus at his side. Ben Onias was bloody from a wound on his head, but the stoop of his shoulders and the emptiness of his expression spoke of something beyond any physical suffering. He tried to meet Simon's gaze, could not bring himself to do so.

'Well?' Simon's voice was like a stone dropping down a deep well into darkness. Ben Onias glanced up, then down again. 'They will not come.'

Silence thundered in Shelamzion's ears. Beneath the streaks of soot and blood, Simon's face had turned ashen. A lesser man might have staggered under the weight of those words. But Simon stood his ground. Then in one smooth motion his dagger was at ben Onias' throat. The Idumaean was no coward, but with the feel of cold steel against his flesh, his eyes flicked nervously from side to side. Hyrcanus demanded, 'What means this?'

Simon ignored him, speaking directly to ben Onias. 'You once described yourself as a simple man. Is it true?'

'It is so. I swear it.'

'Then it cannot have been you who came up with the plan to drip the honey of hope in our ears, knowing all the time we waited for an army that would never arrive!'

Shelamzion's hands tightened around Jathniel. Of course. The scouts who never reached their destination. The promises broken one after another. There was a glaring logic to it. Like the pattern of a face suddenly glimpsed upon a wall where a moment ago there had been nothing but moss and shadows.

A bead of blood had formed at the tip of the dagger. The harsh sound of ben Onias' breathing could be clearly heard echoed in the wetness of the stone walls. He spoke hoarsely. 'You are right. I have led you into a trap with false words of salvation.' The confession, now out, did its damage. Ephraim's shoulders slumped, and Hyrcanus groaned, 'This is a snake I have brought amongst you.' He made as if to draw his sword, but Yeled's hand stayed him. 'That is for Simon to decide.'

Ben Onias' and Simon's eyes were locked. Another bead of blood dripped from the blade. 'I have played you false,' the Idumaean repeated. 'But may the Creator of the Universe strike me down if I did so willingly. There is treachery afoot. I was sent by my master in secrecy, believing I was privy to his plans.' He sighed deeply. 'And you will all pay dearly for my pride. I know now that I am little more than bait set in a trap. Idumaea has made a pact with the Romans.'

Slowly Simon lowered the dagger, though Shelamzion noted that he did not sheath it. 'Yesterday you made promises of unwavering loyalty. What makes you sing a different tune now?'

'This day I received word that my brother had reached the Coponius Gate. I went there, and found him—youngest of my parent's loins—dying of a dozen wounds to his limbs and belly. He paid a high price to tell me I had been played for a fool.'

'And is all the army of a mind to side with Rome?' Ephraim asked hoarsely.

Ben Onias rounded on him angrily. 'There is no army. No hope of rescue. Every messenger sent to me false. Your scouts murdered by Romans who knew their cause before they set out.'

'Yet we are to believe your innocence in all this,' Hyrcanus burst out.

Ben Onias' eyes were back on Simon. 'The rumour that I had no high opinion of Rome was spread as wide as a whore's thighs.' His glance fell on Shelamzion. 'No offence to the lady. But it is my belief that I was sent to you because there is no man so convincing as a man who is convinced he is speaking the truth. So you may kill me now or let me fight alongside you. Either way our cause is lost.'

Simon was silent a long time. Then he shook his head. And the decisiveness of the gesture made Shelamzion's heart beat faster. *He will do it,* she thought. *He will kill him.* She stood up to hide Jathniel in the folds of her skirt. The action drew a puzzled glance from Hyrcanus. He blinked at her, as though he had forgotten she was there, then turned back to ben Onias. Simon was speaking in a low, sorrowful voice. 'You ask me to believe you. Yet how am I to trust a man who admits every word out of his mouth has been a lie?' His hand tightened on the hilt of the dagger.

'No! Simon, you are wrong.' The voice was so sudden and imperious that for the pause of a heartbeat Shelamzion did not recognise it as her own. All eyes were upon her. Simon frowned. 'You see no traitor here?'

'I see one clearly enough. But it is not ben Onias.'

'Simon,' Hyrcanus interrupted. 'It would be better if this were done amongst men.'

'Why?' Shelamzion asked. 'Is it perhaps that you fear I will expose you?'

Hyrcanus opened his mouth angrily to respond, but Simon raised a hand to silence him. He looked to his wife. 'Let us hear what you have to say.'

Then Shelamzion took a deep breath, knowing words can be weapons, used as much to denounce a man as deliver him. 'You commit the sin of pride,' she began, addressing Simon. 'You think Titus wants you dead. But his goal has always been the city. You are a great man, husband, but you are not Jerusalem.' The men before her exchanged glances. And she went on filled with the powerful certainty that it was the truth she was speaking. 'Think on it. Such a short time ago you were of a mind to flee so that we might live as nomads in the desert. Could Titus have asked a greater boon from his gods? Simon gone, and John and Eleazar fallen to fighting amongst themselves. He could have entered as a king and who would have stopped him?'

Simon's eyes were filled with dangerous lights. 'Go on.'

'Yet you stayed. Persuaded by the false words—not of a Roman—but a Jew.' She saw him glance at ben Onias and pressed on urgently. 'And not just any Jew, but one whose hatred of you knows no depths.' And though she held Simon's gaze, she wished she had not. As realization dawned, his look of pain was almost unbearable to behold, and he spat out the name, as though his mouth had filled with poison. 'Josephus.'

She thought she had broken him. Simon, the rock upon which they had built the promise of their future, swayed. The dagger fell from his hand. He sat down heavily, and uttered a long, low moan far worse than any storm of rage. It was the sound of defeat. The sound a man makes when he knows he has lost.

The seconds dragged by. No one moved. Then, just as Shelamzion was beginning to feel the ache of frozen muscles, he asked dully, 'And what has Hyrcanus to do with this?'

Shelamzion inclined her head, and ignoring the Sadducee's antagonistic stare, answered, 'Josephus proclaims his noble lineage to the world. There are not many he would choose to be his spy.'

Hyrcanus' face was full of scorn. 'If this is the evidence that condemns a man then let me seek out the Romans for justice.'

'It may come to that,' Simon said sharply. Then to his wife: 'What more is there?'

'Only that on the day poor little Jonathan was treacherously slaughtered I spied Josephus looking at someone in the crowd, as though he knew him and wanted to commune with him. I took it upon myself to visit Josephus' lady mother to find out who—'

'And the vessel that bore Josephus is pure in thought and deed,' Hyrcanus sneered.

'We will hear this out,' Ephraim growled, his hand on his sword hilt. Hyrcanus fell silent, and Shelamzion continued in a clear, brittle voice, showering her accusations like burning stars.

'I sought out Josephus' mother, and that noble lady gave me a warning. She told me that there was a traitor in our midst. And that I would know him when I found the fatted calf … ' Her words trailed off. Slowly, imperceptibly, the focus in the room changed until all eyes beheld Hyrcanus. And it was so obvious, that there was not one amongst them who did not wonder why they had not seen it before. But it had been so gradual, the changes so slight, that only now when they truly looked did they see it. Hyrcanus' gaunt face was gaunt no longer. Where their wasted flesh pulled taut across the bone, his was plump and fresh. In a city that could not feed its generals, this man was not starving. He had supped at his enemies' table and now he stood before them betrayed by gorged tissue and flexing muscle. Simon stood up. The time for argument was over.

Hyrcanus drew his sword. In one swift motion Yeled knocked it from his hand. But that was all. This was Simon's fight. And Simon advanced upon the younger man holding neither sword nor dagger. This was not to be a quick death. Shelamzion retreated to the darkest corner she could reach. Turning Jathniel into her skirts, and holding him there when he would have broken free. Yet compelled through some sense of natural justice not to look away, to watch the fate of the man her words had condemned.

It takes a long time for one man to kill another with his bare hands, especially when one of them has blood thick with the juices of meat flowing in his veins. It takes a special kind of anger to fuel violence that feels no pain when blow counters blow and bones creak and crack under the strain. An anger that surmounts the desperation of a man fighting for his life and overcomes him little by little until hands meet round the yielding contours of a neck. Eyes bulging above it. Ignored. Pressing down. A pressure of hatred inhuman in size. Communicating itself in fingers unyielding as twisted metal cables, throbbing their tension up through arms and shoulders into the ringing cavern of a man's throat, to give birth to that most profound and piteous of all questions:

'Why?' *Lama* in the Aramaic tongue. Why! Why have you done this? Why, when you were my brother? When I shared my bread with you. Why have you betrayed me?

And no answer, but the twitching, maniac's smile on the dying man's lips and the hiss of death between his teeth.

The body slipped from Simon's grip and lay at his feet in the twisted posture that admits no life. And Simon, dazed and spent, fell to his knees beside it and began to weep. Shock took Shelamzion to his side to kneel beside him. Not to touch. You do not touch a wounded lion. And Jathniel, sensing that something momentous beyond his ken had taken place, did what all small animals do; he fell asleep in his mother's arms. She heard ben Onias whisper, 'Why did he come back? He knew my purpose in finding Simon. Why didn't he run?' And Yeled answered in the steadiest voice she had ever heard him use, 'He wanted to see his face. Wanted to see him broken. The picture he would have painted of Simon defeated would have been worth a fortune outside the city walls.' They fell silent again, and, for a while, the only sound was that of Simon's sobs grown weaker and more fitful.

Chapter XXIX

Of the prisoners [Titus] ordered the leaders, Simon and John, with seven hundred of the rank and file picked out for their exceptional stature and physique, to be conveyed to Italy without a moment's delay, intending to display them in his triumphal procession.
The War of the Jews, Book VII

What is to be done now?

Anxious words. Whispered between her husband's generals, as they stood over the prone body of Hyrcanus. Words that came back to Shelamzion as the great Triumph of the Caesars turned on to the broad expanse of the Via Sacra. All those faces turned towards her. Yet who could she see? Everyone alike. Roman eyes and mouths glistening with venom. Part of a boundless mass of stretched and screaming holes, empty of individuality. A mob reduced to the consciousness of a single thought that exploded from them in an incoherent, carrion burst of hate. The sound of it chased Shelamzion's intellect down dark tunnels where prayers escaped her, petitions evaded her, and harrowing, haunting images lay in wait.

Simon supported between Ephraim and Yeled. No longer weeping, but pale and tight-lipped. Yeled and Ephraim lost as children, gazing at the floor. Then twice-betrayed ben Onias lifting his head and asking,

What is to be done now?

The question was met with blank incomprehension. What is left to do when the world has ended? Then Shelamzion pushed her voice into the stony silence. 'Today we watched the Temple burn, yet we are here. We have not died. So we will do the only thing that can be done. We will try to live.'

They looked at her as though she was mad. And perhaps it was a kind of madness that made her go on—Certainly, walking down the Via Sacra with the last hours of her life bleeding out before Rome's fever-bright mob, it seemed she had been mad. Yet she had spoken urgently, with authority even—

'Simon must approach Titus.'

'To what end?' Incredulity made Ephraim's voice sharp.

'Titus is a soldier,' she went on desperately. 'He came for Jerusalem and now he has her. But there is resistance. His men are still dying. If Simon withdraws. If he offers a … self-imposed exile—'

'John would have to agree to go too,' ben Onias broke in.

'H-he might,' Yeled offered.

Ephraim shook his head. 'Where would we go? It would be death for any who took us in.'

Jathniel stirred against Shelamzion's breast. She steadied his head with the palm of her hand, feeling how fragile was this vessel of her deep love. 'We lived once in the desert,' she said fiercely. 'We can do so again.'

The men exchanged glances. 'What does Simon say?' Ephraim asked at last.

There was a sigh of noise. Simon had drawn a deep breath, like a man coming back to life. He loosened his hold on Yeled and Ephraim and stood straight. And, though his eyes were rimmed red, Shelamzion could see defiance gleaming in them, like a flame in the darkness.

Heralded by the blare of *cornicens* and *tubicens*, the Triumph surged past the Temple of Concordia and flowed across the wide expanse of the Forum, covering the worn limestone slabs with splendour. In the face of such high civilization, the crowds, now ranged along the Forum's perimeter, and so vast they looked like opposing armies, began pelting the procession with petals of rose, sweet orris, violet and lily. Amongst them went hooded priests who, fearing such earthly adulation might ignite the ire of a resentful god, fanned curling offerings of incense into the stifling air.

On a platform reserved for dignitaries and minor notables sat Cornelius. A moment before he had been listening listlessly to the arguments that broke out, sporadically, over bets. They were always the same. Would Simon meet his death with dignity? Would he plead and grovel? Would his merciless god make an unprecedented appearance on the Capitol, swooping down to save him in the final hour? (This last had hopelessly poor odds.)

But, in the enormity of the pageant, all bets were forgotten. With each new wonder—the flaming model of Jerusalem, the tableaux depicting victory, a hundred and twenty white oxen led to sacrifice by painted youths—the crowds grew more voluble, a dark stain of hysteria spreading through their midst. Even Quintus was affected, leaning forward in his seat and drumming his fists when the treasures of the Temple were displayed. Cornelius watched numbly.

In the pomp and self-importance of those magistrates who led the procession, he had found a reflection of himself, and was sickened by it. He sat, crushed between slabs of inescapable sound, and torn between the desire to miss nothing and the urge to bury his head in his hands.

The mob had begun to chant. Two words over and over. A wild, mesmerizing sound, half familiar. *Bar Poras! Bar Poras!* Distorting the lilting Aramaic with their coarse, Latinate gutturals. It drew Cornelius' head forward and he saw the prisoners coming into sight. A sorry lot, for all they had been cleaned up. They walked like a line of broken puppets, these men who had ignited his wildest imaginings. Hard to see them now on the burning battlefields of Judea, wielding swooping sword and cleaving axe.

Craning his head, he caught sight of the women. Shelamzion was amongst them, impossibly small, yet taller than those around her. A queen in bearing, head held erect, as though adorned with a crown of stars. He sent up a silent prayer that she might pause and scan the crowd. To what end? Did he imagine that she would pick out the one face shining with sympathy, lost amongst the infinite constellations of hatred? It was, he knew, the prayer of a ridiculous, conceited man.

In his remorse he almost missed the arrival of the Flavian dynasty. The Imperator and his son sharing a chariot, attired in gold-embroidered togas, their faces daubed red with an extract of Sinopian earth in memory of the blood they had spilled. Alongside them was a youth on horseback, the younger son, Domitian. The cheer that went up from the crowd was like the cry of a maddened god. But now Titus lifted his arm. There was a ripple in the procession, like the flowing spine of an eel. And, though he had known this moment must come, Cornelius felt his heart contract.

Attention turned to the centre of the Forum. Simon, a noose around his neck, was being dragged by an escort of Praetorian guards, who beat him with rods and whips. And while Cornelius cringed from each blow in helpless empathy, ecstatic howls came from the crowd, as though some magnificent feat of combat was being enacted. Two plump, middle-aged matrons to the left of him—they might have been mothers or grandmothers, save for the bright, demonic contortion of their features—brayed for blood.

From the front ranks a shriek of satisfied laughter went up, as a fellow with the scarred face of a street pugilist caught the spatter of Simon's wounds across his balding dome. And Simon—that strange, intricate soul with the trick of looking forward when so many men can only look back—so small now. Diminished by the weight of humiliation and the ceaseless, gouging blows. Writhing on the ground. A mindless brute. Understanding nothing but the need to escape the pain.

In shame Cornelius looked away, and saw Shelamzion sink to her knees. And despite the grand absurdity of it, he began to call her name. Called until he was hoarse. Only to let her know he had come. But his voice was no match for the roar of the crowd. And now another signal was given, Simon was dragged back to his place, and the procession began a stuttering motion forward, leaving Cornelius dishevelled and overlooked, froth at the corners of his mouth, spittle running down his chin, a doddering, despairing Agamemnon watching Iphigenia being led away for sacrifice.

In the days that followed the burning of the Temple a kind of madness drove Simon and his men. Their only hope was to be a thorn in Titus' side sufficient to make him crave removal of its sting. They fell back to Herod's palace, that great monolith on the western side of the city. And it was not long until John of Gischala joined them with the few dozen of his men he could still muster.

Simon and John fell on each other as shipwrecked men, forgetting all old antagonisms in the raw need to survive.

'What of Eleazar?' Simon asked.

John gave an angry shrug. 'Who can say? The Zealots fought hard. No man can deny it. But they fought with their hearts, not their heads. I heard many of them died in the Temple when they might have lived to fight another day if they had fallen back.'

'And Eleazar?'

'There is no word.'

Simon nodded grimly, then forced a smile. 'Then it is just you and I. Ariel will attend your wounded, then we will show Rome that you cannot defeat a Jew by burning wood and stone.'

The words were said lightly, but it was no easy task to contest the solid determination of Rome. The fighting was savage. Shelamzion and Ariel tore up fine linens and precious cotton to make bandages for the wounded. And only Herod's foresight in building his palace like an impregnable fortress saved them. Over and over Simon sent out requests for a parley with Titus, but no word came. He sent scouts out to check the circumvallation of the city, hoping to receive word of a breach. But the walls held, and they were trapped, like animals in a cage.

Then, on the fourth day, a ray of light. A messenger came to say that Titus would hear them out. So much hope resting on that single face-to-face encounter. When he received the news, Simon lifted his wife from the ground with a shout of triumph. 'That he has agreed to see us. It is a good sign. May it please the Lord, we may yet escape this with our lives,' he laughed.

But Ephraim shook his grizzled head, muttering, 'I like it not. They say the priest Jeshua and the Temple treasurer bought their lives with gold lampstands and the vestments of the High Priest. And the Romans took them in exchange for sparing their lives. But what have we to offer Caesar? The treasuries are plundered. And we go empty-handed to strike a bargain with thieves.'

He would have said more, but Simon placed a hand on his shoulder, squeezing the bony knob of flesh with his long fingers. 'Peace, old friend. We have no choice.'

They met on the Tyropoeon Bridge. Twilight seeping across the sky so that the moon was visible, but not yet the star of evening. All day a westward wind had been blowing, cooling the hot embers of the Temple Mount and lifting the ashes so that they now fell across Jerusalem, like a dark, perpetual rain. Simon and John walked through the ashes from the Upper City, followed by an anxious crowd of men and women, whose eyes were too large in their shrunken faces, and who stood on tiptoe to watch the spectacle on which the balance of their lives hung. At the western extremity of the bridge stood Titus, hooded and cloaked in purple, flanked by the men of the XVth.

John and Simon marched towards him, then, in obedience to some signal Shelamzion did not catch, they stopped. Silence held them, suspended in the growing darkness, waiting for Titus to speak. But Caesar's son remained tight-lipped. And after a frowning glance at John, it was Simon's voice that broke the night in two. 'You have our terms. Will you accept them and let us be gone from this city by first light?'

Still no reply. Shelamzion began to tingle all over. Something was wrong. Again Simon asked the question. 'Will you accept our terms?'

There was a sound. Sonorous. Convulsive. It took Shelamzion a moment to recognise it as something as commonplace as laughter. 'Can you possibly still imagine,' the mocking voice asked, 'that having been crushed, you can now invoke the privileges belonging to the victors?' The voice was without accent. Its Aramaic deep-rooted and unfaltering. This was no Roman. And Simon took a step forward, his fists clenched. Immediately the guard of legionaries drew their swords. Simon stopped. 'I came here for Titus,' he said coldly.

The laughter stopped. The hooded figure threw back its cloak, and it was no surprise to see Josephus there, like Pluto risen from his shadowy underworld to stand poised before the smoking remnants of the Temple. He gave a nod to his guard, who lowered their spears. Then, without urgency, he brought his attention back to Simon.

'I *am* the voice of Titus,' he said calmly. 'Be assured that tonight he has sent me to do his bidding, and that I act in his name only.'

'Tell your master if he is afraid to meet with us then it would be better to send a viper in his stead than a traitor, who knows no one's interest but his own.'

The guard tensed visibly. And all expression disappeared from Josephus' face, like water sinking into sand. He forced a smile. 'Gioras' son, you must leave dramatic declarations to those who have triumph on their side. Surely humility is better garb for those disappointed in their ambitions.'

Simon stiffened. Shelamzion thought he was about to turn his back on Josephus and walk away, but John placed a restraining hand on his arm. 'Softly. Let us hear what he has to say.'

A muscle danced in Simon's cheek. He closed his eyes for a moment then nodded. 'What does your master say?'

Josephus gave a slight bow, as though this was a proceeding of court formality rather than a counsel of war. He directed his gaze, not at Simon or John, but to the anxious crowd of Jews hanging on their every word. 'Titus will be merciful in his victory. It brings him no pleasure to be the architect of so many deaths, and he mourns the destruction of the Temple. To this end he makes a generous offer. The ringleaders must hand themselves over for punishment, but the rest shall go to Caesar as slaves.'

Shelamzion felt the confusion as husbands looked at wives, and wives looked at sons and daughters, wondering if life, even the life of a slave, was preferable to certain death.

'No,' said Simon. 'These are not our terms.'

Josephus blinked rapidly several times, his face wide with incomprehension. He looked like a man who had received a blow to the face in response to an unassuming request. For the first time Shelamzion saw doubt clog his features. But he recovered quickly. 'You have lost, bar Gioras. Accept your fate. The fiction that you are free men has gone on long enough. Titus has made you his prisoners, yet he offers you clemency.'

Shelamzion saw Simon glance down at John. Saw John shake his head very slightly. Simon looked back at Josephus.

'No.'

Then Josephus' fury unfolded, like the wings of some infernal creature. He pointed a long, elegant finger at Simon, which shook with the enormity of his emotion. 'Think what you are doing. Your arrogance and your pride have driven you to destroy the holiest site on earth. Will you also destroy the living remnant? Do you know what it has cost me to come here ... what it has cost me to beg Titus on my knees to let you live? On my knees, bar Gioras ... on my knees—'

Simon's body relaxed. He leaned forward, and though he did not speak loudly, such was the crystal silence of the atmosphere that he was heard clearly by all those assembled. 'I am not yet old, but many things have passed before my eyes. I have seen men cut down in battle, dying of their wounds. And I have learned that there is no glory to be found in a man drowning in the torrent of his own blood—'

Josephus opened his mouth to protest, but Simon went on, relentless as the flakes of ash swooping and whirling around them. 'I have seen men wretched with disease, and men who were crawling on the ground because they had no more strength to stand. And yet, Joseph ben Mattathias, when I think of you on your knees before the sneering face of Rome, you, and you alone, do I pity.' And having spoken he turned and walked back through the crowd towards the Upper City. There was a hesitation, then John turned too, and one by one the Jews followed. As Shelamzion joined them she heard Josephus' voice, first angry then growing fainter and more pitiful.

'Simon! Si—*mon!*'

But when she looked back there was nothing to see but the fading light and the falling ash.

Fire had worked well for the Romans, and they were keen to make it their ally. The next day they fired the municipal archive, the Citadel, the Council Chamber and the southern edge of the Temple Mount, known as the District of Ophel. Simon and John made a desperate attempt to hold Herod's fortified palace, but it soon became apparent that this was no better than waiting to be caught. They agreed to go their separate ways. But it was a painful parting. John gripped Simon's forearm, and Shelamzion saw the ravages of regret on his face.

'If we had stood together sooner this day might not have come to pass,' he said sadly. And behind him his men stared hollow-eyed and silent. But Simon, the politician, shook his head. 'No, brother. Do not think it. We were each chosen to be a king of Israel. And we could not have stood long together without tearing one another apart. At least this way we part as friends.'

John's lips trembled. He leaned forward and kissed Simon on the cheek. 'Forgive me, brother.' Then he was gone.

They sat, Shelamzion and Simon, in one of the upper chambers of the palace, talking in low voices. Shelamzion asked despairingly, 'What can be left to us now?'

Simon's face was grim, but he took her hands and held her gaze. 'There is still one small chance. Ephraim and ben Onias came across a map of the sewers, drawn up by one of Herod's architects. I have had some of the men taking supplies down to one of the tunnels. From there we might—' But his words were cut off by an explosion of sound, followed by a clamour of excited voices. Simon stiffened, his head turning instinctively towards the window. 'They've breached the wall. Come. Quickly!'

They ran. Jathniel scooped up in his father's arms. Shelamzion clutching at whatever might help them, as they dashed for the door. Ephraim met them at the foot of the stairs.

'It's not good. We're all but surrounded.'

'And the roads to the west are cut off,' ben Onias added, appearing behind Ephraim. Simon's face was grim. 'Below ground then. We have no choice.'

It was hard to go back down into the darkness. To know that scores of men, women and children followed them there simply because they had put their faith in Simon, and now there was no hope other than the dank and stinking viscera of sewers that writhed beneath Jerusalem's cobbled streets. But down they went. Entering through a drainage outlet on the Herodian Way.

It was a poor expedition. No one had more than they'd been able to grab as they ran from the palace, and half of that was impractical stuff, silks, baubles, prayer shawls, coins. At once Shelamzion grasped their most pressing problem, whispering urgently to Simon, 'The light.' He nodded, and gave the order that the torches were to be doused. Only the most essential would be used until they were certain how long they must be down there.

'But we will not be here long,' a woman's panicked, shrill voice rose up, spooking the crowd. There were murmurs. Shelamzion glanced round sharply. Even in the low light she could see ugly looks amongst some of the men, and many of the women wore hard, inscrutable faces. It was clear that Josephus' poison was working. He had offered them life—even if it was a life worse than death—and now their loyalty to Simon was no longer unquestioning. Simon's reaction was to have no reaction at all. The question was irrelevant, and so he ignored it. He turned on his heel. 'We are wasting time.'

But it was delay that saved them. Rounding a doglegged corner they heard the crunching beat of spades overhead and the distinct timbre of orders barked in Latin.

Simon froze, his arm thrown back to prevent further forward movement. 'Back. Get back!'

They went more quickly and softly than scores of people blundering about in the darkness had any right to. Stumbling against the slick limestone walls until they reached the opening of the main junction again. There they stopped and stood listening.

'Noth-nothing,' Yeled breathed. 'They did not hear us.'

'A miracle,' Ephraim whispered, his old face chalky against the shadows.

Ben Onias had the papyrus he had taken from Herod's palace with him. He spread it out and pointed along a line drawn in lampblack. 'We are not trapped. There is another way round.'

'No,' said Simon.

'No?'

Shelamzion closed her eyes. There was a darkness rising in her head far stronger than the darkness she was standing in. Since the firing of the Temple she had driven her body with fear and fury. But now hunger and exhaustion were gnawing their way back to the surface and she had the powerful urge to crawl into a quiet corner to sleep. Jathniel stirred against her and she dragged her eyes open. Simon was saying, 'They think they know us. Reckoning that we will try to escape by the nearest route then head for Galilee or Bethlehem.'

'Why should we not still try?' a large man, with a broken nose, demanded. 'You can't keep us here.'

The look of contempt on Simon's face made Shelamzion fear that he would ignore the man as he had done the woman. But instead he answered, 'Already those roads will be cut off. It would be certain death to pursue them.' There were murmurs and stirrings, only muted by the mutual fear of being heard. 'We will go east,' Simon announced.

East? Towards the Temple Mount, swarming with troops. Was he mad? There were twitterings of dissent. But Simon spoke on. 'If we can make it as far as the palace of the Hasmoneans, there is a water channel that will lead us near the Temple Mount. There I have left supplies, and our men are digging through to the tunnels that will take us under the Temple itself.' Many eyes looked at Simon. Doubtful. Wanting to believe.

'And is there safety there?' the man with the broken nose asked.

'No,' Simon said coolly. 'There is not. But there are exits that will take us out on the side of the Kidron. And from there we will make for the wilderness … or perhaps we might even reach Masada.'

And so they turned east. Simon in the lead. Shelamzion following, listening to the rumbles of those behind them.

You're a soldier. What do you think?

It's not up to me. Orders is orders.

Well, what of you, the scholar?

When David was trapped by Saul, did he wait for the spear thrust to find him?

David escaped through a window. Are there windows down here?

Fool. Is there but one interpretation of a story? He did what was least expected.

On and on they went. Marching behind Simon. Stopping often when they heard noise from above, sharing their meagre rations. At some point it became clear that Ariel was not with them. Yeled noticed it first and brought the news to Shelamzion. 'We must go back,' she said at once. But Yeled looked to Simon, who had stopped to hear the report, and he shook his head. 'It is not safe, lady.'

'But he might be injured or detained.' She avoided Simon's face, not wanting to see what was written there. She heard his words clearly enough, however.

'There can be no going back.'

Herod's map of the sewers was neither accurate nor complete. Several times they took a new direction only to find the tunnel ended abruptly or twisted back round on itself, bringing them out where they had started. Day turned to night, then day again. They could tell by the watery light trickling in through the drainage outlets. And the further they went, the more Shelamzion found herself wreathed in grey, abstracted thoughts. Lonely, hopeless thoughts, full of unfinished plans and incomplete reveries.

A glance at the trance-like faces about her told her she was not alone in this fractured existence. Numbness had set in. A torpid obedience that was born of lethargy rather than love. Half drowsing, half drowning in the stinking shadows, they marched on. On, ever onwards, while one by one the torches went out.

'Here. We've found it.' Ben Onias' excited voice came from up ahead.

'You are certain?'

But when ben Onias emerged from the end of the tunnel, his torch held aloft, his face was haunted. He opened his mouth several times, but no sound came out, and he repeated this until Simon grew impatient. 'Speak. You are among friends.'

But ben Onias only gestured that he be followed and disappeared down the tunnel. Shelamzion handed Jathniel to one of the women. 'Let me go with you.'

It was a harrowing sight that met them. The tunnel suddenly terminated in a heap of dust and rubble. One of Simon's men—Boetheus, Shelamzion recalled— was lying moaning on the ground. She and Simon bent low, and with his dying breaths they learned the tragedy of what had taken place. Zealots, fleeing Titus, had come across the diggers. A brave fight had taken place, but Simon's men were outnumbered. The supplies were gone, the props smashed so that the tunnel had collapsed, sealing the Zealots' escape route behind them. And burying the hopes of Simon and his men.

There was a long silence when Boetheus had finished. Shelamzion collapsed to her knees, and made feeble attempts to comfort him. There was nothing she could do, but at least it hid her face. From the connecting shaft she could hear the agitated rustling of those who waited. They would not wait much longer. She glanced up. Ephraim and ben Onias were watching Simon. Only Simon could get them out of this. At last he held out his hand. 'Ben Onias, hand me the map.'

The blood drumming in her ears, Shelamzion watched the two men poring over the yellowed papyrus. Several times Simon pointed and ben Onias shook his head. At last Simon said, 'There.'

'It's a tunnel,' ben Onias agreed. 'And it goes in the right direction. But it was never finished. Look, there is no connection to the water channel.'

Simon lifted his gaze from the map and his eyes were grave. 'There is no choice now. We find it. Then we dig.'

So few tools. A hammer and two picks. Pots and bowls for pails. They formed a line. Desperate, hungry people digging for their lives. Their progress painfully slow. A cooking pot filled with earth passed to Shelamzion, who manoeuvred it towards the waiting line of women. So heavy. She had no strength left to lift it. Choosing instead to bend double, pushing it with the palms of her hands. The next woman in line struggling to take it from her, then the next and the next. Until the last, pushing it over, emptying out this sad little offering to the God of frustration, who accepted it then sent them back to begin all over again. Hour after hour. A black wound was opening in the limestone, no wider than a man's shoulders, and progress at the head of the tunnel had slowed to the efforts of a single worker. And so cramped and airless was it that the last man had been pulled out in a faint.

Jathniel began to cry. There were almost no children with them—so few had survived—and he was easily the youngest. 'Hush now. Hush.' Shelamzion tried to placate him. Found she could not. He was hungry and there was nothing left to give. She left her place in the line, angrily pushing her way back up the tunnels to where those who rested were waiting. Someone must have a crust upon them. And by the God of all Mercy she would wring it out of them for her son. But only a few paces towards her goal she stopped. Hesitantly at first. Eyes wandering, not certain. Then turning to run back the way she had come. Jathniel's cries muted by the childish sense for things that are terribly wrong.

Simon was coming the other way. They stopped, inches from collision. 'Simon!' She must speak first. Propriety forgotten. 'They are gone.' He blinked at her and she knew she made no sense. 'I went to the tunnel where we rest. But it is half empty. More than half.' She pointed into the darkness, as though Simon could see what she had seen. 'They have been slipping away while we worked. If they should be caught … ' (In her mind's eye, desperate greedy faces were already creeping out from the earth, eager for reward.) 'If they should *choose* to be caught—' She broke off, frightened by the total lack of reaction in Simon's face. 'Something is wrong?'

Looking down at her, the torchlight moving like a restless animal across his face. 'Come,' he said. 'See for yourself.'

The limestone hills upon which history's most potent city lies were not there when the Almighty took his leave on the seventh day. They grew infinitesimally year on year, the sedimentary sacrifice of crinoids and brachiopods, cephalopods and corals. No High Priest of Jerusalem ever knew it, but the altar where he sacrificed, the Temple where he worshipped, the city he watched turning tawny in the cool light of each new dawn was already an audacious offering of unimaginable proportions. Billions and billions of tiny deaths gifted to an unknown god.

Yet, geologically speaking, limestone is a young rock. Not hard and crystalline, like those forged in the primordial fires; granite, gneiss, schist. Limestone is soft. It crumbles in the hand. It fizzes in vinegar. Sometimes it can be hewn with nothing more than a knife. Yet, once in a while, nature changes course. Unexpected forces come into action. Intense heat. Immense pressure. And then the delicate structures that hold the atoms in their singing spheres dissolve. Magic takes place. Where once there was one rock, now stands another: the maverick child of a prosaic parent. Reddish grey, flinty, marble hard. It has a name in Aramaic …

'*Kepa heli,*' Shelamzion said. Sweet Rock. She was holding a splintered shard in her hand, and her hand was shaking. She looked up towards Simon and Ephraim, saw their faces were grey. And it was no trick of the dusty light. They were grey from within, from the knowledge that this quirk of nature meant only one thing: their flight was over.

Shelamzion felt her legs go weak. She reached out blindly, felt Simon's steadying hand clasp her wrist. 'There must be something more?' He shook his head.

'The formation may be narrower than you think.' Again the shake of the head.

'Good men have been scratching at it for hours, yet it's barely dented.'

'A way round, then.'

He squeezed her arm. 'It is too late. You said yourself. More than half have slipped away. Perhaps we are already betrayed.'

She felt a red mist rise up, making it difficult to think. 'This cannot be. It cannot. It cannot.' There were too many eyes on her. She struggled to compose herself, knowing that the wife of Simon could not give into grief publicly. But two hot rivulets burned down her cheeks, and her words drowned in them when she tried to speak.

Simon's arms were round her. His breath close to her ear. 'Be brave,' he whispered. 'Just a little longer.' She managed to nod, and he led her back through the tunnels towards the small alcove where they had taken their rest. As they walked, she was aware of a hum in her brain, a strained, chafing sound that chopped and sliced at her thoughts. Simon was looking at her, and she managed a tepid smile. 'I am well.'

But his thoughts were elsewhere. 'Ariel. Has there been word?'

She looked away, shaking her head.

'Ah,' he said softly, almost to himself. 'So many gone. I ask myself sometimes, what can be worth all this death?'

But she could not hear this. 'Simon!' Stopping, pulling him round to face her, tears forgotten. Everything they had been through. Everything they had suffered. Not for nothing. 'We have struck at Rome's heart. As Moses taught the Ægyptian to fear the Jew, so have you taught the Roman.'

He smiled, and his smile was as painful as sunlight caught between storm clouds. 'And what is a Roman save flesh and blood and bone? Believe me when I say that I have looked over the dead of many a battlefield, and I am yet to see the thing that makes one man better than his brother.'

'How can you say that? You—You are better than a thousand men.'

'Am I?' His smile faded. 'Have I not raised my sword against the innocent?'

'For the greater good.'

'What tyrant has not claimed that? Men have died following my will.'

'They were glad to do so. Their lives were always yours—' She faltered. 'As is mine.'

'No, sweeting. Don't offer that. I thought once death might be an answer for us all. But now—' He got no further. Yeled was forcing his way up the passage towards them, his face all weary dragging lines, his eyes standing out round and large with fear.

'Th-there are legionaries massing on the avenue they call the Purse of Solomon.'

They were directly below it. Yeled and Shelamzion looked to Simon. What would he do? He looked upwards, as though he could penetrate the limestone rock above his head. Then he turned and glanced back the way they had come. And Shelamzion found she could follow the train of his thoughts. Simon, the *strategos*, could not find a way out. It was hard to breathe. Every inhalation sawing tension across her lungs as she waited for him to speak. Every nuance of his expression taking on wild, improbable significances until his lips parted and he sighed. A strange sigh, much in the manner of a man who has tried to crack the complexities of the universe and is surprised to find himself defeated by the picturesque enigma of it all.

'My time is over.'

No. No. What was he saying? Shelamzion felt her throat constrict, words choking out of her terror. 'But you said—You believe in life.'

'Yes. And that is why I must go.'

He was making no sense. He was ill. The strain of everything growing too much. 'This is madman's talk.' Her voice was rising. Simon caught hold of her shoulders, too hard, hurting her. 'Yeled, leave us now.'

Yeled, who had obeyed Simon's commands without hesitation during the fever-pitch of battle, stood now, rigid and appalled. And Shelamzion had to give a brief, stiff nod of reassurance before he would go. But the sight of his retreating back, shoulders slumped, head bowed, frightened her in a way that bluster and argument could not have achieved. She watched until he disappeared, and even then she could not bring herself to look into Simon's face.

'Shelamzion?' She would not look up. 'Sweeting?' He was silent for a while, then, 'Perhaps if ours had not been such a strange, sad union I would have the words with which to comfort you at its end.'

Her head snapped back. 'Then do not go,' she said coldly.

His face clouded. 'Did Moses enter the promised land?'

She laughed, high-pitched, hysterical. Pulling a hand free and waving it at the gloom. 'Is this the promised land?'

'No, not this. Do bricks and mortar make a land? You—you are my land. And all those who have been driven this far for the love of one thing. The thing we sought when we left Ægyptus.'

'Not for that. For you.'

He drew her near and rested his head on hers. 'You called me a monster once,' he said softly.

'I was wrong.'

'You were right. I saw a new way for men to be. And I would not be altered in my path.'

She could not answer. There was a storm inside her head, and it was left for Simon to continue. 'Have you never wondered that the Almighty would lead Moses towards something marvellous yet prevent him from reaching it?'

'It was His will.'

Simon's brow arched. 'Or was he a man, like me, caught between two worlds; belonging to neither.'

'You are not Moses.'

'Yet I have brought you to a new world, have I not? A better world.' He tapped her just behind the temple. 'In here. Will my son refuse to look a woman in the eye? Will he place men in bondage beneath him?'

His beating heart was against her chest. 'I cannot go on without you.'

'You can. You must.'

Disbelief brought her features upwards. She took a step back. 'Can it be so easy?'

'No, never easy. Never that.' He took her by the shoulders again. 'Not easy. Only right.'

Yeled reappeared, Ephraim by his side. The older man's face was grim. He looked like a man who has encountered the Angel of Death and seen his own face reflected there. 'Is it true?' he asked.

'It is the end,' Simon said simply. 'We will do what we can to save the remnant.'

There was silence. Shelamzion waited for Ephraim to bluster and argue, to remind Simon it was his duty to fight. But, at last, he lowered his shaggy head. 'I see the sense of it,' he said, but his voice was hoarse and his bottom lip trembled.

Chapter XXX

So Simon, thinking to frighten the Romans by a trick, dressed himself up in several short white tunics with a crimson cape fastened over them, and at the very spot where the Temple had once stood he appeared out of the ground.
The War of the Jews, Book VII

Everything happened so quickly after that. There was only time for the briefest of goodbyes. A stolen moment as they waited beneath the outlet that led on to the Temple Mount. Shock holding her grief in check, Shelamzion watched Simon drop to his knees to kiss his son. Absorbed in some childish game that had narrative only inside his head, Jathniel resisted his father's embrace with ill grace. Yet when Shelamzion made as if to chide him, Simon's warning look stayed her rebuke. 'Do not let him remember his father as a source of tears.'

Heart breaking, she nodded.

'Shelamzion?'

She tried to look into his face. So strange to see him, dressed as he was in a soft, white tunic, a cloak of crimson hanging down his back—the finest of the vestments gleaned from those brought below ground—The tunic was a shade short, yet Simon carried it with sad dignity. A forgotten king shrouded in allegory and ambiguity. She struggled to meet his gaze, blinking slightly, as though trying to focus on something that was already receding. 'Can this work?'

'Romans are a superstitious people. If they can believe every stick or stone embodies a god, why not this?'

'And if you fail?'

'You know what you must do.'

Ephraim and Yeled appeared. Ben Onias was with the others, awaiting word. Yeled's eyes were red, and it was left to Ephraim to speak, which he did brusquely, a soldier in the battlefield. 'We are prepared and ready.'

Simon nodded. 'I would expect no less.' But he said it lovingly, as a man speaks to his brother, and the old man's chin quivered. Next he turned to Yeled. 'I fear freedom has brought you little happiness, friend.'

Yeled's voice shook, but strangely his stutter had vanished. 'When I was a slave, all that I felt belonged to my master. Not even my hatred was my own. Freedom has given me all the happiness I ever had.'

Simon reached out and squeezed his arm. 'You have been our rock in troubled times.' Yeled swelled a little under such praise, but they were not sentimental men and time weighed heavily upon them.

'My wife.' She looked up blindly and found Simon looking down at her. He did not move to embrace her. Still too much a son of the East, despite his maverick ways. He had kissed her earlier in the brief instant of privacy afforded them, and the ghost of that kiss still burned on her lips. Reaching out her fingers to touch his chest, she tried one last time. 'Is this the glory the Almighty calls you to?'

His eyes were beautiful with pain. 'No, not that. In truth, I am not certain now that there is any glory beyond a man's beating pulse.'

She gave a little, despairing laugh. 'Even now, I truly do not know what it is you believe.'

He did not answer, but closed his hand about hers, squeezing the fingers tight, hurting her. And she understood something of what he was trying to communicate because, though there was pain, there was also life. He pulled back. And this time she made no attempt to dissuade him. She was coming to understand something of the shocking nature of the human condition, consumed as it is with the Eternal, yet, at the same time, so fragile, so fleeting.

'Go now.' Her voice was harsh with grief—*Jephte calling after his daughter. Abraham crying aloud as he lifted the knife above Isaac's swelling chest*—Or the wife of Simon wringing the last drop of courage from her soul to set her husband free. 'Go now.' Repeated, her words became an incantation loosening the bonds between husband and wife, so that actions took on the somnambulant hues of a dream. Simon stepping back, as though pulled by an unseen force. Her half involuntary step towards him, and Ephraim's hand on her arm. The distance between them lengthening until the harrowing moment when she stood blinking at nothingness and trying to tell herself he had gone.

A noise at her side. Ephraim clearing his throat. She turned to him distractedly.

'It would not be good to delay too long, lady. Let Yeled take the boy.'

She nodded, forcing her voice over the monstrous pounding of her heart. 'Keep him close. We must be ready.'

Ben Onias appeared. 'We await your signal, lady.'

Another nod. She saw the game they were playing, these grown men, these hardened veterans of battle. They were obeying Simon's commands, as though he was standing amongst them, issuing orders. Simon, their anchor, their lodestone. It was easier to obey his ghost than to contemplate the loneliness of going on without him. So be it. With a sweep of her skirts she turned and walked the path Simon had taken, leaving the others to follow behind.

The drainage outlet was a semi-circular construction, leading out on to the Temple Mount. The ornamental grill had been removed, and they lowered themselves on to their stomachs, peeping over the ledge. Yeled's strong hand was across Jathniel's mouth lest he cry out. But he, like them, was dazzled by the severity of sudden sunlight—lightning flashes: diamond bursts—and remained quite still.

'I see him.' It was Ephraim's throaty whisper. Shelamzion forced her gaze through the glare and glister, and made out crimson sails against the brutal backdrop of naked light. Simon's cloak billowing behind him as he walked towards a knot of legionaries. They had just caught sight of him, this strange creature erupting from the earth, like a sulphurous Vulcanic god, and they approached him cautiously.

Too far away to hear what they were saying, but she could see the curiosity in the cocked heads, the puzzled glances. They were demanding to know his name. From behind, Shelamzion heard ben Onias leading everyone towards the outlet. She gripped Jathniel's hand. Let it work. Let these artless Roman boys be overcome in the presence of this unanticipated deity. If only they would break and run.

Yet, heart sinking, she saw they were too bold. Here in Jerusalem, they had tasted the bloodlust of chaotic gods, and they were not so easily overcome by mere strangeness. Simon was refusing to give his name. This much they had rehearsed. Let them summon their general, Terentius Rufus, before he would speak. Only first let them take fright, caught up in the flushed excitement of it all. Running off, forgetting they were soldiers just for a few precious minutes. But the discipline of Rome could not be shaken off even for a god. A small contingent left at a run, but the others remained where they were, swords drawn, wary.

Shelamzion glanced at Yeled then Ephraim. 'It's not working.'

Ephraim's eyes were fixed on Simon, his face drawn with concentration. For an instant she thought he had not heard, then he rubbed his chin and slid his eyes towards her. 'It was the Almighty who sent Simon out there. It is part of His plan. We must be patient.' He went back to his vigil, and she thought, *O, Ephraim. To have a tenth measure of your faith*—But her thoughts were cut short by Yeled's cry. 'L-look! The general.'

Terentius Rufus had the squat, barrel-chested appearance of a soldier of Rome. But his complexion was fair and his close-cropped hair caught the sun in coppery flashes. He stopped a few paces from Simon, chin lifted, hands on hips, a busy man with better things to do. A question, barked loud enough for Shelamzion to hear.

'Name.'

Simon answered. In her head Shelamzion heard that cool, dark voice saying, *Simon. Son of Gioras.*

There was a stunned silence. The general's hands fell to his sides. He took a step forward, as though proximity would verify what his eyes were denying.

Without turning, he called one of his officers over. There was a whispered confab between the two, the younger man's gaze turning repeatedly to Simon, his head nodding, until finally the general seemed satisfied. Then all hell broke loose.

Legionaries running towards Simon, yet stopping short. No man willing to be first. They surrounded him, weapons drawn, exchanging glances; not certain what it meant to see this man, grown so large and terrible in their minds, standing pale and silent amongst them, clearly unarmed. Then a snarled order from Terentius Rufus brought the largest of the legionaries forward. Expressionless, he flipped over his *pilum* and clubbed Simon squarely on the side of the head. For the briefest instant nothing seemed to happen, save the clenching of Shelamzion's belly and the look of horror on the legionary's face—was this, after all, a god he had struck?—

Then, like a pillar of stone crumbling with age or an ancient terebinth going down before the viciousness of a storm, Simon fell. Face first. Limbs sprawling. Consciousness snuffed out, like a quickly drawn breath over a candle flame. At once the legionary's companions sprang forward, grabbing Simon's arms and securing them tightly behind his back, binding him, as though he was the most dangerous of beasts, which to them, of course, he was.

'Lady, this is our chance.'

Shelamzion blinked. She was still gazing over the space of the Temple Mount, though Simon had long gone. Only a small contingent of legionaries remained, and she stared at them, feeling that everything she had seen was part of some senseless dream—Disturbing, dissonant events, unnatural qualities of light—All unreal and far away.

'Lady!' This time Ephraim's voice was harsher. She pushed him away.

'Not now.' Could he not see she was in no condition to think? But Ephraim was like the battering of a tempest.

'How long before they come to their senses and realise that Simon was not alone? Is your husband's sacrifice to be as nothing? Look to your son.'

Shelamzion was on her feet, not knowing how she got there. She took a staggering step, then righted herself. 'Yeled,' she called, and her voice was steady, though her hands shook. 'Bring me my son.' And only once his hot hand was imprisoned in the tight clasp of her fingers did she turn, seeking out ben Onias, then lifting her arm in a single, emphatic gesture. 'Go!'

The warriors went first, those ramshackle men of arms that were left. Ephraim, Yeled and ben Onias in the lead. And any man who owned a knife or had the strength to wield one went with them. Thin, weary men charging out towards their last battle, like the skeletal defenders of some sombre king of the underworld.

Shelamzion followed, leading the women, the weak and the wounded in a reckless race across the Temple Mount. Choking down lungfuls of heat-charged air, the slap of their sandals ringing against the sandstone slabs. Emaciated bodies blowing like feathers through a whirlwind of blades. From behind a tangled web of shouts and cries from voices so painfully familiar that Shelamzion had to fight the urge to look back over her shoulder. But hesitation was death. And already the burden of carrying Jathniel had lost her the lead.

Up ahead she could see the opening of another sewer outlet, an escape into the Mount itself and ultimately below the Temple. It was less than thirty feet away, but her strength was flagging. Her feet tripping over each other in drunken disobedience to her will. The grill that covered the outlet was already loosed from its housing, wrenched free by the first two men to reach it. And already the stronger and more able were disappearing down the sewer's stone gullet.

She called after them. Without effect. No one came to her aid. A woman, only a few steps ahead, slowed her pace, glancing over her shoulder then cutting her eyes away guiltily before running on. And the thought went spinning through Shelamzion's head that her guardians were gone and she was now alone. Then a cry, more terrible than the rest because it was heartbreakingly familiar, caught her unawares and almost sent her sprawling on the ground.

'Sh'ma Israel—'

The voice was ben Onias', suddenly and sharply cut off.

'Elohainu,' she finished through her tears. *Adonai Ahad.* Not daring to turn around. Wanting with the last breath in her to defy Abaddon, that wanton demon of death, who would fill her memories with blood. Then the outlet was upon her, and she plunged inside, still clutching her son, half crawling, half falling down the steep incline until strong arms caught her at the bottom. 'Lady … Lady … Praise the Almighty you are safe.' They were ashamed now, wanting to make amends for their cowardice. But Shelamzion, emptied of strength and pity, could only sink to her knees and weep. And now they were frightened. They stretched their hands towards her, whispering, 'Lady, do not weep. We are safe. We have saved ourselves.'

Then Shelamzion got to her feet, shoulders hunched against exhaustion, eyes flaring with the fires of burning worlds. Taking Jathniel by the shoulders, she pushed him forwards so that he stood in the middle of them, blinking up at their faces with his father's watchful eyes. 'Who amongst you went out to meet your enemy, as David met Goliath, as Moses met with Pharaoh?' she asked, and the coldness of her voice burned, like ice. And when they did not answer, she continued, 'Saved yourselves? No. It is Simon who has saved you. Simon.'

With care, she smoothed the skirts of her overdress, a queen once more. 'Remember that.' And while they still gaped at her, their gestures furtive and shamefilled, she took her son's hand and began to make her way along the tunnels deeper into the Temple Mount. After a few paces she heard the groaning shuffle of footsteps following in her wake. But she did not acknowledge this surrender to her will, save to squeeze her son's hand more tightly.

Two days later, legionaries of the Vth Macedonica, marauding through the Temple precinct, came across a locked door. They forced an entry and found to their dismay that they were in a chamber filled with charred wood. But a noise from below attracted their attention. They duly prised up the flooring, only to discover a huddled mass of Jews hiding in a narrow, stone passage. It became clear that they had been trying to reach a connecting chamber that would lead them out on the side of the Kidron Valley, but part of the tunnel had collapsed during the firing of the Temple, and they were hemmed in, unable to go further.

In obedience to orders, and as no bribes were offered, they seized them, setting some loose to make sport of them around the Temple ruins. Later, those who survived were sent on to Caesarea to be sold in the local slave markets. Among the captured Jews was the wife of Simon.

With each step she took on the winding path that led to the summit of the Capitoline, Shelamzion felt a dull throb of pain in her chest. A deep, loathsome ache, discordant as a chord of music plucked over and over. Echoed in the mocking jangle of the chains about her wrists and neck. Whilst inside her head a desperate struggle was taking place. A shrill, siren voice, that might have been her own, was screaming. There were no words, but there was a warning. An admonition to stop, to go no further, for the consequences of disobedience were dire.

She understood the warning. After all, she was marching to her death. But it was hard to believe in her own fears now that Simon was gone. She had watched the legionaries dragging his limp body towards the Capitol. And since then numbness had spread through her veins and arteries, suffusing her brain with opiated detachment. So when she thought *I will die today* the only thing that struck her was how little the words meant.

The path was growing steeper. A sweat broke out on her forehead, and it was hard to keep up with the jangling momentum of the procession. But still she moved with the blank expression of a dreamer, letting the pitiful weeping of the captive women wash over her, like the sound of waves crashing on some dark, receding shore.

As the procession neared the summit she jerked violently, as she had done several times before, her mind sensing things were not as they seemed. A jarring collision of reverie and reality, and a blessed moment of forgetfulness. Perhaps it had all been a dark, labyrinthine nightmare? Then lights and sounds rushing in—spears of sunlight, the gloating trumpet blasts. And the querulous voice of a woman praying. *Baruch Atah Adonai Eloheinu Melech ha-o-lam*. Blessed are You, Lord God, King of the Universe.

The worn path suddenly levelled out. Shattering the dull rhythm of her steps, sending her blundering forwards, chains pealing out an alarm. One of the purple-robed escorts yelled at her in Latin, and she pulled back sharply, caught up in the sudden confusion, as men and beasts, ferculae and tableaux, drew to a shuddering halt at the summit of the Capitol. But it was the act of stopping that brought her awareness of the monstrous shadow that now lay across them.

Slowly, drawing her eyes upwards so that the megalithic proportions were revealed bit by bit, she took in the full glory of the Temple of Jupiter. Newly rebuilt. Corinthian columns, roof inlaid with gilt bronze, its pediment surmounted by a statue of *Iuppiter Caelestis*. Heavenly Jupiter, astride a *quadriga*, poised to leap into the arc of heaven. Blinking in the strong sunshine, Shelamzion stared up at the god, thinking, *You brought us low. You—A gilded lump of stone.* And she wanted to laugh, but her hands were trembling and it was hard to breathe.

A silence was descending over the summit. In front, the trumpeters lowered their instruments with the last mournful notes still shivering against the flaring brass. The priests ceased their ritual wailing, hurriedly silencing the silver rings on their *sistra*. And even the captives muffled their sobs, looking about, bewildered and fearful. Glancing back, Shelamzion saw Vespasian and Titus dismount and begin to make their way towards the vast altars set up in front of the temple. She followed their progress until they disappeared from sight, then dared to take a couple of crab-like paces, placing herself with an unobscured view of the podium.

They had taken their seats, the Emperor of Rome and his son, each on a throne worked from ivory and gold. Saturnine kings at the gates of hell. And they sat in silence. A silence that rebounded off the stone pillars at their backs, like a deep, dolorous note trembling in the air above the Capitol. In that silence, tiny sounds became incredibly magnified so that Shelamzion could distinguish the studious drone of a bee from the rasping breath of the men in front. And when one of the escorts spoke to his friend, his voice boomed in her ears, though she knew he only whispered.

'You can't tell me it's right though. Gischala killed as many of our men as the other one.'

Shelamzion's ears pricked up. It was John they were talking about. When had she seen him last? On the bridge over the Tyropoeon with Simon and Josephus. The ash from the Temple swirling about their heads. The second escort shrugged and pulled at the sweating collar of his tunic. 'He got what was coming to him.'

'Imprisonment?'

The other man paused to hawk then spit on the ground. 'Imprisonment's just slow death to Jews. They're like Celts. I heard it said he had family in Rome that beggared themselves for his neck. Wasted money. He won't last past Neptunalia—' He would have said more, except that something was happening up ahead.

A man dragged out by legionaries. Head bowed, steps faltering with the unmistakable brand of the broken. The hairs on the back of Shelamzion's neck rose in panicked response. Until this moment she had moved with the torpid awareness of a dreamer, certain Simon was already dead. Now seeing that he still lived, she stood bolt upright, her senses jangling with supernal clarity. And when the legionaries threw him in the dust at the Emperor's feet, she gasped as the hard earth jolted his fragile bones.

Simon. Every tender, savage emotion she had ever felt for him welled up then. She wanted to run to his side, to cradle his head in her arms. To scream at him, *Why? You knew the world is mired in corruption and compromise. Why did you go on fighting when you couldn't possibly win? We might have run away. Just the three of us. Now everything is lost. And I must stand here and endure losing you.* She wanted to beat him with her fists. She wanted to fall at his feet. Glancing about, she dared to take another step. But a growl from one of the escorts froze her where she was.

Simon lay in the dust unmoving, the Emperor and his son studying him in silence, as though they could not believe that these bloodied rags of flesh had once had the temerity to stand against them. Vespasian turned to his son, saying something inaudible, and the younger man made a gesture as if to say, What is it to me? From where she was standing Shelamzion could see the Emperor's jaw working, his lined face a mask. An old soldier used to the justice of the battlefield, she guessed. Finding it harder to kill a man with words. She craned her head forward, saw Vespasian suddenly get to his feet, then step down off the podium.

He stood before Simon and addressed him. But silent as it was atop the Capitol, his words did not reach her. She saw him try again, and once more the urge to laugh rose in her. All this conflict, this posturing of men's egos and the shedding of rivers of blood, ending here with a foolish man addressing an unconscious one. Vespasian glanced at Titus then back down at Simon, and shook his head. And he would have turned and made his way back to his throne except for one thing: the fingers of Simon's hand clawing in the dust, not erratically, but in a deliberate gesture that beckoned the Emperor of Rome to come closer.

Vespasian stiffened. Shelamzion saw him frown. But the gesture came again. Those long fingers that had wielded a sword for freedom, fingers that had gripped her breasts and opened her thighs, now moving in the dust. For an instant she thought Vespasian would choose to ignore the invitation, but he bent forward, deep into the shadow cast by the temple, and spoke in Simon's ear. And Simon heard him.

Shelamzion saw his slumped body tense, saw his head turn. Slowly, like a man dragging himself up through the dark strata of unimaginable pain, he turned towards the voice that summoned him. Vespasian bent lower. In a strangely loving gesture he stretched out a hand and pushed the hair from Simon's face. Simon's eyes were closed, but his lips were moving. Dropping to his knees, Vespasian put his ear to his mouth. Like that gnarled old Trojan king, Pylaemenes, kneeling at his son's side after battle, straining to hear his dying words.

Shelamzion's heart was a hammered anvil pounding at the back of her eyes, tingeing the detail of her vision with violent flashes of red and brilliant white. She struggled to concentrate on Vespasian's face. Deep lines scoring the flesh from nose to mouth, drawn tight in concentration; the cleft between the brows deepening as he struggled to make sense of what was being said to him. Then the sudden change. Eyes widening in surprise. Pushing himself to his feet. Too quickly. Like a man scrambling back from a sheer drop even as the small stones beneath his feet tumble and fall into the abyss.

Next, a bellowing bull's rage. Praetorians running towards him, swords drawn. Dismissed with an angry gesture. Vespasian's arm stretching out, like the arm of Jupiter, forefinger pointing at Simon's undefended head. Words—scalding, burning words—spat out from the fires of deep wrath. *'Fiat iustitia.'* Shelamzion's heart skipped a beat. Let justice be done.

They took hold of him. Two of them. Puffed up with pride. Playing to the gallery. Rough boys from the mean streets of the Subura made good. Snatching Simon up by the wrists and ankles, as though this was not a man they took hold of but something unwholesome, a rejected sacrifice, a rotting carcass. As they hoisted him aloft his eyes fluttered and he moaned a little. Alive … just. Shelamzion's face was rigid, her hands clamped to her sides. The red-rimmed eyes of the captive women were boring into her. She ignored them, speaking to herself harshly, deliberately. *No tears. Will tears save him? Will cries and lamentations change a single thing that must happen this day?* In her belly there was a stone, and her mouth was filled with a sulphurous taste of decay. She closed her eyes.

And when she opened them again Simon was already hanging over the escarpment's vicious edge, the Tarpeian Rock, where all those who stood against Rome lost their lives. He was thin and broken. A corpse stillness about him. Yet somehow she knew he still lived. The two who carried him were stock still, their faces turned towards the Emperor, awaiting orders. Shelamzion waited with them, seconds crawling over her skin; anticipation throbbing inside her skull. And memories, like screaming birds, bright white, chaotic, morphing and flowing into each other with the sound of beating wings. The white house in Gerasa. The flames of Idumaea. Jerusalem. A certain way he looked. His smile echoed on his son's lips …

From the podium came a gesture she did not catch, understanding it only by its effect; the indrawn breath of a thousand gasping mouths. And the escorts swinging Simon's body to and fro, to and fro. Like a game played amongst children under a summer sky. *And what else are we,* she thought, *save children forever playing beneath an eternal star.* The arc of momentum was reached, once … twice … Shelamzion found herself counting along with it. Three times—He was gone. Let loose into the lapis skies above Rome.

For the instant of an instant his image was frozen in her pupils. Hanging in space, limbs thrown out. An angel in flight. Then he disappeared. And out of the stunned silence came the sound of cheering. Uncertain at first, then growing louder and more daring. Competing with the ululating grief that broke out amongst the Jews. But Shelamzion was only empty, empty. And her heart was a stone cast into a deep pool of blood. She could feel the ripples, red and black, spreading throughout her body and beyond. Breaking free across the summit of the Capitol. Across the world. A world where Simon was no more.

'Shelamzion.'

She blinked, startled to find her head sunk low on her chest. It was heavy and she had lost the will to lift it. 'You came,' she said at last, and her voice sounded sluggish.

'You surely knew I would.'

For a long time she was silent, staring down at the ground, where the shadow of a bird flew beneath her feet. Then she nodded. 'It is strange,' she said, and she might have been speaking only to herself. 'When I think on it I must have known.' Her gaze lifted and her eyes were the clear eyes of a doe. 'If anyone would come, I knew it would be you.'

Chapter XXXI

Thou didst boldly love the wild leader of the savage herd. Fierce was he and impatient of the yoke,
lawless in love, leader of an untamed herd; yet he did love something …
Seneca the Younger, *Phaedra*

In ancient times there dwelt a maid, who went by the name of Phaedra. As daughter of a royal house, she was joined in marriage at a young age to Theseus, that legendary king of Athens. At first the marriage was happy, or at least so it was claimed. She bore him sons. Nor did she neglect her duties as stepmother to his child by the Amazon Antiope. This child, Hippolytus by name, was some years older than his stepbrothers. A comely boy, who grew into a comelier youth. But not until he was in the first bloom of manhood did things begin to change.

Some say it happened because Phaedra withdrew her allegiance from Aphrodite in favour of Artemis, inspiring the former's jealous ire. Others say it was the fault of Theseus, who abandoned his young wife for the pleasures of war. And, yet again, there are those who claim that the answer is much simpler. For all the divine streak in her maternal line, Phaedra was a human woman subject to all the quirks and weaknesses of the human heart. Hippolytus was young and comely. His reputation for valour only exceeded by his reputation for virtue. In the end the mystery was no mystery at all. Phaedra simply fell in love. And even the dullest wit amongst us knows that love is the one crime the gods never forgive.

The actor playing Phaedra was a tall, gangling youth, whose voice had not yet broken. His position was centre stage, and when he spoke, his words floated with eerie clarity across the vast, echoing spaces of the grand reception hall that was the centrepiece of Vespasian's palace. A little apart there was a second actor, also dressed as Phaedra, with a stiff, white face of shaped linen and a flowing golden robe. He mimed a series of attitudes in accompaniment to the spoken word: the distraught queen; the pitiful girl mourning her true love.

Cornelius, seated near the back, could make out the rear of Vespasian's party. The princes on either side of the victorious father. Favoured nobles and senators accepting goblets of snow-cooled wine from liveried slaves. And Josephus in their midst, sitting upright, hands in his lap, an image of the scholar entranced for the dramatic merits of the play.

Throughout the performance Cornelius' eyes moved restlessly, returning again and again to the motionless back of the Jew. To be so still. Had Simon's death made no impact upon him? Or was he secretly shaken, seeing the shape of his own death again and again in that falling body? For an instant Cornelius closed his eyes, and there was Simon falling, falling. Arms outstretched. Icarus, his wings melted by the unkind sun.

When he opened them again, Phaedra had fled the scene, and Theseus had reappeared, face set in rigid tragedy, ready to receive the news of his son's death. Cornelius' stomach lurched. So soon. It was much nearer the end of the play than he had realized. He had always considered Seneca's work overly verbose, the play dragging in places, with too many interruptions from the chorus. How many times, sitting morosely at Quintus' side, longing for the final act. Now the scenes seemed to fly by, accelerating the minutes so that they rushed on, more like seconds in length, charging undisciplined as barbarians towards the moment when Phaedra would die—when Shelamzion would die.

He leaned forward, not caring that he earned himself a frowned rebuke from his neighbours. It was clear that the actors all made their entrances through a door on the left, presumably leading to an antechamber where they awaited their cues. Shelamzion would be waiting in there. Still bound in chains, no doubt. As though she might yet escape. As if the streets of Rome thronged with friends of the bandit queen ready to spirit her away.

Cornelius stared at the door through inflamed eyes, as though the pressure of his need alone might be great enough to break it down. How easy was the world of the playwright. He had only to summon a nymph, a gorgon, a god, and all earthly laws might be set aside. No Sophoclean hero ever found himself standing helplessly on the side-lines watching the ineluctable unfolding of events.

Now, in Vespasian's grandest chamber, he sat gripping the edge of the bench until his fingers lost feeling, Cornelius tried to calm himself by concentrating on the play. Impossible. The words—words he knew by heart—came to him in the riddled patois of a fever.

Suddenly the door to the left was flung wide, and out stepped a woman. That it was a woman, and not a youth with down-stuffed breasts and curling wig, was evident by the subtleties of her gait, and the smooth plane of her jawline protruding from beneath the mask. She was dressed as Phaedra, her mask and jewels having been swapped with the actor who had performed the mime. But she wore a simple wool shift. Cornelius winced when he saw it, knowing that the cloth of gold had been removed to prevent it being despoiled by piercing blade and clotting blood.

On either side she was flanked by two attendants, one carrying a sword. This, of course, was artistic license. Overcome with guilt, Phaedra should have carried the sword herself. Doubtless the company were afraid that Phaedra might plunge it into her breast too soon, robbing them of the play's piquant rhythm as it reached the grisly finale.

Phaedra? Was it easier to keep calling her that? To make her a character of fiction rather than the flesh and blood creature she was? The question was immaterial. His body was not susceptible to the tricks his mind might play. No matter what he called her, Shelamzion was there before him for the very last time. And he leaned forward, straining the unused muscles of his body trying to narrow the distance between them.

She was looking about, the pale mask twisting this way and that, searching the audience. And he tried to make himself conspicuous by sitting up as tall as possible. She mustn't think she was alone. Let him succeed in that at least. But, for all the honour, his seat was a poor one, and he knew his face was only one amongst many. 'Shelamzion.' If only he had the courage to shout it now. The word was barely more than a shape on his lips. And now the final lines were being spoken. *O death, thou only solace of evil love, O death, thou chiefest grace to damaged honour, I fly to thee; spread wide thy forgiving arms …*

A sweat broke out on his forehead. His heart hammering a perpetual *no, no, no* against his ribcage drowned out the final words. In a blur he saw the attendant who held the sword approach Shelamzion. She stepped backwards, her head still turning, but clearly searching now for a way to escape. The audience went wild, thrilled by this human twist to a dry moral tale. And Cornelius set his fingers over his face in bars, agog and aghast. *Not like this,* he moaned. But the second attendant had grasped her arms behind her back, and now she struggled violently against him. Every kick and twist like a note of music prolonging the ballad of her life, like an anthem that quickened the hearts and thickened the blood of those watching, even Cornelius. It brought him to his feet, and he called out in the hoarse ecstasy of a lover, 'Shelamzion!'

Her head turned, and he had the briefest glimpse of dark, terrified eyes before the sword's vicious blade was thrust inside her belly.

It was not a clean death. Her arms were released, but she remained stiff and unmoving, as though she had not understood what had happened. Suddenly she jack-knifed over, clutching the bloody wound of her belly in one hand, while the other tore at the mask. It would not come off, and she gave both hands to the task, fighting with it, as though it was a living thing suffocating her.

The muscles of Cornelius' face were rigid with shared pain, his jaws clamped so tightly that a white agony of shooting stars stabbed behind his eyes. He was aware that all around the audience held its rapt, collective breath. While on stage the actors kept their positions in stiff repose, only allowing nervous, darting glances between one another to give clue to their true feelings.

The mask was off. Relief whispered round the audience. Gulps of breath taken in unconscious imitation of the choking gasps of dying Phaedra. A red froth had erupted from her lips. Shivering, scarlet bubbles blossoming at the corners of her mouth. Her jaw working, as though she was trying to say something, or perhaps she was only trying to gulp at the air. And all the time, her eyes held Cornelius', sharing their pain and humanity in those last, ugly, vile moments of death. Without knowing he did it, Cornelius held his arms out to her. She made as if to take a step towards him, then her legs crumpled beneath her, and down she went. Down on to the hard marble floor, her body following the anchor of her legs until, finally, her head rolled, quite gently, on to its side, leaving her sightless eyes gazing up at the audience.

Applause was instantaneous and tumultuous. And Cornelius stood there, his arms hanging limply at his sides, knowing somewhere in the back of his brain that he wasn't applauding and that it was being noted that he wasn't applauding. But he couldn't help it. His hands felt like plumb weights sunk into a depthless shaft. He was incapable of changing his position, even by a fraction. And instead, stood where he was, staring down into the dead face of a woman he had never seen before.

Even as his knuckles grew sore from knocking on the door, Cornelius had no expectation that they would let him in. It was therefore a surprise to be led directly into a comfortable chamber, and there to be offered a seat, a cup of wine. His instinct was to refuse the wine, but he was stiff and exhausted, and quite beyond melodramatic gestures, so he nodded, waving away the slave with a weary gesture of his hand. The slave bowed, and Cornelius became conscious of the redness of his hair. A Gaul perhaps, or even a Briton. The slave who had greeted him at the door had been blond, Germanic. Naturally there were no Jewish slaves in this household. Cornelius might have laughed had he not been so near to weeping.

The wine, when it was brought, was excellent. A plum-coloured Rhaetic, mellow enough to draw a flush to the deadly pallor of his cheeks and rich enough to slow his heart's frantic pace. So when his host entered the room and stood looking down at him, he was able to look up and ask quite calmly, 'Who was she?'

Josephus did not answer at first. Nor had Cornelius expected him to. He dismissed the waiting slave then helped himself to the Rhaetic. Again Cornelius asked, 'Who was she?'

Josephus settled himself in the chair opposite. He looked over the rim of his cup. 'Does it matter?'

Cornelius felt the flush of wine spreading through the capillaries of his face. With unpremeditated violence he brought his fist down on the arm of the chair. 'Yet I would know.'

An exasperated look crossed Josephus' face. 'This is not the reason you have come here.'

'Nonetheless.'

For several moments Josephus stared into his cup, as though about to commune with some bacchanean nymph, then looked up sharply. 'She was the daughter of a merchant family, taken when trying to flee Jerusalem. I was able to communicate to the parents that if the daughter was willing to sacrifice herself it might be possible to save the sons.'

'And did you?'

Josephus put his cup down with a little thud. 'Am I brought before you, some slave to cringe at his master's interrogation? By what right do you question me?'

'The right of a man whose words have been stolen.' It was out now. And only too late did Cornelius consider that a concoction of wine and exhaustion might possibly combust in lethal combination. After all, who knew he was here? And a man who had just deceived the watchful eyes that ruled the world would hardly find it difficult to dispose of someone accusing him of plagiarism. He swallowed hard, waiting for the storm to erupt.

Yet Josephus' expression did not falter. Rather, something glacial overcame his bearing. He looked at his guest coldly. 'And what would you have done with those words, Fabius Cornelius, citizen of Rome? No, do not attempt to answer. I know you better than you think. What a noble creature the Jew would become under your pen. With your victor's magnanimity you would have painted us in heroic colours, would you not, until the head of every young man left in Judea was turned again to war. What arrogance, what hubris is it in the Roman mind that drives him to crush his enemy then compels him to bring the interred bones back to life with eulogies and praise?' He leaned forward suddenly, making Cornelius flinch. 'I tell you it is a rare man who senses his purpose in this life, and a rarer one yet who finds it. But I know mine. I will write my history of Judea's war. And, believe me when I tell you, a thousand years from now, when scholars come seeking their answers, it is my name they will reach for.'

'And when you are the only voice left,' Cornelius whispered, 'who will be able to gainsay your version? You will make Simon a monster in the eyes of the world.'

Josephus shrugged. 'And how very little that will take when the work is already halfway done for me.'

'You cannot mean that. For all your quarrel, you know Simon was a man trying to do right.'

Josephus' lips tightened in a mirthless laugh. 'And is there anything people despise more? Why else do they kill their prophets and give power to politicians instead?'

Cornelius had fallen silent, but Josephus scarcely seemed to notice.

'Yes, I will slander Simon and John, and every zealous heart still beating. I will crush the dream and they will hate me for it. But they will not rise again, and Judea will be safe because of it.'

Cornelius' hands were trembling so much he had to put his cup down, but he found it in himself to ask, 'Tell me, is it because you love Rome or fear it, that you would destroy the dream of freedom?'

Josephus pinched the bridge of his nose, as though wearied by childish argument. 'Roman, do you even know what Rome is?'

Cornelius shook his head. 'I scarcely know what it means to be a human being any more, and you talk of Rome?' He spread his hands. 'Tell me, *Flavius Josephus*. You, who are so eager to join us that you would turn traitor against all you hold dear, what is Rome?'

Josephus' skin was grey. He took a long time to answer, and when he did his voice was low and furious. 'Rome is an iron-shod sandal, forever marching across the nations of the world, relentless and unstoppable. In Galilee I saw it for myself. And what was Judea then, but a speck of sand waiting to be crushed?'

'And so you will change history to satisfy Rome's ego.'

'It is not so strange a thing. For all we deny it, we Jews have a tradition of reinventing history. Believe me when I tell you that I have studied our lore and traditions until my eyes were burning in my head. And the cracks are there for those who would see them. There are those who whisper that Enoch's hand sometimes belongs to another, that there was no true queen called Esther. They even speak of a time when the commandments numbered more than forty. So you see, my friend, Plato was quite wrong. History, more than beauty, is in the eye of the beholder.'

Never in a lifetime devoted to the scholarly pursuit of *akademeia* had Cornelius wanted so much to kill a man, but he found it in himself to stay calm, to lift his cup to his lips and to drink long and slow from it before asking, 'What have you done with the wife of Simon?'

Josephus had his hand around the wine jug. He looked up, black eyes glittering, mouth stretched in a wolf's smile. 'I did what was expected. I killed her.'

The planks of the jetty shifted and creaked beneath Cornelius' hurrying feet. A cool mist was rising just before the break of dawn, extending cold fingers deep into Cornewlius' lungs, making him cough, and cruelly reminding him that he was no longer a young man. In front, swathed in the dark folds of his cloak, Josephus had taken on the qualities of a shadow, lithesome, gauzy. Cornelius could barely keep him in sight. He kept vanishing in the thickening air and disappearing between groups of ferocious-looking sailors, so drunk on the day's Triumph and Rome's power to oppress that they barely noticed that they themselves were amongst the oppressed.

Skirting his way around one such group, avoiding their hostile stares, Cornelius found that he had lost all sight of Josephus. Then panic seized him, and he began to quicken his pace again.

'Come.' Josephus' voice, full-bodied, urgent, somewhere up ahead. With difficulty Cornelius stumbled towards it, almost colliding with an elderly whore, who leered at him lopsidedly then hissed when he eschewed her favours. So many people. Cornelius looked anxiously about. Was it safety in numbers or eyes everywhere?

Josephus was waiting for him at the end of the jetty. He was speaking to a broad-faced fellow sitting in a rowboat. As Cornelius neared, he saw the man's features stiffen into a mulish aspect, then he shook his head violently. His accent was thick. And, even straining, Cornelius only made out the gist of his complaint, something to the order that it was not what had been agreed; there was danger to be thought of. With the prickling on the back of his neck, Cornelius hardly needed reminding of that. He looked towards Josephus, who ignoring him, bent forward, and with consummate grace slipped a ring from his finger on to the hand of the seated man. Cornelius hesitated, expecting Josephus to make the next move. To get into the boat or to issue a command.

Instead Josephus waited, until it became apparent that it was Cornelius who was to get aboard. Cornelius hesitated. It was one thing to follow a man who played with history as casually as other men play with words, a man who destroyed reputations and obliterated lives with a stroke of his pen. It was quite another to put your life in his hands by getting into a boat with a crafty-looking stranger, not certain where you were bound. But he thought again of Josephus' words. *I did what was expected. I killed her.* Then he swallowed hard and stepped off the jetty.

The boat, flimsier than he had been expecting, rocked violently as he got in, and the stranger looked up from beneath scowling brows, muttering a reprimand. But Cornelius heard nothing of the rebuke, his fingers clutching at the boat's narrow sides, and Euripides' famous line—*Happy the man who from the sea escapes the storm and finds harbour*—thundering through his head. He cast a last, imploring glance at Josephus, but he was already looking out across the dark water towards a ship moored beyond the shallows. 'We are fortunate,' he said, without turning round. 'I had feared you would be too late.'

After what seemed like an eternity to Cornelius, with nothing for company but the stranger's grim face and the slap of oars on the water, they pulled up beside the ship. Cornelius paused to read the name, *Kymethoe*, written in fading letters along the side before following the stranger on board. They were met with the curious stares of sailors until the stranger—Cornelius now understood him to be the captain—growled in an unrecognisable dialect, sending them scurrying back to their tasks. It was clear that they were preparing to leave. And the thought made Cornelius give an involuntary glance back towards dry land. There were figures on the jetty, but it was hard to see if Josephus was amongst them.

The captain led the way, Cornelius taking up the rear, crossing the slippery planks of the deck, and bending his head to clear the crossbeam above the door to the cabins. A Nubian slave stood on guard outside one of the doors. He was familiar, and Cornelius recalled having encountered him on his first visit to Josephus. Without preamble the captain dismissed the slave then banged against the door with his fist, barking in guttural Latin, 'Marcella Velia, you have company.'

There was a pause, then an echo of assent, sounding small and muffled though the thickness of the door. The captain turned the handle then stepped back, giving a little, one-armed shrug, as though to say, Do what you will do; I wash my hands of this affair. Cornelius watched him silently, caught in one of those strange moments that peel back, like a palimpsest, towards its original, so that while his feet were planted on the creaking decks of a sailing ship he was also standing outside a prison door, watching it fall open, through an infinite series of moments, as Zeno would have it, to reveal a woman more dead than alive—

'Cornelius.' She was sitting at a tiny writing desk, dressed in a damson-coloured gown, her hair caught up in curls beneath a headdress from which fell a transparent veil of gold, and she had spoken his name quickly to prevent him from speaking hers. He blinked, trying to recover himself. What had the captain said? 'Marcella Velia, you look well.'

'That I am.' She stood up. And he entered the room, shutting the door firmly behind him. The cabin was small, but well-furnished. Apart from the writing desk there was a narrow bed, luxuriously draped. And a number of cedar-wood chests filled what little space was left along the walls. A pale, flickering light came from a dozen candles set around the room. She was looking at him expectantly, but he could not speak. For all he was a man of sentiment, he was not a sentimental man, and it therefore took him by surprise to discover that he was weeping. Instantly she was at his side, crossing all the boundaries that separated them to take his hands in hers. 'Do not weep, for I have wept all the tears there are in the world and none can be left.'

'I did not—' he began when he was finally able to speak. 'When Josephus said he had killed you, then he claimed you were still alive… I did not know what to believe.' He broke free of her grasp to wipe at his eyes. 'You must forgive me.'

'Here.' She lifted a cup of wine from the desk and held it out to him. 'You are only tired and misused … as indeed are we all.'

As he took the cup, he looked more closely at her face, and saw that, for all the careful arrangement of her curls and smears of colour along her cheeks, she was pale as death and her eyes were glassy from weeping. He started to say something, but she brushed her fingers against the cup, still held rigidly in his hands. 'Drink. This wine is from Josephus' cellars. Unlike the man, it will be beyond reproach.'

Cornelius lifted it to his lips and took a long draught. As always, it was exquisite. Shelamzion was watching him, a faint, sad smile on her face. He smiled back. 'You are so brave.'

'No, not brave. Only alive and free.'

'Those sound like Simon's words.' The moment he said it, he regretted it. The smile left her face and she turned away. 'I have been here alone since Josephus brought me, and all I can think of is Simon. The voyage will take weeks and I cannot imagine how it will be, all alone here with nothing but my memories.'

'But where are you going?'

Her eyes slid away from him. 'Far away.'

'To hide?' He made a gesture of confusion. 'You need not go so far to be hidden.'

'But Josephus—' She broke off, as if afraid to go on.

Cornelius felt something hardening inside. 'Josephus,' he repeated. 'What part has he to play?'

'He freed me.'

'That was little enough.'

She threw up her hands. 'Do you believe that Josephus does anything without a price? I stand here before you alive and free for one reason only. Josephus has a task he wishes me to perform.'

'A task?'

'He needs me to find my son.'

The wine cup stopped at his lips. He slowly lowered it, untasted. 'Surely I am dreaming. Even if it were possible—To trust Josephus with knowledge of your son?'

'You don't understand.' She pushed her fingers into her hair, disarranging the careful curls in a way that made his heart ache. 'It was by Josephus' hand that he was saved. As he lay dying in the Temple courtyard he was discovered by Aelius Celatus. Not a centurion, no. But an agent of Josephus, acting under orders to find Simon's wife and son.' She paused. 'Of course, it was too late for me. But he took Jathniel and hid him until it was safe to move him to a more permanent sanctuary.'

'The Britannic Isles. Do you think Paulinus cannot make the connection?'

She threw him a quick, frightened look. 'You have heard something?'

'No, but Josephus is not always as opaque as he thinks.'

Visibly shaken, she nodded. 'I am at the mercy of his skill at intrigue. But Paulinus has not found him. I am sure of it. You see, they made it ashore at Dubris and headed for Caledonia. They thought to make it to an island off the western coast.' Her voice lowered, and she gave an involuntary glance towards the door. 'A place known as the Isle of the Yew. A strange place. There is a Druidic community there, not yet subject to Roman rule. Josephus believes we would be unknown. Invisible.' A fleeting smile, then the joy left her eyes. 'They got as far as Eboracum. There was word. Then nothing these several months.' Suddenly her eyes grew very bright. 'But it is no cause for alarm. Paulinus has spies everywhere. Aelius Celatus—I do not even know his real name—may judge it unsafe to send word. That is Josephus' guess. But I will be able to discover the truth once I am there.'

Cornelius, who had been absently running his fingers over a mermaid crudely carved into one of the slanting, overhead beams, looked up sharply. 'I cannot let you do this.'

She stiffened. 'I am not a child to be told where I will go.'

'No. You are a lone woman, who will soon be prey to every cutthroat and brigand that walks the shores of Britannia.'

'Am I not the bandit queen?' She looked at him appealingly. With her hair swept back from her face, he saw for the first time that the features he'd once thought too strong for any classical depiction of beauty were simply of a different order, a beauty proportioned to the fierce, waterless landscape where it flourished. 'I must go,' she said.

'I will not allow it.'

Colour flooded her cheeks. 'Are you the *archon* now to order this poor little captive's life?'

He was stung. 'Shelamzion—'

'Hush!' she cried, alarmed. 'Shelamzion bat Judah is dead. You saw her die with your own eyes.' The look on his face made her press her fingers against her temples, and she continued in an anguished voice, 'I did not know the lengths he would go to save me. By the time I found out, that poor girl was already dead, I swear. And what was I to do? Throw myself on Rome's mercies and forfeit my life as well?' She made an uncomfortable motion with her head, as though she felt the grip of something unpleasant on her neck. 'Please understand. I had no choice. Josephus brought me back to life. I am Marcella Velia now.'

'Velia,' Cornelius repeated coldly. 'It means concealed. The name he gave you is a kind of game. Even our lives are a game to him. I tell you he cannot be trusted.'

'And this time I tell you he can.'

'Is it your one true god who has spoken?' He was being cruel now for cruelty's sake. He saw her draw breath to argue, then she closed her eyes, and the corners of her mouth drooped. When she opened them again she was smiling at him sadly. 'I do not need the Lord to tell me what I have seen with my own eyes. Josephus has need of my son.'

Cornelius brought his cup crashing down on the desk. 'As a bargaining chip to buy his life should he fall from favour.'

'You are wrong.' She sank down on to one of the chests. 'He had many opportunities to use his knowledge. And you yourself said he need not have contrived to hide Jathniel in far off Britannia when he might have kept him close at hand.' Her hands were clutching restlessly at the folds of her robe, but she went on steadily. 'Can you not see how clever Josephus' game is? It is not the Romans he needs to bribe; he has taken what he wants from them. No, it is with we Jews that he must make his bargain.'

'Bargain for what?'

'His life.'

Cornelius lifted his cup and drained it in one long draught. 'I don't understand.'

'Don't you? There is not a Jew alive who would not pay dear to see Josephus' traitorous head roll loose from his body. But soon there will be whispers. Just a grain or two of proof pushed into the right hands.' She leant forward and her voice became low and persuasive. "'Simon's son lives. And it is Josephus' doing. Simon's wife is there to vouch for the truth of the matter." We are still a tribal people, you see, overly fond of our bloodlines. To many Josephus will become a hero, the instrument of the Lord's will.'

Cornelius felt the vinegar of revulsion gathering at the pit of his belly. 'But such a risk. Not all will believe. And should Paulinus get wind of it—'

'Then Josephus will deny everything. You may be sure he is clever enough to have covered his tracks.'

So cool. She spoke of her future casually, as though her relationship to it was that of a cruel mistress indifferent to a slave's fate. Cornelius stared at the creaking floor beneath his feet. 'He told me he wanted to crush the dream of freedom in Judea.'

That made her smile. 'You must not believe all Josephus says. Remember, he is all things to all men. It is nothing to him to raise up hope with one hand then dash it with the other. Besides, he is not a fool. He knows that freedom is no simple fire to be put out. Oceans of blood may kindle it as much as douse it. He is waiting for the Jews to rise again. And who better to hold the reins of power than the man who saved Simon's son?' To Cornelius' surprise she smiled at these words, and a strange, faraway look came into her eyes.

'Something amuses you?'

She glanced at him sharply. 'Do you really believe the son of Simon could ever be Josephus' puppet?'

'But if you are wrong. If Josephus merely wants you as security against falling favour…'

But she shook her head wearily. 'Please, do not lecture me. Please, Cornelius. I have suffered so much. All I want now is my son and a little peace.'

He opened his mouth to protest, then snapped it shut. More than anything he wanted to ask, *And if you don't find him? Will you come back to me?* But she was looking at him with that aloof, impenetrable expression that excluded the world. He recognised it as one of life's rhythms taking him back to the very beginning, when he had trembled before the scornful eyes of a ragged queen. Surely he could not leave it like this. There must be something that would dissuade her. He opened his mouth to speak, but there was a sudden, sharp knock on the door, and they jumped, exchanging glances. How late was it? With a start, Cornelius realized that several of the candles had guttered and died yet he could see her face quite clearly. Dawn was stretching itself over the waters. The captain's voice came, loud and gruff through the door, and they drew together, as if by some unspoken, mutual consent.

'Unless you intend to voyage with us, you must leave now, Fabius Cornelius.'

'A moment.' His voice harsh and lonely-sounding in the sudden silence of the cabin. Shelamzion was looking at him with a kind of wildness, as though she had thought all their talk of goodbye nothing more than a game, and the dreadful certainty of the moment had only just come clear to her.

'My dear.' He took her hands in his. They were ice cold.

'Cornelius—'

There was a sharp edge of panic in her voice, and he thought her about to say, *Don't leave me. I need you.* Then a wild arc of fear and hope lit up his heart. Could he do it? At this late age, give up everything and sail away into the unknown, a latter-day Paris with his Helen at his side. His legs felt weak, and he could not tell what expression was on his face.

'Cornelius.'

'Yes.'

'I want to say—'

He nodded encouragement.

'Thank you.'

'Oh.' His shoulders sagged. But even in the crashing disappointment wasn't there a faint, unacknowledged awareness of relief? He squeezed her hands. 'What possible reason can you have for thanking me?'

'For helping me see that the world is not all a savage place. That good men still prevail.'

'Ah.' He opened his mouth, but suddenly it was difficult to speak. So many things he wanted to say. Words boiling out of the depths of him, cascading and colliding in the trembling vessel of his throat. *Tell her,* screamed a voice in his head. *I love you. I can't live without you.* Such simple sentiments. But Fabius Cornelius Grammaticus, the scholar, the *historicus* who wielded his pen, like a smith of words, a literary Hephaestus, found that he could not utter a sound. He breathed deeply, trying to loosen the rigour of his lips. But then, as so often happened between them, she answered his unspoken thoughts.

'Even so, I cannot stay.'

His mouth fell open to protest. But there was a second explosive series of raps against the door. He glanced towards it in surprise, as though he had forgotten its existence, then brought his gaze back to her face.

'Let me go,' she whispered.

There were cold talons clawing at his liver, and the room grew visibly darker. He was frozen to the spot. To make a move was to set the future on an irreversible course. Orpheus sending his beloved into perpetual darkness with a single, lovelorn glance. He started to shake his head. 'I can't. ' But what he meant was, I am too old. Too selfish. I have only just found you. I cannot lose you now. Not to that remote, barbarous isle. In search of ghosts.

The dawn light was not yet strong enough to reveal the world's sharp edges, so that she was all paleness and shadow, a memory of herself conjured up from sleep. She leaned towards him.

'Please, Cornelius.'

'I don't—' he began, then stopped. There was a lump in his throat and he was filled with the knowledge that victory sometimes lies in strange places. He swallowed hard. Then, with the plunging grace of dreamers, lowered his head and pressed his lips against her cold fingers. 'Go in peace.'

The door opened and the captain appeared. He was frowning, and he glanced at them suspiciously. 'We are out of time.'

'Thank you,' Cornelius said quickly. 'I am ready to leave.' He turned to follow the man through the door. But Shelamzion, who had not moved since he let go of her hands, suddenly sprang to life. 'Wait! I have something for you.' She ran to her writing desk, and retrieved a scrap of folded papyrus. 'I thought to get this to you somehow,' she explained. 'My Latin is poor. But you will understand—' She held it out and he took it from her. 'You will understand,' she said again urgently. And realizing that her words were in part a question, he nodded vigorously. But the captain was thrusting him through the door. She came after him. 'I will wave from the deck.'

'No. It is too dangerous.'

'I must—' There was a hollow thud, as the door swung shut, cutting off her words.

The boat bumped against the jetty, sending a thin vibration though its passengers. Cornelius, who had sat silent as any wraith taking its final voyage across the Styx, suddenly came to life, getting to his feet, and tipping the sailor who had ferried him far more than the journey was worth. Then, ignoring the man's wide-eyed expressions of gratitude, he got out and stood at the jetty's edge, entranced by the nightmarish forest of his thoughts. He would wait, he decided, though it wasn't safe, until Shelamzion's ship sailed. Shelamzion? Should he call her that? Or should she now be Marcella Velia even in his thoughts? Perhaps she would want it that way. To be obliterated even from memory, a more exacting erasure than death.

'Can it be wise for you to stay here?'

The soft insinuation of the voice was unmistakable. Cornelius turned, and found Josephus had come up behind him. Where had he been hiding? Certainly Cornelius had not seen him when he climbed out of the boat. He shrugged and turned his back, muttering in a low but audible voice, 'Any danger I am in will pass soon enough. Can you say the same?'

'I cannot,' Josephus replied with surprising candour. He joined Cornelius at the edge of the jetty. 'As you know, there have been attempts on my life.'

Cornelius had not known, but it was scarcely a revelation. He did not answer and they stood some time in silence until Josephus remarked, 'In every generation there are men who are born out of their time.'

Cornelius glanced at him in surprise. Josephus was looking out across the water and did not return Cornelius' gaze. 'Would it be beyond the bounds of strangeness if I should describe myself as such a man?'

'You are so many things,' Cornelius answered coolly.

Josephus' eyes flicked towards him, flashing with anger, but he continued smoothly, 'I do not expect you to understand. It is a lonely path I have chosen and I do not easily forget that.'

'As lonely as leaving behind all you know? As lonely as a woman travelling alone and friendless to a hostile land?'

Josephus looked at him strangely. 'The woman you talk of will never be friendless. She has the gift of making men fall in love with her.' He paused. 'Even when they do not wish to.'

They were silent for a while. There was movement on the ship; they were hoisting the anchor. Cornelius strained forward. So much activity. Small black figures scrambling about the decks and rigging, like frenzied demon forms loosed on the world from Pandora's box. Yet there was one. Were his eyes deceiving him or was this figure different from the others, isolated in some way, shrouded. He squinted. Perhaps the blunted outline was a cloak? He couldn't be sure. Josephus was saying something. 'What was that?' He kept his eyes on the figure.

'She was not the only one I saved. There were others. I claimed them for cousins and had Titus cut them from the crucifixes. Not that they showed appreciation for what I had done.' He gave a sour laugh. 'One was even involved in a plot to murder me.'

'And Shelamzion, did she thank you?'

Josephus was silent so long that Cornelius turned to look at him.

'I brought her to my house. After the Triumph,' he continued softly. 'I wanted her to understand what it had cost me to save her. Not financially, though it is true that I paid dearly for her release. I wanted her to understand—' He paused, as though uncertain how to go on. 'I wanted her to know that what I had done was for the best. For the good of Israel—How odd it is to say that to a Roman—I wanted her to understand that I intend my history of the war to be her protection. Her cloak, if you will, hiding her from the prying eyes of the world.'

Cornelius' ears pricked up. 'Then you will exclude her from the work?'

'I will mention her in passing. The wife of Simon is too well known to keep her entirely from the page.'

'And Jathniel?'

'The son is another matter. I think it best for now that I use every means at my disposal to conceal him.'

'You mean, of course, until you have need of him.'

Josephus made a pious gesture. 'That is for the Lord to decide. It is enough that I may play the role of protector.'

They were so close. When Josephus' eyes narrowed, Cornelius saw the skin crumple into yellow creases, like the edges of an antique papyrus. At his temples the hair was quite grey. *You have aged,* he thought with the open astonishment of a child. *Grown old before your time. Joseph ben Mattathias, you are not the pillar of ice everyone takes you for.* And he asked again, 'How did the wife of Simon thank you for your protection?'

Josephus bent his head, looking down into the black depths of the water, and when he spoke, his voice was so soft Cornelius was forced to strain forward to make out the words.

'She spat in my face.'

Cornelius stared at him for several seconds, then nodded. Quite expression-less, he turned towards the ship. A sharp pain caught in his chest as he realized it was moving, the first rosy fingers of light grazing the mast. And suddenly all else was forgotten. He was alone in the early light of day, searching through the mist, hoping against hope, yet angry with himself for wishing something he had ex-pressly forbidden. He found what he was looking for on the stern, a lonely figure wrapped in a cloak. His hand lifted, not so much in farewell, but with that basic human need to reach out, even towards those things that can never be grasped. The figure—the light was still fickle; he couldn't be sure—seemed to lean forward, raising an arm in acknowledgement. Then the image quivered, drawn in by the gathered shadows, and was gone.

Hopelessly, Cornelius gazed after it until there was nothing left, and he found himself entranced by the emptiness. Absence had become a thing itself. There was a sudden emptiness in the world, as though he had stamped his foot upon the ground and heard the earth beneath ring hollow. Then gradually, finding the weight of his suspended arm unsustainable, he lowered it to his side, and stood staring fixedly at the horizon with the expression of a man who does not know what to do next. Josephus' question, when it came, tore across his brain like a roaring tempest, though in fact it was very softly spoken. 'What is it you hold?'

Slowly, he looked down, half puzzled to find his left fist clenched. Rough fibres of papyrus grown warm against his palm. Of course, the note. He frowned. The one he would understand. Unfolding it, he felt so many emotions that he could not separate them. Fear of what it might say. Fear of what it might not. There were two lines that he instantly recognised to be from Ovid. Barely read-able in the pale light. Not quite accurate, a deliberate paraphrasing that held meaning only for him.

Iamque opus perfice, quod nec Deus ira, nec ignis,

Nec poterit ferrum, nec edax abolere vetustas.

Now finish the work, which neither the wrath of God, nor fire, nor the sword, nor devouring age shall be able to destroy.

He looked up to find Josephus watching him curiously. There was something avaricious in his expression, the gluttonous need of a man who has sold his soul to the highest bidder and is filled with desperation for the intimacies of others. He leaned forward, Mephistophelean before his time.

'What does the note contain?'

Cornelius laughed, like a child on a beach coming across the wonder of a pebble windswept from the dawn of ages.

'Hope,' he said. Then he tore the note to pieces and threw it out over the black, churning water.

Fin

Historical Note

The one question I am always asked is, how many of the characters in this story are real. The answer is a simple one—all of the major characters were once flesh and blood, with the exception of Cornelius and his cousin. Cornelius is an invention allowing Shelamzion to tell her story. That the eponymous wife of Simon once lived and breathed seems certain. Much more of her cannot be known. Josephus' history of the Jewish War is the history of men. Women, such as they feature in it, come from the highest ranks of the nobility or go unmentioned. Thus, that Josephus spares Simon's wife a few lines of ink makes her jump out of the page at the reader. He does not name her (his arrogance would not allow it), but he tells of how the Zealots took her, and of how Simon raged against Jersualem's walls until they sent her back. In an age where there were more lines written to 'comely youths' than to young women the relation of Simon to his wife is strangely touching.

As for Simon, I have chosen to make him a hero, while Josephus is determined to portray him in the role of monster. It is with glee that Josephus records Simon's more equivocal acts. Yet even he cannot help a passing admiration for his enemy's courage and daring in the face of impossible odds.

Monster or hero? I suspect Simon was neither, but rather a flawed and complicated man, who was capable of terrible deeds yet also capable of acts tinged with the divine … as indeed are we all.

Glossary

Benjamite	Member of one of the twelve tribes of Israel founded by Benjamin, Son of Jacob (Israel).
Essene	A movement of Judaism that began approximately 2200 years ago. It died out shortly after the destruction of the Temple.
Gan Eden	Lit. Garden of Eden. A place of spiritual reward for the righteous dead. This is not the same place where Adam and Eve lived.
Hillel	One of the greatest rabbis recorded in the Talmud. His more liberal views of Jewish law are often contrasted with the stricter views of Shammai.
Kettubah	A ketubah is a special type of Jewish prenuptial agreement.
Levite	A descendant of the tribe of Levi, which was set aside to perform certain duties in connection with the Temple; also, Son of Jacob (Israel). Ancestor of the tribe of Levi.
Moses	The greatest of all the prophets.
Pharisee	A movement of Judaism that began approximately 2200 years ago. It is the forerunner of rabbinic Judaism, which encompasses all the movements of Judaism in existence today.
Saducee	A movement of Judaism that began approximately 2200 years ago. It died out shortly after the destruction of the Temple.
Shabbat	The Jewish Sabbath, a day of rest and spiritual enrichment.
Shammai	Stricter contemporary of Hillel.
Shema	One of the basic Jewish prayers.

| Talmud | The most significant collection of the Jewish oral tradition interpreting the Torah. |

| Temple | The central place of worship in ancient Jerusalem, where sacrifices were offered, destroyed in 70 C.E. |

| Torah | In its narrowest sense, Torah the first five books of the Bible: Genesis, Exodus, Leviticus, Numbers and Deuteronomy, sometimes called the Pentateuch or the Five Books of Moses. In its broadest sense, Torah is the entire body of Jewish teachings. |

| Tribes | The Tribes of Israel are the traditional divisions of the ancient Jewish people. Biblical tradition holds that the twleve tribes of Israel are descended from the sons and grandsons of the Jewish forefather Jacob and are called "Israel" from Jacob's name given to him by God. |

The twelve tribes are as follows: Reuben, Simeon, Judah, Issachar, Zebulun, Benjamin, Dan, Naphtali, Gad, Asher, Ephraim and Manasseh.

Tables

Months of the Year in Hebrew			
Name	No		Equivalent
Nissan	1		March-April
Iyar	2		April-May
Sivan	3		May-June
Tammuz	4		June-July
Av	5		July-August
Elul	6		August-September
Tishri	7		September-October
Cheshvan	8		October-November
Kislev	9		November-December
Tevet	10		December-January
Shevat	11		January-February
Adar I (leap years only)	12		February-March
Adar (Adar Beit in leap years)	12/13		February-March

Months of the Year in Macedonian (Common useage)			
Apellaios	November	*Daisios*	May
Audynaios	December	*Panamos*	June
Dios	October	*Artemisios*	April
Peritios	January	*Loios*	July
Dystros	February	*Gorpiaios*	August
Xanthikos	March	*Hyperberetaios*	September